Gathering her men

"Mr. Vooms, the deck is yours. Mr. de Weevil, keep to the helm with Mr. O'Shea. Dirk, steady by the hatch. If, and only if, you see me raise my right arm up high—give the order to fire. The range is a stretch but possible. Remind our gunners—disable, not sink. Hit the ship but not the men."

"Where will you be?" asked Dirk, uneasy.

"Over there, Mr. Dirk. Where'd you think, prithee?"

"She means *on* the Frenchy," said Whuskery, even his mustache scowling. "She means by herself."

"No, but who goes with thee, Art?" asked Walt.

"None, Mr. Walt. It'll be a deal simpler to get off with only myself to think of. And I doubt they'll let more than me aboard."

Plinko, Forecastle Smith, Peter, Whuskery, Dirk, and Walter had small arms ready out of sight by the rails. Jack and Mosie were leaning on the deck cannon as if lazy.

Art cast a quick glance around to check, and Walter bleated, "Arty—you'll get yourself killed. *Don't,* Arty. Just 'cos Felix ain't coming back—"

And Art found herself darting around on him, slapping him hard across his left cheek.

FIREBIRD
WHERE FANTASY TAKES FLIGHT™

Piratica II
Return to Parrot Island

Being: The Return of a Most Intrepid Heroine
to Sea and Secrets

Presented Most Handsomely
by the Notorious

TANITH LEE

FIREBIRD
AN IMPRINT OF PENGUIN GROUP (USA) INC.

*For my husband and partner, John Kaiine, who has
sailed so brilliantly through these voyages with me.
With endless thanks, and love always.*

The author wishes to express great thanks to Kate Jarvis
of the Maritime Museum, Greenwich, England.
And also to the wonderful ship the *Cutty Sark*—simply for being there.

FIREBIRD
Published by the Penguin Group
Penguin Group (USA) Inc., 345 Hudson Street, New York, New York 10014, U.S.A.
Penguin Group (Canada), 90 Eglinton Avenue East, Suite 700, Toronto, Ontario, Canada M4P 2Y3
(a division of Pearson Penguin Canada Inc.)
Penguin Books Ltd, 80 Strand, London WC2R 0RL, England
Penguin Ireland, 25 St Stephen's Green, Dublin 2, Ireland (a division of Penguin Books Ltd)
Penguin Group (Australia), 250 Camberwell Road, Camberwell, Victoria 3124, Australia
(a division of Pearson Australia Group Pty Ltd)
Penguin Books India Pvt Ltd, 11 Community Centre, Panchsheel Park, New Delhi - 110 017, India
Penguin Group (NZ), 67 Apollo Drive, Rosedale, North Shore 0632, New Zealand
(a division of Pearson New Zealand Ltd.)
Penguin Books (South Africa) (Pty) Ltd, 24 Sturdee Avenue, Rosebank, Johannesburg 2196, South Africa

Registered Offices: Penguin Books Ltd, 80 Strand, London WC2R 0RL, England

First published in Great Britain by Hodder Children's Books, 2006
First published in hardcover in the United States of America by Dutton Children's Books,
a division of Penguin Young Readers Group, 2006
Published by Firebird, an imprint of Penguin Group (USA) Inc., 2008

1 3 5 7 9 10 8 6 4 2

Copyright © Tanith Lee, 2006
All rights reserved

CIP Data is available.
ISBN 978-0-14-241094-3

Printed in the United States of America

AUTHOR'S NOTE

As you will see, the world of this book is very like ours, and also, it isn't. Names may be familiar—or weird. Some may be authentic old names you might find in a history book—others may be like games played with existing names. Almost all the places that are mentioned can be found on a world atlas . . . even though the names aren't quite what you expect. But some are in slightly different geographical positions.

So, this isn't exactly a historical novel—but it's not exactly a fantasy either. And it takes place in a time we never had. . . .

Two further points. (1) The French and Spanish used in this book *are* from a parallel world (a bit); and translations, too, are pretty free. (2) In our world, of course, it was the French who had a revolution and England who took fright and (along with other still-Monarchist nations) declared war on the French.

It's also a fact that, in *any* world, whatever the excuse or need, and despite the songs and speeches, flags and gallantry, a war remains one of the very worst things that can happen to any country, people—or person.

Last, the fragment of the poem by Coalhill (in our world known as Coleridge) is itself known to *us* as *The Rime of the Ancient Mariner*.

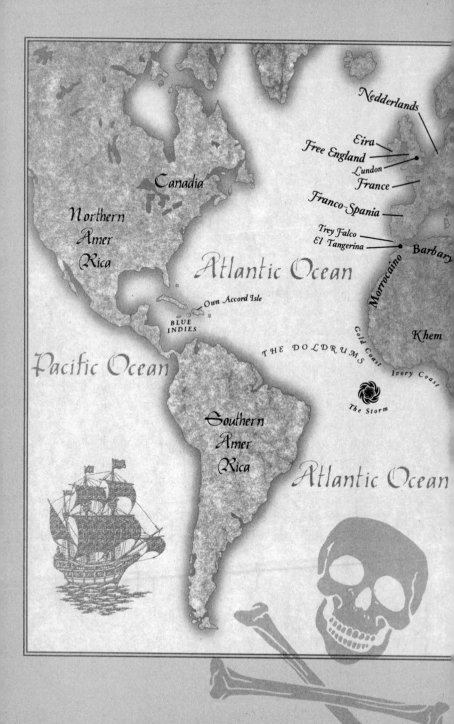

N

W   E

S

Egypt

Persis

Cathay

The
Inde

THE
SPICE
ISLANDS

Africay

Indian Ocean

Mad-Agash Scar   Treasured Isle

EASTERN AMBERS

CAPRICORN SEA

Free Cape Town

Cape of Good Hope

I7L3

~ CONTENTS ~

STAGE THREE: *The Shes*

The action of this novel takes place in a closely parallel world, beginning in the year 1743 (Seventeen-Thirtenty)—approximate, in our dating, to 1803.

"We want that treasure and we'll have it—that's our point. You would just as soon save your lives, I reckon, and that's yours!"

Robert Louis Stevenson
Treasure Island

STAGE ONE
The Shores

~ ONE ~

Night Owls

"*Nnn-nh!* By the Bull's Rushes—"

"Shush, innit. Let 'em go by."

The three owlers stood frozen in the hot summer night. Behind them rose the tall cliffs of Dragon's Bay. On either side ran the shingle beach of the cove. In front, the night sea opened, the waters of the Free English Channel under a pale half-moon.

Something moved far out over the water.

"'Tis a ghost—Tinky, it's a ghost!"

"Shut it, Billy."

Glad Cuthbert stayed silent, and remembered that weird time off the Cape, after the storm. He and the rest of the crew had seen the phantom said to haunt that place, the *Flying Dutchman*. The vessel had been full-sailed, and luminous with supernatural light. *This* was—yet wasn't—the same.

For one thing, she had no lights at all.

She was black, a low three-master, her sails black, too, or very dark, even under the moon. No flags or anything you could identify. And—she seemed draped all around by a kind of cobwebby *something* that trailed down the rigging and floated after in the moonlit sea.

When Cuthbert and the rest sighted the *Flying Dutchman*, they had recalled an old superstition: whatever crew saw that ship, one of them must die. One had an' all, Cuthbert thought.

Tinky spoke in his ear.

"Well, Glad, what d'ya make of it?"

"Meself," said Cuthbert, "I couldn't say. But she's no ghost. She's a real 'un. That's for sure."

Where was she bound, the lightless black ship? Farther along the coast eastward, from the look of it—even toward Good Deal and Till'-Bury. Certainly not to France. Since the spring, Free England had been at war with the French.

But she was farther off now, and a cloud had covered the moon.

The ponies were already loaded, waiting on the beach by the rocks. A narrow path went up there, on to the Fire Hills.

"One lucky thing," said Tinky as they walked back across the stones, "our boat was off and away afore that black 'un came along."

Cuthbert cast Tinky a sideways glance. Tink was a trustless bloke, dark-haired and squinting, with a spotted rag around his neck. He had got Cuthbert in on the owling (smuggling), having met him in the Duck and Sandwich Tavern at Hurrys. Cuthbert swore he himself only took on the job to get away from his missus. He'd thought it was the nearest he would get to the sea now, too, owling. Since Art had given up her ship.

Beside the ponies, and leaning on one, Jollup, the light-owler who flashed the lamp to guide boats in, had gone snoringly to sleep. As usual.

Tink kicked him awake. "Anyone could've come by and 'ad the lot!"

They toiled up the steep path between the sinews of the cliff. Twenty minutes later, emerging on the hills, everyone took a quick look around. The Fire Hills of St.-Leonard-and-the-Dragon had been quiet and mostly deserted before the spring. But with the coming of war, low towers were built up here, and beacons ready to signal a French invasion. If you weren't careful you could also run into a patrol of Free English soldiers. But then, most of *them* would let you off for a cut of the money, or some of the owled brandy, tea, coffee, and tobacco on the ponies' backs.

Just visible from here, off along the hills, one big house, a mansion, shone with lights. Cuthbert gazed at it a moment, incredulously thinking of Art Blastside, his former pirate captain. That was *her* house now. She was a rich celebrity. Cuthbert shrugged.

The smugglers turned into a gulley among thicker undergrowth and walked the ponies on toward the concealing inland woods of Holly Town.

They were a good mile inland when Tinky made his next comment on the strange black ship. "Puts me in mind of something, Gladdy. Some tale I heard once."

"Oh?" asked Cuthbert.

"Yeah, by the Will's Gills. What were it now? A black ship with a woman captain." Cuthbert said nothing. He had not confided in Tink that his own previous ship had had a female captain. Tink was ignorant of newspapers, too, and though he had probably heard of Art, he would have forgotten or never known the names of her crew. "She's a widow," Tink continued, "so I heard. Dresses her ship in black like herself. Roams the seas looking for the pirate killers of her husband. Catches 'em, maybe."

Billy said, "By the Bull's Rushes, that's a good tale, Tinky."

"D'ya think?"

Cuthbert said nothing. But something now started to nag in the back of his mind, worse than his Gladys when she got started. Then the something flamed like a spark.

The woods were closing in.

Cuthbert said, "Listen, mates. I've decided. I'm off for a bit."

Tinky rounded, scowling, on him at once. "What's up with you? You'll lose your cut of the goods if'n you go."

"That's all right," said Cuthbert. He winked at Tinky in the vague glow of their covered lantern. "Got a nice woman I want to see. Get my drift? You pattle on to Lundon and have my share."

Tinky nodded. "No fool like a love fool."

"Too right, forsooth," agreed Billy.

Dozy Jollup, who had fallen asleep riding the lead pony, now fell off with a thump into some bushes.

Cuthbert used the noisy diversion to wish them luck and make his exit.

As he loped back along the track to the cliffs, he did not see Tinky Clinker turn and squint after him, sneering a little as he did so. Now and then Tinky spoke to himself, under his breath. He always found himself his own best listener and adviser. This happened now.

"So you're off to tell your Arty Piraticay, are ye, Glad? Well, good cheer. I'll have a lady to see, too, about that black ship, when I gets to Lundon. And *my* lady is *your* lady's closest enemy. Only you don't know I know that, do ya, Gladdy?"

Glad Cuthbert did not. His head buzzing with a remembered horror story, he was trotting now along the Fire Hills, making for the golden windows of Art's mansion.

House and Pardon ⌐

Every time she saw her house across the sweep of its grounds, day or night, Art was both amused and perturbed. Thankfully it wasn't at all like the house of her father, Richman's Park. Even so, it was grand, large and pillared, hung with carved stone wreaths, and surrounded by an army of statues. She'd tried to get to know it.

"Hail and hi, Diana," Art called lightly to the marble hunting goddess up on a plinth. Diana, of course, took no notice of the young woman cantering by on the black horse.

The trees poured down, oaks, cedars, pines, to the long-sloping lawn, silver-gray in moonlight and stained yellow where the house windows were beaming. On the far side of the mansion the ground was rough and few trees grew. The headland framed a view of the black circling sea.

Felix was on the terrace here. You could hardly miss him. Several stands of candles had been arranged, and by their light he was standing painting, his head bent toward the canvas.

Art rode in and Felix, not looking, raised his hand in greeting.

"Just let me finish this detail. . . ."

She sat on her horse watching him, Felix Phoenix, her beautiful husband, who, by his wit and courage, had saved her from the gallows.

Was he happy now?

She wasn't quite sure. But then, how could she judge? They were so different, and he so intent on his work, these wonderful paintings of views and people. He had even painted Art up on her black horse. (This picture now hung in the Republican Gallery in Lundon.) But Art had called her horse Bowspirit. That said it all. If Felix had mislaid the sea—which anyway he had never been that keen on—she had not. No, the sea was in her hair and skin and bones and blood.

"That's it," he said, stepping back from the easel. "What do you think?"

"Perfect. As always."

"Oh, Art. That's no use. What do you mean? Surely it *isn't*?"

He stood there, smiling up at her, his handsomeness framed by his pale torrent of hair.

Why can't I be content, she thought fiercely, with him—with all this? I'm alive, too. That should be enough—I nearly wasn't.

She smiled back. She loved him. She would *pretend* to be happy.

"Well, dear sir, that lace there is painted a little thin . . ."

"Right."

". . . and that shadow—look, just there. No, that shadow is *much* too dark."

"Suddenly, my lady, thou are an art critic?" He frowned.

"Art," she said. "Art the art critic."

She swung off the horse, and from nowhere a handy groom came rushing, to take the reins and lead the animal to his stable. 'Night, Bowspirit. Thanks, Badger—" This to the groom. Art jumped onto the terrace and caught Felix by the hand. "Your picture is wondrous. 'Tis a joy to the beholder. Nothing's wrong. How fortunate you are to possess such talent. That's where you go when you want to travel, isn't it? Into your work."

They stood a moment, hand in hand in the intense candlelight, he with his moon-white hair, she with her dark brown hair through which the single orange strand—caused by a long-ago cannon blast—flamed on the right side. His eyes were blue as a calm evening sky, hers cool as the steel of a polished sword. Even in their colors, they showed their separate natures.

"You're not happy, my girl, are you?"

Her own thought. So why lie? "Nay. Not much. But with you always, Phoenix."

"You don't regret we wed?"

"Why should I? We seem to have been married before we even met."

"Indeed. I agree. But this . . ."

"Oh, this."

Together they stared up at all the glittering facade of their over-the-top house. And recalled, too, its insides—more than a hundred splendid rooms, with endless objects and luxuries.

"I lived so long without such stuff," he said quietly.

"I *never* lived with it. For me . . ." She took a breath. She said, "For me, one tall ship is room enough."

"Ah. Sweetheart. I know." He put his arms about her and she put her arms about him. "What shall we do?"

"Run away," she said.

"England would never forgive you—nor me, for allowing it."

This was true. Free England, and its people, had responded to Felix's outcry as Art stood on the scaffold at the Lockscald Tree. Risking his own life, he had persuaded the still-revolutionary crowd to rise against the tyranny of an unjust law. Though a pirate, and so automatically condemned, Art Blastside had never killed anyone, nor sunk any ship; all her robbery was done by cunning and tricks. She was already a popular heroine who had selflessly enabled her entire crew to escape the noose. The crowds rose and overpowered the representatives of justice. And presently Landsir Snargale of the Admiralty appeared, assuring Felix he had known Felix's father and would now gain a pardon for Art and make Felix himself rich. Which he did.

What with these riches and the general popular acclaim, the couple found themselves set up for life. They need never do another thing except live as lords and ladies had before the English Revolution.

When they had married (refusing East Minster Abbey in embarrassed horror), the streets around the tiny church were impassable, thousands of people crammed in every available spot. Children were lifted up to see them. Other artists than Felix had climbed walls or got on roofs and were drawing them furiously. "By the stars," Art had said, "this reminds me of my hanging." "Thanks a bundle," said Felix. So they laughed and made the best of things.

Their new home had to be kept secret from the public. Even so, occasionally, uninvited persons arrived. They wanted autographs or to do sketches of Art, Felix, even the horses, even the rabbits that bounded about the nearby woods.

When war—long expected—was announced, most of this stopped. Jolly soldiers hustled sightseers away for security reasons, saying they might well be taken for spies of them Avey Voos—as the French had recently become christened.

However, once in a while, Art and Felix were called into Lundon by the government or the Admiralty. They drove in stuffy summer carriages through packed crowds, attended yawn-starting banquets, were asked to make speeches (which Felix did charmingly and Art did professionally, learning her lines beforehand in the actor's way). Both of them loathed every second.

On these enforced jaunts they sometimes met the rest of Art's crew—all but the Honest Liar, who had apparently gone to earth in the West End. The crew, too, was there to be shown off. All actors; Eerie, Pete and Walt, and especially Dirk and Whuskery, performed with a flourish and seemed not to mind. Yet Ebad soon vanished on some journey, leaving Art only an uninformative letter. Glad Cuthbert as well, their only nonactor, finally escaped to somewhere on the coast and became a smuggler.

Muck, the Cleanest Dog in England, had disappeared, too. None of them had seen *him* since the first days after Art's pardon.

Plunqwette, though—

"Duck!" Felix exclaimed.

"*Parrot*, you mean!"

Still embraced, both of them ducked their heads and bowed over, to avoid collision with a green-and-scarlet-winged explosion.

Plunqwette had always seemed quite pleased with the mansion. She flew from room to room, invisible for days, apart from droppings and dropped feathers on the curtains, chairs, and marble floors. Or she would flap through the trees of the grounds. You found her at unexpected moments, sitting on the head of a statue of a Greek god or a stone griffin, one eye open.

The park was where she had come from now, out of night and trees and around the house. She landed atop Felix's canvas with a flail of wings, leaned down, and pecked a small, neat hole in the faultlessly painted sky.

Art shouted.

Felix shrugged.

Plunqwette announced, "Pieces of mate! Glad to meet you."

"And what does this mean?" asked Felix, stroking Plunqwette's head with one paint-spattered thumb.

"It means *that*," said Art, looking back along the cliffside.

Someone else was rushing toward them, waving one arm like an injured windmill.

Near midnight, Art sat at the desk in the library of the house. The room was ridiculously full of elegant books that she had not read. Only Felix sometimes did, or the servants who liked reading. One of the maids sat even now by the open window, devouring a novel about romance and swordplay.

Ebad's letter was spread on the desk.

My dearest Art, my Captain and Daughter, the letter began. The first time she read that, Art had felt a kind of gentle smugness. She liked the idea of Ebad Vooms—the black once-slave, who claimed he was descended from the Pharaohs of Egypt—as her father. He wasn't her real father, of course. But he had been her mother's true love. And Art's actual father—the vile George Fitz-Willoughby Weatherhouse—she seldom even considered. With good reason.

But the next paragraphs, as they had done the first time she read them, took the grin off her face.

I know, Art, that you need no man to take your part, or look after
you. And, by the Topgallants, if ever you do need one, Felix is
there, and no guy better.

Looking at this now, Art wondered if Ebad had been jealous, as
real fathers sometimes were. But she thought not. Small jealousies
weren't anything to do with such as Ebadiah Vooms.

So I'm off, Arty. Off on a short voyage. Don't have any care for
me, 'tis nothing either bad or glorious. But this Lundon game—
feasts and parades, sham and jam—I care not for it, to act myself
in front of a crowd. Fame is double-edged. I'll see you at
Christmas, if not before.
    Yours, sincere as the sea is changeable,
    E. Vooms

"Dad, thou are a pain in the royal," said Art softly to the letter.
"When I really want to talk to you, there you are, gone."

By the window the maid sighed and raised wild eyes. "It's a
lovely old book this, Missus Art."

"Good, but stow the 'Missus,' Jane. Plain Art'll do."

Art thought, But that's my title now. Phoenix is a landsir, and
I am a landmissus. *Landlocked.*

Her mind went back then to Cuthbert's story, told earlier that
night.

He had erupted onto the lawn. Rather as Plunqwette had. Cuthbert was a lot less collected.

They sat him down, and Felix poured him coffee. They said they
were pleased to see him; he should have dropped by sooner.

Glad Cuthbert sat there, brown and strong and getting his
breath back. Then he said, straight out, "Last winter, just after we
all got pardoned from the jail, Cap'n, I hears a tale in an inn out

Twochurch way, near Rowhampton. Thought it was an ol' pack of lies, like everyone tells. Forgot it. But tonight—tonight I think I sees the very ship."

"A ship?" said Art. "This is the coast, Mr. Cuthbert."

"Cap'n, this 'un ain't like the rest. She's called the *Widow*, and it's a widow captains her. *Her* name is Mary Hell—used to be Mary Hellström, for her dead hubby. Pirates killed him off the Scandinavias."

Art had sat down, her long legs in their boots and breeches resting easily on the terrace balustrade. She said, "I've never heard this yarn, Cuthbert."

"Not so many have. It's apparently supposed *bad luck* to tell it."

"Then—"

"No, Cap'n Arty. You may need to know."

"Why?"

"I'll come to it. The pirate what slew Mary's better half, he was the Golden Goliath."

Art swore. She glanced swiftly at Felix. He had gone white as the white on the palette. Goliath remained well-illknown even after his death. When living, he had robbed and sunk countless vessels, condemning every man, woman, and child on them to a deep-sea grave. Felix's uncle, too, died at Goliath's hand, and through that Felix's father had been ruined, and presently also died. Meanwhile Goliath's one daughter carried on in the pirating trade. She was as filthy as he, or even—Art had sometimes thought—*worse*. Little Goldie Girl.

"These are old enemies, Cuthbert," said Felix in a low voice. "Why rake this fire over? It's done."

Cuthbert shook his head slowly. "It's me bones, Felix. Like some people can feel rain coming by an ache in their bones . . . like that. This story. It makes my neck ache as if the noose is back dangling over it—it makes my ribs ache as if a bullet's flying at 'em."

"Speak up, then," said Art. "Let's hear all about Mary Hell, the Widow."

Telling Tales

Three days after Cuthbert told the story to Art and Felix, Tinky Clinker was telling it to another young woman—but both of *her* close men friends were out of the room.

Tinky had always thought Little Goldie was a beautiful creature, with her thick black curly hair, apple-blossom skin, and light green eyes—but he would rather have kissed a hedgehog. *On the back.*

"Do you have something to say, Clinky?" she asked him, when he appeared in her parlor, shown there by the servant. She always said his name the wrong way around: *Clinky Tinker.* Trying spitefully to irritate him, he guessed, but he wouldn't ever rise to the bait. For even when teasing him like this, Goldie Girl was horribly, nightmarishly dangerous. And she had powerful friends.

"I might have, Mistress Goldie. I'm not too sure, you understand. But—you hear these tales. . . ."

"Especially in your line of work," she idly said, narrowing her eyes. She was like a cat and he the mouse. But Tinky was more a rat—even he thought so—thus a better match for this nasty little witch than she knew.

He'd met her first because he often brought smuggled goods to sell at the judge's house. The judge, Lawlord Knowles, always wanted things on the cheap, though he was loaded with coins and power. A skin flinter, the judge. Goldie, a vicious pirate queen of the Seven Seas, had escaped hanging because she played up to Knowles in court, and he, the muffin, judged her blameless.

Now she was his companion in the fine house. She, who had stalked in silk and plumes, sword on hip, gun in belt, now dressed always as a modest young maiden. Her beribboned hair, growing longer and more lush by the week, hung in demure tresses over her shoulders.

Only when you looked very, very near could you see the tiny little crisscross kiss Art Piratica had cut on Goldie's right cheek, above the upper lip.

But Tinky just knew that not a day, perhaps not an hour, went by without Goldie examining this, frowning and seething for revenge.

Tink had offered to be helpful to Goldie soon as he had seen her and could get five minutes alone with her.

She had said she had no need of anything. Her "darling friend," Lawlord Knowles, was her protector. However, she had murmured she might one day "ask" Tinky's services in some small matter, and any general news he might bring was always interesting.

To explain their chats, she told the judge she was persuading Tinky to drop his price on the owled coffee and brandy. It seemed the sprout-brained miser believed her.

Tinky sat down only when she told him he might.

"You ever heard of a ship called the *Widow*? During your days at sea, innit."

Goldie shuddered. "I was a slave aboard my father's ship, Clinky. I don't recall." This was also the sort of lie she fed Knowles. Others had heard she adored her dead father.

"Well, since you mention your worshiped da, this tale of the Widow's black ship *concerns* him, if'n you take my meaning. It concerns his *death*."

Goldie turned wide eyes on Tinky.

"*How?*"

"Y'see, Missus G, though half the French Navy went after the

Goliath and sinked his fleet, the tale goes yer daddy, by his great cunning, survived."

Goldie stood up. Her face was like clean gray paper.

"Do you say—my father—still *lives*?"

Tinky nearly smacked his lips. 'Twas fun to see the witch wriggle. He said, "Well, I'll give it to yer straight."

Goliath's small pirate fleet, and his own cutter, the first ship named the *Enemy*, blasted by shot and shell, went down to the sea's bottom off the coasts of Inde.

Wounded in the left arm by a musket ball, the Golden Goliath yet managed to swim clear of the wreck. He had no worry for his crew. They meant nothing to him as people, let alone mates. To GG, men and women were like ordinary tools, or household items—a stick, a saucer—either useful or not. And if any got broken—well, there were always plenty more to be had.

Stray planks, oars, and casks floated on the dark blue water. Goliath held to a cluster of these, lying under them and keeping his head under the sea as much as he could.

Paddling with his feet, he veered slowly off from the grouped French destroyers. The air was still thick with cannon smoke, and the French were so sure of victory, already celebrating. He had got clean and far away by nightfall and, so the story went, was even laughing when he hauled himself up on his isle of planks. He'd always had the devil's luck. All he required now was a helpful passing rescuer.

Just after moonrise, he spied a solitary ship there on the wide ocean. She slunk in from the east, with the new moon at her back, a slim, low, European craft, perhaps a merchantman or other trader, heading for the Arabian Sea from the shores of Cathay. He would have liked to pirate her, if he'd had his own ship still, but for now he would act like a poor fellow fallen overboard and abandoned by a heartless captain. (Just as he would have abandoned a man overboard himself.)

The dark ship sailed nearer and nearer. Goliath thought he would swim over. Maybe, since the sea was so serene, he could grapple onto the hull like a limpet. He always kept a couple of climbing hooks about him. It might even *be* possible to take her, if she was lightly crewed—for no one seemed visible on her decks, or even up aloft. . . .

Was the Goliath at all superstitious? Had *he* listened to stories of the oceans?

The way Tinky told it, the way *this* tale of GG went, he wasn't, hadn't.

In any case, at the moment he was deciding to swim, the advancing ship seemed to turn her shoulder to him like a scornful girl.

"Goliath cursed then," Tinky said solemnly. "You'll know, mistress. He never liked not to get his own way."

And already the dark ship was getting smaller. Goliath lay back on the planks, nursing his hurt arm and cussing her to damnation. But other ships would be by. The sea-lanes were busy here.

It was some minutes after he felt the tugging under his planks.

"He looks over the side and sees then he's caught up in a great black raft of drifting weed."

What does mighty GG think now? Weed travels and unravels all over the Seven Seas. It means nothing much. He leans out a little, and with his cutthroat's knife tries to hack some of it away.

But the weed's very tough. Peering down through the waves and the thin moonshine, he sees then it's odd stuff for seaweed.

He tries it with his hand, shows it to the moon, and whistles.

This isn't weed at all. It is a great net, unusually made, and with slimy black pods and tendrils somehow all woven into it, like something natural. It must be for fishing, he thinks. Some numb-skull on the dark ship has lit it drift away. . . .

However, the huge net isn't adrift. It is still trailing out from the ship's stern.

"What a pretty bit o' luck, thinks yer dad," said Tinky. "The net has him and seems like it'll pull him in, right to the ship's side."

Goldie stared at Tinky.

Behind her green eyes she's watching Goliath, pulled in like a prime catch.

" 'Tis the Widow's ship, yer see. Get it?"

Goliath relaxes, *lounges* on his raft, and lets the net do the work, and the sailors, too, who are drawing it home. When he bumps gently against the ship's side, he's only tickled to be hauled up and up to the ship's rail and over to the deck. It's saved him a climb.

There are no lights on that deck, though. Not the proper lamps aft and for'ard. The shadow sails tower up, not even lightened, as the sails of the *Enemy* had been, by white-painted shapes of a skull and crossbones.

Men like shadows, too, wait all around.

"Cheery evening, mateys," cries the Golden Goliath.

But no one wishes him one back.

And then, out of the silent crowd of sailors, a woman comes, gliding along just as the ship had over the sea.

"Mary Hell, that's her name. Her husband was a rich merchant, three ships he had. Off the coast of Scandinavia your da found 'em one afternoon. He took their gold and killed every soul aboard and fired 'em, and all three sank. Seems when the news reached Mary she ups and says, I'm a widder woman now. I'll use the last money I have for one more ship. And she'll be a widow, too."

Mary Hellström did what she said. And when the vessel was ready, she set out with a crew of men who were skilled in the work of seafaring—and other things.

All this Mary herself tells GG, when he stands there dripping blood and salt water on her deck.

"You left me nothing better to do," she says, "than search out your kind and remove them—like warts—from the face of the earth."

"Remove?" says the Goliath, still jolly. "Do you mean kill?"

"Aye. Kill's what I mean. There's many a wicked one I've rubbed out from the page of life. But I don't rob them, even if they have anything worth taking."

"You're a merry pirate!" chortles GG.

"No," says Mary Hell, "I am the Avenging Angel. And never till now did I think I'd ever come up with *you*. But behold, I have."

Goldie sat in her chair. She gnawed her fingernail a minute, then realized she'd spoiled it. Stopped.

"Did she?"

"Kill him? So she did. Or so the tale *says* she did."

Color was blooming back into Goldie's face. She said, "So it comes to the same thing. He's still *dead*."

"It's *how* she kills 'em," murmured Tink.

For a moment Goldie, puzzled, looked only like a young woman out of her depth. Then she snarled, "Well, *how*?"

"None will speak of it. It's that—*'orribubble.*"

Quick as a snake Goldie sprang up, pulled off her shoe, and slung it at him. Though the shoe was made of soft satin, the heel was hard and caught Tinky a clank on the nose.

"Say then how you know all this is a fact, you lying scum-pot!"

Tinky cowered, holding his injured snout. "'Cos I *seen* the Widow's ship! Not three nights afore—off shore, near Hurrys."

"Seen her? What can you know of ships—"

"I know *that* 'un. Couple others did, too." Tinky hesitated, not wanting to reveal right now that one of these other witnesses was connected to Art Blastside, Goldie's mortal rival.

Besides, Goldie had had enough. "What use is this rubbish to me?" she screamed. "These fanfaronadoes and fibberies! By the Wheel's Wood, if you were on my ship, I'd skin ye alive, yay, by the Toad's Ratchet!"

Abruptly her yell ended.

A heavy series of footfalls were coming along the passage outside. With no other preliminary, Judge Knowles flung wide the door, tall, large, upright, and stern.

Tinky leaped to his feet, bowing and mumbling. Goldie flitted back into her chair and put her hand faintly to her head.

"What is this improper noise?" demanded Knowles, who was named in certain quarters Judge Know-All, or more accurately, Judge Know-Less.

"He told me," Goldie whispered, "my father lived."

Tinky grimaced at the fine carpet. "Box of Blatters."

The judge frowned on them both, making a judgment.

"This man's a scoundrel. You should not be talking to him, Goldie. Get out, man. Your wage is in the kitchen. Never let me see you in the upper rooms again."

Tinky fled. Only on the stairs did he produce a choice word or two for the judge. Tinky knew, anyway, this was *not* the last he had seen of Little Goldie.

For now Knowles leaned over her, his face engraved with thunder.

"I don't expect such behavior from you, Goldie. Such hackbucket backstreet yowling. And I've already had more than enough of loudness and idiocy. My carriage was stuck for an hour in the Pell Mell crowds—this nonsensical fad for dressing as pirates—the city has gone mad. *Piratomania*, the *Lundon Tymes* calls it. Nonce and stuffence!"

"Oh, forgive me, sir, I'd rather wither than fret you. But I was so terrified by mention of Goliath—"

"A woman must learn self-control at all times. Particularly if she has such a background as your own."

Goldie gazed up at him, sad and trembling at having angered him, and watched her beauty bind him again. "Though the Goliath was a tyrant, sir, he was, after all—my father. A father must always hold a special place . . ."

"Yes—yes . . . very well. I shall overlook your lapse."

Twenty minutes later Goldie, in her bedroom, was busily sticking a tiny dagger, kept from her pirate days, over and over in a small sketch some artist had made of Judge Knowles. (She had begged the judge to give her the sketch. When he subsequently asked where it was, Goldie said she kept it always with her. She added it was so printed with her kisses it was now nearly a rag. In fact, only the dagger had reduced it to this.)

Having loosed her rage, Goldie sat down to write a note to her other man, her pet ship's captain. She had met him when he kept her prisoner during the voyage back to England, on his gunship destroyer, Free Republican Ship *Total Devastation*. Captain Nunn was young and not bad-looking. He had fallen under Goldie's spell as badly if not worse than wise Judge Knowles. But Goldie had also mentioned the treasure maps to Captain Nunn—how the peculiar tides of the Treasured Isle would very likely sweep them in again to the shore, when once the sea pulled out. Maybe Captain Nunn had fallen even more deeply under the spell of this idea.

Goldie felt enough time had passed. The tale Tinky had recounted convinced her of this. After her trial and release she had had to be careful. But now, by the Whale's Wink, she'd had enough of flattering Knowles—and wearing this dress!

Goldie finished her letter and sat up. The kitchen boy could take it for her, he was always ready for a silver coin—luckily Nunn had seen to it that Goldie was not deprived of all her pirate wealth.

Then, from deep in her past, she heard her father's remembered and appalling voice. "Eh, Goldie Girl. Who's my girl, then?"

She leaned back, crushing her fist over her mouth.

Yes, she had feared her father. She had hated and dreaded him. He was pitiless even to his own, the Goliath kin. He used them, too, as he did everything else. (Sticks, saucers, no matter if they got broken. . . .)

Goldie turned and stuck the dagger once more through Judge Knowles. She was no longer seeing his face, but that of her father. But if Knowles had seen *her* at that moment, he wouldn't have thought her beautiful.

Tinky caught the kitchen boy around the throat in a dark alley beyond the house. "I'll just have a peek o' that."

"But it's sealed—"

Tinky paid no heed. He lit a stub of candle and held the paper up against it, studying the words inside.

Tinky couldn't read, but he had long ago learned the knack of memorizing the *shapes* of the meaningless words and letters. Soon, at the Cup and Kipper Tavern, he would find a reader who could explain them.

For a long while Tink had suspected ex-pirate Goldie had the key to something rich and strange. That was why he'd stuck close.

Tonight he'd rattled her. And perhaps at last the treasure chest was about to open.

~ TWO ~

Wagging Tails ~

"Yo heave ho
And a Bottle of Woe!
All the way down in a Whale's tum-tum!"

"You're in good voice—and a good mood, Eerie O'Shea," said the barman at the Coffee Tavern.

"Yes, dear boy. Off again, to rejoice the Admiralty. One more command performance."

Eerie, formerly Second Officer of the *Unwelcome Stranger*, the most famous pirate ship of modern times, downed the last of the jet-black brew and swung into the street. He was dressed, of course, as a pirate still, a-clunk with medallions, gold muhuras, knives, bullets, lace, and silver braid—but in the tavern or elsewhere, he no longer stood out very much. This was because almost every man in the tavern, and on the Lundon streets—not to mention nearly every woman, child, and animal—was dressed in a similar way.

Inside twenty paces, Eerie swerved around ten cutlassed and beplumed persons, three with stuffed parrots glued to their shoulders, one with a real parrot standing on her head, two pet monkeys in boots with small sword belts, and a carriage horse with a feathered three-cornered hat and black eye patch.

Eerie viewed all this with the kindly contempt of the successful professional watching amateurs. What could you do anyway? Piratomania had taken Lundon over in the spring, about the same time that Monarchist France declared war on Republican England.

Eerie met Dirk and Whuskery, Salt Walter and Salt Peter, in Shooters Lane.

Here D and W had opened a small theater, but truth to tell, their attempts to interest the theatergoing public in what Dirk called "culture" failed. People wanted to dress as pirates and also to *watch* pirates on the stage. So Whusk had to put on pirate plays, as they all had in the past. Though the girl who now played Molly's part of Piratica, Dirk declared, was useless. Didn't know her asp from her eyebrow. "And Art won't do it, *oh* no. I wouldn't dare even *ask*."

"Look at these receipts for the audience last night," wailed Walter to Eerie the moment he saw him. "Three men and a pigeon."

"We have to get the roof fixed," said Whuskery, blowing through his black mustache. "That's how the pigeons get in. How some of the *audience* get in, too, and then they don't pay. Then there's this new antipirate organization—they picket the theater some nights, and *no one* can get in, even if they want to."

"And when I think," commented Dirk as the three of them now strode up Butter Walk, "we could all have been rich as a French king. But *oh* no—*oh* no. It can't *ever* work out like *that*."

Peter said, "We were lucky not to hang. That's where all the luck went. But I've said, Whusk, we could train those pigeons as messenger birds, make a bit of extra cash, mayhap."

Silence fell, the strides turning to trudges, as each of them recalled how they had nearly been rich—richer than any king on earth. Those fantastic treasure maps on the Treasured Isle, found in the great chest—but cast out to sea when the law closed in.

"Well," Whuskery said, "still got each other. Any tidings from Ebad, Eerie?"

"Not a line. Not a stage whisper."

Gloom threatened to settle, even on en-coffeed Mr. O'Shea.

Dirk said, "I suppose *she'll* be there, too. At the Admiralty bash. Frankly, I'm surprised Art does it. *She* hardly needs the free meal."

"Yes"—Eerie sighed—"but *we'll* wag our tails for the meal like dogs."

Art and Felix had offered each of them huge sums of money, once Landsir Snargale made Felix wealthy. But all the men of the crew had refused. To be *given* money wasn't *it*. Though maybe, Whuskery now thought, he could get a loan from Art to fix the theater roof.

"Then there's Honest," said Peter. "Where is *he*?"

"And Muck, the old dog, where's *he*?"

"And our ship, the real true splendid *Unwelcome* . . ."

In chorus they moaned together, "Towed to the breaker's yard and mashed to splinters."

"That's no fate for any good vessel," Eerie said, the coffee high leaving him completely. Whuskery wiped his eyes. Dirk examined his nails. Peter ruffled brother Walt's red hair, as if to comfort.

They cut corners now with leaden boots, toward High Admiralty Walk.

The message from Snargale had come in the morning to the house on the cliffs.

Presently Art was given it at the breakfast table in the east parlor, where Felix and Cuthbert sat reading the *Tymes*.

"They goes on and on about this mystery man that rescues French revolutionaries from the rest of the French," pondered Cuthbert.

"He's called the Purple Daffodil, isn't he?" asked Felix. Before Cuthbert could deny this, Art broke in. "This letter is from Snargale."

"We're to go to town again," said Felix. He sighed.

"Well, I'd rather be off back to my owling," said Cuthbert. (He had stayed over and spent the night tossing and running in a hot, wide, four-poster bed, having horrible dreams that Gladys had refused to have a row with him, or a cuddle, and had instead gone off in a lean low black ship, to kill pirates.) "If it's all one."

Art said, "Wait a moment, Mr. Cuthbert. I think"—she looked up, holding them both with her gray eyes—"this may be a different kettle of haddock."

"How?" asked Felix.

Art read aloud from Snargale's letter.

And as she did so, Plunqwette flew in at one of the sunny open windows and settled on the back of a chair, head cocked, listening too.

"'As you will be aware, Art, we are at war with the French. Although our valiant ships hold them off from these shores at all times, and our soldiers engage them at every opportunity abroad, other more subtle attacks can be made on any enemy of England.

"'To this end, you, madam, with your skill, seacraft, and nearly magical knack as a thief, may once again flourish: this time not only to your own benefit, but to help your country. Free England threw off her chains. France still wears hers. I invite you, Art Blastside, to visit the Admiralty and learn more of this. All your former crew are similarly summoned. Let me assure you, as I shall every man of them, this is no idle dinner date. This, Art Blastside-Phoenix, is the Touch of Destiny.'"

"Wow," said Cuthbert. "The old chap knoweth how to put his words together. What's it mean?" he added.

"It means," said Art, "we're to go to sea again. That's plain enough. The rest—who knows?" She saw Felix looking at her very seriously under his dark brows—the brows that still startled her, as did his black lashes, when his hair was white. "Don't panic, sir.

I can leave you here if you'd prefer. I'd regret the loss of your sweet company, but I wouldn't want to put you out."

"Put me *out*? Art, for God's sake . . ."

"The sea wasn't ever really your thing," said Art.

Felix went red. This happened rarely. It didn't mar his looks.

Cuthbert stood up. "Yeah. I'll take a totter round the terrace. . . ." To his surprise Plunqwette followed him, settling on his shoulder reassuringly. "The sea . . ." said Cuthbert, gazing out at it beyond the headland of the Fire Hills. Behind him he could hear Felix being angry and upset and Art being ice-cool and immovable.

Plunqwette made little soothing noises she had probably perfected by listening to local doves.

Finally a chair went over with a bang.

Out flared Felix in a blizzard of hair.

"There's no reasoning with her!" He joined Cuthbert to stare at the rim of the sea, dark blue under the turquoise summer sky.

Just visible, a small naval patrol was cruising past, scanning southeast for French invaders. Along the hills, too, Cuthbert could make out a patrol of English soldiers marching about by the nearest watchtower.

"Busy times," he said.

Felix said, quietly now, "She won't refuse whatever it is Snargale suggests, if it means getting back—to *that*. To water and adventure and danger . . . It's the breath of life to Art."

"Better let her go then."

"*Let* her go? Do you think I could *stop* her?"

"Well," said Cuthbert flatly, "you maybe, if no man else."

"I *can't* stop her." Felix's eyes were full of rage and pain. Cuthbert hadn't seen that happen for a long while. "I'll *never* be able to stop her risking her neck."

"You took the *hangman's rope* off her neck once; saw it meself."

Felix patted Cuthbert on the Plunqwette-free shoulder, then stalked away around the terrace. Indoors, Art, too, was gone from the room. Plunqwette left Glad Cuthbert, flying back in to investigate the remains of the bread and beef.

In the end Cuthbert traveled with them. He was lured by the notion of the sea, and a ship. He told himself he was there to keep the peace between Felix and Art. But they didn't quarrel. She sat with her chin in her hand, obviously thinking of a shippy future. Felix sat pale and stressed. As for Plunqwette, she slept on Art's knee.

The fast, smart carriage bounced along behind four spanking horses. (Art had considered riding Bowsprit, but Felix looked so fed up, she decided to ride in the carriage as usual on their trips to Lundon.)

They made good time, sprinting through historic Battle-of-Senlac with its abbey and tall, ancient monument to the last true English king, through lanes and along tracks, among emerald woods drawing in and fanning out. Waddlehurst flew by, and other villages. The dusk was falling when they drew off the road at an inn in Seventeen Oaks. Here they spent the night—this time Cuthbert much happier in his room on a nasty, narrow, lumpy straw mattress like bad porridge. With the dawn they were off again. Cider Cup went by, Iris Town, Avlingham, and Come-Here Green. They passed the New Cross about lunchtime and entered Lundon on the stroke of two o'clock.

Nobody had talked much.

Felix by then was thinking of his dead father, Adam, and Art of her dead mother, Molly Faith—the first Piratica. Cuthbert was thinking of the good dinner they'd get at the Admiralty about four in the afternoon, and—Cuthbert couldn't help it—of the sea. Madness. There you were.

The houses in May-Fair were fashionably diamond-glitter win-
dowed, and white as ice cream, and out of one of them that day,
about two-thirty, ran a yellow dog, bright himself with cleanness
and full of a late breakfast.

There was still something in the dog's mouth.

It looked like a very large bone.

Off down the street he and the bone trotted, between the legs
of strolling gentlemen done up as pirates and fine ladies ditto.
Over sunlit squares planted with shady trees, under a couple of
nicely designed arches, went the dog, heading always in a certain
direction.

Last year Muck, Cleanest Dog in England, had fallen on happy
times. Going back to the May-Fair area to unearth the bone of the
giant parrot he had brought from the Treasured Isle and buried,
he next found a public fountain, and there washed it clean of mud.
In the middle of this, a lady, *not* dressed as a pirate, had seen him.
"Look, Hamlet! What a delicious dog!" The gentleman (also not
dressed piratically, but as an officer of the Free English Navy)
peered at Muck with a certain insulting doubt. "*Is* he?" "Oh,
Hamlet," the young lady cried, "you *know* he is." "No, I don't."
"And look, he's got such a lovely meat bone in his mouth—isn't he
clever—aren't you *clever*, my doggy?" "Gadsocks, forsooth," remarked Hamlet Ellensun, Third Officer of FRS *Golden Beak*, "put
the creature down. You don't know where it's been, Emma."

Muck, soaking wet, already lifted up by the pretty, dark-haired
young lady in the yellow dress that so charmingly toned with his
coat, kept teeth firmly clamped on the bone, yet still managed to
smile at her.

"Look, the brute's snarling!"

"Nay, Ham, he's *laughing*, innit. Oh, he's brill."

Thus Muck had been adopted by Miss Emma Holroyal.

For months after that he'd lived a life of overeating and silk-cushion sleeping, petting and spoiling and being worshiped. Emma didn't get tired of any of this; but Muck, gradually, felt the need for his own life back. This morning, knowing—as Muck always uncannily knew—that something was now afoot, he licked Emma's cheek a last friendly time, grabbed back his bone out of her desk—where he had stowed it when she wasn't looking—and made a break for the street.

Heartless Muck. Poor Emma. Poor *Hamlet*—what a tragedy he would have to listen to when he called this evening. But Muck's tail wagged, and he ran fast as any horse toward the Admiralty.

The Navy Building stood at the center of Lundon's High Admiralty Walk. Today someone was up on a ladder, polishing the silver oar fastened over the doorway. Muck eyed the sandstone statues of Egyptian sphinxes either side of the entrance, made a decision, and lifted his leg with an air of great generosity against the left-hand sphinx.

"Here—you can't do that!" howled the man on the ladder. But it was done.

Muck shot through the door, which had opened at the ladder man's loud cry, between a new selection of white-stockinged legs, and up the steps, patter, pounce, skid. At the top he collided with one more group of pirates. But he *knew* these, and they him.

"It's Muck!"

"It's Muck the Cleanest Dog in England!"

"Where hast thou been *this* time, my dogabout?"

"Somewhere posh," Dirk concluded. "*Look* at that yellow bow!"

She was angry with him. Art hadn't felt this anger with her husband since the previous year, during their voyage out to the Isle. Since then his rescue of her, the wedding, *being in love*—had made anger seem impossible forever. But now—he appeared not to understand her at all, despite everything he had said. And she—well, she didn't understand *him*, did she. He wanted the dry land, and she wanted the *world*. It was hopeless.

Art thought, furious and dismayed, It was all right to show sympathy for how I felt, how I missed the sea and being my own person—all right so long as I was stuck with it. But the moment a chance arrives that I might get my life back—oh, Phoenix doesn't like it.

They hadn't spoken above forty words on the whole ride here. Even in their room at the inn in Seventeen Oaks. Then he had thrown wide the window, which looked on a Kentish night orchard, and declared, "How paintable."

And she had answered, "Better stay and paint it, then."

They lay separated by a few inches of bed and ten land miles of mutual irritation.

In the morning she had said, "I'm going to breakfast."

He had said, "I'll find Glad Cuthbert."

There. The sum of their conversation. Sixteen words, that, sixteen words at Seventeen Oaks.

We should have said one more, she wryly thought. Just to make it up to seventeen.

And what would the word have been? *Darling? Pest? SORRY . . . ?*

Oh, to Mars with it.

Having together stonily climbed the marble stairs of the Navy Building, Plunqwette and Cuthbert left in the annex below, they went in to see Landsir Snargale alone, as requested.

His office was hung with paintings of ships, and strewn with models of ships and *bits* of ships—a wheel, a flag, a rope knotted in a bunny splice. Snargale in his white wig rose to meet them.

Art was never quite easy with this man, despite his noble behavior toward her and his evident affection for Felix. No, that wig spelled unwelcome authority to Art. It reminded her of her hated father.

"It's good of you to come," said Snargale, embracing Felix and shaking Art by the hand. "In such weather—a 'Blue-Indian Summer,' the *Tymes* is calling it. And the city is packed with—"

"*Pirates*," said Felix in a cold voice.

Snargale smiled. "Well, live and let live, Felix. It's a craze. 'Twill pass."

"You've mellowed, sir. Was a time you loathed every idea of pirates."

Snargale raised his brows. To himself he decided, Ah, they have rowed over this. Well. It was perhaps to be expected.

"The true pirate I do indeed detest. But as we know, you and I, not quite all are wicked. And our Lundoners are only dressing up. The war, too, has made the city excitable. Generally it was hoped the French would not react as they have. But of course, for twenty years our own successful revolution has threatened their Bourbon monarchy. Their people are still oppressed, as were the English, by that unfair system, and opposition to the French king grows. He therefore means to teach us a lesson so that we cease to be an inspiration for French revolutionaries. Naturally, however, *we* must see their king's plan doesn't succeed."

"If you say so, sir," said Felix.

"And don't you say so, my boy?"

Felix looked bleakly at Snargale. "Forgive me, but any war causes so much destruction, misery, and death. I'd always prefer there were other means to settle it."

"And what would you suggest, Phoenix?" Art broke in icily. "We surrender to France and become one more conquered country, like Spain? We are no Spain."

Snargale said, "I'm glad Art at least is in agreement. It brings me to the matter I must put to her. Your crew, Art, are already here—all but Mr. Vooms and Mr. Honest, but we'll come to them."

"Fire away," said Art.

Felix glanced at her. She looked wonderful, bold and steady and ready, a glow on her like gold.

Snargale nodded. "I didn't commit it to my letters, either to your crew or yourself, but I think you at least guess. You were a pirate, Art Blastside, and a very resourceful and canny one. You robbed any ship you fancied and could take. That was unlawful, naturally. It nearly got you hanged, and only your blameless record of nonkilling, plus your husband's extreme courage and wit, saved you and made a pardon possible."

Art frowned. Precisely then she didn't want to be reminded of her husband's virtues.

But Snargale went on swiftly.

"Now England asks something of you, Art, in return. England asks you once more to become a pirate. A *legal* pirate, going by the name of privateer. A ship you shall have and a full crew. But this time only one prey will you seek. The ships of the French and the Spanish." Snargale paused. Her face, though alert and set, was unreadable. What a remarkable girl she was. "Other captains have already accepted this commission. But this is a fly, fraught enterprise, where every jot of your intelligence, and your luck, will be needed. And, given the best chance in the world, you may still lose your life on those war-torn seas. This game is far more dangerous than the one you played before. Think about it now. Today we'll all take a quiet, private dinner with your first crew. Discuss this news with them at your leisure. You have until midnight tonight either to accept or refuse."

It was Felix who said hoarsely, "And if she refuses?"

"Then we'll forget my words were ever spoken."

And Snargale saw Felix turn away, tears of rage in his blue eyes. They all knew, though none of them yet voiced it, Art was only more likely to refuse than she was likely to turn into a swan.

Breaker's Yard, Unbroken Hearts ⌐—

At Chattering, the evening river was broad and green. Gulls blew over, shrieking of the nearness of the estuary and the sea. Along the right-hand southern shore ran the Republican Shipyard. Here bright flags flew over the clean, attractive skeletons of half-completed ships, where men swarmed and there rose the sound of hammering. But along the left-hand north shore, tucked in behind a jetty of tall black sheds, lay the other side of the coin. This was the breaker's yard. If ships were born on the south side, they were finished off on the north. And from there came the unpleasant noises of smashing and grinding and collapse, and thick smoke rose from burning timber. Boats sometimes crossed over from bank to bank. Some things ripped from a vessel before she was broken up could be used in furnishing a new one.

Eerie O'Shea, shedding tears, stood on the deck of the steam tug.

"Oh, 'tis shame, such ruin for a fair gallant ship, whose heart is oak! Mine breaks."

"There, there, Eerie," said Whuskery. "Chin up."

"Never. That was the fate of our own *Unwelcome*, that crashing and smoke over there. And she wasn't an old ship, even," Eerie added indignantly, "but in her prime."

"She was a *pirate* ship," said Peter. "That's why they broke her up. She was sentenced—like us. Only she—"

"Whoops, here herself comes," said Dirk.

Art prowled along the deck. She ran her eyes over the assembled portion of her crew.

"Why are you crying, Mr. O'Shea?"

Eerie snuffled in a mauve handkerchief, pointing at the left-hand shore.

"No ship dies," Art said, "while she's remembered."

In silence they were chugged in to the other bank.

Felix had remained in Lundon. He had told them he needed to see someone about a painting of his that, like the portrait of Art and Bowspirit, was due to be hung in the Republican Gallery. This was obviously an excuse. But no one protested, except Walt, whom Pete had quickly kicked on the ankle.

The Admiralty tug brought them downriver, bravely flying the Republican Jack of Free England—red, white, green, yellow, and blue. Art's men were full of excitement and unease. None of them had exactly *said* they wanted to go back to sea, let alone to rob and harry the French and Franco-Spanish. None of them had said they didn't, either. Only Cuthbert announced it "wasn't a bad 'ol chance."

Eerie soon became emotional. Even about the steam tug: "Ah, by the Eel's Bells of Eira—to feel the tide under us again!" He began to reminisce, telling them all what they had been like going down the river the first time on the Coffee Ship. Even recalling how Art thumped the mutinous Black Knack on the chin and knocked him out. But Black Knack had died on the Treasured Isle, shot in the back by Little Goldie. He'd betrayed them, too. A superstitious gloom descended.

Muck, meanwhile, ambled about sniffing planks and ropes with an air of refinding. He had brought his bone, but now and then put it down to inspect something else. Plunqwette sat on the rail, glaring at the tug's puffing smokestack.

Art hadn't told her men everything. She had partly wanted it to be a surprise. Now she chided herself that this had been the wrong thing to do. They were grown men, not little boys. But no—they *were* boys, and she was their mother, as Molly had been their mother.

The Admiralty officer who accompanied them guided them off the tug and along the walkways, over bays of building ships. Interest in this lightened the mood. One ship, still fragrant with the smell of sawn wood and new tar, not yet masted but flagged for launching, was shown with pride. "She has the latest copper-bottoming," said the officer. "Sea-proof even in the verminous oceans of the Indies."

"And our vessel, sir?" inquired Art.

The officer pointed. Last in the line of new ships, this one stood up from the bay with an unmistakable valor. She was fully made and finished and fully masted, wanting only rigging and sails.

"Why," said Art innocently, "a windjammer . . ."

"Like our old *Elephant*, who became our *Unwelcome Stranger*!"

"Indeed," said the officer very seriously. "A three-mast windjammer—different from the four-masted WT in her length of spar and mizzen topsail angle."

"*Unwelcome* was a three-mast windjammer," repeated Walter wonderingly. As they got nearer to the big ship, he added, "And this one is ever so like. . . ."

"She has—even unrigged and sailless—that same inner *whiteness*," Eerie murmured, "like a pearl, so she is."

They moved along the vessel's side. Muck padding behind them. Plunqwette flew suddenly up, to perch high on a spar.

"Well, the bird's decided it's OK."

The for'ard end was reached. The group halted, staring at the figurehead that, recently repainted, was familiar to them all as their own faces in a mirror. A veiled figure all darkness and menace, holding out her right hand in a gesture like a beckoning grab.

"'Tis the very figurehead of the *Unwelcome*. . . ."

"They must have taken that from the ship before they broke the old girl up!"

Art gazed at the figurehead. Originally from the tiny Coffee Ship, it had been a woman holding out a coffeepot. But when the Coffee Ship sank at Port's Mouth, the lady lost the pot, and came back to them instead covered in the black mud and veiling weeds of deep ocean. Perfect then, they had made her the emblem of their *Unwelcome Stranger*. Now here again she was.

"The brass trim on the rail looks the same, too," said Peter uncertainly.

"Aye, and the cabin—that sort of mark on the wood . . ."

The men were gaping. Only Glad Cuthbert, oddly, had pulled back. There was a weird look on his brown face. Art had no time to spare for it right now.

"Gentlemen," she said, "I have to tell you that—"

And stopped. Because Ebad Vooms had just appeared from behind the deckhouse. Black as ebony, tall, princely, and dressed as a pirate, he waved as if the meeting had been arranged weeks earlier. Maybe in Ebad's scheme of things it had. Art did not wave back.

They went aboard to the sound of the pipe, the Admiralty officer laughingly saying this wasn't quite proper, as the ship was not yet afloat. The Honest Liar, who had also just appeared—what a stage entrance!—hooted the whistle.

His moon-round face was all goodwill. Nor was he dressed in pirate gear, apart from the familiar brass earrings.

"Where've you been, Honest?" cried Walter, aghast.

Honest beamed. "Just with people."

"But . . ."

They were on the deck of the ship. Above them soared the naked masts. Everything smelled of salt and scrub-soap, wood varnish, metal, tar, and paint.

Art looked at Ebad. "Hi, Dad. I suppose you've just been with people, too."

"Who else is there to be with?"

"You always were a one for secrets."

"I told you the best one."

"You and my ma. Yes. It was the best."

The others were off already, moving up and down the deck, measuring with their steps, calling to one another. The Admiralty man paced along with them.

"Have they figured it out yet?" Ebad inquired.

"It finally seems like it," said Art. "Yes, look at Walter dancing. And Muck's run straight through into the galley. And Peter's gone down after him. . . ."

"'Tis the original same identical ship, Ebad! 'Tis *Unwelcome* herself!"

"She's been cleaned and cured keel-over," said Art. "She, too, has a copper bottom now, and if you care to count the gunports, Mr. O'Shea—"

"Twenty-two!" shouted Peter, emerging from the hatch. "Two aft, and nine on a side, plus—"

"Two deck cannon. Twenty-two exactly." Art nodded. "We'll need a bigger crew with some trained gunners. Do you know where all this is bound?" she continued to Ebad.

But Eerie was informatively singing out, *"Oh, the life o' a privateer! We'll sink the Frenchies with a cheer! Poo to the lot of 'em all, and poo, To ev'ry flaming Avey Voo!"*

"Back to sea, Art, that's where it leads," said Ebad. "Where you like to go best. How's Felix taken it?"

"Like a punch in the head."

"Will you talk him round?"

"He can do as he pleases." Plunqwette fluttered down to meet Muck coming up from the galley. Muck let go his precious bone, and dog and parrot flew at each other's throats. It was one of their traditional hearty fights—which up till now neither had started. Fur and feathers fizzed through the air. Art said, "This isn't only for me. Besides, it's what we all want, isn't it?"

"Mayhap," said Ebad. "Or not."

"What else are we good for? A stage, maybe, but we've tasted the real thing now. Dirk and Whusk tried to revive the Piratica show, and Walt and Pete, but it wasn't going well. As for you and Honest and Muck—you three vanished. There now, look at Eerie; he's overjoyed."

"Or thinks he is."

"Well," said Art. She shrugged. "There is the other matter. And I don't mean bravely worrying the French for the war effort."

Ebad's face was unreadable. Art, too, had this ability. She must, she thought, somehow have learned it from him in her childhood, when he and Molly and Art were at sea, or acting in their plays. So it was no use finding his unreadableness exasperating.

"I mean the Treasured Isle," said Art.

They leaned on the rail, looking over at the green water of the Thamis.

"All those maps," said Ebad. "We sent them off to sea."

"Things go out with the freak tide there and then come back, like the jewels and coins we found on the beach. I've been thinking, Ebad—why not the maps?"

"Why not?" echoed Ebad. "But then, Arty, would not every other pirate on the Seven Seas have the same idea?"

"Like Mr. Hurkon Beare."

"Like Goldie."

"This is a good ship. Twenty-two gunner now. *Legal* now."

"At war now."

Art smiled. "It's fine to see you. Tell me what you've really been doing, Da."

"Sailing between here and France, with that fellow down there in the red shirt."

Art turned sharply. A tall young man with black hair tied back in a long tail was down among the sheds, inspecting some of the shipwright's tools on a long table. "He legally worries the French, too," said Ebad. "Wild Michael, he's called."

"So for you this war is personal?" Art said.

"I was a slave once, Art. England had her revolution and set me free. In France I'd still be chained. Plenty more like me are. Yep. 'Tis personal, my lass."

In the lamplit inn their table was merry. Hearts were high, and the beer passed. All around, the Chattering caulkers and joiners were toasting their own shipbuilding work and boasting. Very few wore pirate gear. Names of ships were bandied about—"D'you hear tell of the Indian man-o'-war *Pakora Sullier*? I helped fix her once in the Arabian Sea"—"The best at sea nowadays is the *Golden Beak*, she that fought the Avey Voos off Franco-Spania"—"They say the Amer Ricas have a new fast ship—six masts"—"'Twould never sail—would sink like a clatterbug!"

Wild Michael, who was dining with Art and Co., called across, "Have you heard of the *Ow Blast*, lads?" They had not. "Launched to sea, and as she goes down the slipway, the guy christening her sings out: "I name this ship—" and stubs his toe. The *Ow Blast* she is to this hour, and a nicer tub you couldn't find."

"There be one called the *Lily Achoo*," vowed a shipwright in the corner. "Much the same, reason of a sneeze."

"And I heard tell of a vessel sailing under English colors called the *Is That A Wasp*."

Others shouted. "Lady-missus out Grinwich way names a ship, or starts to, and sees the love o' her life, not met for thirty years, waiting in the crowd. Ship's called *Is That You Edgar Aah*—swooned she did, ya see."

"Me brother swears he met a ship in the Blue Indies named the *I Knew I Shouldn't Have Had That Last Sausage*—the *IKIS* they hail her as, for short."

At the table's end, Cuthbert sat writing to his wife. He had written her the same line three times, each time phrased and spelled a little differently.

My deer Gladys, I am hoff ter sea . . . .
Me dar Gladys, well yam over to sea . . .
Glayds, y'm off.

Something had interrupted Cuthbert's thoughts. He confided it to no one. The party was jolly, and Ebad's friend Wild Michael seemed a good enough bloke, in a sinister way. But there was no one Cuthbert felt he could take aside to share the cloud that had abruptly sat down in his brain.

It was when he had looked at the figurehead on the newly beautified *Unwelcome*. He hadn't made a connection before. And really, it was daft to do it now. So he must be getting fanciful. In a way he wished he had never heard that tale at Twochurch. Never put it together with the black ship he and Tinky saw go over the horizon at Dragon's Bay. He had thought *her* important enough to tell Art the story about Goliath and Mary Hell. It was because of Goliath's filthy daughter, Goldie, that was why.

Yet somehow . . . real or phantom, the *Widow* seemed to be

casting a long shadow over them. In fact, she seemed even to have been there *in their past.*

For *Unwelcome*'s figurehead might have been *modeled* on the Widow herself. Draped in veils, in widow's *weeds*, like her ship, those fearful nets that dragged in her pirate victims . . . This wasn't the omen Glad Cuthbert would have chosen for their voyage, whether they went to fight the French or to search out their lost treasure maps. But he couldn't tell the rest. Actors and sailors— superstitious to a man.

Cuthbert saw the black eyes of Wild Michael regarding him. Not really wild, not unfriendly; nor to be trusted.

Cuthbert nodded, and bowed his head again to his letter. Firmly he scrawled, *Door Glady, m'off.* And signed it with a flourish. He never for a moment thought this would upset her.

"What is that?" Art demanded.

She had just entered their guest room in the Navy Building to find Felix dressed in a manner as alien to *him* as it was known to *her.* As a pirate. He had put on the lot. Loud scarlet coat, torn lace shirt, breeches slung with sword belt, sling of bullets, knives, pistol, gems and bangles, and over one eye, a black eye patch—like the horse she had seen that evening in the Strand.

Or . . . like dead Black Knack.

"What? Why, only what the well-tempered murderer is wearing this season," Felix said. "Maybe not the eye patch, though." He took it off and dropped it.

The hour was late, nearly one in the morning. Art had returned from several days at Chattering. Felix, too, had been busy.

"Why," said Art, "have you bought this clothing?"

"Because it's what I'll be wearing when I come on your enchanting jaunt."

"I see. But you're not coming with us, Phoenix."

"Yes, I am."

"No. You are not."

"Oh, believe me, I have no *wish* to go with you. But go with you I shall."

"And I might wish you would, but you won't. Do you think I can concentrate on anything with *you* underfoot? You won't fight and you don't know a ship's aft from her anchor."

"I'll have to learn, then. God knows, I saw enough of it last time."

"Last time you were a liability, sir. I can't risk you. It's too dangerous."

Unpatched, both his eyes flamed.

"And do you think I'll risk *you*? What do you think I am? You hazard I'll sit meek at home and paint and doze, and not go off my head guessing what's become of you?"

"Oh." Art deflated. She turned her back on him. "I'll be fine, Phoenix. I'm charmed safe."

"I am coming with you."

"And you are *not* charmed."

"No? Who got *you* off the bloody rope?"

"Oh, that again. Don't use that as a weapon, Felix. Stow it. Belay and shut up."

They stood. Minutes dripped by.

He said softly, "Let's leave this, Art. It's heartbreaking. We'll— argue again in the morning. If you want."

They got into the bed, kissed each other a dispirited single kiss, and lay once more back-to-back, separated now by the width of a war and Seven Seas, and all the baggage of two different lives.

At the Edge ⟶

Very many discussions went on in small, gilded rooms or shadowy large ones, with gilded and sometimes shadowy men who represented the republican government. There were papers given and documents, sealed and unsealed. All this to authorize Art Blastside and her ship in their new patriotic work.

Everyone scattered to tidy up their lodgings and last arrangements. Art and Felix rode home in their carriage to the house on the Fire Hills. This time they did not stop on the way, but made on through the night.

She looked at Felix, sleeping, in the jolting carriage, Plunqwette also asleep on his chest. The bird went up and down with Felix's breathing.

Melancholy, she thought. At least the parrot will be nice to him.

The rest of her crew, apart from Ebad, seemed in high spirits— or were they acting? They certainly seemed to want to get away from the boredom and skint state of failure. None of them had done well since the great shiny days following their pardon. Only Cuthbert had made a profit at his owling. And Ebad—well, he had made his own adventure with the mysterious Wild Michael.

Art wasn't sure what she thought of Michael.

He was good-looking and strong, and the life and soul of the party, cracking jokes, telling stories, being gallant and amusing with everyone. But he was dangerous, too. Art could see it on him, his dangerousness. He "worried" the French, did he? Well, he worried *her*, a little. She had asked Ebad about Michael, when they'd taken a walk along the riverbank that second night at Chattering.

"Is your Mr. Wild a safe bet, Ebad?"

"No. But who would you say was?"

"Listen, Dad. I don't want you mixing with people who'll get you in the way of trouble and then leave you in it."

Ebad laughed. "Molly! By the sole Pole Star, you sound just like your mother sometimes."

"My ma would want you to be careful."

"No, Arty. You can't tie up a man's life. Nor a woman's, either. Molly knew that better than most. We do what we must, and can."

It seemed Wild Mike came of a good family, his parents a rich landsir and his landmissus. They, too, had a cliff-top house, but along the southeast coast, near the Estuary Mouth at a place called The Edge. The *Unwelcome Stranger* was due to sail down to this very bay in less than a month. The shores of France lay close across the water there, and navy patrols and war fleet, too, marshaled the area.

"I've seen a map of the place," said Art. "Snargale showed me. There's a treacherous undersea bank not three miles out."

"The Badloss Sands. Aye, many a neat ship's been smashed there to splinters. It helps keep the French off. But I've sailed by the spot many times. You only need a proper chart, and to know what you're at."

"Sailed by with Michael, do you mean?" Art asked herself if *she* was jealous.

But Ebad just then drew her attention to the fresh Chattering-built ships lying out on the river. Conversation turned like a sail to another wind. She let it.

Ebad had said he would be sailing now with *Unwelcome*. Would he rather have gone back to his voyages with Michael?

Forget that. It was arranged. Art and her officers were to recruit extra crew at The Edge and provision up there for the journey.

In the homeward-bumping carriage, the moonlit fields and hop yards of England lolloping by, Art herself tried to sleep as Felix and Plunqwette did. Couldn't.

For the first time she wondered if she was seriously wrong. Then pushed the idea away. This was the life she wanted, or soon it would be. "Wish me luck, Ma," she whispered.

Once they arrived at the house, the preparations and packing began. Art went to the stable and bade farewell to Bowspirit. Feeding him apples, she promised Badger would ride him regularly. She considered Bowspirit would probably forget her. "If you were a dog or a cat, I would take you, my friend." But Bowspirit disapprovingly shook his noble head.

She slept that night and had one bad dream. She dreamed *Unwelcome* coursed bravely out of Edge Bay and was instantly wrecked on the Badloss Sands. All around masts and canvas cracked and fell, timbers shattered, and black seas rushed in. Dirk was screaming that his nails would be ruined. Somehow Little Goldie Girl was standing on the shore, high white cliffs behind her, and she was tiny as a pin yet clearly visible, smiling.

Waking, Art shook herself. There would be a pilot to guide them out of the bay, and Ebad Vooms as well. A childish dream.

The *Unwelcome Stranger*, who had weathered so much, was indestructible—charmed, like her captain.

Felix and Art neither argued nor discussed anything anymore. It seemed they had each accepted the other's position. They were polite to each other. They even talked about small things . . . weather . . . food . . .

She considered outwitting him and flying off a day early to The Edge and her ship.

Before, the crew had called Felix their lucky talisman. But that time he had meant to give them all over to the law. In the end he relented and pleaded for them. And rescued her. As he had reminded her.

The crew still loved Felix.

He was worthy of love.

But she so wished he wasn't going with them.

The Thamis flowed semi-eastwards to the sea, past Grinwich, Rottenhythe, and Till-We-Bury Docks, whose defensive fort now was lairy with the blue, green, and red uniforms of Republican soldiers. Guns poked out seaward, and two-thirds of the ships lying at anchor were patrol vessels. Some way beyond this point the estuary eventually widened in an unnerving yawnlike gap. And there swung the wide, wide waters of the Free English Channel, and the Strait of Dove.

England was fortressed here by the Dove-White Cliffs. They cascaded up, castles of chalk, whose pale faces were blinding in the summer sunlight. The Edge was located among them, and below, the land curved to form deep Edge Bay. Which was as full now of warships as a broth of potatoes.

The town of Good Deal joined here with the village of Edge—urban sprawl. And the pirate craze had come here, too. It was as bad—or worse—than Lundon. But at least, Art saw, she went unrecognized, as she might not have been in Lundon or Port's Mouth.

Unwelcome, temporarily crewed, was on her way from Chattering. Art and her crew, already at The Edge, put up at the Hog in Heaven. Here the recruitment began.

Into the hot and sunny inn room lumbered, bumbled, or stamped tarry, salty types who had sailed for years on this ship or that. Or, on the other hand, naive types who hadn't sailed anywhere ever but had picked up news of a privateer. Such a spree might get them killed—or make them rich. A female captain was great, too. They had mostly heard of Piratica—Art Blastside—but didn't know this was herself. Some of them besides thought her a young man—and far too young to know what she was doing. Many of the less experienced interviewees were dressed as pirates and strutted about, slapping their thighs and waggling cutlasses. "Avast me pilchards, by the Shark's Shirt!" "We will take ye Frenchy ships and *eat* 'em, by the Cod's Carpet!" And so on.

Art regarded them all levelly.

"With whom," she usually asked, "did you crew before?"

"Ah—to the far east, to fabled Cathay, and later to the Isles of the Canadee—"

"No. I said with whom."

"Whom? Oh—er—with Captain *Hume*. Quite right."

"I have been told of no such captain. Either naval, merchant, or pirate."

"Have you ever," added Ebad, looking piercingly in the applicant's eyes—or the one eye that had no eye patch—"*been* to sea?"

"But of course—"

"—not," finalized Art. "We want experience, sir. This is no pleasure trip."

The genuine old salts were often as bad, however.

"Ye're a lassy, ain't ya? 'Tisn't what I'm a-used to. I can't be doing with a girl aboard a ship. The sea's a She, a ship's a She, and woman's a She—and that's one She too many."

"And you, sir," said Art, "are one too many for my vessel. There is the door. Good day."

Others stood glowering. "I bin sailin' since me fourth year on this earth. I don't take no nonsense from any cap'n."

"You will be given none. There is the door. Good morning."

At noon, stretching, Art rose to her feet.

"What a rain shower of fools."

Felix, notable by his absence at these interviews, joined them for lunch. Maid servants of the inn, dressed also (approximately) as pirates, fluttered around him. (Handsome Felix. Any woman would be proud to have won him. Any *other* woman would have been happy to make *him* happy.) "Pass the bread, please," said Art. Felix passed the bread. Neither looked at the other.

Ebad said, "There were five possibles in that batch this morning. And one other who might have been some use to us. But . . ."

"You mean," said Art, "that very young boy in the silk coat."

"Aye, yeah. The very young *boy*. He gave his name as Bell."

"Yes," said Art, "I marked him on my list, too. But he's never sailed before, I'd take a bet. His hands—"

"Were smooth and clean and excellently manicured."

"Would put even our own Dirk to shame."

Ebad said, "What, Art, you of all people—no, I suppose you, of all people, *wouldn't* have guessed."

"Guessed what?"

"*Mr.* Bell. 'Twas a girl."

"A girl," said Art, cool as ever. "I see."

"There was another such in the passage, waiting. Only her mother came in, toting a rolling pin and they left with some noise."

"I suppose," said Art, "there's no reason a girl shouldn't sail with us. *My* hands were soft before I started to work a ship. And *I'd* never sailed save as a tot."

"Nay, Arty."

"And she could hardly object to a female captain."

Felix said, in a dark, low voice, "Few of them would object to sailing with *Piratica*. Why don't you open the secret?"

Art said, "Not the plan, Phoenix. This secret is meant to hold until we're at sea."

Ebad said reasonably, "Every fake pirate this side of Australia might want to join up with us otherwise."

In the afternoon, three gunners with some experience on warships of the line arrived. They, like Glad Cuthbert long ago, had been taken off by Franco-Spanish pirates, then freed by, and served on, an English destroyer. They liked the idea, they said, of serving now with a vessel that was both legal *and* a pirate. Another man came in shortly after who had served previously—on merchant trader FRS *Elephant*. He bowed to Art and announced, "I reckoned it would be you, missus. And I know the *Elephant*'s the *Unwelcome Stranger* since you took her from Captain Bolt at Port's Mouth. I crewed under Captain Bolt, and a stupider turbot I never did see. You took him fair and foul, a pretty sight, and hurt not a hair of any man's head—just the cap'n's hat your parroty doo-dahed on. Laughed myself daft, I did. Had to make out I was sobbing with rage. Never forgot that merry day."

Art looked the man over narrowly.

Those traders that carried the FRS of Free Republican Ship were all under the direct authority of the Admiralty. They took their cargoes and their orders from that source. Generally their crews were disciplined and well trained.

"So you enjoyed it when we took your ship. Is that enough," said Art, "to make you want to sail with us?"

"Oh, aye. I loved her—your ship. She was—*is*—a good ship. Lucky as a lamprey out of a stew."

"And what is your sea trade?"

"Carpenter, Cap'n. Name's Bagge—Oscar Bagge. I'll keep it quiet, too, who you really are."

Evening fell with a clear blue-green dusk. Stars sparked over Edge Bay, and carriages full of uproarious wannabe pirates went thumping up and down the town. As the lamps were lit, all the skull-and-crossbones flags that dressed the place like bunting fluttered in a soft breeze from the strait.

Under cover of this first darkness, a ship stole lightly in toward the bay. She anchored some way out. One blinding star—Venus—tipped her mainmast.

Art saw her from a window of the inn.

The *Unwelcome Stranger*, now rigged and clouded with sail, hung between sky and sea as if weightless. A beautiful phantom. At Chattering she had been reborn and wonderful. But now—*now* she was *alive*. Art rejoiced that she'd waited to see her vessel fully dressed.

That's who I really love, then, she thought with a twist of the heart. Not my amazing Molly-Ma, not my adoptive half-unknown Ebad-Dad, not my exquisite husband Mr. P. No. It's her out there, with the water under her and the star in her hair. My ship. That's who. Welcome, my *Unwelcome*.

Wild Michael reappeared next morning. He strode into the Hog in Heaven and bowed to Art with a *wild* flourish.

"Good day, sir. Surely you don't intend to volunteer as crew?"

"Alas not, Mistress Blastside-Phoenix. I only bring a humble invite for nosh at the family pad."

Art was taken aback.

Ebad said, "A house worth a visit. How's your lovely ma, Wildy?"

"Lovely. The cook's still good, too."

"So, we're going?" said Art.

"Aside from my glamorous family," said Michael gravely, "there's my younger sister's blokey. You might like to meet him. He's a rising star in the Republican Navy. Just promoted this very morn to Captain of Ship of the Line FRS *Golden Beak*, innit."

Art told the rest of her crew, and her partner, of the invitation. Whuskery declared, "They're an important family, those Holroyals. Covered in bling, by the Rat's Tattoo."

Everyone dressed in their best. Art didn't quarrel with Felix when he, too, put on *pirate* best. She only remarked sweetly, "And where do you prefer this earring, Phoenix? In your ear or through your *nose*?"

High above, on the white cliffs of Dove, the Holroyal homestead turned out to be a palace, carved, porticoed, and the orange color of gingerbread. It was surrounded by gardens and grounds that sloped away behind to meadows, woods, and orchards. White birds burst from the trees like cannon shot as Art and Felix left the carriage, and a large golden animal came running from the house.

"What a nice doggy . . ." began Eerie.

Walter added, "Lovely coat."

Dirk said, "If it jumps up, *my* coat is *ruined*."

Cuthbert, who stood there with his old companion the hurdy-gurdy in its box under one arm said, "Er—that ain't a dog, mates."

"It's some sort of small lion," Art agreed.

The small maneless lion reached them. Waving her lion tail, she leaped at them all with huge paws. Walter fell over at once, screaming. Peter sprang to defend him. Muck promptly split for the trees. Cuthbert drew his pistol ready to fire. Dirk pushed Whuskery behind him, dragging out a cutlass, while Whuskery pushed *Dirk* behind *him*, likewise, until the two of them became hopelessly tangled. Eerie said, all astonishment, "A *lion*—like in Africay? By the Eel's Heels . . ." Ebad only sighed.

Honest, who until then had hung back, stepped forward, crouched down, and called the lion to him. She went. They embraced.

"It's tame," decided Peter.

Honest stroked the lion's head. "She doesn't know she's a lion."

"Thinks she's a dog," clarified Eerie, doubtfully.

Plunqwette, who had taken up sentry duty—or refuge?—on

Art's head, flew off into a nearby arbor. Muck skulked in the distance, barkless with affront.

The lion eyed everyone kindly. Then, seeing Wild Mike emerge from the pillared portico, fired herself straight back at him.

He led them into a cool marble foyer (where the lion now skated about in insane skiddings of enthusiasm).

The Holroyals were a dark, attractive family, a-drip with jewels.

Landsir Chrysothemis and Landmissus Malvera received their visitors in the gardens. An elder sister, Kassandra, was at Stratt-Ford, it seemed, acting Shakespur to great acclaim. The younger sister, Emma, rose with a shriek.

"There is my own dog—my yellow dog from May-Fair! Oh, heartless doggo! Where hast you been, *bad* boy."

Muck, who had slunk in behind the others, looked instantly guilty. He had left his bone at the inn for safety, and now had nothing to distract himself from the horror of the mad lion or this new embarrassment. He ran behind a strawberry bush.

Art's crew were also embarrassed. They tried to explain to Emma that Muck always did this. He would go off and lead a life of his own, lying to people that he was a poor stray creature and needed mothering, but always returning to the pirates. "Cleanest Dog in England," Walt added lamely.

Emma's huge dark eyes brimmed with tears. Landmissus Malvera's huge dark eyes fixed on her daughter. "Come, Emma. No laments. What will Hamlet think? He'll expect you to cry only with joy at seeing *him*."

Luncheon was served, with champagne and peaches.

All around, the doves settled like summer snows in the green trees. The air was full of the distant breathing of the sea, of cooing and lion purrs, and Muck's dim snufflings from his thicket. Plunqwette patrolled the table. No one seemed to mind.

It was very pleasing, there in the garden. Art sat alert. The amusing conversation was full of jokes and wit, and no information of any sort. Michael was like this. She didn't, she thought, trust any of them.

A moment later an unnerving yell broke the peace of the afternoon. It seemed to be some frightening warning, echoing from the direction of the house, then proceeding swiftly along the line of trees, which loudly crackled and rustled. Doves catapulted into the sky.

"Another lion!" hooted Eerie.

"No, it's a *monkey*—must be—look, it *swings* through the boughs!"

"Or one of those dog-men-Lemon things from Mad-Agash . . ."

"Lemuras, they were," said Whuskery.

But out of the leaves a slim youth appeared, easily advancing hand over hand from tree to tree. Reaching the closest branch over the table, he called carelessly, "Emma's Hamlet Ellensun's just ridden up."

"Why, thank you, Calm," said Landsir Chrys.

"*Calm*, did he say? That monkey-lion boy is called *Calm*?" exclaimed Eerie.

Calm swung over and was gone among other trees, now melodiously whistling as he went.

Out on the lawn walked a smart young man in a naval captain's uniform, his hat in his hand.

Wild Michael introduced him to Art and her pirates. Hamlet viewed them with undisguised interest. Then turned to Emma. "Why are you crying?" he asked.

"Delight," snapped Emma resentfully.

Hamlet sat down and ate a hearty late lunch. One by one the family drifted away, to "fetch" something, to "see to" something. The crew were lured off as well, into an orchard to inspect apples, into the kitchens to try a new cider . . . Even Emma floated with her mother toward the house, Walter and Peter somehow going with them.

Presently Art, Felix, and Ebad sat alone with Wild Michael and Captain Ellensun.

"Elegantly stage-managed," said Art.

"This family is the soul of tact," said Hamlet. "But that yellow dog in the bush, by the way (*Muck*, did someone say it's called?), I think it bites."

"So do many of us, sir," replied Art. "What goes on here?"

Ebad murmured, "Better put it on the table, sirs. My daughter won't stand any nonsense."

Plunqwette fanned her vivid wings and squawked: "Pieces of bait!"

"Bait?" asked Hamlet. "Well, I can offer that. But first"—he met the eyes of Art with a steady, sea-gazing stare—"*first* I'll tell you, Captain Blastside, your main plan is known." Art said nothing. Felix, too, kept silent. "By which I mean, your plan to wiggle through the French lines and head back across the globe to Mad-Agash, and thence to the island commonly referred to as *Treasured*." Hamlet folded his hands together neatly. Waited.

Felix spoke. "Why would you think we'd do that? We found no treasure on the Isle. That's common knowledge. They sing *songs* about it."

"Do they, by the Messy Mizzen?" Hamlet smiled.

Art said, "I think, Captain Ellensun, the government of Free England is too hopeful. Nothing's left on the Isle but an empty chest—which is how we found it. Naval officers were our witnesses, just before they arrested us."

Hamlet's neat hands unfolded. He took a small piece of paper from his pocket and began to fold it into a tiny paper boat.

"Does this knock a knocker in your mind, Captain B?"

Art glanced at Ebad. Ebad shrugged.

She said, "Let me guess, sir. Some of those boats we made from the treasure maps have been rediscovered."

"What else. A Free English naval destroyer, patrolling off the Amer Ricas, brought up three maps on her anchor chain, still somewhat in boat form, and with much of their information washed out. A fishing fleet off the Indies took seven in a net—five sodden and unreadable, two quite clear enough. The captain sold them to persons unknown, but we, of course, got to hear of it. There have been a few other instances. One story runs a single map sailed into the Thamis by itself and was flown off with by a nesting goose."

"Mmm," said Art, flat as the tabletop.

"Mmm. The government of England is, as you said, indeed hopeful. It seems the tide also returns things to the Isle. Bits of this and that, maps made into boats . . . A war's costly, and this one we have now with France has been on the cards for years. It's got to be fought. It's got to be won—by *us*. Have you heard the French king's words on the matter? He said, 'I will destroy England and her revolution. I will destroy the *future* of England.' "

"War's your job, I think, Captain Ellensun. Yes, I'll board a few French ships, rob them, and let them go. You'll know my methods. No man is killed, no ship is sunk."

"And when you reach the Treasured Isle, Captain Blastside, you will claim any treasure map you may find there, and generously bring it home to assist your country. Yes, you and your men will receive a fair share of any resulting loot. But, you'll agree, you're in England's debt. England spared you the rope."

"My husband here, and the *people*, sir, spared me the rope."

"Then for the sake of those same *people*, you'll deliver."

Michael said, "Now, Ham, offer the lady some bait."

Hamlet said, "Have you heard of the Green Book?"

Again, silence.

Ebad: "*I've* heard a rumor of it. In the past, I can't recall when. And again in the last six months. Just one more story, the sort that circles in taverns when the gin or the coffee flows."

"Maybe," said Hamlet, "or not. The Green Book has been mentioned now and then in recent times of war. That's when everyone most wants to get their mitts on it. It's said to contain the ultimate clues to almost every treasure ever carried to sea and hidden. Including, naturally, every treasure map once buried in that chest on the Isle. Or so they say."

"This sounds like a fancy," said Art briskly.

"The tale's strange, I agree. The Green Book also has, reportedly, a very strange owner. Find the owner, you might get the book. But *she's* elusive as a blue kipper." Every eye stayed on Hamlet. He said, "Ever come across talk of the legendary pirate slayer Mary Hell? She has a black ship, the *Widow*, that travels without a single lamp across the night seas, draped in black weeds and trailing black nets. I've never caught sight of this bark myself, but I've spoken to sound, sane men who thought they had."

Art said, "I've heard of the *Widow*. I've met a trustworthy man who saw her."

Hamlet reached across the table, the little paper boat he'd made held out in his fingers.

"What's this, sir?"

His turn to say nothing. Art took the paper. It was an ordinary scrap that anyone could have used to write a message on. Something was written on it, too. Art unfolded the boat.

Familiar and disturbing, a line of letters marched across the paper. The ink was recent, black and fresh. It might have been written yesterday.

Ebad and even Felix craned close to inspect.

(Through the trees a faint music sounded, Cuthbert's hurdy-gurdy. A boy was laughing. Squinting against sunlight, you could just make out Calm Holroyal dancing the new dance, the Walzen, with the lion.)

"We're both aware, Captain B, your original treasure map gave its clues in letters. This may be the same. 'Tis supposed to come from that mysterious Green Book, copied from it by one of Mary Hell's—er, guests. His bones were found, you understand, with some of his personal clothing attached. This note of letters was in a hidden pocket, wrapped in greased cloth to waterproof it. What you hold is my own copy, an accurate one, made from that first note."

Art ran her eye again along the extended line:

N E T Y A V—

and so on.

On the map of the Treasured Isle, which had taken them to the chest *full* of maps, the letters had represented numbers, the number each letter was in the alphabet. If these letters were of the same kind, who could know?

Muck gave a stifled yap in his bush.

Laughter was now sparkling on every side, people returning into the gardens. The family and several servants became visible. Strawberries were being brought, crimson on silver trays, jugs of cream, chocolate—Hamlet stood up, nodding politely. Michael turned helpfully to take a tray. Landsir Chrys advanced, beaming wolfishly. Business, apparently, such as it had been, was now over.

❦ THREE ❧

Feathered Friends

"Goldie, I am most disappointed."

Judge Knowles scowlingly confronted his meek companion in her parlor.

Meekly, she murmured, "How have I annoyed you, sir?"

"Our aim, I had thought, was to change you from your former ways—those manners taught you by your appalling life at sea—into a proper woman. Yet the womanly virtues go unnoted. Look at this book of corrective sermons I gave you, penned by the Reverend Smoal—thick with dust and unread. . . ." Goldie lowered her eyes sadly. "And here, this embroidery—why, a four-year-old could do better! A *parakeet* could do better! Besides, I hear you were seen on the street dressed in *male* clothing."

Goldie shook her head. "Sir, whoever said that lied. I'd no more don such garb now than I'd put stinging nettles into your bed."

"Tush and pash. What rubbish are you uttering? Nettles kettles. My own servant, Crabbe, saw you in Shepherd's Shrub Market, clad as a lad."

Goldie wept into an itty hanky. "Such wicked falsehoods."

Knowles loomed over her. "You'll mend your ways, girl. I'll not be made a nut-hat of. I'm off now to my sentencing. Five felons in need of hanging. Think upon it."

Half an hour later, the judge was in his carriage and on the way to the Law Courts. Goldie, her female attire torn into rags and strewn about her chamber, was dressed in breeches and boots, shirt and coat, and her bag already mostly packed. She went next into the adjacent room, the judge's own. From his night table she took up such jewelry of gold and silver as he left off when out judging. From his wardrobe she took his three best lawn shirts and his second wig. From a loose board by the fireplace she clawed up a hearty cache of coins and banknotes and a small box of rubies—whose position he had unwisely given away in a tender moment. A few other items Goldie gathered. A couple more surprises she organized.

Left to her own true wishes, she would have shot the judge dead, but common sense told her the hue and cry such a desirable act would cause. And no suspect would be more obvious than herself. Maybe in the future, some chance to be *thoroughly* avenged for these boring months might arise. Almost regretfully, then, Little Goldie remembered Mr. Beast, her First Officer aboard the *Enemy*. Beastie would've seen to Mr. Judge Know-Less. But Beastie, too, had hanged at Oldengate from the Lockscald Tree, thanks to Knowles himself. A shame, really. But after all, it served the Beast right. He'd denied her, made all her men abandon her on the Treasured Isle—simply because that thicko Arty Blasty had beaten Goldie in a—completely not fair—duel.

However, there still remained one small joy.

Mr. Crabbe, who had spotted Goldie going to see her pet Captain Nunn in male clothes and told his master, now learned Goldie was asking for him in her parlor. It seemed she was grateful that he had uncovered and reported her improper dressing up—for it was a vice she *longed* to conquer. Therefore she wished to reward him.

So Mr. Crabbe, the fool, scuttled up the stairs and, on entering the parlor, met Goldie's boot full-on in the stomach area. Once he was down, Goldie leaped on him. She gave him a nasty whack, he later whined, in every painful bodily spot, and ended by pouring glue into his hair.

That done, leaving him stuck to the carpet, Goldie toted her bag and bounded out into the street. Here she donned cutlass, pistol, and plumed hat. She now fitted in entirely with Lundon's fashionable piratic scene.

Marching toward the Old Bull and Shrub Tavern, where anxious Captain Nunn was already waiting, Goldie was only challenged once.

The PIRATE, or Pirate Intolerance Regiment and Teatotalers of England, had a stand set up by the tavern door. A group stood there shouting about ordinary citizens being the victims of "Buccaneerafear," afraid to "Step outside into this tumult of cutlasses and feathered hats—see there—come, lad, come. Take off your ridiculous gear and, pray, don't enter this den of vileness, where foul alcohol and coffee are served to puddle the brain! Tea is the only wholesome drink." About six huge teapots were balanced on the stand. The teatotalers, who would drink only tea, swigged from their spouts constantly, snorting with approval. Another feathery "pirate," passing Goldie, called, "Coffee and wine's nothing to them lot. Addicted as haddocks to that tea! You watch, once they've drunk it all, they'll go running off for a fresh brew."

"Listen not, O curly-haired youth!" cried the loudest-shouting PIRATE member, making a huge lunge at Goldie. His tea-mad eyes blazed. But Goldie reached past and, with drawn cutlass, smashed every pot at one blow. Black tea exploded in all directions. The PIRATEs dropped any pretense at preaching and fell to the ground, slurping the tea remains frantically from the street and pushing one another out of the way to get them.

Unhindered, Goldie went into the tavern.

"Miss me, Nicholas?" she inquired of Captain Nunn. "Or is

your new friend to take my place? What are you doing with a pigeon?"

Nicholas Nunn, Captain of the Destroyer FRS *Total Devastation,* cleared his throat. Goldie always made him uneasy, despite her looks and her treasure-hunt plans. The pigeon, too, had rather unnerved him, suddenly flying in at a window and landing on his table. Actually, it was a white dove, NN thought. He said, "Do you see what's on its leg?"

"My, a piece of parchment. Can it be a message from someone? Do tell who, Cappy Nicky Nunny. From a new girlfriend, maybe? Better not be, baby, by the Cat's Portal."

Captain Nunn tried to capture the white pigeon-dove. But as had already happened many times, it evaded him, flying up in the air. Now, though, it made for Goldie.

"Nick, thou are a twit." Ungently grabbing the bird, Goldie prized the bit of paper off its leg. Then dumped the dove back on the captain's empty lunch plate.

She opened the paper. Now Goldie was surprised.

"What is it, Goldie?"

"Well, tain't for you, sir. It's for ickle me. Odd."

She read the tiny scrawl, frowning, and Captain Nunn kept quiet, watching the dove sitting on his plate. ("What a useless cook they must keep here," remarked a passing drinker. "Look, they ain't even cooked it.")

Goldie, when the captain dared glance at her, was staring into space. Her face showed a weird mix of horror, anger, and excitement.

"Er—bad news?"

"Some well-wisher."

"Er, yes? You mean someone who makes wishes at wishing wells—er, do you?"

"I mean, you hack-squawk, he or she says they wish *me* well. I'm addressed by my name, *all* of it." She read out softly in a cold, thin voice. " 'Little Goldie Girl, Pirate Captain, Daughter of the Golden Goliath.' But," she went on, "he or she doesn't reveal who she or he is. Nevertheless the information is—perhaps valuable."

"May I know it?"

"You'd better, Nunny." Goldie clenched the paper now in her fist. "I've tried before to learn where she took herself, that rat queen Artemesia Blastside. Oh, I even went and saw the mob cheering her, when she wed that wretch Phoenix. I was the only one didn't cheer. And my neighbors turned quite unfriendly. I had to whisper I'd lost my voice—*couldn't* cheer. But oh, I'd have liked to have shot the pair of them, there on the church steps."

"Yes. Captain Blastside is your enemy—"

"My *Enemy* is my ship, you twern-bat."

Captain Nunn was now truly confused. He opened his mouth, shut it.

Goldie said, "Art's off at Good Deal and Dove, in her own bloody revamped drat of a ship. Legal Privateer, pirating for flaming Free England, by the Wheel. Him, too, that Phoenix. All of them. Well"—her eyes scorched over the captain—"at least I know now she's due to be at sea. My kind *well-wisher* has done that for me. So we'd best hurry and get your own vessel on the waves. Drink up. We're off."

"But—I'd ordered a roast dinner. . . ."

"No time. Eat that pigeon, if you're hungry. Or"—Goldie's face now glittered with a kind of diamond cruelty—"let *me* have it. . . ."

There was no reason she should hurt the dove. But her boiling thoughts of Art, who had outwitted, beaten and shamed her, and cut on her perfect skin that miniature cross, needed expression. The dove was for it.

The captain looked squeamishly away.

And so he missed Goldie's second grab at the bird, and how the bird now evaded her. Rushing up in a furious white clatter of wings, it turned and slashed Goldie deeply with its beak across the palms of both her hands.

She shrieked, and the more sober persons in the Old Bull and Shrub looked around. *"My sword hand . . ."* Goldie spat as blood dripped.

The dove was gone, a flying summer snowball. Goldie wasn't to know that the one who used such doves as messengers had trained them all in both self-defense and attack.

In this way ten further minutes were lost as Goldie was bandaged and given brandy. Then she and her friend were in their own carriage, rumbling through the pirate-choked streets, going southward. The ship waited at Port's Mouth—a long journey. And it wasn't any destroyer. Captain Nick had taken unofficial leave from his naval captaincy in order to disappear on Goldie's quest. He hoped Goldie wouldn't be too upset. But she was going to be, for she had naively imagined he'd steal the destroyer for her, as she had suggested. NN was in for a bumpy ride.

Another upset and bumpy ride was had that evening by Judge Know-All. Getting home, he had found himself made a nut-hat of after all, his servant beaten up and glued down and most of his best valuables thieved—all by a young woman he had saved from the gallows last winter.

Tumbling to bed after midnight in a state of combined rage and unwilling embarrassment, he encountered Goldie's last treat.

His bed had been stuffed full of the fresh green thousand-needled nettles grown for soup in his garden.

Howling, the grave and clever judge bolted back out of his bed, scarlet from top to toe with stings, and fell down his own stairs. The roaring and crash brought every one of his servants, even the unglued Crabbe, out to see.

Carried moaning to a couch, Judge Knowles knew that, inside twenty-four hours, he would be the laughingstock of most of Lundon. For once he judged correctly.

Tinky Clinker had taken a little stroll along the late Port's Mouth dockside. The night was fine, the moon high—a round silver coin. He had a few of those, too, in his pocket.

He looked at the assembled ships, sleeping there, sail-furled or unrigged, like beautiful birds. But Tinky didn't see any of that—like that. He had already located the ship he wanted, for you could usually find the right information, if you knew how. A couple of questions, a couple of free drinks.

The *Rose Scudder* was a cutter, lean and well timbered, elm on her keel. No sails tonight, either white or black and Jolly Roger'd—the skull and crossbones. Who knew how that dotty danger Little Goldie would want this ship to look, once out of port? A replica of the *Enemy* seemed likely. But maybe not. You couldn't tell with the Goldies of this world.

And his interest? Tinky, though wary, felt now he had a bargaining card for getting on that ship, and sailing on the treasure quest.

It had been the luck of the devil, how he'd got it.

Those three afternoons before, selling off the owled goods at back doors high and low across South England and Lundon Town, Tinky had called on his final client.

The Republican tax on coffee, alcohol, chocolate, and lots of other nice things might bring the government money—but a smuggler made sure they didn't get much. No one wanted to pay through the nose, not even to help the war effort. As for the tea, it was taxed worse than anything. And those teatotalers—well, they couldn't get through half a morning without three or four strong pots of the stuff.

Clinker had been recommended to this particular client. The man was a member of PIRATE, and he welcomed the owler with glee. "You'll have a cup?"

"Don't mind if I do," said Tinky.

Outside in the yard, some geese were strutting about.

"Prime ol' geese," said Tinky. It often paid to be friendly.

"Pride and joy they are, sir. I'll let you into a secret. You and I, we both like to get under the law a little."

"Oh yus?"

"Every one of these fine geese is marked as a celebration dinner for someone. They all pay me, and then they come for the goose. Which I hand them—in, as you might say, its wrapped state." Tinky looked blank. "I mean, in its feathers and alive."

The boastful, teaed-up Pirate-Intolerant then explained that the goose buyers always made a fuss. They said they had understood their goose would have been killed and ready-cooked. The PI claimed this was a mistake on their part—a live goose was a *fresh* goose—but assured them anyone could deal with the bird and packed them off.

"Inside two days, generally, back they come."

"That good a meal? That *bad*?"

"No, sir. I mean my geese come back. They are trained to escape, and fly off. Homing geese, one could say."

"Then don't yer customers turn up and cause bother?"

"Nay, innit. You see," said the PI modestly, "my wife and I move house a lot. And the geese with us. Once the sold bird's back, off we all go. The ex-customer can't find us. Only trouble we ever had," he added, "is with one particular goose. Bubbles, he's called. See, there. That's him."

Tinky gazed through the open door. All the geese were, to him, identical. "Oh ah."

"Now, Bubbles had been sold twenty-six times. And always returned to me inside three days. But on the occasion of his last sale—winter just gone it was—the naughty chap went missing for over five months. I knew the customer hadn't eaten him. We had to stay put, you see, waiting for Bubbles to return, and the man turned up ranting about his goose disappearing. But I said quite truthfully, 'There are the geese, sir. You can plainly see Bubbles isn't among them.' And he had to admit this was a fact. I gave Bubbles up for lost. Then, this summer, there he was. Knew him at once. 'If only you could talk, old fellow,' I said to him. 'Where hast thou been?' In a way he did talk, though."

"Oh yeah?"

"By St. Eddible's Oyster he did. Bubbles brought a waxed parchment in his beak. Folded into a paper boat it was. A map, I think. He let me take it and waddled off with the others. I have the curiosity still."

Tinky had changed to stone. Of course he had heard the legend of the goose and the treasure map—he'd always reckoned it a joke. He unstoned himself slowly so as not to draw attention, sniffed, and said vaguely, "Well, I'd give something to see that, I would. Bubbles's map."

"Would you? My dear boy, I'll fetch it. You can *have* it, if you like. It's some theater tosh, what else, from these endless awful pirate plays, which we of PIRATE picket to get taken off, for the good of a Buccanighted nation. Yes, here the map is in this jar. Take it, take it. I've never liked it in the house, really. Pirate muck. Now, tonight I have a goose being collected, that one—Mabble—do you see? So a few more days and my lady wife and I will be drinking your admirable tea in our next house. I'll be sure to send you the new address."

Bell and High Water ———

Interesting Mr. Bell—who was not a mister, nor named Bell— stood at the edge of Edge Village, looking out at the Festival of Ships going on in the sunlit bay.

There had been some aggravation about this, among the captains of the warships there, and also the navy patrols.

But a Celebrity was here, after all. *Piratica* was here. And the authorities had meant to hush that up. Ha ha.

There was her ship, the *Unwelcome Stranger*, known in song and story, poised upon the outer water, waiting, they said, for tonight's high tide to leave England and begin her now-legal piratic assaults on the Avey Voos.

And so, the festival, in Piratica's honor.

Mr. Bell watched this, quietly at first.

Her long black hair was tied back; her hazel eyes were clear. Her boots were polished. And so were her cutlass and her flintlock.

By midafternoon she'd know if she had been accepted into Piratica's crew.

Mr. Bell had great self-control. More than might have been expected—for though she was nineteen, in male attire she looked much younger.

People were all around now, pointing out the peculiar festival ships, laughing.

Mr. Bell, accustomed to presenting her/himself as the center of attention, laughed too, pointed, was splendid.

"This house is full of Frenchies!" hissed Glad Cuthbert.

Art said, "Why do you think so, Mr. Cuthbert?"

Glad Cuthbert drew Art into a side room off the hall. No one else was about. "After lunch-dinner, I goes off by meself. Takes a look round. I always do, new place. Amazing what you see."

"And you saw?"

"Nothing. *Heard.* Up there in the library room. Two men talking Fringlish with that Wild Michael."

"Fringlish . . . oh." Art had been taught real French by her mother, along with other languages. But Fringlish was a combination language of French and English, often incomprehensible to true speakers of *either* French or English.

"One of 'em says *'Je ne sais quoi do wot?'* Then Mikey says, *'N'importe. None'll voos attrapeh. Trusteh moi.'* And the third chap, he says, *'Mais ils on our heels, n'est pas innit.'*"

Art mused. "So one of them was baffled, but Michael said it didn't matter, to trust him and no one would catch them. And the third said, 'They're on our heels.' And then?"

"*Then* that lady Calm and that lion come springing upstairs. So I pretends I'm a-tuning the ol' hurdy. And we go out and I play a bit, in the garden, like you saw."

"Where's Ebad?"

"Talking with that Michael. Cap'n—is there any chance Ebad Vooms could be—"

"No, Cuthbert. None. If the Holroyals are in some way assisting the Monarchist French to spy on England, and then to escape, Ebad of all people wouldn't be helping."

Two servants wafted through the hall.

It would soon be time to leave this elegant (and sinister?) house.

"Say not a word, Cuthbert, to anyone. Get me?"

"Aye, Cap'n."

They strolled out. "And so," Art said clearly, "your wife threw a *cat* at you, you say?"

"Great big tabby."

The servants passed.

Wild Michael appeared.

"And what did you *do* with the cat?" (Art)

"Kept it. Nice old furry thing it was. But it ran off with the black tom belonged to the horse-bus driver."

"Hate to chop your fascinating chat," said Michael.

"No chop, sir. 'Twas done."

"I'll bet," said Michael. He smiled at Art. The smile perhaps said, *And I believe you weren't talking of cats a minute back.* "I've been hearing," said Michael, "such tales of your artistry with the sword, Captain Blastside."

"Have you."

"All Free England rings with praise of it. You can best any man—or woman. They say."

Art smiled, too. "Some will say anything."

"I have to mention, I've longed to see you in action, Cap'n Art."

"And alas, we must instead go our separate ways."

"Then perhaps, before we do, you might indulge me."

Wild Michael stood lightly, amiable still, balanced on the smooth, wide, shiny floor, his hand casually at rest now on the hilt of a fine lean blade. Art, dressed as ever as a man, also had a sword at her side. She, however, didn't put her hand across to it.

"And what would your gracious mother say, sir, if we took to brawling in her house like ferrets?"

"Ma would laugh. Dad would probably start to gamble—on *you*, Captain. Emma would scream for joy and Hamlet become stern. Calm would sit on the highest step for the best view. Look. There he is already."

Art glanced up and saw Calm Holroyal had indeed somehow appeared from nowhere and was perched at the top of the stairs. None of the others were visible, though. Let alone any Frenchmen from the library.

It seemed Wild Michael meant either to threaten or to test her. He must guess, or have himself overheard, Glad Cuthbert's message.

Art drew her own sword with a lightning movement. The flash of afternoon sunlight on the blade lit up the hallway like a soundless cannon blast.

She could see—had seen from the first—that Michael was fly and quick and would certainly be no less than a good fighter. But he had been trained, of course, in the sensible way, not like her—on a stage.

Art Blastside walked toward him. Four feet off, she spun on the spot and, rounding on him, brought up the blade at a slant that nearly knocked Michael's sword right out of his hand.

He stepped quickly back. "Geezer! You're one cool dudette, I trow."

But next second he slewed hammering in at her, the flick and slice of his sword lashing like a dragon's tail of steel.

Art jumped clear. She leaped directly at the wooden banister, swung herself around on it, and landed a cracking kick on Michael's right shoulder.

He yelled. "By the Goat's Garter!" Even now he had not dropped his sword. He was strong.

Art let go the banister. The thought uncurled through her head that she was enjoying this.

She grinned at Michael and he grinned back.

"Now," she said sweetly. And dropped like a stone, ducking the swing of his blade, rolling like a ball, slamming into him—all in one single riot of motion. As his legs went from under him and he toppled over backward, she reached up and batted the sword after all from his grip, as idly as swatting a gnat.

The entire fight had taken two and a half minutes.

They sat a few yards apart on the marble floor, laughing at each other.

"I see 'tis all true. Brill, Cap'n. We must meet again."

"Anytime."

"But not this one."

The new voice was cold as frost on iron.

The people in the hall, and Calm on the stair, looked up and along the gallery above.

Felix Phoenix stood there, a fashion model in his pirate clothes, his face matching all the white marble.

"Hi, Phoenix. What's afoot?"

Felix stared at Art. "Oh, *nothing*, it would seem."

He turned and strode away along the gallery.

Art said, "What bites *him*?" Felix remained a mystery to her.

Glad Cuthbert leaned on the banister and watched Wild Michael and Art Blastside shake hands. Whatever had needed to be proved here had been, apparently. But Felix? Cuthbert understood. Felix was jealous as hell. And from the look of Wildy and Arty, any man might be, yeah.

In the boiling room at the Hog in Heaven next: Art and Felix.

"Haven't you enough men to play at swords with?"

"Plenty. I told you. Michael wished to prove me."

"Managed it, too."

"Phoenix, you are being—"

"What? What am I being? A *husband*? God forbid. I'll tell you, Artemesia—"

"Don't call me that!"

"—you can go off on your privateering and get yourself and all your hapless fellow actors killed by French warships. Good luck to you. I'll remain in England."

Art's mouth fell open. She slammed it shut.

"So. At last you see reason," she muttered, through nearly closed lips.

"Yes, I see *something*. I see I'm not *fit* to be aboard your scrug of a ship, not fit to rob and ram and bully across the seas. Maybe ask your Michael to help instead."

"Michael . . . Don't be an idiot. He has his own ship—oddly called the *Invisible*—and a pack of plots going from the sound of it. Cuthbert told me—"

"I don't give a cinnamon damn for what anyone told you. *I* am telling you. I'm off."

Art felt a deep, sore ache begin inside her heart. Strange. So long since she felt this, but at once easy to remember. It had been during that journey home as a prisoner, seeing Felix on the other ship, thinking he hated her, knowing she mustn't look across at him or she'd break in pieces, and *that* she would not do.

Same today. *Molly wouldn't have stood for this. Neither shall I.*

"Do as you please, sir. When are you going?"

"This moment. My bag is packed."

"Don't let me keep you. The wooden thing in the wall is the door."

Felix grimaced; his eyes were *black*. He pushed one beautiful hand through his fantastic pale mane, slung his bag over his shoulder, and stalked from the room.

Art found she was shaking.

She mastered herself in three furious breaths.

Outside the window, some peculiar things were happening on the sparkling bay. She watched, not really knowing what she looked at, as lopsided small ships were towed up and down by rowboats. The vessels were dreamlike—or nightmarish—colored all wrong and all out of proportion. People on the shore cheered or jeered and threw their pirate hats in the air. *Am I going off my head?* Art asked herself, peering at the inexplicable sight.

At least, out beyond the major cluster of ordinary, sane-looking shipping, the *Unwelcome* remained, a perfect silhouette.

The summer sun was going over. Only six more hours till eleven o'clock. They would sail then, she and her men, and the extra crew that was hired. Not Phoenix. Not her partner. Well, she had wanted him not to be there. Hadn't she?

Under the inn window baby voices fluted.

Then a mother's shrill cry: "Anchor! Leave Cannon-Ball alone!" And then an older child saying with disapproval, "Mizzen-Mast's just been sick all down my skirt."

There was this fad, too, since Art was freed from the gallows and piratomania began. Newborn babies were given nautical names; some children had even had their existing names altered. Such was the case below the window, for now the mother yapped, "Cutlass! Don't eat that! You don't know where it's been."

"It fell off that bacon ship, Mum!"

"No, Cabin. It can't have."

"Yes, Mum. Mum, Mum—look, that gull's got a bit! And there's a bit o' fish in the road."

Someone else shrieked, "I bin stung!"

Then from the bay came the vague swelling roar—of a familiar name.

Art straightened, nearly unnerved.

"*P-i-r-a-t-i-c-a,*" they were shouting.

Someone thumped on the door Felix had closed with such crashing quietness.

Art threw it open.

Salts Walt and Pete were bouncing there, with Honest and Eerie.

"Art—come and see. They're having a festival in your honor. There's ships sponsored by all the trades and businesses . . ."

"A baker's ship made of loaves of bread and buns . . ."

"One of meat—that's the Butchers League . . ."

"*Flowers*, from the Flower Girls' Collective . . ."

"And a fish one—choice—you should see the sails—whole shark-skins—'Tis charmingly done, Arty."

About six bees soared into the inn room.

Art and her men ducked and wove, avoiding them.

"They're after the flower ship," Eerie explained as they hastily exited from the room, leaving the bees in possession.

Art didn't want to go down into the town, let alone be acclaimed right now as Piratica. Yet somehow she didn't have the energy, suddenly, to resist.

Instead she seized Eerie by the throat, dislodging his lace ruffles. "If you—or *any* of you—say who we—*I*—am—I'll run the poached ranter through."

The street glowed and throbbed with the heat of five o'clock. Out on the blue water, the red and brown meat ship circled with the silvery, white, and black fish ship. The ship of loaves was already soggily coming undone and going down. The flower ship smelled marvelous even from this distance. It was every color of red roses and yellow and cream lilies, blue lavenders and purple, late pansies, stock, and vines. A paper ship was also afloat—just barely. It had been constructed from old and current newspapers and was the work of the *Good Deal and Dove Tymes*.

Gulls swooped in a swirling frenzy, ripping off chunks of roast beef or prime cod or newspaper (perhaps a mistake). Laden with goodies, the big birds next came arrowing in over the town. Slices of ham dropped into hats. Half a plummeting leg of lamb stunned a gentleman standing at the waterside. Wasps, bees, and flies droned in droves to and fro, drunk on nectar from the flower ship, sting-ing at will, flying into hairdos and up noses.

Peter was now alarmed. "Bit of a fish-up, if you ask me."

The jolly noises of the seafront were changing to yipes of out-rage and dismay.

From some of the routing shipping farther out, an occasional sharp smack of small gunfire sounded as attempts were made to keep off insects and gulls. In their rowboats the Butchers' League, too, was firing in the air in a vain effort to save some of their vessel—a whole roasted ox now tilted into the water in a screeching froth of birds.

England has gone mad, Art thought bitterly.

"Someone has to judge the prizewinning ship!" declared Eerie. "Look, there she goes. Why, Art! She's supposed . . ."

"She's supposed to be *me*," agreed Art in a growl.

She glared at the dark-haired young woman dressed as a male pirate and carried along by the crowd toward a stage hung with pink-and-black skull-and-crossbones bunting.

"*Piratica!*" yodeled a thousand voices, between bee beatings, while the rain of wet bread, bacon, and gull poo continued to descend.

Honest said, in his mild, uncritical way, "It's Mr.-Mistress Bell."

Mr. Bell had been nabbed by the crowd just as she left the Hog in Heaven with her paper of successful recruitment.

" 'Tis she! She be Piratica, Queen of the Seas! Cool!"

Mr. Bell found herself lifted up shoulder-high, to the pleasure of the clapping audience. Why not? It wasn't the first time she'd been the center of attention.

Her mind was, though, a little preoccupied.

About half an hour before, in the main room of the inn, she'd paused for a cup of coffee. And while she sat there, through the room had stridden one of the most handsome young men ever to grace a pirate coat. He, too, barked for coffee, then slumped at her table, slinging on a bench a traveling bag.

"Excuse me," he said after a moment, not glancing at her. "I didn't mean to alarm you."

"You don't," said Mr. Bell firmly. "I was just reading some good news."

Then the blond-white-haired man gazed right at her with eyes of midnight blue.

"That's gladdening. But then, I see you're one more of these piratomaniacs."

"I have a place on a ship," said Mr. Bell.

"Oh, really? What's that? The *Eye Patch and Catflap*?"

"Nay, sir, by the Wheel. The famous privateer *Unwelcome Stranger*. I'm off to harry the French."

Felix cursed.

"You seem upset," Mr. Bell suggested.

"No, no," snarled Felix, "I'm merry as a bat in biscuits."

Mr. Bell rose. "I'll take my drink elsewhere."

"No, take it here. I apologize for my outburst. The *Unwelcome*, you say."

"Mmm."

"So am I. To sail with her, I mean."

"Oh? Really? A fellow member of Piratica's crew?"

"Not quite. Piratica's husband."

"Then you must be Mr. Phoenix, the famed painter."

"Yeah. That's me."

"I am quite awestruck."

"No, madam," said Felix, "you're too lovely to be that. Or to be such a liar."

"Oh. Am I lovely, Mr. Phoenix? You should know. A painter, and so on."

"And may I ask your name?"

"In *your* case, Mr. Phoenix, I think you may use my female name."

"Which is?"

"Belladora Fan."

"Do you flutter like a fan, Mistress Fan?"

"Not often. Just my heart. Occasionally."

The coffee was drunk. Mr. Bell got up. Mr. Phoenix, who had obviously changed his mind, then returned upstairs and repacked his bag, in a room full of fourteen bees, one wasp, and a muddled dragonfly. Unlike the last packing he had made here, now he got ready for a voyage.

Outside, soon after, on her little stage, Piratica-Bell judged the flower ship the winner. It was by then the only one still entirely afloat.

Two seconds after the judgment, the poorly angled shot of a flintlock missed ten gulls, and instead set the barely-above-water remains of the newspaper ship afire.

The papers had been waxed, if not very well. They took the flame sluggishly at first. Thought about it, liked it—and gulped it down.

Over the bay astonishing fire ran spangling. Three rowboats went up instantly, and rowers from the Bakers' Association hurled themselves off into the water. The bread ship remains caught, too, sending up bursts of black smoke.

The day had been a scorcher. Everything so dry . . .

What happened next happened in moments.

The mass of rowboats provided unfortunate stepping-stones for the fire, which rushed headlong at the sinking prow of the meat ship. The fats of cooked lamb, beef, and pork threw fireworks drizzling into the sky. Then, with a fizzing thud, the entire dinnery craft exploded.

Stinking fat, slivers, minces, and dagger-sharp bones arced over the bay, striking men already struggling in the water, hitting the crowd along the waterfront so screams broke out.

The fish ship, too, was now on fire.

No one was near enough to tackle it—the Fishmongers' League, or whatever they were, had already left their own burning boats and were flailing in the bay. The fish ship drifted, as if guided by some horrible unseen hand, through the open water, to where six merchant vessels, a naval patrol of five cutters, and seven tall warships of the line stood at anchor.

Such shipping was either too bulky to maneuver very fast or hemmed in by other ships that were. Cries of anger and panic rang out on the decks. Poles were produced, and long grapplers, and with these they tried to drive the mindless fish ship away.

But with a dreadful unhurriedness the flaming, spitting fry-up slowly—inexorably—circled in first to one, then—driven off—to another.

As men shouted threats at one another from ship to ship, the fish ship finally sidled by and was in among them.

"No, Art," said Eerie, trying to grab her.

"*Yes*, Mr. O. Let go or I'll fell you." And she was gone, over into the bay, and swimming like a slender snake for the outer water.

" 'Tis the *Unwelcome* she fears for," said Honest.

Something bumped into them, hard. It was Cuthbert sprinting from somewhere. "Come on, mateys. Yes, I've got the swimming now. Over we go!" Pushed and shoved and already half jumping, they splashed into the water in an untidy heap.

As they floundered and set course after Art, the whole massed crowd on the front, and all those now packing the windows of every waterfront inn, shop, and house, gave a bellowing groan. The FRS Merchant Trader *Siren*, first to be fully touched by the ship of burning fish, caught light like a candle.

Art lifted her head from the water as the noise came and the color of extra fire lit her path. She veered aside. Her object was solely to rescue her own vessel. She passed by *Siren*, but the fire was moving ahead of Art now. As she came level with her, FRS Warship *Killer Instinct* was also growing garlands of flame. Her crew were seething her with seawater, and foams of steam rose. The whole sea was darker, puddled with greasy fires, and the air thickened, full now of the bees and wasps of *sparks*. . . .

Behind Art came the sound of a mast splitting with a terrible crack. The warships, and some of the merchantmen, had cannon. How long before those guns primed themselves from the fire and self-detonated? Not long. Art turned in the water, saw her five crew fighting through a plunge of swimmers going the other way. Two men rode on a crisped side of beef, and one aimed a punch at Cuthbert, who avoided it by diving. A shower of blazing timbers rained over. Art could see, far off onshore, that something else had caught alight. She raised her arm, then pointed down. *Go under*. Honest got the message. Cuthbert, just coming up for air, got it and returned subsurface. Eerie dithered. Salt Walt pulled him below and Pete went with them. Art herself dived. Undersea, she swam at a rate of knots toward the *Unwelcome*, the ship farthest out along the bay. In Art's sight, the image of burning, the clouds of smoke. Noise and alarm rang in her ears. *War will look like this*. Then she dived deeper, swam faster.

In fact, FRS *Killer Instinct*'s cannon held out. But not her store of gunpowder.

Art was far enough away, and deep enough, that when the colossal boom came of the warship blowing up, it had the impact only of a single slammed door.

Night had fallen, after the sun sank bloody in a curdle of smoke.

Parts of the seafront still burned.

Vivid flames like crimson tongues licked at the smoke-blind stars.

One whole terrace of shops and houses had been destroyed. Four ships had been lost. Nine ships had been damaged. On human casualties, figures varied.

The Deal and Dove branch of the Pirate Intolerance Regiment and Teatotalers of England waited on a little hill overlooking this hellish vision of torched town and bay. Their visiting preacher, the Reverend Beast, was poised above his flock on an upturned cart.

Ignoring the calling and bell ringing below, every eye was fixed on the priest.

He drank from his black glass, blackened, as he had told them, from long years of tea drinking. "My insides're as black, no doubt," he had said, "but once my filthy heart was blacker. *I* was a pirate once. But I've mended my ways. We know, don't we, my good friends, that every pirate must be removed from the tablecloth of life. And every one of these pirate worshipers, who put on their garb and go about pretending to be pirates, too—they must be *brought to their senses*."

The assembly applauded.

Behind them, before them, crimson smoke, ruin, and distress.

"*This* is what this madness brings," cried the reverend. He raised his arms against the fantastic backdrop. His beastly, shaggy, craggy head was either inspiring—or revolting. The PIRATE members clearly thought *inspiring*.

"First Mate of God I am now," cried the Reverend Beast, who had been First Mate aboard Little Goldie's ship, the *Enemy*, less than two years before. "I tell ye again, this pirating about is what brings destruction!"

They had doused her with water and taken in her sails. They put down ship's boats and rowed her out, out beyond the bay, careful, drawing her along as they had in the Doldrums.

More than a mile off now, the smudged red rose of the town. Even the white owl faces of the chalk cliffs had a faint blush. But the *Unwelcome Stranger* was safe. She still had the luck she had always had. And Art Blastside—well, she still had the luck, as Hurkon Beare had said, of seventeen devils.

High tide turning at eleven gave them easy passage.

Everyone had reached the ship by then, including the new recruits. Including Felix.

Art gave him only one look. She did not show the jolt that went through her ribs. She didn't know if she was glad or sorry he'd joined them after all. But then, *he* didn't even *look* at her. He went across to Ebad, greeting him affectionately, as if someone had to be greeted like that and it certainly wasn't going to be Art.

They passed the flower ship, still floating another mile from the bay. It hadn't burned, but had sunk quite a lot. It wore the appearance of a floating wreath.

"The Badloss Sands will probably snag her," Eerie whispered. "Flowers for all those ships already broken there."

So, ship and crew pilotless after all, it was Ebad who guided them by the deadly sandbank.

Art had forgotten, till then, her dream of being wrecked on the Sands. Now she recalled it. But it was a silly dream. They skirted the unseen treachery without a hitch.

Unwelcome always survived—storm, battle, fire . . .

A last rose hung on the lilies in the water, a last rose smoked in the town. And quarrels—let them fall behind, too, and plots and mysteries. . . .

Before Art now, at last, at last, was the open sea.

Interval: Roll Call ⏤

Scene: The Deck. Morning. Fresh and cloudless blue. Sea frisking. Sails unfurled. Making good speed.

Present: Captain, officers, and crew.

Art Blastside: "Name by name, Mr. Vooms, Mr. O'Shea."

Ebad Vooms, First Officer of the *Unwelcome Stranger*, hands Eerie O'Shea, Second Officer, the crew list. Eerie hands it to Glad Cuthbert, unusually both gunner and promoted Third Officer.

Mr. Cuthbert calls the roll:

"Forecastle Smith—quarter master!"

"Aye, sir."

"Mosie Dare!"

"Present."

(Tazbo Lightheart, an experienced primer, ten years of age, jabs Mosie Dare, a young black man of nineteen, in the ribs.)

Tazbo Lightheart; "Say *Aye*, yer box of earwigs."

Mosie Dare (blushing): "Aye, sir."

Then—

"Ert Liemouse!"

Hoarse: "Aye *aye*, Mr. Bert."

"Doran Bell!"

Musical: "Aye aye, Mr. Cuthbert."

"Shemps!"

Silence. Some looking around. Shemps, one of the eleven gunners, is discovered asleep beside a tar barrel. Dragged to his feet, he starts a fight with de Weevil and Gideon Squalls.

Art Blastside utters one ringing roar.

Quiet happens.

"Shemps!" offers Glad Cuthbert again.

"Aye, Mr. C."

For a minute after this everything proceeds rhythmically through the following:

De Weevil and Gideon Squalls in person.

Sikkars Eye, the second primer (which is the job of priming and maintaining the cannon; a boy this time of twelve).

Mothope and Stott Dabbet, and the sole Cathay crew member, Plinke (whose actual full name is Pey-Lin-Kee).

After this, something else begins to occur.

Almost everyone begins to hear an echo start after each called name, but in the *wrong* order. The echo has neither the voice of Cuthbert—nor the name's owner. As so:

"Grug!"

"Aye, sir."

"*Grruggg . . .*"

"Oscar Bagge!"

"Aye, sir."

"*Baggy-baggy Bag-bag . . .*"

"Boozle O'Nyons!"

"Aye and yay, m'sir."

"*Boozle-Ony yons . . .*"

"Lupin Hawkscoot!"

"Aye aye, Mr. Glad."

"*Lupinn Hawk Scooooot . . . hoot . . . root . . .*"

Art touches Cuthbert on the shoulder. He pauses.

Ebad calls, "Who is repeating the names?"

"Taking the mouse, sounds like," shouts Lupin, fierce as a fork. "Jus' let 'im walk out and face me!"

But no one owns up, let alone walks out.

Cuthbert goes on, rather warily now.

"Larry Lully!"

"Aye, sir."

"*Larry Lully, Lully Larry . . .*" tootles the weird echo voice. It changes all the time, not only in tone—now rough and low, now high and piercing, now squeaky, now with two or three strange non-English accents—but it also *alters position.*

Whoever is doing this must be moving both fast and invisibly among the crowd on deck.

Larry Lully, a big gunner from Own Accord in the Blue Indies, just manages to catch Lupin Hawkscoot as he swoons. Larry and Plinke hold him up, and Lupin revives and moans, "'Tis a ghost— 'tis a ghost of my former cap'n—Cap'n Ahab. . . ."

"What, he's dead, is he?" asks Boozle.

"Nay, nah," says Stott Dabbet, "stood the old horse a drink at the Burglar's Bugle only last week. He wasn't dead. Having a whale of a time."

"Stow this chat," orders Art. It's stowed.

Cuthbert calls the actor crew now:

"Dirk!" "Aye aye, duckie." "Whuskery!" "Aye, Mr. Glad." "Salt Walter! Salt Peter! Honest Liar!" "Aye." "Aye!" "Aye aye."

And the last of the extra crew—Cuthbert going quickly now, trying to outwit the wandering unknown voice, which, oddly, didn't speak up over the actors: "Nib Several! Shadrach Lost!"

Both agree they're there.

But each time, once more, the voice repeats their names in some crazed way.

Cuthbert decides to ignore it.

They're nearly at the end anyway. . . .

"One man still missing, Cap'n," says Cuthbert.

"Not so, Mr. C.," grates another, yes, *visible* voice, shouldering up from the kitchen galley in the shape of a long, lank, grizzled man, age about forty, bristly with stubble and waving a long ladle.

"Here's myself, Feasty Jack, all present and incorrect. Star cook to the bad ship *Unwelcome*. And here's Maudy," adds Jack, holding up one arm.

A parrot, white as any chalk cliff or dove, springs from the crowd of men and straddles Jack's right shoulder with a squawk and flare of wings.

The mystery of the *hidden* voice is solved.

But the relaxed mood doesn't last long.

Off the mainmast launches a parrot green as grass and red as rubies. Plunqwette is plainly miffed.

She hurtles at Maudy, and Maudy hurtles right back.

Spitting, shrieking, clawing, and flapping, a terrible feather ball made of two bad-tempered parrots locked in a brawl clears the central deck area. Feathers, etc. scatter.

"*Two* of the things," mourns Eerie, mopping his coat. "Oh, by the Sacred Eardrops of the Mad Harper of Eira!"

Art sees it will be no use trying to control Plunqwette, so she lets them fight.

Feasty Jack evidently takes the same view.

Muck, who yesterday, bone in mouth, swam to the ship on the high tide just in time before she left the bay, crouches by the deckhouse, scowling through his whiskers. He's remembering his last stolen cuddle with a sobbing Emma Holroyal, by the strawberry bush. She had bidden the yellow dog farewell in a rain of tears. (When Hamlet came by later, also to bid her a tender farewell, Emma dismissed him with an irritated, "Oh, bye then.")

Muck now thinks it would have been better to have remained ashore. One parrot was awful enough. Two . . .

But miles of fair-weather sea now surround the privateer, who flies her usual Jolly Molly—black skull and bones on a pink ground. The coasts of France are a low, clear outline eastward and south.

Felix, un-roll-called, still a passenger, leans on the rail, fairly obviously drawing pretty Mr. Bell. Until Plunqwette, in passing, decorates the paper.

Plunqwette then appears to win the parrot fight. She retires to Art's cabin.

Maudy retires to Jack's shoulder, ruffled but unbowed.

The crew wipe off hats, coats, and go about their duties. (Only pretty Mr. Bell, who doesn't seem to have received any direct pooey hits, is laughing. Mr. Phoenix isn't. He chucks his parrot-messed drawing over the side.)

Art, standing under *Unwelcome*'s bowspirit, thinks, One man *is* still missing.

But he'll always be missing now, that one man. Black Knack lies oceans away on the sea's bottom, just off the changeable coast of the Treasured Isle, where Little Goldie's bullet put him.

STAGE TWO
The Ships

~ ONE ~

Robbery with Violets —

Decks are clean as just-peeled apples. The masts gleam with attention and suitable polishes. Tar, closely seaming up all planks, smells on the air as cozy as a new-baked cake—while the divine scent of actual n.b. cake also rises from Feasty Jack's galley. All's shipshape.

The crew have been busy and able. The *pirate* crew—that is, Art's band of former actors—have stood about with their eyes popping. "We never did it like *that*!" have complained Peter and Walter, Whuskery and Eerie. Even Dirk has had a row with Mosie Dare, who had been skillfully cleaning the gilt trim: "*That's* not how to shine a trim." "Oh, go and trim yer *nails*!" replied Mr. Dare. Whuskery had to stop the fight. Cuthbert, though, was pleased with the new recruits, admiring Grug and Plinke's elegant repair of a tiny rip in a sail.

Felix strolled about, drawing them all. This was all right now, of course. They were legal now—any artwork of their activities couldn't be held against them. No, one day each of these portraits might gloriously hang in the Republican Gallery.

Mr. Bell had strained her ankle, toppling over a coil of rope into Felix's handy arms. Plunqwette stalked the upper rigging. Muck kept hiding his bone in unfortunate places: "*Aah!* I'll never be able to sit down again!" for example howled Shadrach Lost, who had unexpectedly found the bone wedged into his hammock. Or, "No wonder me hurdy-gurdy wouldn't play," from Cuthbert, on pulling the bone out of the instrument's sound box.

Muck was definitely unsettled. He brought the bone at last to the captain's cabin. "Shall I place it here, Mr. Woofy?" queried Art, offering to put the bone into the sea chest there. Muck wagged his tail, uncertainly. The bone was placed. But Muck returned an hour later, drew it out—after much scrabbling and finally falling head-first into the chest among clothes, books, and maps—and ran off with the bone to the lower deck. "Dog's mad," said Gideon Squalls. "Cleanest Dog in England," growled Salt Walter. Ebad separated them. "Gentlemen, save your fists for the French."

Art had her cabin to herself, just as she'd had in the past. She was glad of it. If Felix had become her unfriend again, she'd rather he kept out of her way.

She watched him flirt with Doran Bell. Chilly with disgust and unadmitted hurt, Art ignored them both. Bell was useless, of course, after all. Not a seaworthy muscle in her whole cute frame. Why had she wanted to come with them?

Art spoke to her as Mr. Bell, still clad as a savage pirate, sat with ankle propped up, reading a book of poetry by Mr. Coalhill.

"At the first likely port, Mr. Bell, we'll put you off."

"Oh dear," said Mr. Bell, looking through thick dark lashes. "Captain, I must assure you, your husband's interest in me is purely—"

"My husband's interests don't *interest* me, madam. Either you pull your weight on my ship or you go off. The ports of Morrocaino will probably suit you."

"Oh, *Captain*—"

"That's it."

"But I've yearned to sail with you, by the Wavelet's Wobble."

"Whatever."

Mr. Bell looked down at her book.

Art strode away. Ebad, standing smoking his pipe under the foremast, watched Art go by.

Two days and nights also moved over the ship.

Art spent hours at the rail or on the quarterdeck, her eyes on the sea. *This* was her life. *This* was her family. She shut her heart in a sea chest and, unlike Muck with his bone, left it there.

There hadn't been a sniff of the French.

The long, intricate jigsaw piece of the coast, sometimes nearer, sometimes farther, showed only vague hints of life. There was little wind. The ship herself began to dawdle.

Art said to Ebad, "What do you say, Mr. Vooms, we set course at once for the south and east? There are no French here—the English patrols must have scared them off. But there'll be French traders aplenty that way, toward the Afric coasts." Ebad, Eerie, and Cuthbert nodded. They gazed intently at the map she had spread before them on the cabin table. It was recently drawn, a copy done from memory of the first map of the Treasured Isle. Inaccurate and guessed at; yet it was a powerful symbol.

"D'ya think we'll make it?" Cuthbert asked. "I mean—*twice*, like?"

"If we mean to," said Art.

"And the rest of these men, this newfangled crew, do *they* get shares?" said Eerie, still smarting that Lupin Hawkscoot oiled the masts in an unfamiliar way, and had given every gun a name.

"If the maps have come back to the Isle, there'll be enough treasure to go round," said Art.

"Nay, Cap'n—no, there won't," insisted Cuthbert. "Think of all the maps that went down. And besides, that Hamlet Ellensun—he said, you say, we must give 'em all over to the government."

"Never mind that. We keep to the pirate code, sir. Fair split for all. The government will come second."

Ebad said, "Honor among thieves."

That afternoon, the coastal jigsaw piece produced a slender point, around which two ships appeared, flouncing heavily up the Channel. They were French traders and flew the Bourbon Lily of the French king, gold on a blue ground.

"Not fifteen guns between them," said Art, staring through the spyglass. "Strike our colors," she added.

Down slipped the telltale pink-and-black skull and bones. Up soared a little handkerchief of flag, with a gold lily on a blue ground.

"Salut! Comment ça va?"

"Greetings," translated Ebad in a gruff voice for the others massed close, "how are you doing?"

The First Officer of the French trader *Parfait* (*Perfect*) smiled broadly. He answered across the interval of sea in a stream of French.

"We thought you were the damned English," translated Ebad softly. "Already the cannon were primed. The lookout shall be lashed."

All Art's crew belly-laughed. English? *Us?*

"Lashed?" gobbled Ert Liemouse, furious at the notion of the French whipping their lookout for being right. Tazbo Lightheart covered this gaffe, throwing his arms up and yelling *"Veevler rwah!"*

"Veevler rwah!" thundered Ebad.

All the crews on the French ship, and the Franco-Spanish trader behind, began to shout the same thing.

The crew of *Unwelcome* hastily joined in.

"What are we shouting, by the Gnat's (G)nightgown?" demanded Nib Several. "Long live the king," grunted others who had understood.

Just then Art jumped on the rail, seized the rope, and flung herself on it over the fourteen-foot seagap in one acrobatic flight.

She landed with the elegance of a lion by the slightly startled, but not-too-put-out captain, who was now on the deck of the French *Perfect*. "*Alors, vous êtes une fille!*"

"Well, well, you're a girl," said Ebad, resignedly.

"Not blind, then, the Monarchist carp!"

Art was going confidently on in the French faultlessly taught her by Molly. "But yes, Captain. And we are a privateer in the service of the king. We search the Channel and the mouth of the Atlantic for so-called Free English ships. And then"—she spread her hands—"we *eat* them."

The captain, very taken with Art, inquired her name.

"*Je m'appelle Artemise.*"

"First time I've heard her admit to her proper name," grumbled Eerie.

"May some of my fearless crew come aboard your ship, Captain? I can tell you, we've longed for a civilized chat. Also, we're obliged to offer any French trader captain goods taken from the stenchful English. Wine and tobacco, a cache of small gold boxes . . . we need to lighten our hold."

"He's greedy, too. Look at his eyes light up."

The French captain was all for a handover of pirated goods. The second captain on the Franco-Spanish ship, the *Perfecto* (again, *Perfect*) was happily of the same mind. The guns, still visible at the ports, looked unmanned by now and sleepy.

All bonhomie (*"That's good-will, mates!"*), thirteen of Art's men grabbed ropes cast to them and swung over onto the neighboring decks, six or seven to each ship.

Fifteen men remained aboard *Unwelcome* looking on—most of these at the gun stations below.

"Your crew is quite small, Captain Artemise," murmured the French captain, sliding a very friendly hand onto her shoulder.

"*Pardonnez,*" said Art regretfully, and set a pistol nose to nose with him.

"*Que faites-vous?*"

"What ya doin'?" translated Cuthbert.

"Talk English!" now bawled several irked voices as other unwelcome *Unwelcome* pistols and flintlocks poked at French nostrils, ribs, and backsides. "Or Fringlish! Likeh-voo cette ici?" "And, c'est à dire, stop trying to draweh votre pistol."*

On the Franco-Spanish ship, *Perfect 2,* resistance was attempted, and quickly ended when Shemps put a bullet through the planking an inch from the second captain's foot.

"Donneh, mon sir, or I'll pad you with troos."†

Art's new crew had also been sworn to the rule of Piratica. To rob while threatening, but never attempting to kill. Things were going so well.

Next minute the general merrymaking froze as de Weevil, up in the crow's nest, screamed: "South'ard! Big gunner!"

Art called, "Keep your eyes on our French sirs here." She did not shift her gaze at once. "*Cher capitaine,*" she whispered, "one unwise move and I will send your head skipping over the water." He shrank. *Then* Art looked back, around the point.

Yes, she was a sight, this fresh arrival. A vast whale of a destroyer, flying broadly the blue and gold of France. Thirty guns at least, and all snouting ready from her ports.

The French captain glanced, too, and breathed a prayer of thanks into the muzzle of Art's pistol. "*La Maman Trop.*"

"*The Bossy Mum?* Is *that* her name? Why, Captain," said Art, "what a sad thing for her and you—"

---

*"Do you like this 'ere?" "And, that's to say, stop trying to draw your pistol."
†"Give, my sir, or I'll pad you with holes."

She knocked him down with one swift blow of her fist. At this signal the others similarly felled their nearest opponents on the *Perfect* and the *Perfect*.

The scramble came, grim and savage over the rails, swinging from ropes or simply dropping into the narrow lane of sea between the vessels, and racing back toward *Unwelcome*. They managed it in the wake of the shock that had stayed the traders, but moments after a hail of enemy bullets began, and there sounded, too, the worrying clank and grind as French gunners reorganized the *Perfect* guns.

Art was one of the last to vacate the French ships. Ebad had been covering her, she saw, and Cuthbert. As the three of them now plunged off and into the strip of water, rapid fire whined over their heads. Art felt a red-hot scorch part her hair; then the sea closed her in.

Around her she glimpsed swim-kicking legs—then a dull, intense rumble told of a first French cannonball, shot low. Art somersaulted. Something like a boiling iron shark dived by her, not twenty feet away—missing them all, yet setting them spinning. Art desperately righted herself. The ball had gone wide of everything. Surfacing, she saw it bounding along the tops of the waves in a hiss of steam and speed—making apparently for Africay.

The *Unwelcome*, alternate plans previously decided, now began to slew away herself. The last yards of the swimmers' race were urgent. The privateer pirate's crew lugged themselves aboard across the gunwhales and fell onto the home deck.

From the French *Perfect*'s flank three more cannon barked—still aimed at too strict an angle for the crazily careering *Unwelcome*. Now that her own men were out of the water, however, the privateer's guns finally spoke up. Angle still told; most of the volley went wide—but a single shot split the Franco-Spaniard's bowsprit—

"Cuthbert," Art guessed. Down it went, hauling the flying and outer jibs off with it and leaving the inner jib and staysail flapping like the wings of a mad gull. Celebration burst from *Unwelcome*. Then she swung again, heeling around as if to kiss the sea with her mast tops. Men rattled over the deck cursing, but the privateer came up gracefully from her curve, turning now only her narrow stern toward the plunging French ships.

Art squinted back. They were out of range, and *Unwelcome Stranger* had had the last word. Nearly.

For in fact the real last word, like a golden ill-wish, was the great sea beast called *Bossy Mummy*, who drove on toward them. She had not yet passed her own floundering traders. Art knew *Bossy* would spare them not a glance. *Bossy* was now keen only on reaching Art's privateer.

Washed up amid her jangled crew, Art shouted orders. Ebad took the helm, which Boozle O'Nyons had so ably managed till now.

More men dropped down into the ship's insides, to be ready at the *Unwelcome Stranger*'s guns.

In one small fragment of her brain, Art noted her bickering pirate actors worked with the new crew in frantic harmony.

Oscar Bagge passed her, yelling, and Art ducked as a third of the fore lower stunsail, damaged by some previous hit, broke apart, the canvas slapping down across the deck. The trader's revenge for their bowsprit.

"Thanks for the warning, Mr. Bagge." They got up, and pulled a slightly stunsail-stunned Forecastle Smith up with them. "What's the plot, Cap'n Art?"

"We run," said Art. "She's big, their mother ship. But not so fast."

Felix was suddenly beside her, pale and raging, seizing hold of her. "You're bleeding, woman! Are you hurt?"

"Hurt? No. A bullet combed my hair. Get below, and take that idiot Bella Bell with you."

"You're the idiot, Art. To cause this—"

"*Below*, Mr. Phoenix." Art's face and voice were things of stone. He let go of her. "We do not argue in the midst of battle. Hold your row."

Something—what? pain? contempt?—crossed his face.

He turned and walked away over the waddling deck. She thought— a silly thought: How well he keeps his balance. He always has.

She thought, Do I like this? Speed and awful danger? Death in the shape of a French destroyer rushing near?

Shut up, Art, she thought. Hold your row.

And went to the quarterdeck.

The two trading vessels had by now fallen far behind, obscured by low necklaces of smoke. Beyond which the outline still towered of *La Maman Trop*. Advancing, always advancing, her black guns held high above the sea.

They ran.

They ran for three hours. Then three more. Longer. Sunset painted the west. Darkness drew in. Eastward, the coast of Franco-Spania. Little prickles of light along the evening shore—beacons, warnings. Stars matched them with warning beacons of their own.

Behind, at the world's rounded edge, the shape was still there, *Unwelcome*'s shadow, much larger and blacker than she: *La Maman*.

"She won't give up."

"Nay, too right. That one, I've heard of her. Like a bloodhound she is. Hunts till she can fix in her teeth."

Art stayed on deck. She arranged the watches, to give her men food and rest. She and her officers drilled the men. Rehearsals.

Feasty Jack came springing up to the quarterdeck, while Maudy claw-gripped to his collar, to bring Art a slab of warm bread plastered with meat stew.

"Cheers, Feasty."

"Least I can do, Cappy. May be the last meal ye ever champs on, once that mother catches us."

"How many guns do you think she has?" Art asked of Ebad.

"Thirty-seven, so I've heard. If she's using the right shot, her range could be well over a mile and a quarter."

"We can outwit her," Art decided. "Perhaps. . . ."

He didn't argue.

In the belowdecks Muck wailed. Plunqwette strode the rigging, her feathers on end.

The sky was blue-black, a vast dome. If only they could fly up into it—

But then, *La Maman Trop* would no doubt fly right after them. No escape. A heavy silence lay over the *Unwelcome Stranger*'s grunting, straining decks.

For a robbery, this one had gone badly.

Art slept two hours on the quarterdeck, woken at her instruction by Eerie.

He'd given her ten minutes extra, out of kindness.

She swore at him. Kindness left Eerie.

As the sun rose, it showed the unrolling coast. Nothing helpful there, no friendly harbor as yet, willing to welcome pirate and privateer, like the truce ports of the Morrocains. No islet to slip behind and hide.

You hoped a moment then, stupidly, that the pursuer had somehow melted away in the dark like a bad dream. But she hadn't. There she was, a bulky blodge on silvering sky.

Art called her officers and some of her most experienced new men. Eerie wouldn't look at her. Oscar Bagge, the carpenter who would double as ship's surgeon, waited, agitated, polishing up certain things from his trade—saws, blades, needles . . .

"I regret, gentlemen," said Art, cool as ever—or seeming so—"we have only one gambit after all. We'll turn and fight."

"Fight?" said Eerie in an awful rasp. "Fight that great big bully ship out there? She'll blast us apart, by the Milky Streams of the Lost Lands of Eira. Shiver us like—like a *stage prop*!"

Glad Cuthbert said loudly, "Whatever you say, Cap'n."

Shemps said, with a lurid scowl, "Let me at 'em, say I, by the Seal's Sandals."

"Aye!" shouted many voices.

Astonished despite herself, Art stared around. *They* were ready, then—the new recruits, these real sailors, these real pirates—these real Free English who hated Monarchists. Even Glad Cuthbert.

Oh, and after everything, her own crew, Molly's boys—they were wilting, as at the very start.

Whuskery and Dirk said nothing.

Salts Pete and Walt gawped, horror-faced.

Honest looked—sad.

Only Ebad was—Ebad. Unreadable, *blank*.

And it was Ebad who shouted, "Clear decks for action!"

Men pelted to obey.

The fake French colors had been taken down by now, and the skull and bones was bravely flying. Tazbo and Sikkars Eye had been oiling and coddling the cannon. Every man had had some sleep—or said he had. Muck and Felix and the useless Bell were below in passenger quarters. Plunqwette, refusing to settle, circled the masts. Art had tried to call her down, but Plunqwette knew by this time that calling in at battle stations meant shutting away for safety.

Art thought, We've had it anyway. She might as well stay on deck. If we go down . . . better chance to get away. Then mentally she slapped herself. *We shall win.* Against all odds. "I am Piratica," she breathed aloud. "Unbeatable. Eh, Ma?"

Up in the sky, as if she heard, Molly's parrot screamed, "Queen o' the Seas!"

Feasty Jack had appeared, and manned the aft-deck cannon. Maudy sat in Jack's pocket now, just his white head, with black beak and red eyes, stuck alertly out. The foredeck cannon was in Ert Liemouse's charge. Tazbo, Sikkars, Hawkscoot, Mothope, Lost, Squalls, Dabbet, Lully, Grug, and Nib Several were at gun ports below.

Art thought, We'll hit her hard, the *Bossy Mum*. But she'll—miss somehow. We'll take off again, get up coast, hide. This is possible. I have—the luck of seventeen devils.

In her head, Felix's voice. "But you never kill, Art."

I shan't.

The pirate band, with instruments, was assembled on deck.

And over the waters, a faint *rat-tat-pat*—the enemy war drums. Was the *Maman* inside her colossal firing range yet? Surely she was—

"Strike up!" Art shouted.

The band's drums too began to beat, Honest's hands whirling. Whuskery's trumpet gave a caterwaul. Walt's piercing whistle played a skittish tune. And then came the deep animal gurning of Cuthbert's hurdy-gurdy.

The huge French ship was near enough now that Art seemed to see, without the spyglass, the men up on her decks, the glint of handguns. But no longer could you hear her drums beating time for her advance. *Unwelcome*'s band had drowned them out.

This was music for a dreadful dance, ship with ship. Twenty-two guns to thirty-seven. (Why hadn't the French ship fired? Cat and mouse . . . ?)

The muskets of Dirk, Peter, Eerie, shining in the broadening day. Art's flintlock, cleaned in the hour before she slept, with a kind of tingle in its grip . . .

At the wheel, Ebad, with extra wheelman de Weevil ready to add weight.

Eerie had slung off temperament. He stood at Art's side. He was now in his role. Abruptly he roared, with an actor's flawless pitch, "Come, lads, let's sing 'em a pretty song—" and broke out his grand full tenor to launch them.

> *"Here's all poo to the Avey Voos—*
> *To every cowardly one of yous . . ."*

Every seaman's voice, even those of the gunners below, joined Eerie's.

Art turned and squeezed Eerie's shoulder. He only grinned and warbled on:

> *"No I don't care a jot*
> *For the French king's lot,*
> *Let them come along and meet us if they wish.*
> *For we'll take 'em by the hair*
> *And throw 'em in the air*
> *And sink 'em all and feed 'em to the fish!*
> *And I don't care a cod*
> *For any Frenchy bod . . ."*

A different voice sang out.

It was much deeper than Eerie's. Deeper than any voice on either ship.

The sea shook.

Singing stopped.

"By the Bunny Splice!"

"Do they have that much *range*—?" (Oh. Someone didn't know.)

La Maman, just about one mile from them, had loosed her opening shot, seventeen cannon mouths' strong.

"Starboard evasion, Mr. Vooms!" Art's cry came high and metallic over the general noise.

The water and the air between them and the French ship was coming undone as if seventeen enormous claws dragged through it.

"They only boast," lied Art to the astounded men around her. "The balls will be spent before they reach us. Hold tight."

Unwelcome spun to starboard.

Ebad and de Weevil hung on the wheel. Sky and sea and the on-rush of shot sprawled over and by. It was true. The balls had lost their immediate power and direction. (Poor ammunition?) One only touched—*touched*—*Unwelcome*'s keel, soft as a gentle hand—and she rocked.

Too soon to retaliate. Art's privateer *didn't* have the range.

Art looked only at *La Maman*, spoke to Dirk. "Mr. Dirk, to the gun deck, if you will, and tell them count to thirty. To thirty, come what may. No more and no less. Then fire. Full broadside. As we rehearsed it."

"Aye, Cap'n."

Cuthbert sprinted for the aft section—gunner now, no longer bandsman.

How brave they were being at last, she thought, her actor crew. Brave as the pink flag. She shouldn't have doubted.

One—two—

On deck, other men were counting in their heads.

Ten—fourteen—

Feasty Jack counted, Maudy nodded in tempo.

Seventeen—nineteen—

Twenty—twenty-three—

But I, she thought, did I—

The huge mass of *La Maman* gained on them, the wind behind her blowing from the northeast. For such a monster, in fact she was very quick.

Twenty-five—twenty-seven—

"I can't see their eyebrows yet. . . ."

Did I make a mistake?

Thirty.

THIRTY.

Unwelcome's cannon coughed a nine-throated united thunder. A gout of fire and metal smashed the sea to breaking glass—this time running away from her. Reloading speed was good. The nine-throated thunder came again.

Then *Unwelcome* did her little jig. She rotated steadily and presented her lean backside scornfully to the French destroyer—yet positioned just slightly askew, in case the bigger ship tried to rake her with a shot stem to stern. *Unwelcome*'s two aft cannon boomed, not wanting to be left out. She was a narrow target, that at least. . . .

She had fired twenty pieces of shot.

Dizzied by the spin, her men hung on to the rails and masts, craned at the gun ports, looking to see what effect this concert had had. A long, low vocal grimace rose.

Balls were cascading like diving dolphin, splashing *La Maman*—nothing else. Too low. And—

"Still too far."

Art: "We repeat the maneuver. Port swing, Mr. Helmsman."

She thought, Yes, a mistake. I should have waited. Where's my judgment? Where's my luck?

Below came the rumble of primers and gunners staggering to the opposite portside station.

Ebad had given the wheel over to de Weevil and Mosie Dare.

Ebad said to Art, "Do you see the flag the French are raising?"

"Yes, a white flag with a green key on it."

"It means they want to talk."

Why? she thought. They have the advantage. . . .

Across the narrowed space of water another voice came, this one human, propelled through a canvas horn. He used English.

"Greeting to the English rebel ship. We hold fire. You are a valiant vessel. We are willing to accept your surrender."

"Never!"

"Never, by the Whale's Warm Undies!"

"Rather marry a chicken!"

"Rather *be* the chicken you marry!"

All around they shouted denials. Art let them. They needed their fierceness. She watched the French ship—now near enough surely, even with the wrong ammunition, to blast her ship to splinters. Yet frustratingly still not quite near enough to be hurt by their answering fire.

So what now? Agree. Let them in close—*then*—

I can't think. What's wrong with me? Ma—give us a hand—

Art showed none of this inner turmoil.

She called in her own actor's voice, which covered the distance well, "Indeed, monsieur. And your terms?"

"Terms? Ha ha ha! *Alors*—here they are. We offer you a lovely holiday in the fair land of France. Our prisons, I assure you, are very tasty."

"How are the guns?" said Art to Whuskery.

"Hot as Indian mustard."

"You have five minutes," the French voice bawled. "Then we take you all apart."

"Art—what's that?"

"Walter, not now."

"No, Art—Cap'n—look! What *is* it?"

"Yay," said Oscar Bagge, gazing out where Walter did, toward the coil of the coast. "Something—but what?"

Art turned impatiently.

She thought her eyes played tricks from stress and lack of sleep.

A part of the sea, and also of the sky, seemed curiously cut adrift. It wavered there, riding the waves, approaching—or was it?

"It's nothing."

" 'Tis a cloud," Eerie said.

"On the *sea*?"

"Fog, then. Mirage. By the Blue-Eyed Sheep of Connor— shut up."

Art shook herself. She lifted her hand to the French. "Five minutes—*cinq minutes*—yes, monsieur."

"Four now!" the Frenchman bellowed playfully.

Art said to the men about her on the deck and grouped below, "We wait until they're close. Then loose our guns again. The same as last time. Double broadside, then aft guns."

"They'll rake us—blow us to bits, Captain."

"To bits of bits."

"Yes, Mr. de Weevil, Mr. Bagge. Very likely. Do you prefer jail and the gallows? Not even a nice friendly Free English gallows, at that?"

Feasty Jack cackled from his deck cannon. "I've not taken a pot at them yet. Want my turn. Like to cook a Frenchy ship."

"Mr. Plinke, go below. Our gunners fire as *they* judge, soon as *Bossy*'s near enough."

"Aye, Captain."

Whuskery and Dirk looked into each other's eyes.

"I *said* we shouldn't have come."

"Oh, go on," said Whusk, "it's better than acting with that girl who played Piratica in Shooters Lane. That Marigold Worthytown. Her ma *forced* us into letting her act—not that she *could* act."

"Another bossy mother," agreed Dirk.

"And think of the glory," said Eerie. "Sad we won't live to hear of it."

"The *Lundon Tymes* will carry it," said Mosie Dare.

"Piratica and her gallant crew sunked by a thirty-seven gunner."

"All hands lost."

Lightning erupted on the sea.

Brooo-mm Crack-crack-craaar—

Eastward, between them and the shore, fireworks and noise—

"That drifting-cloud thing must be some little storm keeping all to itself—" Walt, losing his fear in a weather report.

"Nah, yer tickposset—'tis another bloody ship—that's her *guns!*"

Plunqwette shrilled by overhead—a cannonball of feathers. "Pieces of Fortun-ate!" squawked the parrot.

Ebad said, quiet and somber, "You can never be sure of her till she's near. Even I wasn't. Her masts and sails are painted like a backdrop—clouds and sky, and the sides of her like the sea. It's the *Invisible*, Art, Wild Mike Holroyal's brig."

Every one of them had stretched their necks to gape.

The mirage ship was coming in swiftly, and her guns—"How many, Ebad?" "Seven on a side, one aft and a pair on deck"—were quacking and belching out shot—straight at the bulk of *La Maman Trop.*

Alarm grew clearly visible on the French deck.

Her own cannon spat back. But—at what? It was a messy volley.

"This *Invisible*—she's a devil to see. *What?*" asked Pete indignantly.

"That's the idea."

"Every man to his station!" Art shouted. "We're not the audience, gents. We're part of the show. Mr. Plinke, Mr. Vooms—helm and steady. Double broadside. Then again at will. We can get her now—she has *thirty-nine* guns out here to match her own thirty-seven—and they're facing two ways."

From the sea and the sky, eastward and closing, something, mostly unseen, cannon blaring, visible only as they fired. In front, the pirate ship that *La Maman* had hoped to capture. They had not fired on her too cruelly, hoping to take her intact. And this pirate vessel was still avoiding their barrage by weird balletic moves while herself keeping up a continual port broadside.

The first time they'd seen this English ship dancing round, stem to stern, the French destroyer had been amazed. *"C'est impossible!"* No ship of any bulk, let alone a windjammer, could *pivot* like this and at such speed.

Then the French got it. "By the Sacred Blue Heaven—that ship is none other than the *Unwelcome Stranger*. We have, in our sights—*Piratica herself!*" For even in France many had heard of Art Blastside. What a prize!

Now, though—well. Shoot *La Maman* did, but nothing seemed to strike either the unseen ship or the pirate ship that danced.

While *bang-bang* went the guns of the *Unwelcome*. *Boom-thud* went the guns of the invisible *Invisible*.

La Maman Trop found herself holed, port fore and aft. The mainmast had been shattered and, going down, had taken the top off her mizzen.

Everyone thought the *Unwelcome* was an uncanny thing. And she had, obviously, invisible friends.

La Maman had given only five minutes for Art to surrender. Inside ten more, *Mummy* herself turned heavily and, badly listing to her port side, limped off along the rolling hills of the sea.

If the French captain reckoned the two English ships would not give chase, he was correct. Back along the coast other French vessels would no doubt come to the aid of the wounded bully. "And so we must allow them to go. *Quelle* shame," Fringlished Wild Michael as he jumped aboard Art's ship.

Every man of Art's crew was now up on deck and staring.

This near, yes, you *could* see *Invisible*. Just. Her masts and sails, as Ebad had explained, were expertly daubed to resemble blue skies with occasional puffs of cloud, and here and there a tinge of darker cloud—enough to fit should an overcast come up, but not enough to give anything away under a clear sky. Her sides and planking were sea-blue, sea-green, sea-gray. She had oar ports as well as gun ports. And even her oars—and guns—were blue-green. But oh—the final camouflage—

The men on *Unwelcome* began to laugh and clap and cheer.

Michael was quite used to this. He bowed, doffing his sky-blue, cloud-painted hat from his blue-and-white powdered hair. His face was also blue and white, blending to a blue-and-green-sea neck, shirt, coat, and breeches.

All the rest of his men were the same, except those perched up in the rigging, who were entirely sky-colored.

The brig's sea-green-blue oars pointed idle now at the water.

Felix, also on deck, spoke like a spike. "Quite an artwork, Mr. Holroyal."

"True, sir. And one day we may even be hung—though not, I think, in any art gallery."

Art came off the quarterdeck and shook Michael's blue-green hand.

"Did my dad, when he sailed with you, do himself up like this?" she asked.

"Yes, our Ebad. Blue as a cornflower, I promise."

"We owe you our skin, Mr. Mike."

"'Twas nought. Sorted. But I do have a favor to ask in return."

"Ask."

Michael looked over his shoulder. "Louis, come and introduce yourself."

A short, stocky man, blued and greened like all of them, stepped forward. He bowed with a great flourish to Art. "*La Piratica!* Enchanteh, innit."

Though he had said he was enchanted in Fringlish, the accent told. *"French,"* said Art.

"Aye, Art," said Michael, "but before you run him through— this is Louis Adore, one of the three prime revolutionary leaders now active in France. Their symbol is a violet, the Flower of the People. A fellow Republican, Louis is intent on freeing his country from its royal oppressors, the French king and all his cronies." Louis bowed again. There was a violet in his collar. Michael went on, "France is too hot for him now. So he must travel to Morrocaino. There are those who'll assist him, in the port of El Tangerina."

Art looked the two men over. Did this explain the French talk Cuthbert had overheard in the Holroyal library? "You want my ship to take this man there."

"Mine is needed for other work. What dost say? Or will ye bottle out?"

Art frowned on Michael. Undeterred, he smiled at her, his white teeth gleaming through all the blue makeup.

A Selection of Monsters

Captain Nick Nunn backed away and tripped over a chair, landing hard on the floor at Little Goldie Girl's furious, daintily booted feet.

Which kicked him quite hard.

"Ouch! Goldie—don't—" Scrambling for cover behind the desk, Nick Nunn covered his head with his arms.

"*Cretin!* By the Wheel's Whirl—I should nail you up on the masthead."

"But, Goldie—"

"Button it."

Goldie paused, her lovely face alight with venom. The cabin of the cutter *Rose Scudder* was not really big enough to contain her poison. It seemed to crowd the room, leak out on deck, so the crew Nunn had hired, a rough-and-ready lot, still quaked and cursed and sidled away to other areas of the ship.

They knew, all of them, who Goldie was. The Goliath's daughter. A pirate queen who had nearly been hanged—let off only through her cunning. Lethal and untrustworthy—and perhaps the very person to lead them all to riches beyond the dreams of the average. They were scum, this crew. Nunn had thought he was clever, getting them, but really he had taken a horrible chance. In fact only Goldie's reputation kept him safe.

He had wanted her to like the ship. The *Rose Scudder* was light, a cutter of a similar type to the old *Enemy*. But LG had set her heart (did she have one?) on a Free Republican Destroyer, like Nunn's previous command, the *Total Devastation*. Forty-two guns and a hide like a rhino.

Curled up under the table in the cabin, Nunn wished he was somewhere else. But they were already at sea. Little Goldie Girl had saved his punishment till he had nowhere much to run.

When she spoke again, though, her voice was calm.

"All right, you uncool jupey. Go and fetch Tinky for me."

"Yes—Goldie."

"*Captain* Goldie. *I'm* the one in charge now."

"Aye . . . Captain."

Alone, Goldie picked up the chair and sat on it, studying the chart. She wished again—this was becoming a bad habit—that old Beastie had been with her. *He* could read a chart *and* plot a course, and no mistake. Which was peculiar, as he'd never been able actually to *read*.

Tinky came in, respectfully knocking first.

She thought he had potential, otherwise she'd never have let him aboard. The map he had got off the goose guy was a beauty. And a lucky sign, too. Oh yes, Goldie would reach the Treasured Isle, and this time she would pick up every returned treasure map and every drop of spilled booty otherwise to be found there.

"Any sign of the French?" asked Goldie.

"Not a whisker."

This hadn't been the case earlier. Leaving Port's Mouth, *Rose Scudder* had instantly spotted four French ships sneaking through the Channel. Nick Nunn was all for taking them on, but the *Scudder* wasn't equipped for that, as Goldie pointed out sharply. And "I'm not at sea to fight the French. Who cares who wins the war anyway?" Nick had been (foolishly) shocked at Goldie's attitude. But they took off quickly along the English coast, heading southwest to the Isles of Scylla. It was a bleak place, even in summer, the sea frilly with submerged rocks and the Isles scattered like gray-green stones. One great fort glared down at them.

Named for a Greek myth, the English Scylla was also said to be the haunt of a sea monster.

Now it was evening, the moon up and the anchor down. Tomorrow they would break back across the Channel mouth and head for open seas.

Goldie wouldn't be easy, she thought, until Mad-Agash Scar was in sight, and not even then. For that bag of boils, Hurkon Beare, who had his lair on Mad-Agash, was to be trusted less than a monkey.

Tinky had sat down.

"I like your cheek," said Goldie, sweet as a knife in marmalade.

"Eh? What's on my cheek, then?"

Goldie was about to demonstrate, violently, to Tinky that he had sat down *uninvited*—when a white piece of the just-risen moon dashed in at the open door.

"Hey!" cried Tink.

Goldie gave one of her rare and surprising girl-like squeals.

The white thing landed on the desk.

"'Tis a dove," Tinky told her.

"Belt up, forsooth! Do you think I'm blind?"

Goldie gave the dove a look fit to change it to stone. The dove ruffled its snowy feathers and let go a snowy poo on the chart.

It was the same kind of bird she had been sent in Lundon, at the Old Bull and Shrub Tavern. And this one, too, had a little roll of paper attached to its pink leg.

Goldie reached toward the dove with murder in her cat's eyes.

The dove wafted into the air, back out of the door, and up, up to the top of the mizzenmast.

Goldie and Tinky Clinker came erupting up on deck.

Nicky Nunn, standing by the wheel, gave a low yelp, thinking Goldie was still after his blood. All the other men stopped what they were doing, too, staring at her nervously.

"Trashadders!" squalled Goldie, in good voice now. "Bring that bird down! 'Tis mine."

Hands hurried for pistols. One crew member, eager to win favor, began to clamber the rigging toward the tiny white blot above. The dove watched all this with a bright black eye, then let go another snowy offering on the climber's head.

"I must have that message!"

A pistol cracked. Captain Nunn, getting the better of himself, shouted, "Hold your fire! By heaven, don't let the fort hear a load of guns going off—she'll think the French are coming, or we *are* the French—and blast us out of the water."

Goldie seethed. Tinky again helped everyone out with a description of what everyone could already see. "Look—it's flying off."

Metal yapped, and a bullet whizzed by his ear. Goldie, not caring for Nunn's advice or Tink's ear, had aimed for, but missed, the dove. Up in the navy-blue sky it fluttered, heading away now, back toward the southeast coast.

"Goldie—*Captain* Goldie—look." A flake of paper, loosened from the dove's leg, fell into Nick Nunn's outstretched hand. She snatched it from him.

By the light of the aft port lantern she read:

rt Blast is bound for El Tanger
ke haste. Your well-w

The rest of the message, it seemed, remained stuck on the leg of the escaped messenger. But here was enough.

"El Tangerina. Could be no other spot." Goldie's eyes now gleamed.

Nunn noted the gleam. Perhaps only the lantern light made her eyes seem in that moment like those—of a demon.

But a sound started then, out of the night and the dark water, that drove off even his worry about Goldie.

It was a strange sound, like the call of some huge beast, but low and muffled and hollow.

It had no true direction, either—one minute it played out from around the islands, then a continuous echo furled away into the open sea.

"What—was *that*?"

Nobody, not even Tinky Clinker, gave an opinion.

Nick Nunn had been at sea some years. For that matter, so had Goldie and most of the men on the *Scudder*.

The sound fell silent in long, eerie stages. And was not repeated.

Instead—

Westward, through the mild wavelets of tonight's calm Atlantic, a moonlit humping, surging, coiling mass rose up and wallowed and went down again, leaving behind it a half mile of creamy wake that vanished slowly.

"The monster of the Scylla Isles!"

Goldie, pale with fear, clutched Nick's arm. "Is it gone?"

"Let's hope so, Gol—Captain Goldie."

"Raise anchor," she said. "Let's get out of here."

He didn't argue, nor did the crew.

Goldie went back to her cabin. In the small space, where the rest of them could not see her, she trembled. Outside, the reassuring shouts and rumbles of the ship getting under way again. In her head, bad images from her past. "That's my Goldie Girl," said her terrible father, bending toward her. "Leave me alone," she hissed to the memory, "you're dead, *Daddy*." She encouraged herself: "Think of Art." But the sea monster, too, kept rising in her mind. A dark *un*lucky sign.

She should call Tinky back. She hadn't really wanted him for anything. More—for company. Goldie didn't much like to be alone. She found she felt this more and more. The presence of a suitably frightened and admiring underling steadied her.

It was worse here, at sea. How she missed her old crew of pirates. Mr. Beast and Mr. Pest, Tattoo and Rotten and Yucky and Basher and the rest. All gone now. Gone where her daddy had. She went to the chest and took out a mirror. Goldie studied her face. Flawless, but for that one little crisscross scratch of a scar Art had given her. *Think of Art.* Yes, that was better. Think of killing Art Blastside. Almost with affection, Goldie thought of it. And the Isles of Scylla drew away behind.

El Tangerina

Plunqwette and Maudy were locked in combat in the blue air above the *Unwelcome Stranger*. Feathers—green and scarlet or white—rained on the ship's crew. "Could trim a hat with all these," Dirk remarked. No one knew what had started the fight this time—or ever. Sometimes the two parrots came across each other strutting or sunning themselves on yards or rails, or on the longboats strapped atop the deckhouse or cabin roof, and neither bird reacted. But then *this* would happen. One would rush screeching from Art's cabin or out of Feasty's galley, and the battle would once more begin.

"Its full name's Maudyce, Jack's parrot," Mosie Dare had informed Art. "Comes from 'more dice,' y'see. Jack likes gambling ashore. Won Maudy that way."

But Jack had told other tales to other members of the crew. For example: Maudy was really Maud*ie*—once thought to be a female. Or Maudy stood for Lord Maudynning, who had given the parrot to Jack—the referee—after a successful duel.

Only Eerie gazed up at the aerial war and muttered, "By the Silk Socks of St. Savage, 'tis them up there, and the other two same in her cabin."

"Yeah," said Walter. "At least *they* keep the noise down, though."

It was true. Fighting with words only, neither Art nor Felix had raised their voices. But the verbal blows were probably as harsh as anything landed by parrot claws and beaks.

"You gained nothing by trying to rob those French traders, Art. And nearly lost your ship and all your men to the French destroyer. So *fortunate* your best friend Michael turned up when he did."

"What's *this* lecture in aid of, Mr. Phoenix?"

"Lecture? Do you think, Art Blastside, when you and he were firing on that ship, she took no casualties?"

"I never aim to kill."

"And do you think no man *was* killed? Wake up, woman. You can play that game only so long."

Art, dissatisfied, bothered. *Had* men died because of *Unwelcome*'s guns? She had thought not. Or . . . *trusted* not.

Molly's code. Easy on a stage . . .

"Mr. Phoenix, I've things to do."

"More ships to attack. More guns to fire, blood to spill—"

"You've said enough."

"Don't speak to me in that way. You're not *my* captain. You're my wife, for my sins."

"*My* only sin, it seems to me, is in wasting time on your chat!"

"*Artemesia*—yes, don't call you that. Do you know what your name comes from? I'll tell you. It comes from a plant called *Artemesia absinthium*, from which can be made a deadly poison. It tastes *bitter*."

"*You've said enough.*"

"True. For you never listen, do you. By the stars, Art—Art—"

"Get out," she said quietly. "Go and read poems with your clever Mr. Belladora Fan Bell."

And he, straightening, white as ice, fixing her with his dark blue eyes, said, "Yes. As you know, she and the French fellow, Louis

Adore, get off at the Tangerine port. I'll be leaving your ship along with them."

"And very much along with her."

"Indeed. Why not? Bella won't rob a merchant ship or fire a cannon, and she even wears a dress at parties. What a change. And she talks to me as if I'm a human being. Also what a change. Good day, *Captain*. You and I are through."

The door slammed this time.

It was as if he had taken away every muscle and bone from Art's body and carried them off with him. Her heart had stopped beating.

What would Molly have done? Said be damned to him.

"Be damned to you, sir," whispered Art.

Mr. Doran Bell, or Belladora Fan, had proved something of a revelation.

No sooner had the sky-sea-tinted *Invisible* pulled away than the deck of *Unwelcome* had been in uproar. The crew, old and new, loudly crowded around the French revolutionary Louis Adore, who spoke up bravely in both Fringlish and English. Into the scene abruptly had stepped Mr. Bell, tossing her tail of black hair over her shoulder.

"Stand back, if you please, sirs."

"Eh?" was the general reply.

Mr. Bell had always been so—*gentle*. Now she was firm and even quite fierce-looking.

"I am," said she, with a sudden excellent actor's pitch that carried right across the ship, "Citizen Adore's minder. No, none of you think I can fight, but I *have* been trained—" and into her slim hand leaped her sword, whippy and impressive. The crew, used to Art, prudently edged away. "From now on Citizen Adore will be known simply as Lewis Daw. Since the captain is kind enough to take us to El Tangerina, he and I will get off there. You need know nothing else. Except that I can protect this man, who anyway you should be a friend to. One day there will be a Free Republican France to match Free Republican England, and he will have helped create it. If you help *him*, you help your own country and disable her foe."

"Quite a speech," Art declared. "And I see your poor little ankle's quite better. This is why you came with us, I think. For Mr. Daw."

"Just so, Captain."

"And Wild Michael lay in wait for us, of course, for the same reason."

Mr. Bell shrugged her slender but now obviously strong shoulders.

Louis or Lewis Adore/Daw couldn't conceal a grin. He, unlike Bell, didn't look very dangerous, more bookish; his nose seemed specially made to wear the pair of spectacles he presently put on.

Art felt herself outfoxed. But told herself this wouldn't matter. For El Tangerina was pirate-friendly and a good place to call at for supplies, fruit, and water.

So the seas grew bluer and greener, turquoise with a peacock lining, with wave-hearts of lettuce green. And Felix no longer drew pictures of anyone. He strolled the decks with Lewis and Mr. Bella, all of them reading aloud from a poem entitled *The Ballard of the Glittery-Eyed Old Sailor* by Mr. Coalhill.

> *"And every tongue, through utter drought,*
> *Was withered at the root;*
> *We could not speak, no more than if*
> *We had been choked with soot."*

"Let's hear it for giving 'em some soot, then." Stott Dabbet, not a poetry lover.

But "Nay, they have each a fine voice." Eerie, all approval. "And that poem is a wonder."

Warm days, soft nights. Spangle stars and moonglow. The faint ghost of the coast. Morrocaino drawing near.

Overhead, two parrots fighting with claws.

In the cabin, two people fighting with words.

And then, silence. Silence.

"Art—you can win him back, you know. He's only a man. Make him alter his mind."

"Is that what Molly would have done, then, Mr. Vooms?"

"Maybe. She and I never argued much. No. We never argued."

"You and she were happy then, Dad. And—you and she—better stuff than he . . . or I."

El Tangerina curled behind her indigo bay. From miles out they could smell the tangerines.

Old brown walls were overhung by cascading knots of orange fruit in netted frames. Above the harbor, the twisting brown streets, squiggling up to the old brown fortress, were lined with tangerine trees. In courtyards and gardens they grew in tubs or grouped in orchards.

The town seemed lit by their flamey-golden glow. The scent on the shore made the mouth—and the eyes—water.

Belladora had undone her black hair. It streamed over her back and shoulders. This way, in her male pirate clothes, she looked oddly fiercer. Louis-Lewis had shaken hands with Art and Ebad, bowing, promising them that the New French Republic, once formed, would never forget them.

"I am to find here a man named Rogé de Jolie, a great scholar. He'll write down *votre grand service à* me."

Felix, too, shook Ebad's hand. Ebad spoke gravely to him, aside from the others and under cover of the noise in the port. "I'm sorry to see you go."

"It's for the best."

"Whose best, Felix—yours or hers?"

Felix said. "Don't prolong this, Mr. Vooms. I wish you well." And with that he strode off up the scribble of street. Belladora and Lewis fell into step with him. There they went, toting their bags, getting smaller and smaller, becoming one with the colorful crowds.

Art was apparently completely in command of herself. She went around with Forecastle Smith and Feasty, checking the stores to see what was needed. She had organized who stayed on the ship and who might go ashore, in relays, so all got a turn.

Back on deck, "Do you notice up there?" said Feasty Jack, pointing in at the higher town. "That's the rhino-ring. You can see the flags. It's on today. Might take myself there for a bit of sport."

Walt wanted to know what Jack meant. Others gathered around as the cook, Maudy on his head, explained an old tradition of Tangerina that was part Spanish and part Afric.

Everyone seemed pleased. A holiday air took over. It was always the same, Art thought, with men who preferred to be at sea: all they wanted when there was to be back on land.

Not me, she thought.

It was her duty, she had decided, to go ashore. To look around, behave as if intrigued. And then it would be her duty to sail on, robbing French ships where she might, returning piratically to the Treasured Isle, with its hundreds of parrots and returned maps.

No one must see what she could feel inside herself. The empty room where her happiness had been.

Fool, she thought. It'll pass. He's only a man. I'll get over it. He's better gone. I'm better alone. And I'm stronger now he's not with me. I just don't feel it yet.

The town was alive with rogues and ruffians, pirates and the crews of privateers, some of which were no doubt French. But in the Morrocains, as here and there elsewhere, by the truce code of their hosts they seldom made trouble. And if anyone did, it was quickly shelved till the antagonists were out at sea again.

In the market, Forecastle, eagerly and greedily assisted by Tazbo Lightheart, Sikkars Eye, Boozle O'Nyons, and Grug, staggered under the weight of slabs of fresh meat, bananas and limes, and long chunks of white nougat set with candied peel. ("Now, ye can leave off o' eating that, Mr. Eye, or you'll get a *black* eye offa *me*.")

Tangerines they *had* to have. It was a terrible need because the smell of them had by now swamped everyone. There were tales of men who had devoured these fruits and been unable to stop until they made themselves sick. Tales of men *dreaming* of tangerines for days after leaving the town. The locals were immune. They seldom wanted them, bored with them, and the favorite color of El Tangerina was blue.

Art ate a tangerine. Didn't taste it. Said she'd have another. Ate it ditto.

She had left Ebad on the ship, and Eerie, too. She hadn't wanted their eyes—Ebad's unreadable, *knowing* her; Eerie's all ashine with distress for her—hadn't wanted those eyes looking out for her all the time. Checking her, as if she'd been wounded.

This will pass.

Walter was stroking a piece of silvery brocade hung among veils and linens of every shade of gray and rose. "What a good color this'd be for a coat for—um, Felix," he finished flatly. Walt blushed. Art said, raising her eyebrows, "It will save some money then, not having to buy it for him."

The Badgerigar was a strangely named wine shop tucked behind three winding alleys.

Felix had never heard of it, or its English name, but Belladora and Lewis had, and were to meet here helpful, scholarly de Jolie.

"He's known to me as Roger Jolly," Bella said. She smiled at Felix, and he smiled back. She was a gorgeous creature. He liked very much to look at her, to draw her. As he had always found himself looking at and drawing Art.

Art didn't have this beauty. Art wasn't beautiful. And yet— what a face, what *presence* Art had. Misguided, wrong, difficult, inflexible, perhaps insane—yet . . . had she been here—

Felix pushed the memory of Art from his mind.

They entered the tavern.

It was a wide, low-ceilinged room, colored darkest yellow, fawn, and black from tobacco smoke, coffee fumes, and time. Sailors— and pirates—sat about in the usual tavernly way. Morrocaino traders, whose caravans came regularly to the marketplace, played games with painted counters on long slate boards, puffing on the stems of tobacco pipes cooled in bubbling glass vessels. Chickens marched about the floor. But in the far corner a huge cage of gilded wrought iron, door open, contained not a bird but a large, shadowy animal.

For a moment Felix forgot Art—oh, the relief.

"*What* is *that*?"

"It's a badger, Mr. P," said Bella. "It was the pet of a sailor from England, who trained it to sing. Look, here it comes."

Out of the cage the badger shambled, the rough gray fringes of its coat bouncing. On vast claws it ambled toward them, lifting its lean, black, snakelike head with central white chalk stripe that didn't seem to belong to the rest of it.

Various people in the tavern stroked the badger as it passed. One offered it a piece of pomegranate, which it guzzled.

Then it sat on the floor before Bella, Felix, and Lewis and—it *sang*.

The song was a quite tuneful series of tweets and chirrups and peculiar giggles.

Lewis was delighted. Felix drew a small pad of paper from his coat and began to sketch the badger, which wore a little gold ring in its left ear.

The song ended. Customers laughed and applauded and threw the badger bits of meat and fruit, which it trundled gladly around to accept.

I should tell Art; she'd be amused.

Ah—no. I shan't be telling Art.

They sat in a booth and drank tangerine arrak and sweet mint tea, until Mr. Jolly arrived. He was a serious man with a magnificent mustache nearly worthy of Whuskery.

He, Bell, and Lewis spoke mostly in French. Felix had a little French, not much. He started to draw everyone in the tavern, feverishly filling and tearing off papers, trying not to think.

Then Lewis and Jolly moved away into a corner, beginning a tense talk, this time in Arabic.

Belladora looked at Felix.

"They're arranging things. All's well. And so, sir, this afternoon is open for me to do as I want. Perhaps . . ." Felix stared at her. "I see," said Belladora.

"No, dear girl, you don't. How could you? But . . ."

"You're sure I'm wonderful, but you can't stop thinking of your wife."

Felix drew in his breath, and let it out on a painful "*Yes*. Oh, Bella, you're beautiful. I should be at your feet. But—*but*."

"Don't fret, baby," said Bella. " 'Tis what I've been guessing all morning. What will you do?"

"I don't know."

"Why not," said Belladora, "go back and take her by storm?"

"*Storm? Art?* You must be joking."

"Well, by stealth, then. *Pirate* her."

"How can I?" he said miserably. "She and I will never agree. She can't be happy on land, and I can't be happy on a pirate ship, or a warship come to that. I see somebody's murder round every wave. If she doesn't see that, too—she's blind."

"Alas," said Belladora. "And you such a beauty, too."

She leaned across the table, kissed him gently on the mouth, and walked away to join her companions.

About ten minutes later, the three wished Felix well and went out of the tavern where the badgerigar sang like a budgerigar, leaving Felix washed up, alone among the remains of the tea and arrak and his sketches, his head in his hands.

✑ TWO ✑

Local Color ——

Up to the hilltop above the town, Feasty Jack led his sightseeing group of crew.

He had been in Tangerina before, apparently. But then, he seemed to have been to most of the places on the globe.

Resignedly Art went with them. Like their mother, who must keep an eye on her boys when they want to watch foreign sports events and gamble.

Honest was walking by Jack, and Art saw with a distant, uninvolved surprise, that Maudy was now sitting on Honest's shoulder. Wrapped up in her struggle with Felix, she'd missed the start of this unlikely friendship. No one aboard apart from Jack could handle Maudy, and anyone who'd tried to touch the bird had been thoroughly pecked. (Walter and de Weevil were reduced to tears.)

Honest had begun the surprising relationship by entering Jack's galley in order to pass on to him some message of Art's. Seeing Maudy perched on the rind of a large cheese, Honest went straight up to him.

"He doesn't take kindly to anyone's touch, Mr. H., only mine. We've kept company a long while, him and me. Take care he doesn't go for you. Knew a man in the Australias lost an eye to Maudy."

But Jack had broken off as Honest stroked Maudy's head with one slow finger.

Maudy opened his black beak, hissing out his black tongue like a dragon.

"Watch yourself, lad. I *told* you."

But Maudy closed his beak. He put his head on one side and cooed, "*Told* you. *Told* you so."

Feasty wasn't sure he liked his man-mauling parrot becoming mates with Honest, but Honest was hard to dislike. Jack, it seemed, had decided to make the best of it. After the scene in the galley, he sometimes gave Honest Maudy to mind when he, Jack, was in the wilder throes of cooking, cursing among his pots, slinging spice and cuts of meat about like a terrible, grizzled, stubbly witch with a cauldron.

Now Jack, Honest, and Maudy led the way up the hill to Tangerina's rhino-ring, the nine other men bundling merrily after. Art, at the rear, wondered what Jack had said to them about this stadium. She couldn't recall. Didn't care.

It was brown-walled, like all the town, and hung with clouds of netted, branched tangerines. Flags blared red and gold above.

Inside, the long benches ran in tiers around the ring of the arena below, which was sanded white and glaring in the sun.

"Which team shall we bet on, Feasty?"

"Better bet on the animal, Walty."

The stadium was very full. The crowds whistled and called, to one another and the unseen teams. Sellers of tea and arrak, fruit and sweets, threaded through the benches and up and down the various stairways.

The scent of tangerines was so familiar now, Art had forgotten it.

Jack beckoned over a tall man in clean bright rags.

"This is Trapa Harapo, lads. He wears rags to show he's straight with all customers who place a bet with him, and so he never makes any money. Eh, Trap?" Trapa Harapo smiled modestly. He had several gold teeth, a gold necklace, and rings. "Who's on today?" Jack asked. TH rapped out a list of names. Jack nodded. "I'll take the Zenobius team."

To Art, it was all like a crazy dream. But she couldn't be bothered to ask them to explain. Over the sea, fruit, and nougat, she could smell animals, too. Presumably, from the title of the stadium, these would be rhinoceroses. What was going to happen? Were teams of men going to fight—*rhinoceroses*?

Bets were being placed. Whuskery was trying to persuade Dirk *not* to bet. Shadrach Lost said he always lost. Most of them put money on Jack's choice, but Grug chose another name, and so did Peter, saying whatever Walt bet on wouldn't win. A band rambled around the ring playing a curly Arabic tune.

Then the first bout was announced in Spanish and Morrocain.

"Isn't it Zenobius yet?"

"He'll be one of the last. He's a favorite."

Trumpets sounded a fanfare. A gate was opened in the arena, and out ran six colorful figures. Four were men and two women. Each wore the same shade—four crimson men and two crimson women. The crowd roared and waved.

"See that little bag at their belts?" asked grinning Jack. "That's where it is. It's a real skill."

Art was now so mystified she found herself leaning over to Whuskery to demand, after all, what on earth went on.

But just then another arena gate was undone.

Out galloped, snorting and huffing, an enormous, blackish Afric rhino. And for a moment Art forgot Felix Phoenix—oh, the relief.

A girl from the Badgerigar Tavern had come kindly to Felix and offered to bring him soup. "If you can't pay, dear Englishman, I'll make no charge."

Felix smiled at her. She'd even spoken in English. He thanked her and said no. She left him alone.

He thought, I'd better go.

He thought, Go where, then?

Find a ship, he sternly suggested to himself. *Go home.*

And where's home? he asked himself.

Home's where the heart is, dearie, he heard Dirk say sarcastically in his thoughts.

Well then. No home. Homeless, like before.

Felix put his head back into his hands.

The first rhinoceros of the afternoon's rhino leaping was called Cleopatrus.

The Red Team danced around it, playful, and the rhinoceros dipped and bowed, nodding its head to them in quite a polite way, only now and then pawing the ground with its right forehoof.

"*What's* it called—Cleopatrick, is it?" grumbled Grug, who had a bet on a beast called Esthus and wanted the show to get on.

The four actors present were fascinated, however.

"Art—do you think it's *staged*?" Peter.

"'Tis a put-up job for sure." Whuskery.

"Oh, my gold coin—*is* it staged, Jack?" Walt, terrified.

"No, my boy. It's real as thee or me."

But now the Red Team had separated out.

"Here we go. . . ." shouted Shadrach.

One of the crimson men ran suddenly toward the rhino. A couple of feet from it he sprang—straight up. The rhino snorted and tossed up its head—too late. The red leaper had caught the horn in both nimble hands.

Using his grip on the horn, the leaper sailed over the animal's head in a long, soaring swing, to balance upright on the rhino's now-prancing back.

The crowd cheered as the leaper somersaulted high and landed on the back again, steady as a rock. Something red sparkled through the air. The leaper had pressed the bag slung at his waist and showered his trampling mount with a spurt of crimson—dye or paint. Next instant the man curled into another somersault, which now took him clear off the rhino, to arrive back in the ring, where two others of the Red Team neatly caught him.

All the rest of the team now performed variations of the same act. Some were more sure-footed than others. Once or twice the crowd gave a yell as someone slipped on the soon red-coated hide of the rhino. One leaper slithered down, his acrobatic double somersault coming unstuck. But one of the girls *danced* on the rhino, giving high kicks, and leaping off again to the catchers with the grace of a diving fish. Every mishap was counted against a team. And when at the end the rhino lost its temper and charged all six of them—so they had to scatter—those who had bet on the Cleopatrus Team gave up with a groan.

Esthus, Grug's choice, had a yellow team, who hopped and juggled plates on his back, painting him like a daffodil. But though they made few errors, Esthus eventually got fed up, too, and began rolling gloriously on the arena floor, powdering himself with white dust.

Grug tore up his betting slip.

"It's an art," said Jack, smug in superior knowledge. "Ah," added Jack. "Where has he gone, your Honest Liar, and my parrot with him?"

"I think he went to the toilet, forsooth," said Walt.

"Just let him," said Jack, "be careful of the bird." Then strangely, deeply, he sighed. To Art, Feasty Jack murmured, "Yet never mind that. Maudy can take care of both of them."

Another rhino came barging out, and a green team all in a muddle. Probably this lost them many points at once. But the green rhino, called Isabellus, was if anything *too* well behaved. It stood patiently, often snuffing at paint on the arena floor. At the end of the bout it had a horn and a face that were green, yellow, and red.

"Damn it to Sausage!" cried Peter, ripping his betting slip to confetti.

There was one more bout before the interval. A rhino called Blankus appeared, and a team in white. They worked Blankus nicely and changed him into a snow-white rhino, ending to loud cheering. No one in the ship party had thought to bet on Blankus. But, "Looks like old Zenobius has some real competition there," said Jack.

During the interval Jack rose and went about, trying to find Honest.

Art ate another tangerine. Felix was in her mind again, looking at her with his blue eyes, staring at her with dislike. No, worse. With indifference. *We are through.*

After the interval Honest still did not appear. But a purple team erupted into the ring and gave a spectacular turn with their rhino, Candakus, which managed to be both skittish and playable.

"Stiff competition," said Whuskery. "Eh, Jacky?"

Feasty Jack only frowned now.

Shadrach Lost said, "Told ye, mates. I'll lose me dosh, and so will you."

The afternoon was getting on, the dusty light in the windows densening to old gold. Roars and warbles and shrieking cheers came down the hill in waves from a brown-walled stadium there. What was going on? Felix couldn't get up the energy to ask anyone.

The crew of *Unwelcome* would be visiting the taverns and the market, he supposed. At one point he was even sure he'd seen Muck the dog trot by the tavern door. Provisions would have been taken back to the ship. Tonight, the others would come ashore, the rest return aboard to ready her for departure in the morning.

Art was still here, then—if not in the town then on her ship.

What was *she* thinking?

Was she thinking about that bloody Michael?

Somehow . . . he didn't think she was.

He knew he had hurt her. Oh yes, he knew her well enough now to know that. But she was proud and strong and didn't show it. Just that dull flash in her eyes—as if he'd thrown a stone into their clear gray waters, and it had sunk from sight, only the ripples visible for a moment.

Art . . . the last person in the world he would ever want to hurt—

Felix glanced tiredly around the Badgerigar.

There were few people in here now. Many, he reckoned, had gone off to the bullring or whatever it was on the hill. Shadows sat at distant tables—pirates, sailors. It didn't concern him. The badgerigar itself had waddled out into the courtyard, where it relaxed in the shade of twelve tangerine trees.

Felix remembered Art dragging him half-conscious out of the sea off Port's Mouth, Art on the far deck of the destroyer taking her to England to hang, Art brave and cool as a marble leopard with the rope around her neck by Lockscald Tree. Art when she first took him in her arms.

Felix whispered, *"What am I doing?"*

Something like lightning burst through him. It cleared his head like a deck ready for action. It made his blood move, woke him up.

For what did it matter to *him* if she was nuts and wrong and inflexible and annoying—what did it matter she was a *pirate?* Oh, it mattered everything, but if he couldn't alter her—then he would have to put up with it. He must be there with her, and for her. She was his and he was hers. No choice. Why struggle? Give in. Love's love.

In that second, as he straightened and raised his head, a soft little sound lilted behind him, and a faint perfume tinted the air. And then something hard and nondelightful poked him in the back—

Felix tried to spin around.

The poking object dug in harder, and now went punching quickly up his spine, hitting, it seemed, on every vertebra.

"Don't turn, Mr. P. This you feel—'tain't no banana."

Felix completely stopped moving, as if he never would again.

And the nose of the gun pushed aside his long hair and settled unreassuringly at the base of his skull.

All in blue, the favorite color of El Tangerina, the Zenobius Team stepped out. Three men and three women leapers: sky blue, blue-black, pastel blue, greenish blue like turquoise, mauvish blue like lavender, blue like sapphire.

When the rhinoceros emerged from the other gate, he, too, was an unusual shade. He was a creamy, smoky fawn.

"*White* rhino," said Larry Lully. "He's a star."

He was the largest of the animals seen that afternoon, and though he stepped as delicately as his human team, there was something *dangerous* to him.

The ship party and a great number of the crowd sat bolt upright, concentrating.

At first the leaps were things everyone had watched before. Perfectly performed, they drew applause, but each flare of noise fell back in a breathless hush.

Zenobius then did a curious little dance of his own while the team danced in a loose ring around him, clapping their hands.

After that Zenobius stood still. He had his hindquarters to the bench where the crew sat. They watched his hair-tufted tail flick once left, once right, and become static like the rest of him.

The sky-blue male leaper, the turquoise male leaper—as if lifted by unseen hands, each man vaulted upward—neither catching at, nor needing, the horn. Both men flew at a diagonal angle over Zen's back, left to right and right to left—passing each other with a jolly salute in *midair*.

As Turquoise was flying down again over Zenobius's left shoulder, the rhino turned, the deadly horn striking out—the crowd gave an odd whining gasp—and Turquoise tossed over the horn a snug wreath of blue flowers.

The tiers exploded with joy.

Catchers caught the two descended leapers.

"Springs in their shoes, eh?" said Whuskery.

"Can't fool another actor they can't," said Peter—who had been sitting with his mouth open and hadn't realized.

But the next two leapers now leaped—the girl in black-blue and the girl in pastel—Pastel going up from the front and using the horn for her swing. Black-blue using her spring heels to clear Zen's rump. They landed in handstands on the rhino's back, then also squirted him with palest and darkest blue, before jumping away at either side.

Zenobius veered with alarming elegance to impale the fifth leaper in sapphire.

Down Sapphire dropped on one knee.

The appalling horn passed over his head. Sapphire dodged in under the rhino's belly, rolled aside, stood, put *both* his feet on the beast's flank, and went up his rib cage like a fly up a wall. ("Gluey shoes and hands." "Must be.")

While Sapphire balanced on the rhino, he pulled from his clothes an arrangement of leather straps, which he hand-glued over Zen's back. Then a short wooden pole was slotted into some holder among the strapwork.

While this went on, the last women of the team, who wore blue-lavender, partnered the rhino in a new, stately dance.

The pole wobbled on his back. The man in sapphire swung through three airborne somersaults and sailed down to the catchers.

The last girl leaped, seized the horn, and landed upright gripping the wooden pole. It was taller than she was.

Zenobius puttered. Hundreds leaned forward, eyes bulging.

Lavender climbed the pole in four swift moves. At the top, she upended herself with the ease of a squirrel. Now she balanced upside down, her head on the pole's top, some six feet above Zenobius's back.

Not a sound in the stadium, until Lavender herself shouted.

"Corriendale, Zeno!"

"By the Bee's Six Ankles—she said *run!*"

Zenobius, the lavender girl upside down on the pole above him, broke into a wild charge.

The crowd screamed. Everyone was on their feet. Art was on *her* feet.

Art saw the girl, in total poise, rushed across the stadium, up in the air, her arms and legs neither holding on, but moving with quick jerks, keeping her steady, keeping her safe, only inches from death.

And without preface across this sight, the image of Felix came in a kind of burning whirl. It wasn't like Art's other thoughts of him. *I must find him.*

Now.

Zenobius reached the barrier of the arena and halted like a well-driven carriage horse.

The lavender leaper flew off the pole to land in the arms of the five other members of her team.

The stadium thundered with cheering. Hats thrown in the air. Flowers of all colors chucked down to the ring.

"Glue in her *hair*?"

"No. It's skill, my son. And there are many casualties—at least to the teams of leapers. Never the rhino. He's always kept safe. He's sacred, you could say."

"I won?" jabbered Walt.

"*I* won," said Shadrach Lost.

Jack craned about. "But where is my bloody parrot?" he creaked like an evil door.

Maudy and Honest were in the rhino stalls. The leapers, removing their colors and makeup, cleaning the animals of paints with buckets of water and sponges, had assured him of death from the horns of their animals if he touched them. Honest couldn't speak Morrocaino or Spanish. He smiled and shook his head apologetically, and went to stroke the rhinoceroses. Each creature allowed this, even the irritated Esthus and Cleopatrus.

Then the leapers crowded around, letting Honest feed their beasts, asking how he had charmed them. Laughing when he couldn't understand, as Honest himself did.

Maudy, too, by then had begun to talk, clinging to Honest's red head handkerchief, peering over to chatter in Honest's ear. Maudy didn't speak only in English. He uttered Persian, varieties of Africay, French, Cathay, even Morrocain. So the red leaper who had jumped Cleopatrus first said to the white leaper who had jumped Blankus last, "A chemical formula, that's what the bird is saying—how to turn salt into silver . . ."

Maudy clacked in Honest's ear, "Jack dreamed of his death. Who to take Maudy? Who'll take my bird," added Maudy in Feasty Jack's own tones, "and care for him?"

Honest rubbed his round cheek against Maudy's feathery one. The sharp beak was both rough and smooth.

"Yes, do look about now, Mr. Phoenix. *Here* I am. Perhaps you remember your former sweetheart, Little Goldie Girl."

He'd known her from her voice and her perfume, though any love of his she had certainly never been. Felix turned anyway. He looked into her green cat's eyes, her exquisite, awful face, with Art's tiny kiss of fury cut there.

Behind Goldie stood three rough and beweaponed men from the *Rose Scudder*. Nick Nunn wasn't among them.

One of the men showed his teeth at Felix.

"Pretty, ain't he? Won't be when Missus here's finished with you."

Goldie nodded. "Crude, but a fact. I don't forgive breach of promise, Mr. P." (Breach of—*where* had she dreamed *that* up from?) "But what a chase we've had to catch you up! Open seas and a strong wind at our back helped us. You see, I'm the lucky one now. Oh, you must be so sad you gave me up for *her*."

Felix nodded. He knew he was an idiot, but he'd been so long with them, those actors, that woman he loved, that the dramatic words simply left him like a curse. "Yes, so sorry, Goldie, but you see, my kind heart takes me only so far. I couldn't stay with such an ugly thing as you."

Her face was like a piece of fire.

"What did you say?"

"Ugly as sin, aren't you? Mirror breaking. Make a man sick. My regrets."

She lifted her hand to strike him—maybe shoot him—then checked herself. Primly she ordered one of her crew: "Fancy, knock him out, by the Wheel's Wander." As Fancy thumped and Felix fell, Goldie explained, "Indeed, ugliness is all you can hope for now, *Felix*." Customers in the tavern looked away, turning a blind eye. Goldie ignored them, too. Carrying the unconscious man, the pirates left, unhindered. Before sunfall they would be back aboard the *Scudder*, El Tangerina a mist on the horizon, and the Atlantic wide before them.

They searched the town. Ebad came ashore, and Cuthbert. Art and her crew went to every wine shop, every alley, up to the fort, down to the port, through the market—which was lighting torches for the night. No one had seen Felix, or if they thought they had, he wasn't to be found where these witnesses said he might be. Near midnight: the Badgerigar. The badger was singing to an enraptured audience, and they had to wait till its song was done. The tavern girl came and served a thirsty Cuthbert and Boozle a bottle of wine. Cuthbert had Spanish from the ship he'd sailed with before. "I—I saw him," answered the girl. "A handsome man, and so well mannered. Indeed, he seemed unhappy. But then a black-haired girl—very good-looking and dressed in the pirate way as a man—she came and they were talking. I had to see to customers in the courtyard. When I came back they had left. Oh yes, he went away with her. His sweetheart, I think I heard her say—but my English is poor." Cuthbert looked glum. Boozle drank to drown Art's sorrows. "'Twas that Mr. Bella, like we all thought. He's agone with her. Quit the town by now. Nothing to be done."

Swash and Swindle

Just as a gull would see it, high in the sky, the ocean a great wrinkling, pleating, sparkling mass below, with the white dots of ships' sails sprinkled only here and there. Heading southward, down the hammerhead jut of Africay, the Coasts of Ivory and Emerald and Golden Guinea. (Far south the Atlantic is pouring to the southern seas and the white rim of Antarctica. But the gull will not fly so far as that.)

What does the gull see directly beneath, then, with its heartless, shining eyes?

Two ships there, not twenty miles from each other.

The gull, who has flown lower after fish, could have seen their names, but to a gull such things mean nothing. (*Rose Scudder*, and *Unwelcome Stranger* in the lead. But it isn't a race. Is it?)

Nights fall and days rise, sun and moon and stars wheel over, east to west. The Doldrums are passed. But perhaps this is a new gull now, flying on south. What does *this* gull see?

More fascinating than any ships, a curious bubbling ahead, a kind of arch of water and cloud lifting from the horizon. It's miles off. But the gull, who can read weather if not ship names, turns on a handy downdraft, heading fast for shore.

During the first days out from Morrocaino, the voyage reminded Art's original crew of their previous trip along the edge of Africay.

The sea was warm, and the coasts sweated green reflections into the water. Mangolines and twisted palms straddled the surf, and white bays opened through honeycomb cliffs. Sometimes narrow boats came out to where they had anchored, to offer fruit and coconuts. Art wouldn't go ashore.

She had made up her mind that now she need only act out her duty—her role. She would take them all back to the Treasured Isle—the Island of Parrots, as some of them now named it. Get the maps, if they were there. . . .

She watched the shores drift by. (She saw the past, not the present, and Felix by a lagoon, learning to play Cuthbert's hurdygurdy.) They crossed the Equated Line with toasts to Neptune, the sea god of ancient days. The Doldrums, last time such a pain, went by without a hitch.

But a hot night, electric with stars, brought the sighting of a single French ship.

The moon wasn't up, but starshine was enough, and Ebad read her colors easily—the Bourbon Lily.

"Why's she out alone?"

"Thinks these are safe waters," said Larry Lully. "Most of the English fleet's in the Mediterranean by now, keeping the French out of Egypt. Or that was the word in Tangerina."

The French vessel was heavy and low in the water, not made for running.

"What cunning trick'll our Art play on 'em?"

Art played no trick. She got the band ready on deck, put on more sail, and rode down the French ship's path with drums and trumpet, and cannon already speaking loudly.

The balls were landed deliberately wide, but the flash of fire and smoke and the racket alerted the trader to her likely fate. They took no risks, hauling up a white flag of surrender and howling over the sea that they gave up, while throwing their handguns on the deck.

Art dealt with them in her piratic, theatrical, and courteous fashion, announcing in French they need fear nothing providing they behaved. They behaved.

The ship was loaded with Indian tea and spirits from Afric stills, and a clutch of cut diamonds in boxes.

"Diamond's a poor stone," remarked Feasty Jack. "Give me a ruby every time. You know where you are with a ruby. If you have half an eye, that is." He and Forecastle bore a haul of tea and spirits below into the galley.

They left the trader unharmed and not entirely empty of goods—apart from the stones—not wanting to take on her weight.

Gideon Squalls and Shemps said afterward it hadn't been right not to blast the Avey Voos out of the sea while they had the chance. "Made them cannon *itch*, not to score a hit."

Others said they had had one eye out all the while for some great bumble of a French destroyer, thirty or forty gunner like the *Maman Trop*, to emerge from a cove and nobble them.

Art went to the galley. Maudy stood on a large mangoline, pecking it either in anger or hunger. Feasty Jack looked up. "Your Plunqwette isn't here, Cappy. Nor your yellow dog neither. In fact, I think *he* got off at Tangerina."

"Very possible, Feasty. But tell me what you meant about the diamonds."

"Why nought, Cappy Art."

Art lightly drew her sword and laid it across the cooking area, keeping the hilt in her hand. Maudy winked, and went on with the mango. Jack grunted approvingly. "In that case, Captain, I can tell you those diamonds aren't real. They're *paste*. Oh, there are genius black men along these coasts don't go down any mine, *make* these and sell them for a fortune."

Art said, "Oh." She sheathed the sword. "Can you prove it?"

"Aye, missus. If you give me one of the stones."

Art took a single jewel from her pocket, handed it to the cook.

"You know, Cap'n, a diamond is *hard*—can scratch glass?"

"Yes."

"Then how is it"—Feasty put the gem down on the floor and stamped on it, lifted his foot, and showed her a dozen bits of what now looked like broken ice—"I can do that?"

Art said, "Let's keep this between you and me, Feasty."

"Aye, sir."

So much for the first piracy, then. But the second French trader, anyway, was in sight the following afternoon.

She had fourteen guns, plus an escort, a dark sloop with a fair parcel of top-deck cannon.

"She'll be carrying something more valuable, then, than drinks and jewelry," said Boozle O'Nyons.

"What?"

"Well, Cap'n, something for the Frenchy war, I'd say."

Every gunner on *Unwelcome* went below to his pair of guns, where Tazbo and Sikkars galloped to and fro, to prime. Art put Jack on the foredeck gun and Mosie with the aft gun. The hatches of *Unwelcome*'s gun ports, however, stayed shut, and up the masthead Art had run a Franco-Spanish flag.

Rather than try to pass her, the French ships challenged *Unwelcome* as soon as they were in range, loud-hailing for her details.

Art waved in a friendly way and drew in closer, at which the sloop spat off a barely wide warning shot from three aft guns.

"Keep apart," the hailer yelled in King's French, "you seem to be a pirate vessel."

Art pitched her voice and informed them, in good Spanish, "Just so, señor. A privateer of the king's own choice."

"We see your ship's name," came back the cry. "The *Uncle Strangler*—an English name."

"Just so again, señor. We stole her from an English crew. So busy since, we've had no time to paint out her name."

There was some discussion on both the sloop and the trader.

Finally: "Why do you approach us?"

"We have been looking for a French vessel. We have rare information that may help the war effort."

Twenty minutes then went by, during which the French must have set up a debating team to discuss this. Down by *Unwelcome*'s guns, hands twitched. Ert Liemouse remarked that any Frenchy calling his ship the *Uncle Strangler* should be immediately fired on.

Art went to her cabin and pulled some things from the desk. These included old doodles, practice sheets from when she had tried to learn to read a chart in the proper way. She sealed them hastily with red candlewax.

"Mr. Vooms, the deck is yours. Mr. de Weevil, keep to the helm with Mr. O'Shea. Mr. Dirk, steady by the hatch. If, and only if, you see me raise my right arm up high—give the order to fire. The range is a stretch but possible. Remind our gunners—disable, not sink. Hit the ship but not the men."

"Where will *you* be?" asked Dirk, uneasy.

"Over there, Mr. Dirk. Where'd you think, prithee?"

"She means *on* the Frenchy," said Whuskery, even his mustache scowling. "She means by herself."

"No, but who goes with thee, Arty?" asked Walt.

"None, Mr. Walt. It'll be a deal simpler to get off with only myself to think of. And I doubt they'll let more than me aboard."

Plinke, Forecastle Smith, Peter, Whuskery, Dirk, and Walter had small arms ready out of sight by the rails. Jack and Mosie were leaning on the deck cannon as if lazy.

Art cast a quick glance about to check, and Walter bleated, "Arty—you'll get yourself killed. *Don't*, Arty. Just 'cos Felix isn't coming back—"

And Art found herself darting around on him, slapping him hard across his left cheek.

"Here," snarled Peter.

Walt began to cry.

Dirk said, "Well, what a bitch."

Ebad Vooms bellowed from the quarterdeck, in *French*. None of them knew what he had said, except Art and de Weevil, but they got the message nevertheless.

Art spoke quietly. "Thank you, Mr. Vooms. Mr. Walter, you're insubordinate. And this during an engagement. Men are flogged for that in the English Navy."

Peter said, "You'll flog my brother over my dead body."

"Really?" said Art. "Perhaps that's too drastic. Perhaps instead you can be flogged side by side. Now *shut thy mouth*."

Maybe reassured by the black French officer who had just sworn so grandly on the quarterdeck, the captain of the trader now shouted to Art, also in French, that she might come aboard. *"Seul,"* he added. *Alone.*

And Art thought for a second, Alone? Well, I am. I don't even know myself anymore. Art Blastside wouldn't have slapped Walter.

Then she fixed her thoughts only on the enemy ship.

Still not allowing *Unwelcome* any closer, the trader let down a small boat, which was rowed across and back.

Art climbed up the ladder and stepped in over the trader's rail. The captain eyed her with one raised brow. "You are a woman. I thought this. Then you must be Spiteful Suzette. She's the only female privateer to serve the king."

Art looked him in his clever eyes. He could be inventing this Suzette to trap Art, or Suzette might be real and known to him. Art took her chance.

"No, sir. Not I. I'm His Majesty's best secret. None know *my* name."

"Ah!" cried the captain. "Like this English wretch the Purple Hollyhock, this monster who helps filthy French revolutionary traitors, friend to Louis Adore and his men—but you, of course, are loyal to France."

Art looked modestly down, taking in the captain's sword, well-stocked knife belt, and pair of pistols.

"I have the papers here," she said. She drew them out, put them back. "But we must go to your cabin. I won't pass them over like a cabbage."

They went to his cabin. He shut the door.

"Sit, I beg you."

Art sat. The captain sat. Art removed the papers again and passed them to him. Collected as a closed book of tales, Art stayed motionless and silent as the French captain broke the seal, spread the papers, stared at them, rustled through them, and opened his mouth to explode in an oath worthy of Ebad's own on her quarterdeck.

"Hush, sir," interrupted Art. "As you see, the papers are nothing, just some rubbish found on our stolen English ship. *Here* instead is what I have for you." She pulled the bag neatly from her pocket, undid the strings, and poured out before him seventeen sun-bright blinks of ice-fire light.

"Blue of God!"

"Diamonds." Art filled in the gap. "They are from the king's own treasury and entrusted only to me. For you. In return, of course, you must give me the precious thing *you* carry."

Confused, guard down, the captain gaped at her. "But—how do you know . . ."

"Of course I know, Captain. Why else am I here?"

"But we have carried it faithfully—"

"No one doubts this. But spies are everywhere. The English now know you have this thing. A batch of Republican destroyers are even now on your tail. I was sent to find you. Therefore give *me* the delicacy, and make your escape."

"But I must see some authority from His Majesty. . . ."

Art let out a dry laugh. "I find it difficult to understand how a man of your courage and brains can also be so slow."

"Excuse me?"

"Naturally, the king has given me nothing that can prove his involvement and interest. Should the special item fall into enemy hands, it would be most unwise to let them know how much he counts on this venture."

"I understand," said the captain. He rubbed his chin. "Destroyers, you say."

"Certainly. Five ships, fifty guns apiece, combing the sea for you. Would you like their names?"

"My God." Back his eyes went, for comfort, to the diamonds.

Art thought, He's as ignorant with stones as I am. I even believed that time the red glass in Felix's ring was a ruby—

Pain surged in a wave.

The captain didn't see; he was busy running his hands over the jewels.

Art cleared her throat and her mind, and added, "It goes without saying that the king wishes you personally to keep three of the best stones for your *own* use. The rest must go to the war effort."

Oh, look, like Muck with that bone—

The captain took a few more minutes to play with the paste jewels, then got up and went to the table. Striking it sharply at one corner, he released a narrow, hidden drawer. In went the diamonds, out came a paper, sealed. The drawer was closed.

Is he fobbing me off with tat, as I have him?

"You will . . ." He faltered, half handing Art the paper, half holding it away from her, so she had to wait, ". . . guard this with your very life?"

"Monsieur, I will die a hundred deaths before I give it up."

They parted, each pleased with themselves, each disturbed. The boat rowed Art back to *Unwelcome*. She climbed the ladder and, getting on board her ship, felt dizzy for a moment. An awful vision came into her head then—not Felix this time. It was a memory of the ghastly Angels Academy for Young Maidens in which her father had shut her until she remembered who she really was. There they were, girls in curls and tight-skirted dresses, balancing heavy books on their heads in order to walk straight.

Not one of her crew spoke to Art. The French trader and the sloop saluted in a far more friendly way as the two ships sailed off.

Now to see what this paper shows—whether I've been canny or just been swindled as I swindled the French captain. But first—first I must put things right with Walt.

Even unconscious and lying where he'd been thrown—across some old sacks on the lower deck—by the light of her lantern, Felix was handsome. Goldie inwardly admitted this, then denied it. Then she threw the bucket of cold water in his face.

He came to. And for another moment it upset her, his face with the water running down like tears.

But what had he to cry about? She would *give* him something.

He didn't really react to her for some moments, just accepted that she was there, that he was tied hand and foot, that he was (obviously) aboard her ship. Kidnapped and due for nasty treatment.

Goldie, who had come down alone, not wanting any more insults against her to be heard by others, became impatient.

"Are you awake yet, Felix Phoenix? Better be. You have a busy day tomorrow, and it will be dawn in two more hours."

Felix shook the last water from his eyes.

Was he angry? Scared? She couldn't tell.

He looked at her. "I have to apologize to you," he said.

"You—*what*?"

"Apologize. I'm sorry I called you ugly."

"Aye, by the Wheel's Whatsit, you *will* be sorry—"

With his own strange impatience Felix cut in. "Yes, yes, no doubt. You're a vile and wicked creature, Little Goldie Girl, but ugly you are not. You're beautiful, and you know it, and *I* know it. In an instant of idiocy I said otherwise. Do what you like, but please understand, that was just my bad temper, back there in the town. You're lovely as a spring morning. I could spend my whole life painting you. But I suppose now my whole life will amount to about twenty-four hours."

"Very clever, Felix." Goldie glared. If she had *been* a cat, he thought, her fur would stand on end. "You can't get round me."

"I'm not a total fool. I never thought I could. It's just—well, I had to apologize. I was nicely brought up. Even if you were not."

Goldie sizzled. Then the sizzle went out. She gave a tinkly crystal laugh. "You're more entertaining than that singing badger, Mr. P. But of course *you* sing, too. Don't you?"

Felix sat there, relaxed-looking despite the sacks and rope ties and water trickling down his back. And he sang to her, in his perfect voice. It was some silly song, known in England. When Felix sang it, it became important, magical.

Hypnotized, Goldie listened. Then sense returned.

"Shut thy gob." Felix obeyed. "Now. Shall I send down Fancy or Taggers to keep you company?" Felix didn't respond. One more actor, then, Goldie thought, like the hated Art Blastside. "No," she said. "I think *I'll* see to your punishments. *Mine* will be *much* worse." She went away, taking the lamp, and left him to think about them in the dark before the dawn.

No gulls now. Night holding course for morning. But southward, where the gull had stared—that arch of water and wind, cloud and thunder, still there, running up now to the north. Too far off for Goldie and the *Scudder* to be concerned. Not yet visible to the forward vessel, *Unwelcome*, so heavy with emotions and mysterious valuables. But the Afric coast is muttering low with trees and surf, holding its breath—

As the storm, like a live thing, hunts for prey.

Breaker's Yard, Break of Day

"Where is Muck?"

By the time evening came on, almost the whole crew was searching. It was done in quite a riotous way, for earlier, after Art Blastside had come back aboard, the tensions of the afternoon's piracy had been dispersed.

Art had called them all up on deck. Even Feasty—with Maudy in his hair—the actors, the gunners and the primers, quartermaster and officers. They stood about, most of them with long, bleak faces. When Walt, pale as a peeled banana, appeared, flanked by both Peter and Ebadiah Vooms, a low growl went up.

"This ain't a flogging ship!" Gideon Squalls squalled from the deckhouse roof. Others joined squallingly in.

Art held up her hand. A sort of silence full of held-in noise resulted.

"Gentlemen. You're here to witness your captain beg Mr. Salt Walter's pardon."

Astounded, the crew.

Lupin Hawkscoot swallowed his own pipe smoke and coughed, Larry Lully banging him helpfully on the back. Cuthbert gripped his tar pot. Nib Several wiped his face with an oily rag.

Art waited again, then walked up to Walter.

"Mr. Salt Walt. I wronged you. This is a pirate ship, and every man can have his say. You meant only for the best. Will you excuse my error and forgive the hardness of the blow? You may name your price for the wrong I did you."

Walt didn't know what to do. He looked at Pete, who stammered, "Well, Captain Art—he should hit you back. Shouldn't he?"

Art noticed Ebad's face, like a carving from basalt. He said nothing. The rest of the men now waited, craning forward—an audience, a full house.

She let the pause hang, then said, "Unfortunately, Mr. Peter, if any man here hits out at me, I'm liable to forget myself again and knock him through the back of beyond, by my troth. Shucks, it's just how I am, guys."

The silence held, then gave way to laughter.

"Aye, don't risk it, Walty!" "She's the very devil, our Arty."

Art smiled and added, "It'd better be something more civilized, Walter. Perhaps you'll accept the equal of a captain's treasure share, when we find it—two portions instead of one?"

Men shouted this was generous. Feasty chuckled, so Maudy went up and down, up and down.

"Can't say fairer'n that, by the Crow's Cratch."

Walter came over, looking stunned. He and Art shook hands. "Never meant to upset . . ." he began.

"Nor I. Forget it. We move on."

The routine cleaning and oiling of the ship began in earnest after that. It was an unusually clear evening, the sun huge, a hot, dark pink as it lowered to starboard. Ribbons of peachy clouds decorated the sky, not moving, only gradually dissolving, and coloring the whole heavenly ceiling rosy amber.

This was when Muck's prized bone was found, rolling adrift on the gun deck.

"That's not like Muck. To leave that bone out in the open. He'd been hiding the damn thing everywhere."

"In my grog jug he put it!"

" 'Twas in the apple barrel I found it last week."

They took the bone to Eerie, who accepted it and said, "That dog's gone off again. When he doesn't like the look of things, that's what he does. He must have jumped ship at Tangerina, the faithless hound."

"Nay, he'll be around. He never got off when we did—not with us, anyway."

So they searched.

"Did Muck go after Felix, do you think?" Eerie muttered to Ebad.

"Perhaps. He was always his own dog, Eerie. And he always comes back."

Eerie grew mournful. "This ship is going to hell in a hopsack."

The sky too, apparently.

The Muck search was lapsing by then. Men clustered at the rails instead and looked at the dark pink sun, no longer so pretty, more threatening—like a peculiar huge new planet. It was at least two hours to sunfall, yet all the rest of the sky, east to west and south, was filling up like a glass with thin red wine. Northward, behind them, one oval break of blueness showed in the strawberry-colored murk. Up in the lookout, Tazbo watched this hole slowly swivel inward, getting smaller and smaller, becoming tiny as a button— winking out.

But still the wind was soft and light. The sea was as well mannered as any captain asking pardon.

"I don't like it. This Afric weather . . ."

"Never seen a sky like this—save in the Inde once. And then the wind came and blew the trees down."

Feasty Jack poked his head out from the galley.

He squinted at the sky, wet his finger, and held it up to test the wind. As he had thought from the on-off shifty billow of the canvas, it came now from the south, now the west, north, and east. A *circling* gust.

Maudy also took in the sky. He flew up suddenly to the lookout and perched there. And Plunqwette, who had been sitting on the mizzen, opened her green wings with a screech and came over the sail at him. Tazbo shielded his head as both parrots plunged past, clawing and screaming in the now-usual way.

About then Honest knocked on Art's cabin door. When she called him in, he found that Ebad and she were examining a large paper spread on the desk. Honest glanced at the paper. It wasn't either chart or map, but the drawing of a ship.

Honest said, "There's a kind of storm coming."

Before Art and Ebad could react, across the open doorway hurtled the fighting parrots in a whirlpool of feathers.

"What's caused the tiff this time?" Art inquired. She had no real interest in the fight, or in the search for Muck, or the plans for the weird ship the French captain had given her. The idea of a storm did stir her for a second. Something else to take her mind off—

"Maudy says," said Honest seriously, "he and Plunqwette fight because they're in love. It's how parrots—sometimes—settle things."

"In *love*!" Art began to laugh. Then forgot to. (Is that why parrots fight? Is that why he and I—fought?)

Ebad spoke across her thinking. "Mr. Honest, when you say a *kind* of storm—do you have some notion as to its type?"

"No, Mr. Ebad. But it isn't like most other storms. It's—an *individual*."

Alertness now replaced Art's listless mood. They went out on the red-lit deck, Honest blowing his whistle for attention.

A third French ship came drifting to them a little later, over that reddening darkness that wasn't either night or day—came drifting as if out of the eye of the low, hellish sun itself.

Visibility then was poor. *Unwelcome*'s lamps had been lit. Her decks were cleared, things secured or stowed. The whole crew readied at its stations.

The sea had remained flat, though the waves changed to the color of pitch, spangled with red sequins. And on this the unknown ship merely swam into view. All three of her masts tilted at broken angles; she had not a light to be seen.

Art, through the spyglass, noted the flag. It was a true skull and crossbones, with double skulls, done on black, with a gold lily ironically stitched below. A *French* pirate, then—once.

She passed the glass to Ebad.

"Is it a trick? I don't see anything moving on her decks. Her rigging's torn, and the sails, too. Someone's nearly dismasted her. English ships?"

Ebad took a long while peering at the French pirate. He gave the spyglass again to Art.

"Look carefully, Captain. Do you see that black drapery around her, over the masts and yards, trailing in the water?"

"Yes. It looks like—spiderwebs. . . ."

"By the topgallants, Arty, so it does. A black widow spider."

Glad Cuthbert had arrived on the quarterdeck.

"Is it one of the ol' girl's bits o' work, Ebad?"

"Which old girl?" demanded Art.

"In the tale, Art—remember, I told you. The widow who kills pirates to get justice for her dead hubby . . ."

"Mary Hell," said Ebad. "I've spotted some of her creations before. And this wreck looks recent. *She* must be in these waters!"

"Are we in danger?" said Art crisply.

"I don't know, daughter. How'd she judge us? Pirates who don't kill. Who try *not* to kill."

The ruined ship floated nearer. The motion of the seas was uncanny, waves spooning over, this way and that, as if toward some central area up ahead to the south.

"No sign of tempest yet. We'll board her," Art decided. "Wait until she's closer, check her out."

"I can tell you, Art. She'll be full of good stuff—everything they'd stolen. Mary leaves all that where it lies. They say she's never stepped off her own ship, the *Widow*, since first she went aboard."

There was no need to launch a boat, which Art had judged would be insane, with bad weather about to strike. The broken ship came obligingly nearer and nearer, and soon enough they could look across her unlit decks. They flung the grapplers, sank in *Unwelcome*'s claws. Art and half a dozen of her men swung across the slight gap.

It was a fact. The black nets—like webs, like seaweed (widow's weeds)—were spread everywhere. It seemed these must be the Widow's calling card. The men crept from place to place. Tools and weapons lay scattered. Bottles of rum and a smashed violin, too. Art pushed through into the captain's cabin. Lighting and raising her lantern, she took in the table laid with pewter and good glass, the rotting roast and pools of gluey wine.

Below, it was similar. Empty hammocks swayed, tobacco pouches and pipes clattered on the floor. The guns had fired at least once and recoiled heavily—the materials of gunnery were cast about, primes and cotton, cannonballs and wet gunpowder, stinking. In the hold were bales of embroidered Indic satin, chains of pearls, caskets of money, sacks of coffee, and barrels of withering fruit.

"Take nothing out of her," Art said. "It's cursed."

No one wanted anything.

They came up, crossed the deck, and swung back to the very welcome *Unwelcome*.

The grapplers then wouldn't let go.

They cut themselves loose and found the sticky, ghostly nets had also caught on parts of the *Unwelcome*'s hull. These nets, too, they slashed away.

In the now-almost-windless red-grape dusk, they got free of the corpse ship and left her bumping there, in the ending of the light.

"'Tis bad luck."

"She be like the *Fatty Morgainor*—the demon ship wot vanishes f'rever and ever away—yet be always *seen*, to lure ye on. . . ."

But the French pirate vessel vanished as full darkness drew down.

For the sun was really gone now. The air smelled of struck tinder, or yellow phosphorus matches—the new invention always likely to blow up in your face—

"Take in all sail!"

They skipped to the rigging. Men like crabs crawling, the great sheets rolled up and bound to the yards.

Art relieved Tazbo Lightheart, who sat shivering in the crow's nest.

"Feasty's made Franco-Spanish omelettes and mutton sausages," Art told him.

Down he went, quick and able.

He's still a kid, she thought, ten years old and can fire a cannon. *Like me, once.*

No. I could only act. And, I'm still acting, Am I fine, Ma? Do they believe me? Do—*I* believe me, Ma?

No stars shone through the blackness. The moon, which should be high, was nowhere to be noticed.

Down there, she could hear Cuthbert playing the hurdy after supper, a regular old singsong.

No wind now at all. The ship creaked in a dry, lazy voice. The furled canvas squeaked and sighed. The sea went *slop-slop*.

She's all I have. My Unwelcome Stranger.

The two o'clock bell sounded. Like a cue in the theater. . . .

Art *saw* the storm appear, distinctive and terrible, lifting from the southwest, a hoop of fire and shadow—

Below, at her bellow, shouts, whistles, and alarms. Men who had been snatching sleep scrambled to their posts.

The night had been so uncommonly vacant of noise. And still it was, when the human hubbub quietened.

Unwelcome's crew watched the arrival of the weather in awe.

"It's like a door—into hell."

Lightnings were caught in the hoop of cloud. Waterspouts dazzled off the sea and swirled through it. At its center was a sort of opening, black—a void.

A great red fork of lightning cracked out of the roil of cloud, hitting the sky, scorching it like the whip of a snake's tongue.

Art could see now, the cloud mass was less a hoop than a *tunnel*. It sucked down air currents and electricity, sucked *up* water, spun them all around and around. And the tunnel's mouth, that O of blind blackness—the ship, too, was due to be swallowed up in it.

There was no real wind that she could feel. The atmosphere was thick but sequined everywhere with eerie stitches of light. The tops of *Unwelcome*'s masts bloomed abruptly in filmy white fires.

Art swung hand over hand down the rigging. Sitting aloft had no place in this. She jumped to the quarterdeck.

Ebad and Boozle had the wheel. Mosie Dare stood by, ready to fling in his extra weight.

They could hear the thunder finally, trapped and muffled in the rotating cloud.

All along the ship, men stayed like statues, seeming bolted and strapped down like the guns, the barrels, the tons of sail.

Suddenly the sea *heaved* upward.

The ship was tilted straight up, her bowsprit pointed at the sky, almost standing on her stern.

Despite all precaution, a rumble of objects shaken loose and careering free in the underdecks.

Art staggered *up* along the deck. She caught at falling men in passing and threw them against anything they could cling to. She felt the thrust of the sea under her feet, trying to turn *Unwelcome* upside down. And the ship's resistance striving to force herself level. Feasty had tied himself firm to the mainmast. Out of one large coat pocket, two small beaked heads protruded side by side, one white, one green and red. No battle now.

No longer held off, the lightning flashed strongly, vision coming and going in slices. Glimpses, everything at crazy angles—Tazbo's frightened face, Ert Liemouse clutching a rope, Cuthbert clutching the hurdy-gurdy, Plinke praying calmly in an unheard chant, Mothope with his mouth wide open—like the mouth of the storm—in a howl of rage. Apart from Ebad and Cuthbert, none of the original crew to be seen—oh yes, Dirk and Whuskery lashed to the deckhouse with the chicken coop—

Art hauled herself onto the forecastle deck. Under the bowsprit, she grasped the stays and the rail.

All at once the ship was dropping fully level, plunging her nose down with a grinding thud into the jaws of the tempest and the sea.

Long ago—last year—Art had been fearless. She'd reveled in a storm. Yet this storm, as Honest had said, was an *individual*.

The ship swayed, moaned, and croaked, her stern now driven deeply to port by the combers of the spooning ocean, and her prow dragged over to starboard, so she strained against herself, and the oak and elm and copper of her cried out.

The boiling lightning-veined clouds were all around them at last. The black core of the storm had disappeared—because they were *inside* it, in the tunnel.

Sea slapped Art's face, stinging as wasps. Paying her back in kind, after all, for hitting Walter. The masts leaned. Against her will, the ship began slowly, ponderously, herself to turn.

Water was swilling down a drain there in the sea's floor—that was how the ocean had become here—a plughole. . . .

The pale fire on the masts went out. But just then the red, forking serpent's tongue cracked again, whiplike, from the cloud. The mizzentop took the full force of the strike. It *burst* like a bomb—fire, wood, and iron showered the decks, steam screamed in pillars—stays gone, the mizzen topgallant and royal sails broke loose, unfurling themselves like sheets of white thunder—

Unwelcome, burning, was still sluggishly spinning.

Art could feel the helm protesting—and abruptly something giving in the heart of it, in the heart of her ship. A horrible grunting twang rang out. The rudder chain—

Now other missiles than water, fire, and bits of mast were falling. The pillowed bags of the storm were already full of things it had seized and splintered. Palm leaves rained down, branches with crushed fruit still on them, whole sides of trees—fish showers fell, stones, and coconuts that the storm itself had delicately split in two. And worse than these—the head of a china doll, mysteriously in one piece—till it hit the deckhouse—a quarter of a ship's wheel that, crashing amidships, stove in the planks and dropped through to hole the gun deck beneath.

No time to repair, no chance to save. And the steering gone.

Art couldn't think what she could do. Before, she had always known. No longer. All she had done was crawl up here to face this unconquerable foe—like her mother would have, in the *play* called *Piratica*.

Art, the useless fool. A Maiden of the Academy of Soppy Twits. An actor—

Then the wind came.

The spinning ship, going quite fast now, found herself shoved violently, sidelong down the sea.

The voice of the wind squealed from every direction. It snapped up the last of the mizzen top. The smoldering sails detached and flew out across the water, clearing the ship, a pair of torn-off wings—

But the clouds, too, were being blown right over. They undid themselves and streamed away—and then there was only the wall of blackest night, colliding with the ship, this wall itself ripped high all along the eastern sky in a new, more colossal fire.

The sky is in flames!

No—no—it's sunrise—sunrise—I thought less than an hour had gone by—

But why is the sun rising so high up in the air?

Behind her, she heard her crew keening. They sounded like wolves—dogs—like Muck—where was Muck? Where Plunqwette?

The wind slashed the world apart, one more fragile coconut.

Not only dawn was in their path now. Something else. And *that* was why the sun was rising high up in the air. It was rising that way because it was only just now cresting a tall obstacle. For it wasn't black night after all they were colliding with—

The *Unwelcome Stranger*, who had once been the FRS *Elephant*, a trader turned pirate, liking a life as a pirate better, blew sideways on, graceful to her last second, between the million-knot blast of the wind and the dawn-rimmed rocks and cliffs that here block-aded the Guinea coast.

Her hard, sweet keel of elm, her copper plating, all one broad, gun-speaking side, skating on ancient rock. The noise like fractured violins and vast trees axed in a place of stone, the shriek of metal dying.

She had escaped the breaker's yard. But *this* was the breaker's yard.

Her remaining masts disintegrating, chunks of ash and saw-dust fluttering softly down. The bundles of the sails' white thunder unrolling. Lying suddenly over on her port side, as if only tired, taking a rest. The sea rushing in to make a lace-edged green coverlet.

"She's struck." A whisper. No need to shout. The cliffs know, the listening sky, the air, the sea, and every man aboard. The wind, merciless in uninterest, fades like a sigh.

❧ THREE ❧

The Black Land ——

Molly spoke in her marvelous voice, close to Art's ear. "This ship—she's lucky. She's friends with this sea." And then she said, "And even if we went down, don't fear . . . sleep among mermaids and pearls and sunken kingdoms. You wouldn't mind that, would you, love?"

Art's dreaming. She doesn't often dream, in fact, of her mother. Molly's always *part* of her somehow, so not necessarily to be dreamed of that much. But anyway, Art can't quite make her out, and now everything changes, and here's the awful Academy, that jail of polished floors, tight skirts, and book balancing to learn how to keep the back straight and the brain empty.

Vile Miss Eeble is positioned in front of her.

"Pray, what is this?"

"Artemesia banged her head!" A chorus of many silly girly tones.

"You've no business, Artemesia, to bang your head. A *lady* does not bang her head on anything."

Miss Eeble grabs Art and lifts her clean off the floor.

"Put me down, madam, or I shall make you!" Art thunders.

How on earth has this skinny wretch picked her up at all? How dare she—

"Keep still, daughter. This is the tricky bit."

Not Evil Eeble's voice after all. A velvet male voice at actor's best calm pitch. He's black, this man, holding her, carrying her—

"Dad," says Art. Oh, that's all right, then. No, he's not her actual daddy, who is that pain in a basket Fitz-Willoughby Weatherhouse. This is her mother's partner, Ebadiah Vooms, her *true* father by joint adoption.

"I hit my head on an eagle," Art tells him.

"No," he says, "half a foremast hit *you*. Your skull's tough; you're great. Hold still."

Art sees water all around. How odd. They seem to be standing on the sea. The sky is bright, and the waves are like living dark blue treacle with big flounces of white. What artistic rocks and towery cliffs—Felix will like to paint them. . . . Where *is* Felix, by the way?

Something hurts. Head. No, heart. No. Both.

Art lets go again of being awake, and so Ebad finds it a lot easier to swing her around to Eerie and Honest in the longboat.

As day seeps more and more through the walls of the earth, the sea grows polite and much flatter.

A good thing. Men with broken bones are staggering off the wreck, splashing into the two boats that, of four, survived when the *Unwelcome Stranger* struck the rock bank.

Everyone is present, if not quite correct. Even the soaked parrots, huddling together, preening each other in Feasty Jack's best hat that somehow he had managed to save. Oscar Bagge, carpenter and surgeon, is going to be a busy fellow if they get ashore. Several are unconscious, like Captain Art Blastside, who was hit on the head as the ship keeled over and their world fell in. Others, like Grug, Lupin, Whuskery, Nib, Stott Dabbet, and Sikkars Eye went down and under, but enough able-bodied men were left to pull them out or dive and *hoist* them out. Now they upchuck sea or snore or cough. But they've all survived.

A sort of deadly serenity hangs on the two overpacked boats. But some of the men weep, and Ebad Vooms is one of them, as they row away along the slack of the sleepy ocean, leaving their broken vessel stranded. Every tickle of the gentle wavelets now is pulling her apart. As the longboats round the cliff face and find the opening inland and the mirror of lagoon beyond, still across the water they watch the planks drift from *Unwelcome*, the barrels and segments of sugar-icing trim, and rails, and washing bundles of sinking sails and spars.

"Did the figurehead go? Our coffee lady in the black veil?"

"Aye. Smashed right off as the ship struck. Down to the bottom she's gone, to Dewi Jonah's Chest."

In the chicken coop, clasped by Salt Walter, the birds splatter on their wet straw, clearing their throats. In Eerie's pocket, in a watertight packet, the French plan for the very unusual ship. Cuthbert lets water run from his wheezing hurdy-gurdy and talks low to his wife in England. But Forecastle Smith is the one keeping a grip on Muck's once-precious bone. For Forecastle has seen the bone will make an ideal splint for his left, broken-boned forearm.

The coast beyond the cliffs was like other spots they had come across at the hem of Africray. White sands, the blue lagoon, and the trees, which the unnatural storm hadn't touched.

Over there, too, forest began. Heavy green jungle full of green darkness and shafts of green sun.

They stayed by the lagoon.

As the human carpentry repairs went on, amid howls and oaths, and including the making of splints and crutches, fish were caught and pineapples plucked. They lit a fire for Jack to cook. The sun, too, soon sweltered down.

(Did any of them forget that just around that shoulder of cliff, a ruin lay, eaten slowly by the sea?)

Art slept beneath a palm, her coat rolled up by Ebad and under her head. A bruise like a blue flower stained her forehead. Ebad checked on her now and then. The cannon blast years back had put the marigold streak in her walnut-brown hair. Would this blow leave any marker?

Most blows, most shocks, left something, he mused, sitting by her, swallowing some grilled fish he couldn't taste. Molly had left her mark on *him* for sure, invisible but always there.

The sun golded the scene. It showed them all how grand and pleasant everything was, trying to make them lighten up. *Cheer up,* the sun cruelly and ignorantly shouted, *it may never happen.*

"Feasty—that's not your cook smoke, is it, blowing across over there?"

"No, Mr. O'Shea."

"Then 'tis people native to the land here. By the Nag's Nose Necklace, they're often friendly along these coasts."

"Not always," said Grug, who had recovered broken-legged from his skinful of seawater but not entered a happy frame of mind. "Sometimes they *resents* visitors."

They heard drums soon after, the sort that belonged only to Africay. A complex tempo and pattern wove through the jungle. The calling birds respectfully went quiet.

"Here they come."

About twenty tall men emerged from the columns of the forest. They were dressed in white robes and carved wooden jewelry, with a wink of gold. Black in their white, they paused, looking across at the refugees on their shore.

Then three strode over. They spoke in a dialect of the Guinea coast, and Ebad, knowing it, answered them.

At once they stared right at him.

They'd asked if this was a shipwreck or a trading mission. Ebad had said a wreck. But now their eyes blazed on him.

They had handsome, aristocratic faces, carved as if from ebony, like their ornaments.

Ebad didn't realize, quite, that his face was like theirs. Only more so.

They, however, apparently did.

Without bothering to say anything else about wrecks or visitors or trade, the leader of the group drew from his robe a big golden coin or medallion. Moving forward, he held this out to Ebad Vooms.

Ebad got up.

"What is it?" he asked in the Afric lingo.

"Look, and see."

Ebad looked.

He saw—what? The profile of a man cut into the medallion. A profile certainly classically African, the hair crinkled and worn long to the shoulder.

"Forgive a stranger to your country," said Ebad, "and tell me what this means."

But the three men only turned, making a sharp, almost violent gesture to their waiting comrades. One of these spun around at once and sped back into the forest.

Every crewman that could surged to his feet, a watery flintlock, pistol, knife, or sword in his hand.

" 'S all right, Ebad. We're here for you."

The leader of the forest people shook his head impatiently.

"You misunderstand, sirs." He spoke now in perfect English, only a flavor of accent to pepper his sentences. "We mean you no harm. This is the face of a king upon the gold. And you, lord, re-semble him exactly, to the last detail. We're pleased to meet you. Step into the woods, all of you, if you wish. All comfort is there. You will never regret it."

"Don't trust the beggar," said Grug. "Pretty rugs cover rotten floors."

Others agreed.

But Eerie said, "But 'tis a fact, Ebad and this gentleman on the coin—they might be twins."

The medallion was passed among the shipwrecked crew. Only Art, still sleeping under her palm, didn't come to see.

Puzzled and unsure, the men of the late *Unwelcome Stranger* gazed at their would-be hosts.

And in the jungle the drums suddenly began another pattern and a different tempo.

"*I* will go with you," said Ebad.

"Very well," said the black leader.

Twenty-six voices rose in a din that started the birds up again under the trees. "Nay—Ebad—not alone!" "By the Crock of O'Cran—I'll be with ye!" "Don't be a nutter, Mr. Baddy, we're yer mates, and we'll go with you—" "And I—" "And I—" "And I—"

The black leader smiled royally. "I see, lord, they take you as a man of great importance. Their captain, no doubt."

"First Mate. The captain's there. My daughter."

Surprised brows rising. "She? A white woman?"

Ebad frowned. His unreadable face might now be read, if only for a second. "Her mother was white. My wife."

"Then, lord, she is a princess to us, for your sake. She, too, was hurt? Some of us will carry her."

"*I'll* carry her," said Cuthbert, "poor ol' girl."

"And I," said Dirk. "I mean, dearie, I can't get any *more* untidy than I already am, can I?"

Being deep within the jungle occurred inside three or four strides. It closed around like curtains, or another kind of sea.

Trees were tall, ribbed and pocked like sculpted posts, and going up high to a shut canopy of leaves and fronds. Creepers knitted the forest together, but there was a clear path. (Their guides, the white-robes, had already presumably hacked their way through to the beach.) The greenness was intense. Birds buzzed, fluted, and shrieked. Insects that stung rushed from tree boles.

It was a long walk, especially for Grug and Boozle on crutches. And then a village appeared, with pointed roofs, grass-thatched huts. Two or three black cattle stared from a swampy pool, where they were browsing on reeds. Though the crew were brought fruit and water, the leader of the group of white-robes said this was a rest of one hour only.

"How far is it, the place you mean us to go to?" Eerie asked him.

"Some days' travel."

The men from the ship exchanged looks.

"Suppose," said Ebad, "any of us prefer to stay here? Or to return to the shore?"

"Do you know your way? Can you find it? The forest grows quick and thick, and will already be closing the path. This village meanwhile can never afford to feed you. Do you know which waters are safe to drink hereabouts? Which plants are to be eaten? There are snakes and tree cats. Any that don't wish to accompany us, they must take care of themselves."

Feasty Jack gave a gravelly laugh. "A fixed game."

The others gloomed at the trees. It was a labyrinth, and mostly the sun wasn't visible to judge direction from. Besides, what did the beach hold? A shoreline, and a view around the cliff of a dead ship.

After an hour, they got up and everyone went on.

Not long after, Cuthbert called Ebad. Art had come to again. She then insisted on getting off the improvised stretcher they had made of branches. When Ebad got there, she was moving around like a drunk dancer, Dirk keeping tight hold of her arm.

"Hi, Ebad, I'm well. Just getting my sea legs."

"Take it slow, Arty."

"Yes, Dad. But I was getting so worried, you see, lying there gazing at the back of Dirk's coat. I've never seen him in such a mess."

She seemed to know who they all were; no loss of memory, then. She had taken in their position and what had happened. Her vision and hearing were obviously already clear again, and the dizzy nonbalance soon wore off. Presently she unfastened Dirk and next Mosie Dare from her arms, and everyone walked on. No one had asked if she understood about the ship. *Did* she? She seemed more than anything else amused in a sad, withdrawn way. But she could stride now, look at her. Aside from the bruise on her forehead, she was physically not so different.

All afternoon they toiled through the jungle-forest, and by now toil it was. The white-robes hadn't lied; the cut path was already being smothered. The black men, and then some of the crew, began to slash away the ferns, creepers, and silky oar-blades of leaves that choked the route.

They reached a narrow brown river, with banks of drooping, willowlike trees, smoking blue with steam in the heat. Monkeys yattered, unseen. An enormous muscular snake slid down the bank into the water. Soon after two deer, which seemed to be wearing white-striped breeches, bounded over a glade. (Walter, Ert, Tazbo, and de Weevil talked about them for ages, wondering who had dressed them like that. "Someone with absolutely *no* taste," Dirk concluded.)

Art by now was walking with Ebad. She spoke to him in French.

"So they mean you're a king, Mr. Vooms?"

"It seems so. Perhaps they're mad."

"Perhaps we are, never to have recognized it. You always boasted you were descended from the pharaohs of Egypt."

"It's true, Art."

"Awesome."

Abruptly, the leader of the white-robes flung one arm high to halt them. Then pointed straight upward. Everyone stopped.

They stared into the tangle of boughs and foliage. Something dully shone there, a strip of solid dappled sunlight lying along a bough.

Art, too, looked up at it. She knew what it was, either from pictures Molly had once shown her or from actual childhood experience—she wasn't sure which. For it was a spotted leopard.

The white robes led the whole party carefully aside, giving the tree cat a wide berth.

From then on, every few minutes there was some odd happening.

Something flew by through the canopy, for example, its wings swishing like rakes through grass. Or Shemps trod on a snake and leaped in the air yelling. But this snake was only another root. Just as the snake that dropped on Boozle an hour later was only a vine. Then there was the *real* snake, looped around a branch. "See that?" This from Jack. "They call it *Bite-is*. One nip and it's good night, Africay."

The jungle eventually darkened. The sun was going down at last. Shadows rose like screens. Soon it was dim enough that they bumped into things—trees grew invisible, darkness *itself* was more dense—and so they skirted the shadows and crashed into the trunks. Glinting insects misled them further, whirring through the air in flights of sparks. And then from caves or holes seethed a black, clattering cloud, faintly squeaking—flying mouse-umbrellas—*bats*.

When they reached another village set in a glade, over twenty sighs of relief sounded like a small gale.

Once let into a vacant hut, given bowls of some kind of porridge, the men ate, threw themselves on the ground, and slept.

Art didn't eat much or attempt to sleep.

She walked outside the hut, expecting any moment someone would halt her, turn her back.

Two of the white-robes crouched alone by a small fire, one of them the leader.

Art could speak their dialect, too. She went up to them and asked if she might sit down.

"Sit, then."

She sat across from them. She watched the firelight gild their faces, flame on coal. Art had noted the white English of her party were not particularly frightened of these men. But Mosie Dare, the black Englishman, and Larry Lully, the Blue Indiesman, were both wary and unnerved. Ebad, though—Ebad seemed mostly interested in the whole dodgy adventure.

About three-quarters of a mile off, she judged, drums were beating again through the jungle. Ebad had told her the drums sent messages; a kind of code was in the patterns and rhythms. What, she wondered, did these say?

Art fixed her mind on all the current events. It was like holding steady the wheel of the ship. Yes, even of the ship that lay miles off on the rocks, and miles, too, behind the closed door of self-deception and self-protection in her brain. She'd face *Unwelcome*'s ghost one day—not yet. (So much behind that closed door now. Is it getting crowded in there?)

"What is the name," Art said in a little while, "of the place you take us to?"

The leader glanced at the other man. The leader said, "It is Khem."

"Khem . . ." Something slipped across her thoughts. Hadn't Molly spoken of this—some story or legend—wasn't *Khem* the ancient name for Egypt?

"We're going so far north?"

"No. Eastward."

"To Khem."

Khem, she thought, it means something. Black, she thought. *Black Land*. The great River Nile rose to flood the fields of Egypt and make them rich with black silt for a good harvest. So, the Black Land: Khem.

"There's a river there?" she asked.

"The stem of the River Water Lily."

In English, foxed by the phrase, she questioned, "A lily stem?"

"The river's source," said the leader, smiling into the fire.

Art gave it up. She said, "Mr. Vooms has told me you think he resembles a king."

"*The* king. He does."

"But won't your king mind this—a look-alike turning up?"

"There is no king. Not since old times long past. He had then another name, the king in the Black Land of Africay."

"Let me guess," said Art in English. "The king was called the *Pharaoh*."

The white robes raised their eyes, then bowed to Art with the courtesy of the very proud.

Art bowed back, in the ordinary way. She returned to the hut.

The large round space was full of sleeping and gurgles and the occasionally jumpy bad dream.

She crossed to Ebad Vooms and leaned toward him. To wake him or not to? What was best?

As she pondered she saw something flitting across the open doorway of the hut. Listening, she heard bare footsteps next, padding all around the outside of the round walls. Until a ring of men with long spears cordoned the hut and everyone in it. Even across the doorway the cordon ran. Tall, dark figures, a living fence.

Art sat down and leaned her back on the wall. No point now in disturbing anyone. She'd overplayed her hand with the two men outside.

First light was when? Perhaps three hours.

She didn't mean to sleep again but . . .

A trumpet woke her—several trumpets.

The noise seemed to split her skull, and light poured in at her eyes.

Everybody was lurching up from the hut floor. Art got to the doorway first, and the guards—what else were they?—let her peer out between their shoulders.

Behind her, in a horrified wail, Gideon Squalls's voice rose above the rest. "What are *they*? 'Tis monsters—do my head in!"

"No, no, Mr. Squalls," said Feasty, "those are Afric elephants."

"*Monsters*! Look, they got ropes growing on their faces—"

"Trunks," said Feasty. "And do ye see the ears?"

"To miss 'em 'ud be a fine thing, great flappy objects."

"The ears of the Afric fanty are shaped like the map of Africay itself," continued Jack in a collected, knowledgeable way. "*Unlike* the ears of the fanty of the Inde, whose ears are shaped exactly like the map of the *Inde*."

Art dodged nimbly under the crossed spears and out onto the turf beyond the hut. The spears rattled behind her but nothing else. After all, *she* wasn't a pharaoh. Unimportant.

The elephants were enormous, yet orderly. They rose there like the walls of some live castle, gray and sewn all over in tightly organized wrinkles and seams. High up in the old-young faces, little eyes glowed like amber. Ivory tusks curved out beside the rope-trunks, each pair ringed near the face with gold. There were only four of them. It had sounded like forty.

Ebad was already standing among the elephants.

The guards had allowed this, she assumed, because he was also surrounded by the men in white robes.

"The drums last night," said Ebad. "Did you hear them?"

"Yay, Daddy. Loud and clear."

"It seems we're moving too slowly, so the drums called for transport."

"Elephants?"

Ebad walked her quietly through the elephant grove and showed her some wooden platforms set on wheels. They were painted in complicated patterns, scarlet, yellow, white, and black.

"We ride on these and the elephants pull us through the forests. Someone's already cleared the way and kept it clear, or so our guides tell me."

"And did they tell you we're going to Khem?"

"Yes. That's the old name for Egypt."

"I know, Mr. Vooms. So we're going to Egypt-in-Africay and you are going to be a pharaoh." She added in French, "Do we make a dash for it after all?"

"Nay, Arty. There's about a hundred warriors over behind the huts, wearing a kind of armor, and with weapons. And Art—"

*"Oui, mon père?"**

They all speak French, too."

—◦◦◦◦—

*Yes, Father?"

174 ~ THE SHIPS

The jungle had definitely been cleared. An avenue as wide as Pell Mell in Lundon was cleaved through. This path also ran very straight; in fact, it would stay straight all the two further days they trundled along it on the elephant platforms. It was a bumpy ride, the wheels taking every uncleared root and stone, of which there were plenty, at a gallop. The elephants galloped, too, their advance heavy and tireless, feet hammering the ground. Men with broken bones, and Bagge himself, who had done them all up with splints, yelped and swore.

Snakes, annoyed-looking monkeys, birds, deer, stared in disapproval or fled.

The black warriors, in their beaded breastplates and kilts of thin bronzy metal, galloped alongside the platforms and also ahead and at the back. To Ebad, at any pause, the warriors offered clashing salutes with their spears. They also drew daggers shaped like scorpions, serpents, and lizards, holding them high so the blue sky blazed on every sharp scale and point.

None of the crew thought it sensible to argue about a single thing.

"A splendid sight," Feasty Jack remarked, sitting on the second platform, with Maudy on one shoulder and Plunqwette on his head, both parrots glaring in amazement at the galloped-by forest. "A grand sight. And those gents can hit a moving target at a hundred yards."

"With those funny-looking knives?" asked scared Larry Lully.

"No, lad. With the spears. The knives are never used to fight. They have a ritual purpose."

"What's that?"

"None knows but they."

Two days and a night sandwiched between, they galloped.

The escort and the elephants hardly stopped to rest.

Five times men were jounced right off. Without hesitating, warriors instantly caught them all in mid-plummet and dropped them back in place. None of the five had broken limbs, nor got them now.

Art found she laughed at these antics, stupidly. (Once, though, she dreamed of Felix, during a two-minute sleep on the platform. He was playing cards with Belladora Fan—only Belladora had somehow changed into Little Goldie Girl. That *wasn't* so funny.)

As the quick, hot, red sunset began on the second day, the hacked-out avenue came to an end.

It came to an end at the brink of something even more impressive, indeed astonishing.

The elephants slowed and chugged to a standstill. The warriors, too. On the wheeled land rafts every man, and one woman, got to their feet.

The jungle path stopped before two tapering pylons made of cut stone. Pictures and symbols were chiseled into them, and their tops were capped with gold, which caught the ruby sunlight blindingly.

Beyond, there lay a second road. And a *road* was what it certainly was. The most elegant and best made and widest street of any city of the West could hardly compare with it. It was paved in huge regular blocks, and the joins could scarcely be seen. In the setting light, it, too, glowed, like copper. And so did the stone statues that lined it either side, stretching away and away to the narrowing horizon.

"They're like lions, lying down, with the front paws out and the heads raised," said Walter, wonderingly. "Only—"

"They have the heads of men!" Shadrach finished.

"Feasty, you know a lot. What are they?"

"Shesps," said Jack, offhand, preening like his parrot now. "Or you can call them sphinxes."

"Lynxes? Spinxes?"

Feasty simply grinned.

" 'Tis a king's royal avenue, Art," said Honest, soft as the sunset breath of wind that stirred the trees. "It's old as forever."

"It's *Egypt*," said Whuskery. "Like when we did Shakespur's *Antony and Cleopatra*, Dirk, eh?"

"And this time not a creaky old painted backdrop, either," Dirk agreed dreamily.

The warriors were bowing to the avenue. The elephants raised their trunks and greeted it with a fanfare that rang the jungle like a bell. This must have terrified the sun, for it shot suddenly away down to the left, under the walls of trees beyond the road.

At once the sky cooled.

Having shown the road respect, elephants and warriors bounded forward again.

Holding to the platform sides and one another, the whole crew stared in all directions at road and sphinxes. But night was dropping like a black sail, rubbing out the scene.

They must have rushed on then for about fifteen minutes in darkness, before light once more appeared ahead of them.

"It's torches."

But it was more than torches.

The avenue ran to a high, torchlit stone wall, on which were drawn more pictures—Egyptian scenes, that Art, and one or two others, had come across in books. In the wall was a massive oblong arch, and when the procession reached it, Art saw the avenue ended, and one more startling thing began.

It was a small city of straight streets and two-story, flat-roofed buildings, which here and there flowered into much greater buildings, columned and strung with flags. Torch and lamplight made the city golden, and showed all its scores of colors. But it was not enormous by any means, and beyond, visible from the height it stood on, flowed a long, sweeping plain. And the plain, too—*shone*. It glittered and glimmered, right to the banks of a dark river, and on again beyond the river, to the end of the view. What finished the view was also of interest.

The triangle soared up from the spangly plain, up from the jungle that still surrounded everything. It was surely too regular in shape to be any natural hill or mountain. Vast streams of stars were already burning in the sky, and the starlight outlined the triangle, broad base to pointed top, quite clearly.

Art looked at Ebad. "It's an ancient Egyptian pyramid, isn't it?"

But before he could answer, a horn began to blow from somewhere up in the city, and people were running from the buildings, and all the warriors turned to Ebad on his platform, knelt down, and held their special daggers to their foreheads.

"Respect, Ebad!" croaked Eerie. "By the Banshee's Best Blanket, respect *and* some."

A single figure moved out from among the warriors. He was the white-robed leader, who all this while had bounded along with them.

He too knelt, and they learned now he had a voice strong enough for any actor.

"Hail, lord. Hail, Ta Neweh Amoon, King of the Source and the Three Lands! Son of Heaven! Pharaoh!"

Where's Muck? —

He had swum ashore at Tangerina, as a matter of course.

Muck was a nosy dog; he liked to sniff around.

And in the port town, under the scent of tangerines and rhinoceros, he found lots of curious smells that were worth investigating. But—really his heart wasn't in it.

Though Muck was a dog, he had emotions, loyalties, and wants—like most creatures. Like most dogs. Basically now he missed Emma Holroyal. Despite treating her quite casually as an "owner," going missing often, burying the special bone in her desk in the May-Fair house, and finally running off altogether to rejoin the crew, Muck had been stricken with a fatal love—that of the pack animal for his preferred pack leader.

In El Tangerina, Muck trotted about, stole a sardine, was chased, fell into a rubbish heap and found a lovely cheese rind to go with the sardine, and had a wash and brushup at a public fountain, where he showered some smart passing ladies with shaken-off water. All pleasant. (At one point, too, going by a doorway, he had glimpsed Felix Phoenix sitting inside. Muck had behaved as if he hadn't known Felix at all.)

Later, Muck sat under a vine-and-tangerine-clad wall and overheard some talk.

Muck was one of those wise or working animals who learned languages—or bits of them. He learned names, too, because it was only sensible to pick up from chat just who might be about to leave or arrive.

So, under the wall, Muck heard the English crew of a small frigate at anchor in the bay discussing how they were about to join the English fleet patrolling in the Mediterranean Sea. "What do you think of that Hamlet Ellensun?" someone asked. "Made Admirable of the Fleet." "*Admiral*, you asp." "Well, hake me."

Muck's ears were by now like those of a rabbit. Naturally he didn't follow every line, but Hamlet's name he'd grasped, and he knew, too, about a sea called the Med.

He hopped in at a window and pattered to the frigate crew's table.

"Hey, 'tis a cute old rat-better down here, see, by my missing leg."

"Yellow as butter," said others thoughtfully.

Muck made himself charming, standing on hind paws and doing a brief dance, smiling at them. They fed him scraps of their meal. "Who's he belong to?" Muck leered adorably at them, and when they eventually reeled out of the tavern at sunset, he trotted in a familiar way at their heels.

Muck had often got in with crews. He'd traveled to quite a few spots like this, if always in the end finding his way back to his own actor-pirates. How he always *could* find them he didn't know, and had never bothered to worry over it. This evening, for example, he knew they were in the town, but he didn't seek them. He accompanied the frigate sailors instead to their ship, which had a curious name that Muck, obviously, didn't read—the *Ow Blast*.

Here the dog was presented to many deck personnel, and up the ranks as high as the First Mate, who patted Muck and gave him a tangerine.

Yet again then Muck was a hit, and that night he set off with the frigate, sailing due northeast.

As it turned out, word came from a passing vessel before they'd gone too far. All English fighting ships were being called to Franco-Spania. Admirable Admiral Hamlet Ellensun had already been victorious in the Med; the French had fled and were reinforcing and regrouping off the coast of Jibrel-Tar, just across from the top of Morrocaino.

"There's some old island there," the men of *Ow Blast* told one another. "That's where they think we'll find them Avey Voos. It'll be one dolly of a battle."

Muck, who knew the word *battle*, now managed to unlearn it fast. He sunned himself on the deck and watched the sky and water, and at gun practice, when all twenty-four guns bellowed, he hid under a bunk and maybe recalled the bone he had left behind on the *Unwelcome*—but there was no going back, not now.

Hamlet, too, belonged to Emma. Hamlet, therefore, was the person to head for. Only instinct told Muck this, but the instinct was *very* strong. Oddly, too, Muck was thoughtlessly aware that now he could locate Hamlet as easily as in the past he had always located his actors. Hamlet, as Emma's property, presently meant more to Muck than the actors. Or even—incredibly—than the bone!

Ow Blast's sailors had decided to call Muck "Lucky." This sounded enough like his original name that Muck soon realized it was meant to be his. (Emma had only ever called him Doggy, or, to others, *My Dog.*)

The charging blue rhino of the sea dashed about the sides of the ship. Muck listened, hearing Hamlet's name more and more often. He had even by now learned the name of the offshore Morro-Spanish island where the next big engagement with the French was expected. "A haunted isle, off Jibrel-Tar," the sailors said. "Eh, Lucky? Old Roman ruins there, statues and columns, and a great square—a plaza, they calls it. Sea washes right across sometimes and gushes out again in big spouts. . . ."

"Look at that dog, listening. I'd swear he gets every word."

But Muck-Lucky didn't. He got what he needed, which were *Hamlet* and, by now, *French fleet*, and the island's name, which was Tres or Très—or Trey Falco.

Asleep in the basket he sometimes accepted use of in the officers' quarters, Muck dreamed of hunting across the neat gardens of May-Fair. There was a large dream moon, yellow as his coat, and several of Emma's dresses. Perhaps Muck didn't quite dream that. Perhaps he *thought* he did. Perhaps it wasn't likely that even such a clean dog on a cushion, sleeping under the quarterdeck of the fighting ship *Ow Blast*, could have a dream of any sort. Who could say for sure? ("That dog's dreaming of the moon," said the First Mate. "Look at his paws twitch.") So *there's* Muck, then.

Crew, Crown, and Crocodiles

Overhead, far overhead—about seventy *feet* overhead—the ceiling was dyed a deep indigo and had been painted with gold and silver five-rayed stars. Columns with carved, leaflike green stone tops held it up. As the columns went down to the floor they became red, gold, and sky-blue. The floor itself was of sand-colored stone, smooth as mirror. Everything but the ceiling was covered with pictures of people and animals. You could stand alone in this room, and in others here, and feel *crowded*.

This was the palace.

His palace.

The House of Ta Neweh Amoon.

Art looked into a small square pool. Even this was full of golden fish, and pink water lilies.

They had all been here about ten days. But it felt like ten months. Or—weirdly—ten *minutes*. Always some unusual thing to see or stumble across. And yet the same.

Egypt in Africay. The Land of Khem, the Third Land of Egypt, where sprang the source of the Nile—

"Those fish look tasty, Cap'n."

"Shut it, Mr. Shemps."

Art, and most of the others, hadn't altered their dress. It was still shirt, coat, and breeches, even the normal piraty eye patches, cutlasses, three-cornered hats, lace, earrings, and rings.

Some, though . . . Eerie O'Shea had really thrown Art, appearing at supper yesterday clad like the locals. In a white pleated kilt, heavily beaded and glass-jeweled Egyptian necklace-collar, his hair done like that too, cut at the shoulders, oiled, and with a flower behind one ear. If she'd considered it, she would have expected *Dirk* to do that. But Dirk said he'd had *quite* enough of Egyptian dress when he and Whusk had acted in *Antony and Cleopatra* at the West Bacon Odeon. They'd got over their awe and admiration fast, it seemed. Too fast? Was this just sour grapes?

In any case the locals did the Egyptian bit best. On their dark skins the pure white linen dresses and kilts, the scarlet and blue jewels, shone. Their long, crinkly hair was perfect.

Art shifted from one foot to the other and glanced through a long door-window. In the clean, straight streets of Khem City, glamorous people strolled with well-behaved leopards and lions walking on leads, or monkeys held by the hand. Tall, long-tailed birds strutted about, too. Acacias and palm trees lined the walls of gardens, and from the flat roofs of houses, painted all shades of color, creepers heavy with flowers and fruit trailed down. A paradise?

Some of the crew, aside from Mr. O'Shea, had gone down with what the others called Lily Fever. This meant they just wanted to lie about all day on the comfy wooden couches by the lily ponds, brought snacks and beer by pretty servants. The black city had made them all welcome. It was easy to give in, perhaps. Had any of them ever known such luxury? At night, every house feasted, and here in the palace, where the whole crew had been put up, an enormous dining room, pillared and painted like everywhere else, served a supper that started at sundown and went on until, by Mr. Bagge's unbroken pocket watch, it was two or three the next morning.

A clatter in the street. Art looked out again. Two open carriages—chariots—each with a pair of plumed horses, were prancing up the road.

Elephants trumpeted in the royal elephant stables.

Crew, Crown, and Crocodiles ~ 183

Then the thinner notes of horns sounded.

Oh. He was on his way here, then. Himself. Pharaoh.

Art braced herself. She didn't turn to see what her men were doing.

Dirk, Whusk, Honest, Salts Pete, and Walt stood just behind her. She knew they were already partly sneering. Oh, *here* we go, the sneers said. One more dramatic performance. We're *actors*, remember. We've seen it all, *done* most of it. So what if this is supposed to be for real, and has all these lovely over-the-top props—it's a show. As for Ebad—he's just the top of the bill. *Egypt-in-Africay*, starring Mr. Ebadiah Vooms, in His Most Famous Role as Pharaoh.

The others here with Art were hostile. The theatrical side overpowered and made them sullen.

(Ten-year-old Tazbo Lightheart said loudly, "All this Egypt stuff is rubbish for kids.")

Only Feasty Jack, who had stayed with Art's un-Egyptian party, seemed intrigued by the city, the people, and the customs. The two parrots had completely cheered up as well. They spent hours flying over the city together, dipping down to lily pools or small fountains for a drink and giving over hours to mutual grooming on the roofs of the five temples.

Only Boozle, Gideon, Shadrach, Mothope, Sikkars, Lupin, and Ert hadn't bothered to join Art this morning in this room with the star ceiling.

The horn fanfare ended.

Long lines of graceful attendants entered, forming up to either side. Then came a tall chap with a silver palm tree, and one with a ritual sword, and others with symbols of (presumably) kingship. Priests paced through, wearing leopard skins. These were taken, Jack said, from the bodies of animals that had died naturally after a long life. The priests' heads were shaven. They represented all five of the temples, the Cat Temple, Wolf Temple, Bird Temple, Snake Temple, and the Temple of the Goat, God of the Waters and the River Source.

The crew shuffled, muttering now.

"No audience," came Dirk's acid tones, "would put up with so much *business*. It's the *story* they want."

At last out came two men who seemed seven feet in height, bearing vast fans of white and black plumes.

"And here's Mr. Baddy."

Here he was, too.

All noise stopped. They hadn't, any of them, seen Ebad close-up for nine days. Even though he had sat in on the suppers, he'd sat far off. And before, until now, he too had dressed in the old piratic way.

Art felt her heart gather itself and jump up, banging its top on the base of her jaw.

What did she think? Was she proud of him? Angry? *Frightened?*

He was dressed as all of Khem City was.

The stiffened kilt was thick with gold. The gold collar had in it lapis lazuli, emeralds, and amethysts—and even Art knew these ones were genuine. On his arms, armlets of gold and ivory. On his head the striped local headdress, topped by a pharaoh's double crown, blood-red and snow-white, with the images of golden serpent and silver vulture.

Someone murmured, "By the Bat's Two Hats, thou art the part, Mr. V." (Peter?) And someone else (Larry?), "Six foxes on it, in-nit. Pharaoh plus."

Ebad's face, so often unreadable, now simply jet, beautifully carved. The face of a Great King. But never of a pirate, an actor, a friend, a lover, let alone a father.

He walked through the lines of kneeling attendants, and every crewman there hastily knelt down, too. Only Art stayed on her feet, hand on sword hilt, head tipped back, level-eyed.

Ebad Vooms, now Ta Neweh Amoon, stepped right up to her. He spoke as he would on a stage, but in the dialect.

"Greeting, my daughter."

Art said, in English, "Hi, Taneweh. I see you have tickets on you."

His lips curved then. That was all.

The attendants were chanting, some song of praise in a language Art didn't follow—perhaps even ancient Egyptian.

Under the chant, Pharaoh said to her, "I'm to go to the mouth of the river. It's something the king has to do."

"And a king has to do what a king has to do."

"There will be things to see there. Come with me."

"Oh, *wow*! Are you *sure*?"

"Your sarcasm's not quite worthy of Molly's daughter. Maybe of mine. But come with me anyway."

"Do I have a choice? Thee's the law round here."

"In a way."

"What about them?" Not turning, she flicked her head at the groveling men behind her. Even Dirk was kneeling. Even Honest and Cuthbert. She could *feel* they were, didn't need to look.

"Everyone. The others?" he said.

"Those not present have Lily Fever. They sit by the lily pools and eat sweets. How sweet."

The chant came to a finish. Somewhere little bells tinkled with a tinsel noise.

Huge doors, covered in carved, wing-spread birds, were opened. Outside, the city had gathered to honor Pharaoh. Hundreds of faces like dark flowers were turning upward, to offer smiles, glints of gems, and the wave of leafy fans.

—∞—

Ramps ran down from the city to the plain. It was a mini-desert, with rocks lifting from it and dunes lying in grainy folds, like sugar in a bowl. The desert was of a pale sand, but like Pharaoh's kilt, thickly frosted with *gold*.

"Do they tint it, then, the sand?"

"No, Arty. It's gold dust. There are gold mines here, have been for centuries."

Pharaoh and his steely-eyed daughter rode in a single chariot drawn by two black horses. There was a man in the chariot's front, to control the horses. And so they had only to stand there on the bouncy floor, looking around, first at the crowds, then at the ramps, and now the desert of gold dust.

"I bet, when the wind blows, it really hurts if it gets in your eyes."

"Yes, Art. Very possibly."

On the chariot rail, Art's fist, knuckles white. Pharaoh Ta Neweh Amoon must have seen this, but he didn't comment.

"What do you have to do at the river, then?" she asked casually.

"They bless the river. I bless the river."

Art swore colorful as the paint on the city.

Only seven of the men from the ship had come with them. Feasty was one, walking back there with Plinke. Forecastle, Honest, Walter—with a reluctant Peter not letting Walt out of his sight. Walter had brought one of the chickens from the rescued coop. (The other chickens had already run off into the depths of the palace, where sometimes you saw them, flown up on chair backs or nesting in a drape.) But this chicken was apparently now a pet. Stott Dabbet, grumbling but sticking at it, brought up the rear.

Far off over the plain, the pyramid rose like a golden biscuit.

"A pharaoh, Arty, is a god here," Ta Neweh Amoon said. "He ranks with the Cat Goddess and the Wolf God and the rest. And that sort of king isn't like the old English kings, or the French king, who take from their country and do nothing for it in return. Here, the king has countless duties, and if it comes to it, Art, and they need him to, to keep them safe, he dies for his people."

Art swung around. "My God, Ebad—they're going to *kill* you? We must—"

"Nay, Arty. Calm down, girl. It's very unlikely. These are peaceful times. Food's plentiful. No plagues or wars . . . They won't harm me. But, do you see, they've made me a *real* king. It took nine full days and nights to do it. It was much, much longer in the past. And the king they've made me is the servant of his land, not its tyrant."

Art felt tears push behind her eyes. She never cried. She thrust the tears back and they sank, and her eyes burned, as if after all the wind had blown gold dust into them.

"Are you saying, Ebad, that you . . ."

"Not yet. First we must go to the river. They call the river the Lily. They claim this is the source of the Nile."

She tossed her head.

She thought, Phoenix should be here. He'd talk some sense into Ebad. Drearily she thought, Or Molly. But they're not, are they. Just me. And when did I ever talk *sense* into *anyone*?

Rocks edged the riverbanks, with the occasional palm growing there. The river ran quite fast, but the breadth of the watercourse was only about a hundred feet.

"Not very impressive for a source. If it is."

"It widens to the north. They say other waters spring out of the earth and add to it. But this is where it starts." The chariots and walkers were turning to the left now, going in the opposite direction from the flow of water. Over there the jungle loomed—dark, vivid green. There was a dull rumble Art could hear now, and when the chariot paused a moment, she picked it up through the soles of her boots.

In about twenty more minutes, they had followed the river back into the jungle.

The trees grew close to the bank, in parts threatening to come down and smother the river with roots and creepers and hyacinth-like flowers. But obviously many willing hands kept the course clear. There were signs of recent efficient hacking.

They left the vehicles. The priests went first, then Ebad, followed by Art and the seven men from the ship, and Walter's chicken.

A path of steps laid with cut stones wound up the side of a treed and ferny rock. The sound of rumbling grew louder and opened out into the soft crashing of a waterfall.

The trees parted. And they'd reached the Source of the Nile—or anyway, the source of the Water Lily River.

In the shadow under the heavy trees was a mystically atmospheric spot. The rocks cluttered up and jagged down, and halfway between the forest floor and the cliff top stared a series of gaping caves. From each of these, waterfalls of various types splashed out. Some were only trickles, some narrow gushes, but the five central falls were very full-bodied and foaming. And at the middle of the most forceful torrent of all, a carved being gleamed in the rush of white water. He resembled a powerful man, but with the coiling tail of a great fish and the noble head of a goat, crowned by two curling horns. In his hands was an upturned cup. As if he spilled the river out onto the land.

The priests sang again.

"They say," Ebad told Art, " 'Hail, Knoom, Lord of the Waters, God of the Source.' "

Art shivered.

(Over there, across the river, what was that in the trees? Something odd—or just some trick of the half-light—)

She said, "Brilliant theater."

But Ebad had already walked slowly away and begun to make offerings to the river. Priests held out the baskets and Ebad—Ta Neweh—picked out the bread and flowers and flasks of wine and let them drop down, murmuring something. Then instead there were baskets of small gold objects and jewels—not glass? These, too, went to the river, or to the god. Whichever.

Until suddenly part of the brown water leaped up—and took the shape of a great snapping head of nutcracker jaws, decorated with yellowish teeth—

"Aah!" screamed Walter, burying his face in the chicken. "More monsters!"

"Hush, Mr. W," said Feasty. "It's only a croc."

"A—*croc*?"

"Crocodile."

"Aye," said Cuthbert kindly, but looking rather unhappy himself. "I've seen the ol' things afore. Like a thick-scaled snake-fish with legs—you should see 'em race on land—and fangs."

Walter still didn't seem keen.

And more of the crocodiles were now crowding the channel, slithering from holes in the riverbanks, shoving one another out of the way, golluping up whole gobsful of raw meat from fresh baskets.

"'Orrible," said Stott Dabbet. "Reminds me of dinner at home with the wife."

Art heard her seven men laugh. She put her hand on Stott's shoulder. "Well done, sir."

"Nay, Cap'n. 'Tis a *fact*."

Ta Neweh had given over the last of the feeding to the priests and attendants now. He came back to the crew.

"They were brought from Egypt," said Pharaoh. "The sacred crocodiles. As eggs."

"Eggs!" gulped Walter, covering the chicken's head so it shouldn't hear.

(Something strange was in the trees over the river. Something even more extraordinary because it didn't fit this extraordinary scene.)

Art shook herself mentally. Saw what it was. She spoke very quietly. "We're miles inland, Mr. Pharaoh. So why is there a *ship* over there?"

The crocodiles were sinking underwater. The priests and attendants stood aside as Ta Neweh led his adopted daughter and her seven crewmen across the roof of the rocks and down into the jungle on the far side. "I told you, Arty, there was something to see."

And was it Ebad or Pharaoh addressing her now?

"No, Art. I don't know if I belong here. But I know *this*. They won't let me go lightly. Not me. They'll hunt us all. Doubtless kill us all. But if I *stay* . . ."

"Then you're their *prisoner*, Ebad."

"We're all prisoners of something. Yes. Molly's my prison, if you like. I don't mean anything bad by that. You know I loved your ma better than morning and moonrise. But she's gone, and I don't forget her. Don't want to, either. So, it's quite a happy prisoner I am, of Molly's memory. The same for you, I'd guess."

Art nodded. "Yeah."

"Well then. You see, Captain Daughter, I've tried to find a purpose since, on a stage, and with the pirate ship, and in France, grabbing French revolutionaries out of the talons of the French king, along with Roger Jolly and Wild Michael. But what use is it? You throw out your king. You throw your hats in the air. Now the

Golden Age begins—but then you find you've replaced one tyranny with another, one set of bullies with another. Republican England's free, but her government is getting to be as harsh and bossy as any set of lords and princes. It's how it goes, Art. Yet—here . . ."

"You *want* to stay."

"Maybe I do. My best role to date. And, be honest, I act it stunningly well. And if I stay, the rest of you can leave. Besides . . ."

"We get a ship."

They had spent the afternoon walking in the jungle over the River Lily. Here one glade gave on another, all carefully cleared and *kept* clear. And in the glades, guarded by the sacred crocs—in the river, or waddling on the mud banks below—ship on ship perched on platforms of stone. And where creepers came to twine the masts, they were cut away. And where the sticky sweat of the jungle rotted them, their timbers were always replaced.

"They were a people of shipbuilders, the old Egyptians—or my black Egyptians. When invaders threw them out of Egypt, they didn't run down through the continent. No, they *sailed* down, round the coasts, in ships made of reeds with linen sails."

"Those ones here told you that?"

"I've read of it, Art. And, in my blood, I know. I recall when I was a child and I was made a slave, and then they said I could help crew the ship or lie in the stinking hold. I chose to crew—but I was like Molly then, and like you, girl. No sooner on deck than part of me already knew exactly how to go on."

He told her then, whenever a ship came in on the far-off coast—many of them wrecked on the rock banks there—the coded drums relayed the news inland. The villages all had ties with the city in the jungle. And men from the city were often on hand near the coast. They gave what help they could to the shipwrecked crews. But few foreigners were ever taken to the city itself. The wrecked ships, however—

"Are brought here on the elephant rafts—and repaired," Art finished.

"Restored. Though most of those vessels can never sail again."

They stood under the trees, surrounded by the open-air museum of ships, whose masts tapered up between the boughs. Five or six monkeys had just gone by, swinging from mizzen to mizzen of three tall vessels. One figurehead, a fierce warrior woman in a helmet, had dropped away from her lugger into the ferns, but the men of Khem had already raised her, and were mending and repairing her ready to go back in place.

"It's madness," said Art. She had begun to hate the ship glades by the river.

"Perhaps. Or love, Art. Maybe it's a kind of love."

Cold and tense, she said to him, "Did they bring *my* ship here to this—*funfair*?"

"*Unwelcome* isn't here, no."

"Thank God for that. The sea broke her to pieces, then, and spared her this indignity. It makes me *sick*."

He said, with infuriating irrelevance, "You don't get sick, Arty. Like your mother. Molly told me the only time she ever threw up was when she was carrying you."

Art turned angrily and looked at her men. They were ambling about, seeming quite pleased with the ships marooned on their platforms, with monkeys in the rigging. Feasty Jack had even climbed up a ladder on the deck of a low, lean old schooner, examining her planks and caulking critically.

"But as we said," went on Pharaoh Ebad, "if I stay, there'll be a ship for the rest of you. Several are seaworthy."

Peter, who was the nearest, now heard, stared—then shouted to the others, "A ship! We get a ship!" The seven crew, Feasty leaping down to complete the group, excitedly ringed Ebad and Art.

"We can go home!"

"We can reach the parrot island—find the treasure maps!"

"A ship? Which one?"

"Are you sure she'll float?"

Art barked at them. Silence fell.

"Well, Mr. Vooms-Amoon. *Will* she float?"

"Yes. I've looked them over, the ones capable of relaunch. She was the best in my judgment. A two-mast frigate, not more than ten years of age. One year since she hit the rocks and was repaired here."

"*Two* masts?"

"'Twill be enough to get us away," broke in Stott. "I served in one such in the Blue Indies. Robbed our way silly from Sugar Isle to Mexico."

"Does she have guns?" asked Jack.

"Sixteen," said Ebad. "It was twenty, but four were lost. Polished up and in good working order."

"Where is this animal?" asked Feasty.

Ebad looked only at Art. "Already on her way to the coast."

They danced about yipping and slapping one another on the back. Even Walt was glad, hugging the chicken.

But Art looked back at Ebad with her own face of steel.

"Already decided, then. No more to say."

"One final thing."

He drew her aside, down a last overgrown path, leaving the others to rejoice or cluck.

Here the overgrowth was new—it had been cut back perhaps only a week before, then left to grow in again.

"A secret?" she said. She wasn't concerned. She'd lost Ebad. *No* one was left. Anything now could only be a sham.

One more massive rock face blocked the route. No way up. Ebad touched the side of it with a golden ring he now wore, set with a sea-colored stone. The rock trembled, and a little stone slab slipped sideways on its runners. For some reason he said, "There's a far larger entrance, but this will do for us."

There was a black cavern inside.

Pharaoh, a modern guy, struck a light.

Art stopped breathing.

The cavern went in some distance, but near the door-mouth it was neatly piled with tools on trestles, rope, wooden boxes, and barrels. Farther on across the floor leaned stacks of wood and sheets of metal, and there was a forge, currently unoccupied, its fire out. Behind all that, less easily seen in the back of the darkness, a rising shape, narrow, widening, and there a high pole like the trunk of a slim tree, hung sideways with tilted, evenly set stripes of branches—

Art stepped forward, treading softly, disturbing nothing. By the logs and metal, the anvils and unlit fire baskets. She didn't hesitate until she stood under the bows.

How tall she was, the ship. You never considered it much, riding her. Not even the height of her masts—they were familiar as sky.

Art put her hand on the ship. Against cracked oaken joists and little patches of barnacles—seldom touched, unknown. Known.

The figurehead, as someone had remarked, was gone, down at the bottom in the Sea Chest of Dewi Jonah. But her skeleton was saved, and most of her mainmast, and a section of her foremast, too, and strips of her decks, her wheel even—look, two-thirds of it at least—even her guns, lined up there like tired soldiers—

"The *Unwelcome Stranger*," Art said. "You told me she wasn't . . ."

"Not out with the others in the forest, the ones that won't ever sail again. But *she's* repairable. They say it'll take one year."

Stupidly, Art, "So long?"

"Aye, Arty. You see, there's the French plan Eerie brought, for their new-invented super-ship. *Unwelcome* died, but she'll be born again. Different. Stronger. Faster. Unsinkable, maybe."

"This is all lies—it's *theater*, Ebad."

"No. It's all true. It's part of the price I'm worth to Khem, the Black Land. Your freedom, a vessel, and the remaking of your own ship. Do you say I'm not worth it?"

Interval: Close Call

After they returned to the coast, the journey went at speed. They were used to the elephants, the platforms, the warriors, the jungle with its big bladed leaves and coiled snakes, cackles, screams, and leopard snarlings. Nothing really happened on the way back, as if the whole terrain knew they couldn't concentrate on it anymore. Their minds were full of ships.

There were no halts longer than it took to get fresh water or food. They slept as they galloped, doing it better this time.

Art was now firmly in charge. She let them see it, even when she was tolerant or understanding. Both her First and Second Officers were gone. Ebad was Pharaoh, but Eerie had crept into the palace dining room that last night, with a black lady on his arm. "We're wedded, Arty, by the Mules of Mustard. I can't go with you." And then he blushed. The lady, who had gold woven in her hair, stroked his cheek. Art frowned, then shook his hand.

There had been plenty more of that. Other men had fallen in love—with women of Khem, or with the idea of Khemic chariot racing or horse breeding, or simply continuing to lie by the lily pools. They kept saying Art would be back, wouldn't she, in a year. Mr. Pharaoh had given her a special ring; yes, there it was, though she was putting it in her pocket, not on her hand. The ring had only to be shown on the coast, or in the jungle lands, for her to be brought safely back to the city. Good old Captain Arty. She'd take them on again then. Bound to, they were such a cracking crew. And when *Unwelcome* was rebuilt—she'd need them. Next year . . . But for now—oh, she'd never find that treasure again. Those maps 'ud be in bits, feeding the fishes. And the seas were full of war, and every ship stuck like a porcupine with guns. 'Twas better here. Pass the roast duck and brim the glass with wine!

"Don't know the cap'n, do they?" said Nib Several. "Desert her now, and in the future she'd rather sail with a crew o' crocs than any of *them*."

Smug, her *loyal* men.

Only Jack wasn't smug. He had stood at sunfall on the last night in the city, watching the light drain from it, then begin again in every lamp. As he said to Cuthbert, "I'd stay here, if I could." "What stops you, eh?" demanded Cuthbert, angry at the deserters. "Aside from the fact that without my cooking skills ye'll poison yourselves," said Jack, "I have an appointment to keep at sea." "Oh, ah?" But Feasty said no more of that to Cuthbert.

When he called the parrots in from the Bird Temple and presented them both to Honest, Jack did say something, though. It was dark on the palace roof by then. "There you go, son," said Feasty as Plunqwette hopped, closely followed by Maudy, up Honest's arm. Honest's eyes were full of tears. Jack shook his grizzly chops at him. "You take care of the bird, now. He's got his wings full and no mistake with that Plunqwette."

"Pieces of pir-ate," added Plunqwette weirdly. Like a period.

The new roll call then:

Captain Art Blastside.

First Officer Glad Cuthbert.

Second Officer Honest Liar.

Oscar Bagge, carpenter and surgeon.

Forecastle Smith, quartermaster.

Feasty Jack, cook.

Gunners: Shemps, Grug, Stott Dabbet, Larry Lully, and Nib Several. Primer: Tazbo Lightheart.

General hands and crew: Salt Peter and Walt, Plinke, Mosie Dare, de Weevil, Dirk, and Whuskery.

Birds: Plunqwette. Maudy. One chicken, unnamed.

Eighteen men and three birds, and a vessel waiting on the white shore of Africay. A two-masted frigate of sixteen guns.

The jungle flew by, was whisked up and off like a backdrop.

Instead, a day of blasting sunlight and blue water.

The ship lay in a small cove, out of reach of the terrible rocks.

"Not so bad. What do yer think, Cap'n?"

"She looks sound."

Courteously assisted by white-robed men in slender boats with tipped rust-orange sails, the crew boarded the ship. Supplies had already been loaded—fruit and meat, flatbread and fish, water, beer.

The 'tween-deck was so compressed they had to stoop almost double. The guns had a nice shine. And the powder was dry.

What was her name, then, this new ship? Her figurehead was a little leaping horse. Attractive. Was she called the *Horse*, then?

Art hadn't looked or asked. This was wrong. Every ship had a name. Art patted the ship absently, on the rail.

"Who are you?"

An explosion of laughter went up. All the men clustered, honking and mooing with mirth.

"What?"

"Captain—we just looked for her name. It's painted so tiny—"

"You can easily miss it—and no wonder!"

"Seems she was being named—but the feller doing it—"

"Interrupted like!"

Yodels of joy.

"I'm waiting, Mr. Lully."

"Yes, sir. She's called—" Larry bent double, which wasn't necessary as they were not on the 'tween-deck. "She—she's—"

"She's called the *Lily Achoo*, Cap'n," said Cuthbert. He was the only one of them who didn't look amused. "Heard of her. Thought it was a *joke*. The chap sneezed as he was naming her. Not like a stolen ship or a pirate ship—she's legal in that name now. Can't change it."

"Well, *Lily Achoo*. One *more* funny. But you're watertight, and you float." Art, to the ship. What else could be said? They would sail at full tide, one hour after sunset.

Plunqwette sat high on the aft-mast, Maudy on the foremast. They almost seemed to be looking for a *middle*-mast.

Wonderful weather. Not a cloud in the sky.

The boats would guide them out, past any subsea danger of shoal or rock.

I dreamed of Unwelcome's *smash, didn't I? Thought it was to be on the Badloss Sands off Dove. But it was here.*

Tomorrow they would sail south again, down to the Cape, turn the corner of the land, ride out into the Capricorn Sea. And on toward the Treasured Isle.

"I don't know you, *Sneezy Lil*," said Art to the ship. "But then I didn't know *Unwelcome* when I took her first." Probably, she thought, I shall never see any of them—husband, adoptive dad, old ship—ever again.

So, she thought. *Discipline* now, Art Blastside. All this—pretend it's a damned book on your head. *Balance* it, girl!

The sun's rim dips; the stars rush out:
At one stride comes the dark . . .

The *Lily* swam from shore, her sails perfect squares of bleached canvas, sucking up the mild night breeze.

Everyone was on deck. Taking it in that they were back at sea.

Phosphorus on the ocean, a glittering arc of leaping fish.

Art had the wheel, moving oiled and easy, getting the different feel of this vessel. The *Lily* had a kind of *right-handedness*, Art thought, a little tugging sometimes to starboard. *Unwelcome* had been just a touch *left-handed*, then . . .

From the lookout, Larry's voice ribboned.

"Off the starboard bow!"

Art looked. Cuthbert had already gone to the rail with the spy-glass Ebad had saved from the wreck.

"Can't see a thing, Cap'n."

Art called up to Larry. "Mr. Lull, *what* do you see?"

A pause. Then Larry warbled, "I don't make it out. . . ."

Tazbo and Plinke were climbing one mast each, Walt and Mosie not far behind.

"Wait—Cap'n—" Cuthbert. "There's something—"

"Take the wheel, Mr. Smith."

Art at the rail. Cuthbert gave her the glass.

The starred and phosphorus dark sprang into largeness in her eye. And she saw—

It's land—no, no land there. But like a sort of cliff, paler than the night—an *iceberg*, then, strayed up from the far south—

But even as she stared, the clifflike thing began to spread, opening itself out, blending itself in a layer, not really dark, not really light, across the sea to either side. And forward, too. It was coming to meet them.

Tazbo yelled wordlessly from the top at the same moment Art grated out, "*Fog*, Mr. Cuthbert."

"Aye, a bank of the filth."

And how quickly the fog came on. As if, by recognizing it, they'd called it close.

Already Art could smell it, a vapor quite unlike any mist or pollution on the land. The smogs of the seas had other odors. Some were sour, some stank, some had the smell of fish. In some a *scent* of the land had been trapped, grass or warm brick, herbs, lavender—perfume even. In some there were smells that no one could name, as if they'd fallen from the clouds or off the moon.

This fog bank reeked of salt and cinders, and old wet fires and soot—

"Like rain in a hot chimney."

By now the deck and masts were fluffed over by the fog. Outlines blurred. Inside three minutes the bank had covered them. None of them could any longer see farther than an arm's length.

They were well clear of the rocks of the coast, clear by more than two hours. Hold the course, then. The wind still moved them quietly on.

Yes, it was very quiet. Inside the bank, sounds were muffled or made peculiar. A man coughing at the ship's for'ard end seemed a mile off. A coin dropped by someone in the waist of the ship clinked as if it dropped inside Art's ear.

Images formed in the fog.

Their own passage through seemed to produce these. But they were nightmares—snakelike creatures that dribbled down the unseen masts, birds with wings the length of the ship.

Like the jungle, then, the fog. Full of beasts. Or ghosts.

Something in the fog made their skin start to prickle, too.

Cuthbert was at Art's shoulder.

She thought, Last friend, then. When will *he* go off? Back to his Gladys . . .

Something burst from nothing and landed with a green squawk on the wheel, immediately followed by its white double.

"Hi, old girl. How dost thou, honey?"

Plunqwette rubbed her beak over Art's fingers, a raspy caress. Maudy said, "Something's burning."

"Yes, Mr. Parrot. Smells like it."

One more hideous fog face loomed from the dark-pale darkness, and the ship's lanterns described it. Art and the parrots and Cuthbert, and every other man on deck, glared at gigantic fog features that slowly dissolved.

Beyond . . .

A kind of hollow in the fog—

"*What* is that?"

"It's just an illusion, Missus Cap'n."

"*No.*"

No, it wasn't. Slowly, as everything now, in *slow motion*, the deeper core of dark in the pale-dark began itself to draw near and, as it did so, to become another shape.

Art freezes. Cuthbert also.

On the wheel, gently turning a little this way, that, the parrots look under scaly, experienced lids.

From the fog, in the fog, and perhaps formed out *of* the fog— another ship.

She's long and low, yet her masts stretch high. Three masts, full-rigged.

Though fog-softened and veiled over, she's much darker than

the fog. She's black, a black ship. Her sides, her sails, and something that, like fog itself, trails over and around her. . . . *Dark*. In a pool of *dark* she moves, carrying *dark* with her. But no stars. There's not a single light aboard this vessel.

Slowly, slowly, slow, she drifts, feather-weightless, across their bows.

Is she real? One more fog ghost?

Real.

From her half-seen yet too well-seen decks, a voice calls to the *Lily*, a voice that might be a woman's or a man's, that might be an *echo*.

"You are known, English ship. You carry a cargo of sorry souls. But not so sorry you're any concern of mine."

"Who in God's name . . ." Grug, limping on his crutch, staggers to the quarterdeck.

"It's *her*," says Cuthbert. "It's *Mary*."

"*Who?*"

But somehow the lightless ship is close enough to take the glow of their lanterns. And through the wafts of fog, everyone who looks can make out now a tall, thin figure standing there under the bowspirit of the alien vessel. She is clad in streams of black, even her hands covered, and the white, white face seems to scorch out of it all, and two black blots that must be eyes—

Again, the grim voice calls.

"Pass, then. Go to your own doom. I am not your doom. Unless you break your code. *Then* I'll look you up. For now, 'tis others I seek. . . ."

As if some awful thing deep in the sea—a devil, or underwater volcano—puffed out its breath suddenly, a blank smoke of whiteness floods through the fog. It becomes a wall. It hides everything. As for the other ship, she, too, might have changed herself to smoke.

Art can't even see the wheel under her hands.

Yet *on* the wheel, Maudy speaks. He uses an actor's voice, that of Mr. Belladora Fan. And he quotes, as she did, from the poem by Mr. Coalhill:

> *"With far-heard whisper, o'er the sea,*
> *Off shot the spectre-bark."*

STAGE THREE
The Shes

⧼ONE⧽

Lundon Pried ⟋

"Xenophobia. 'Tis too much!"

"Eh?"

"I said—"

"He means, sir"—the fat gentleman butted in on the two thin ones—"a hatred and fear of all foreigners. Though why he must use such a ridiculous word as *that* I've no idea."

"Tush, sir. 'Tis, at the end of the day, a word already in the great Johnson Dictionary. *Xeno*—from the Greek—"

"Johnson made half those words up, I'm sure. Take the very *first* word—*aardvark*—obviously invented."

"Besides, we are *supposed* to hate the French!"

"*Order! Order!*" cried Madam Speaker, Mistress Bess Dancer, once a fine actress on the stage and luckily having a mighty voice.

Between the River Thamis and the winding lanes of East Minster, where the Abbey rose like a great animal sitting up, was the seat of Free England's government, the Houses of Talk. Here everything was carefully debated—sometimes with the help of flung cauliflowers, rotten tomatoes, or eggs.

Today the chamber had been extra noisy, for the war was the original subject.

Now, however, Mr. Cranberry, a gentleman in powdered wig and cranberry-red coat, began to set out his new bill.

"I think every honorable gentleman present will agree, England can no longer endure this disgrace. Even our enemies, the French and Spanish, laugh at us, though our ships thrash them in the Atlantic."

"Hear, hear," growled most of the men in the room. (Sadly, it sounded more like *baa-baa*.)

"Therefore my bill proposes an end to this piratomania, and its attendant buccaneerafear, which has swept the country all summer. You'll recall, no doubt, the several ships burned to the waterline at Good Deal and Dove, due to some pirate festival idiotically put on there. And many of you will be aware of the difficulty even in walking or riding along a Lundon street, where both men and ladies dress as pirates and choke up the ways with parrots and monkeys and fools hobbling on wooden legs—which, by the by, has reduced many persons to having to be carried now in bath chairs, having so injured themselves with hopping."

"Baa!"

"Also, this habit of putting on eye patches. Countless accidents occur every day—those who, unable to see properly, fall down holes or over others, harming *them* also. And who has not, sirs, had his carriage held up for an hour or more behind some wretched horse, itself in an eye patch or wooden leg, that careers all over the road?"

"Ba-aah!"

"Even beyond the capital and the ports, this madness goes on. I have seen men and girls sailing on duck ponds—*duck ponds*, damn them—in flimsy homemade boats sporting the skull and crossbones, while the cows are waiting to be milked and the apples to be picked. Meanwhile, the parrots—"

"Baa baa baaaah!"

"—Which of us hasn't beheld some of the dreadful birds, hundreds of which have escaped their owners and are now living wild in every park and garden and hundreds of the roofs and attics of our cities. Their *doings* fall thick on precious buildings and monuments, which before were only pooed on by our own fine Free English pigeons. Worse news, too, of this. An unpleasing disease is spread by these feathered friends—Parrot Fever. While from the monkeys, I may add, has come a nasty furry itch! Meanwhile, if such is to be believed, there are claims the parrots and our own pigeons have begun to breed—"

"Never! Impossible!"

"Is it, indeed. Madam Speaker, my honorable friend there hasn't, as I have, read the article in today's *Tymes*, which describes peculiar pigeons noted in the Strand, who are red and blue and green—and sometimes in the middle of a proper *coo*, break out in such phrases as *Pretty Polly!*"

Brief uproar greeted this.

Bess Dancer (once known as the Best Pair of Ankles in Europe) bellowed them all down.

Mr. Cranberry resumed.

"The insurance companies, too, are suffering. Most of the workforce seems to be idle due to some piratic injury, for which they demand insurance payments." Cranberry consulted a paper. "'Claim for three guineas, owing to nicking of hand while piratically fencing.' 'Claim for *five* guineas, due to breaking leg falling off small boat; friend also injured, on whom I fell, requires *ten* guineas.' 'Claim for ruined garden and smashed statue due to pirate-obsessed husband digging up said garden in search of buried treasure he was repeatedly told was *not* there, but having bought treasure map from peddler in Shepherd's Shrub Market.' 'Claim for total value of fishing boat stolen by persons pretending to be pirates. Who have also put in a claim for *twenty* guineas, having caught cold when said boat sank.' 'Claim from upset family for three shillings, for a daughter whose nerve gave way when her pirately dressed brother firstly appeared, with his left hand apparently replaced by a hook—and she *then* found a second hook in the marmalade. His reply to her anxious "Whose hook is this, Hector?," which was "My spare one," reduced her to hysterics and she is still in care.'" Mr. Cranberry paused. "There are many further appalling examples."

Even the baaing had dropped to a vague bleat.

"The country has gone mad," said Mr. Cranberry. "My attention's been drawn even to incidents involving *real* pirates, the scum of the seas, who have been invited into fashionable houses, made companions of, and who have then"—he lowered his voice to a bitter snort—"run off with young women already due to marry men of good character."

A sly chuckle slipped around the chamber. It was known that Cranberry's own fiancée, Becky, had done this very thing.

Madam Speaker had only to cough to still the sneer.

Cranberry gathered himself and roared, "We must pry Lundon loose from this horror. England must be freed once and for all from the craziness, and clear blue water put between us and pirato-mania!"

A very warm *Baa* now rose.

"I therefore propose all pirate clothing and actions be banned in public places, especially those where food and drink are consumed, such as taverns, inns, and coffee shops. Our citizens must remember we're at war—and piracy is *not* patriotic! Therefore, gentlemen and Madam Speaker, I present my Anti-Pirate Bill."

Quite a lot of baaing now happened. Only the First Minster, Mr. Blurte, seemed a little worried. Was Cranberry getting too much attention? Should Mr. Blurte have thought of this bill before Cranberry did?

Yet not everyone, it seemed, was in favor.

Voices started yelling from various sides that Free England meant *Free*, and to play at being pirates was the right of every man, woman, child, and horse.

Mr. Cranberry sat down. Mr. Blurte rose, and one or two others.

But before another speech could begin, a shower of cheese parings was thrown—then somebody hurled the inevitable cauliflower.

Mr. Blurte swayed from its path. To his right, Mr. Custard, who had been calling loudly that all that mattered "Is the people!," ducked. Behind them Mr. May caught the cauliflower in midair. A moment of quiet allowed him to make a remark that would be reported in the *Lundon Tymes*. Holding the vegetable high, Mr. May drily observed, "I see someone has lost his head."

But worse than cauliflowers was to come. Through an open window, maybe *attracted* by the cauliflower, or the noise, a cloud of brightly feathered birds came swooping. Parrots—or was one of them a purple-and-yellow pigeon?

Amid the resulting chaos, Landsir Snargale of the Admiralty got up and left the chamber.

Mistress Kassandra Holroyal waited for Snargale in a small annex in the Houses of Talk. The famous actress wore a gown in the colors of the English autumn just beginning. Her black hair was also done faultlessly. She was pretty as a picture—as pretty as she had been in her male clothing, under the name of Mr. Doran Bell, or Miss Belladora Fan.

Kassandra was used to dressing in male costume. She often did it when in the role of Rosalind or Viola, say, in a Shakespur play at Stratt-Ford.

Snargale kissed her gloved hand.

Kassandra beamed.

"Landsir S, you'll be happy to know the revolutionary French leader Louis Adore (aka Lewis Daw) is safe in Morrocaino. The others have been rescued by my brother, Michael, who we otherwise know as the Purple Foxglove. He rescued them with great cunning from the Paris prisons. As soon as I know their current hiding place, I'll inform you."

"Wild Michael used the white doves, as usual, to bring you these tidings?"

"Just so. And there's a new trick, too. We paint them different colors with fruit dyes."

"Ah. The parrot-pigeons are explained."

They glanced around the annex, Snargale with some unease and Kassandra now grinning.

The walls, both here and in the corridors of the Talkery, Mother of Talkers, were plastered with posters.

AA, announced one: AHOY ANONYMOUS—ENTIRELY CONFIDENTIAL HELP IN GIVING UP PIRATENESS. And another read: POLITE NOTICE: THANK YOU FOR NOT BEING A PIRATE (this alongside a rather *rude* notice that showed a pirate crossed out by crossbones).

Pamphlets littered a table. *Wean yourself away from the Harmfully Piratic. Piracy can Seriously Damage your Heath—Seek Help—your Pharmacist or Alchemist can assist you.*

Or, *Try the Pirette Patch—use of this Eye Patch for two or three hours per day is Guaranteed to Lessen your Craving.*

And, *All at Sea? Buy Maroon Marauder—you will find Chewing this Pastil eases the Piratic Habit.*

Kassandra began to laugh.

Landsir Snargale said, "Which is worse, the pirate mania or Mr. Cranberry's measures to stamp it out? There's madness everywhere besides. Have you heard, they're taking the stores of tea and coffee away from the docks? The French king, it seems, has sworn they will be blown up, and England without her cuppa will be brought to her knees. Sacks and casks of the stuff are therefore being held in unlikely places—the Republican Gallery, for one."

At this instant Cranberry rushed by. He was waving yet one more paper.

"D'you see, Snargale? MAGOTRU!"

"I beg your pardon?"

"It's a union—I've never heard of such a thing in my life—the Most Amalgamated Gentlemen of the Roads Union, or so they style themselves, forsooth."

Kassandra and Snargale bent to study the flapping paper.

"Highwaymen!" said Snargale. "Whatever—"

"It seems the public parks and heaths where these chaps do their robbing—Wimblays Common in particular—are now so dug over by treasure seekers, the highway lads keep tumbling off their horses. And there are parrots everywhere, and monkeys even, that steal anything the lads rob as soon as they've got it. They therefore say they have a just grievance against pirates, who should stick to the seaways and leave the roads to their *traditional* thieves. A fair point. Besides, you won't be surprised, Snargale, to know a certain amount of stolen money and goods off the highways is given nowadays to the government, to help the war effort. I doubt this pirate tax I intend to bring in will make up for the losses. Even including the fee for a proof card for any who genuinely *need* to wear wooden legs or eye patches. Look at this list of highway signatures—scores of them. Seems the union has been masterminded by Gentleman Jack Cuckoo."

"Did you know that's really a woman?" asked Kassandra helpfully.

Cranberry gave her a vile look. Lovely young females annoyed him very much now, ever since Becky ran off with that pirate.

"They say," he shouted, blustering off along the corridor again in a small whirlwind of papers, "they're being prevented from earning their living." Around a corner he went.

Kassandra picked up a fallen paper.

"'Landmissus Prudence complains,'" Kassandra read aloud, "'she has always been robbed every Saturday evening, in Hide-and-Seek Park, at nine o'clock promptly, by the Park-Gate Phantom. She looks forward to this harmless pleasure, which also enables her to buy a fresh set of diamonds each week. Lately, however, the Park-Gate Phantom has not stopped her carriage. Instead, a note was sent apologizing for his absence, and saying the Phantom would be laid up for months with a bad back, having fallen over a monkey near Lancaster Gate.'"

"How is the Purple Foxglove, your brother Michael?" inquired Snargale, changing the subject as they strolled toward the exit.

"He looks very well. Though of course, sir, we never exchange any chat, or even appear to know each other, when we're working on a case."

"Quite. But did you talk to Felix at all?"

"Oh yes. He was a most unhappy young man."

Lord Snargale drew up. "Why? What's happened?"

"A cruel quarrel, I'm afraid, with his wife."

"With *Art*?"

"Just so. He swore he was done with her, and I left him brooding in El Tangerina. Maybe he changed his mind."

Snargale said nothing more. At the doorway he put a package into Kassandra's hand. Spies, adventurers, and agitators were expensive, but useful. And Wild Mike and Kassie Holroyal were of the very best.

As he stood there to see her off, Landsir Snargale's mind stayed on Felix and Art Blastside. Those two. Such a curious match, yet one he'd never doubted, once he saw them together.

It had been a long while since any word had come of the privateer *Unwelcome Stranger*. After Morrocaino she had seemed to disappear—and everyone aboard her. Troubled times, like troubled seas, sometimes swept more away than common sense. They swept away the ones you cared about, making them vanish. Felix had been lost before. Sheer luck had enabled Snargale to find him. And that kind of luck, surely, could be relied on only once.

The Owls and the Pussy Cats

Lily Achoo emerged from the haunted fog bank into a dull sea smeared with cloudy sun. She had drifted, despite Art's care with the helm. But the currents had seemed rather unusual, having a strong will of their own.

Now they must turn full southeast.

Art gave the wheel to Mosie and the deck to Cuthbert and went to the captain's cabin.

She stared at it all of five minutes, its shippy sameness, and its complete unlikeness to her cabin on *Unwelcome*, before flopping on the bed and falling into sleep.

Art had slept about an hour when Plinke came to wake her.

"Captain, three ships are in pursuit of us."

She started up. "French?"

"No, Captain. English ships. Destroyers. But even with the spyglass, no one can read their names. Mr. Glad Cuthbert says you have the eyes of an owl and can see anything like that, even *without* the glass."

Art's eyes, if those of an owl, belonged to a very tired owl. But she splashed cold water into them and over her face and went on deck.

Sure enough, she read the names first.

"FRS Naval Destroyer *Shock*," she told her crew. "FRS Naval Destroyer *Bruiser*. And—oh yes, FRS ND *Tiger Cat*."

Just then *Tiger Cat* blasted off ten cannon. It was only a warning, flying miles wide, but impressive. There were coded flags up by then on the masts.

Ebad had taught Art something about those flags.

"It says—'Friend not foe.' And . . . 'Hold still'—or posh words to that effect."

"What shall we do, Cappy?"

"What they say. Take in sail. We'll wait. After all, gents, we're legal now and in the service of the Republic."

The edge of the storm (the very storm that had crashed *Unwelcome Stranger* on the rocks of the Guinea coast) had also brushed the more backward ship *Rose Scudder*. But by the time this had happened, the freakish weather front had diluted. *Scudder* was taken for a bit of a spin, but without much damage.

Afterward, Subcaptain Nicholas Nunn inspected the vessel with a bristling Goldie prowling behind him, threatening him, and every man aboard, with living hell if anything had been spoiled. Seeing a torn sail, she turned to Taggers, who was walking behind *her*, and smacked him in the mouth. Taggers staggered and cowered. Which said it all.

How had Nick ever missed what Goldie really was? He often asked himself that.

What an act she'd put on, though, when he first met her, his prisoner then aboard the good old FRS ND *Total Devastation*. Of course, Goldie had also tempted him with the idea of refinding the treasure maps. So it was his own fault. This self-judgment, somehow, never cheered him up. As well as the rest, he was ultra-bothered over the way she was about this fellow Phoenix.

Just before the storm had hit them, Goldie had gone down into the hold again, where her own personal prisoner, Felix Phoenix, was stored.

But there was nothing new in that. Since Tangerina, she had regularly been doing it.

The rough and rowdy crew were a combination of jealous and jolly on the matter. That she was beating Phoenix up they had *no* doubts. (Awful cries and thuds sometimes rose from the hold during visiting hours.) But her attentions to Phoenix were still pretty frequent. Well. He was handsome. Or they assumed he still was, though probably she had loosened all his teeth and torn out all his hair by now. At least. But none of them had *seen* him since he was first slung in there. Only Fancy and Flag had once tried to sneak down and find out what state he was in—some of them had bets on it—and Goldie had caught them. She had had them flogged up on deck, with everyone else called to witness.

No one ever resisted. She was the Goliath's daughter.

Her visit to Felix, just before the storm, had started like the others.

Goldie sprang through into the dark area in the ship's hold. Only it wasn't dark anymore. A lamp burned on a barrel, with spare oil standing by. In the flickery light, Felix, long unbound, sat drawing something. He glanced up. "Hello, Goldie."

No teeth were knocked out or hair missing. Actually, his hair was combed. His face was even *clean*. His clothes, if the worse for wear by then, were in no more mess than those of the crew. He hadn't been battered.

He smiled at Goldie the way he always did. And Goldie flinched, as if he'd kicked her. But the only violent kicks that went on in here happened when she bashed the ship's timbers or slammed something on the bulkhead, screeching. "You'd better yell," she told Felix the first time. "They expect it. You don't want them to think I'm getting soft, and to come down themselves to sort you out, sir." So Felix, puzzled then, had let out cries of pain. Goldie didn't even laugh.

Again, that first time, she had gone back up the ladder as soon as their dramatic performance was over. But she left him the light. Next time she brought the spare oil, after that some paper and ink pencils, clean water, bread and fruit, cheese, wine. All these treats without explanation. She always threw them before him with a haughty, bad-tempered grunt.

Felix, completely out of his depth, going on instinct only, didn't argue or question. He just spoke to mad and frightening Goldie as if she were an ordinary, fairly decent girl.

He kept thinking, One day she'll come in here and finish me off. But she didn't. And in the end he realized that maybe she wasn't going to.

The evening they caught the storm's edge, before that happened, Goldie arrived and acted, with his aid, a really ghastly attack, flinging things, howling. Then, while his ears still rang from the noise, she'd sat down facing him on the sacks.

"Do you know, Mr. P, how long you've been down here?"

"No. You see there's no day or night to tell by."

"*I*," she said, "would have found some way to measure time. Your foul partner, Blastside—do you think *she'd* have sat here all this while and not reckoned it up?"

"Very likely she wouldn't."

"You, sir, are a simpleton."

He only looked at her. In the dark lamplight, his eyes were black.

Goldie then said nothing for about a minute. The ship creaked around them, her stays and planks sharply grumbling. If Felix had known enough, he might have realized the weather was turning. If Goldie did, she took no notice.

Finally she rapped out, "Why do you think I've spared you punishment? Isn't it a *vast* mystery to you?"

"Because you believe I don't deserve punishment?"

"*But you do.* Oh, by the Wheel's Wailing—you *do.*"

"Then, if you think that—I've no notion why you've spared me."

Another pause. Goldie, ice-cold: "Why aren't you afraid of me, Mr. Phoenix?"

Felix frowned slightly, startled. "Am I not?"

"The only one who didn't fear me—aside from morons who should have and were too stupid to, like great Judge Know-All— the only one, Mr. Handsome, was my *father.*"

"Your—"

"And he, dear sir, was evil. As you're *well* aware. But you are not evil. I doubt there's a bad drop of blood in your whole body."

"Thanks."

"Don't mock me!"

"I didn't, Goldie. I said, Thank you."

She stared at him. She said, "We're like two people from two different countries, and neither can speak the other's language."

"Don't you think that's often so, not only with us?"

She folded in on herself. She was—*thinking*?

She said, slowly, "Normally I boast of the Golden Goliath's wickedness. But he was—he was *scum.* He was a *devil.* I used to be so—afraid—but I was only a child then. I grew out of it."

"He treated you cruelly."

"Oh, just a bit." She raised her cat's eyes. They flamed. "Worse than you'd *ever* guess. Worse than I—would ever tell you. I can't— *speak* of it. *There's my Little Goldie,* he'd say. *There's my lovely Goldie. Daddy's girl,* he'd say."

Felix lowered his eyes from the green furnace of hers.

"I'm sorry."

"So you should be." The usual rage snapped her up again. "And for your own behavior, too. You lied to me and promised me your affection—"

"Not quite."

"*Don't dare debate with me!* By the Wheel—I'll *skin* you."

So he looked at her again, full in the eyes, and said as steady as Art might have, as steady as the already storm-licked *Rose Scudder* no longer was, "Better do it, then."

What Goldie might or might not have done he never found out. Exactly in that second, the *Scudder* gave a great kick of her heels, putting even Goldie's kicking to shame.

Rather than roll them over or throw them down, the buffet somehow tossed them both to their feet. Felix grabbed the lamp as this happened. He thrust it on a hook in the ship's wooden side, for safety.

But no sooner was this sensible action taken than—something seemed to punch him directly above and between the eyes. He felt the blow—it came from nowhere, certainly not from Goldie; perhaps some falling thing, he confusedly thought, had struck him— but his brain was full of an image, deadly, fearful, inescapable—a pale ship of three tall masts that hurled forward into the teeth of black rocks below a tower of cliff. He heard the scream of the ship, saw the crack of masts, the gaping wounds in her side, and the gush of sea.

Felix dropped backward on the floor of the hold and lay still.

Little Goldie, who had been about to give all her attention to the weather, stared at him. She was quite clear nothing at all had hit him, yet he was plainly out cold, and on his forehead, a blue star of a bruise was already rising.

She surprised even herself then.

Goldie sped over the jumping floor and knelt beside Felix. When he groaned, she found she drew him gently up into her arms.

He lay then with his head on her shoulder, eyes shut, not moving. She looked at him. She had never chosen to hold any man in her arms. Never wanted to. Where she had felt she had to, in order to deceive, her sense of anger had been lessened by the knowledge that she made fools of them.

This wasn't like that.

Felix opened his eyes without warning. They were like turquoise now. He and she gazed at each other. She said, "Something struck you."

"A mast," he said, in a dull, empty voice.

"Nay and no. No masts in here. But your head's bruised." She hesitated. "Or I thought it was. A shadow, then. 'Tis gone." For the blue star had vanished.

He sat up, not pushing her away. Too *kind* even now, she smartingly wondered, to be rough?

"What's wrong with you, sir?"

"Nothing, Goldie. Just . . ." He turned away. He was crying.

Goldie, not kind at all, seized his arm and shook him. "No games, Phoenix. What's up?"

"The storm," he said.

"'Tis nothing, just a bit of busy weather. 'Twill be over in half an—"

"It carries a memory. Something it remembers near here— somewhere else it's been, somewhere with high cliffs and banks of rocks in the sea . . ."

"Guinea coast. Southerly."

"There, then."

"*What*, by the—"

"She's dead. Her ship's gone down. The *Unwelcome Stranger*. Art is dead."

Goldie drew away from him. Superstition, so common with sailors and actors, made her spine shiver.

Felix wept, and Goldie abandoned him and darted up the ladder back to the upper deck, where the wind was already ripping at the canvas, the sky like boiling lead.

Now, three hours later, after the storm had blown itself away and the inspection of the *Scudder* was complete, Nick Nunn watched Goldie going back down into the hold, presumably to visit her captive one more time.

With both anxiety and venom, Nick muttered, "She's fallen for him. Flog me with a red-hot kipper if she ain't."

Goldie didn't hear. Just as well.

Felix was her hostage, with whom she had meant to blackmail her old enemy, Art. If Art *was* dead, then other uses might be found for him. This was the reason she took care of him. Of *course* it was *nothing* else.

Nothing.

By the later afternoon, the three Free English ships had drawn up in a line by the *Lily Achoo*.

All three flew flags that more or less said, according to Art's calculations, *Hi, mates! Nice to meet you!* But their gun ports were open and the decks rather full of uniformed guys with shiny swords.

Nearest, over to port, stood the *Tiger Cat*. Some of Art's crew were admiring the figurehead—a leaping black-and-orange tiger with brilliant gilded eyes.

Jack's Maudy lowered the tone by squawking very clearly, "Give it a saucer o' milk," then flying across to perch between the tiger's ears, quickly followed by Plunqwette. The tiger now looked as if it wore a feathered hat.

The two ships were now only about twenty feet from each other.

Tiger's captain strode to the bow and shouted across.

"Hello, the ship *Lily*, we know the cut of your jib. Thought you were lost these several twelve-months, innit."

"Bit of a mishap," Art called back, "off the Golden Guineas."

"But all shipshape and Bridge-Toll fashion now. Do I address *Lily*'s captain?"

"You do, sir."

"I see you're a woman, sir. We don't boast many such among our ships of war."

"Is our old *Lily* a warship?" came the buzz at Art's back.

She was thinking, too. *How does that captain see I'm female so fast? He's the one with the owl eyes!*

She shouted, "My own ship sank. The *Unwelcome Stranger*—"

At which loud exclamations bounded across the twenty-foot gap.

"*You* are *Art Blastside*? Here, lads. Three huzzahs for the Peerless Piratica, Dudette of the Seven Seas, and all her Merry Men!"

And the huzzahs sounded—over and over, as the other two ships, *Shock* and *Bruiser*, picked up the news and reacted.

Art's crew also broke out in spontaneous cheers for themselves, pleased to be made a fuss of.

Art stood bowing, her heart feeling like a little dry nut. Once this acclaim might have meant a great deal. No longer. But she must go on pretending.

"Thanks for your generosity," she called when the hubbub eased. "It will warm us on our travels. We're bound for the Eastern Ambers, Mad-Agash Scar—"

"No, *no*, madam. By the Gull's Gullet!" The *Tiger*'s captain was all excited suddenly. "You must come along with us. I will consider it a mighty honor to escort so famous a privateer captain."

"Along with you *where*, precisely?"

"Ah, 'tis out of it you've been during your repairs. You've not heard. A great battle is arranged to be fought, just off the tip of Jibrel-Tar. The island and local seaways are booked. Not to be missed! And our patrol is one of several, gathering up now every ship able to assist in this ultimate sea fight against the French."

Art could *hear* jaws dropping on the *Lily*.

"We are, as you say, a privateer. Our task is to rob and harry, not to—"

"No longer, Captain Piratica. Forget any other plan. Now you'll sail with us north by northwest and east, to Jibrel. Each cannon counts. Each fighting man. England expects every ship to do her duty."

Art, Cuthbert, and Feasty—and all the rest—glanced about at the three Free English Destroyers, their guns staring from the gun ports, the Free Republican Jack flying on the masts. Southeast, the placid blue sea, the Cape, the Treasured Isle. No use thinking of it now. *England expected.* "Rat's Rowlocks!" spat Grug, lamming the foot of the mainmast with his furious wooden crutch.

"Cap'n Arty, there must be a way out of this," said Cuthbert a while after, in her cabin with Oscar Bagge, Forecastle, and Plinke.

"Maybe. But you see how close the *Tiger Cat* shadows us. She's a big vessel, forty guns. Do we want to take her on?"

"Not what ya said, Missus Cap'n," rumbled Forecastle, "about the *Maman Trop*."

"Quite. And look what happened. We must play along for now."

Bagge leaned forward. He was busy retying Forecastle's splint, adjusting the huge bone that had once been Muck's keepsake. The more Bagge saw this bone—from a gigantic fossil parrot, the first crew had said—the more curious he became about it. He had a brother who studied such things.

Other men came to the cabin from time to time to tell Art she ought to get them away from the *Tiger Cat*—risk her guns, run for it. (Not the Salt brothers or Dirk or Whusk. And Honest had charge of the deck, so he didn't appear either.)

Art said, "No, not yet." Over and over. It wore her out.

For her own mind, too, kept saying, *Go on, take the risk—they won't expect it. And the wind's brisk, blowing southerly. We can out-race them.*

But she couldn't make herself agree, with the crew or herself. *What's amiss with me? Have I lost my courage?*

In the end, evening fell. Jack had created a vast, tasty supper, and the men poured off to eat and left Art alone.

Then she sat in the ship's cabin, listening to the ship's noises, which weren't like *Unwelcome*'s, and the two parrots billing and cooing sickeningly on the deckhouse. That—or the smell of the food—was making her feel . . . what was it? *Strange.*

Or was it the light twitch and tumble of the *Lily*'s deck—

Abruptly Art felt—not only sick, but *sea*sick.

She tried to thrust this off. Seasickness didn't happen, not to *her*. But then the nausea grew so awful she could only drag the washbowl out of its cupboard and stare unseeing into its depths.

At least no one was watching Sea Queen Piratica—*puking.*

Presently, raising her head, Art dismally thought, What do you say to that, Ma?

And the sickness ended as if someone had turned off a lurching pulse in Art's insides. Instead she heard, deep in the hollow of her clearing, disbelieving head, the quiet voice of Ebad in the Black Land. "You don't get sick, Arty. Like your mother. Molly told me the only time she ever threw up—

"Was when she was carrying you."

Tinky Clinker had lurked around on Goldie's current ship all these months, often lost in his thoughts, which were mostly of treasure maps. From being his own man, a high-up in the important trade of owling, with men who took his orders, Tinky had been brought down to the station of Goldie's dogsbody—or *cats*body, perhaps, since she was such a rotten little cat.

He had given her the goose man's map, of course. That had bought his passage with her, and also convinced Tinky himself that this venture was worth trying.

But Goldie—she'd really disappointed him.

Yes, she was as unreliable and vicious as he had always known she would be. But as cunning and as *lucky* as he had also thought? No way, neither up, down, nor sidelong.

She'd muddled and screeched and dithered along, faffing off to the Scylla Isles to avoid French ships, wobbling across to the Morrocains—and then she caught this captive, this Mr. Felix Phoenix the well-known artist. Now *Scudder* trodged along the Afric coast, and Goldie, the infamous celebrity daughter of the mighty Goliath, had neither pirated a single ship nor blasted a single port. She had robbed no one, and didn't seem in any hurry to get where they *had* to get to. The Treasured Isle.

All she seemed to be concerned with, Tink eventually decided, was slapping her men around and hanging about the belowdecks with that Mr. Phoenix.

Tinky was disgusted.

He'd expected ruthless—if potty—cold-blooded dedication from Goldie. If she killed a few people along the way, he had no problem. (Mr. Clinker had never had much of a problem with others killing a few people, providing none of them was him.)

But this. She was—he could see it, even if the others were too dumb or scared of her to do so—longing to be Felix's main squeeze.

And like any twit in *lurve* (Tinky had *never* been in *lurve*, and proud of it), she was letting everything go to pieces while she sat about and fretted over Felix.

TC had therefore gradually foreseen the two things that could happen. One, she'd simply lose control of the crew and the ship—

especially if that perjuzzy Mr. Nunn at last became angry—or worse, Mr. Fancy did. Two, and *even* worse, Goldie would merely wipe everyone else from the picture and run off with Mr. P and all the loot.

Tink knew his duty. That was, his duty to himself.

He would have to take things in hand.

Goldie was just emerging from the belowdecks. It was two days after the bit of storm they'd gone through, and ever since she had been popping below about five times a day.

She looked all somber and dreamy and sort of—was it poss?—vulnerable. And this time she hadn't even hidden the sandwich she'd tried to get Phoenix to nosh—only he had obviously refused.

How Felix had got to her Tink wasn't sure. Looks? Charm? Nah. Who cared, anyway?

Now *Tink'd* get to her.

"Mistress Captain?"

". . . What?"

"Can I have—"

"Wasp off. I'm busy."

"No, Missus Captain, *truly*. This concerns yer safety and yer honor—*and* the treasure on the Isle."

He watched her brain wake up inside the mist of *lurve*.

Rounding on Tinky, she slammed him back against the ship's rail.

"All right, Clinky." (Still that wrong use of his name.) "What's your gripe?"

Tinky dropped his eyes. "It'll pain me to say—"

"It'll pain you more agonizingly if you *don't*."

"Aye, Missus Cap'. Well. I know you're a clever woman. Seen that afore. So—you judge."

And from his pocket Tinky drew out the very map he had given

her previously, the map the goose found, the map from the Treasured Isle.

Goldie gaped at it.

"How the—"

"Nay, lovely Captain, 'tweren't myself. How'd *I* get it off yer, poor
old Tink?" (Inwardly he grinned. Who *else* had got it off her?
Before becoming an owler, Tinky C had been a very talented pick-
pocket. And as Goldie always kept this map about her, not trust-
ing any other hiding place, it had been mouse play for a pro like
him to lift it.)

"Then—"

"I *found* it, mistress. Look, if'n I own up, are you going to tear
me limb from limb like?"

Goldie was herself again, fizzing into fury. "You'll think you're
blessed if I *do*, Tinker. *Speak up!*"

"I found it in the hold. I went down for some extra grog.
Y'know what it's like—a long voyage like this. And I sees that
feller down there—"

"*Mr. Phoenix.*"

"Yeah, him. He's fast asleep. But that map I gives you back in
Lundon—well, I *know* that map. And it's in his pocket." A most
bizarre sight. Was she swelling or shrinking? Swiftly TC went on:
"I admit I tried to rob him. Didn't think you'd mind. I mean, I
meant to offer you anything really classy I found on him—anything
you'd been too busy to get off him yerself—"

"*You say you robbed Phoenix while he slept and you found the map—
which somehow he'd stolen from me?*"

"Yes. I can't read—but I know the shape of that map." Tinky
added, ever tactful, "I guess he slid it off you when you was beating him up. I mean, even a brill lady like you can't think of everything when she's smashing a chap about."

Goldie gave Tink another push that nearly sent him through the side of the ship.

But as he collapsed on the deck, gasping for breath, a drift of happiness washed across his mind. *She'd bought it.*

Indeed she had.

Goldie had only ever lived among male villains or male wimps. None of them were to be trusted.

And Felix, it seemed, was no different.

She thought of the many times she had been close to him recently, urging him to drink water or Budgerigar wine, or eat something—and when he had seemed to swoon during the storm, she had even held him in her arms. . . .

It had been an *act*.

Art was an actor, like her accursed addirash of a mother. And Art had taught Felix how to act, too.

Goldie writhed inside as her heartless heart burst like an overheated cannon, showering her with bits of scalding emotional metal.

She glanced back only once at Tink.

Her face was no longer that of a spiteful, beautiful cat. It had become the face of a starving, hunting panther.

Nick Nunn on the quarterdeck noted this with alarm. (So did Taggers and Fancy.) But they couldn't read her thoughts—even she couldn't. And yet, amid the white-hot hurt and rage, Goldie wished once more that her dead First Officer, Mr. Beast, were with her. He'd have been loyal. He had only let her down—that once. And not—like *this*.

Lying on the deck, Tinky pretended to snivel. But he knew his mission was accomplished. Now Goldie had no purpose but to reach the Isle. And as for that Phoenix—*he was a dead man*.

Dead Men Talking

Below the Guinea coast, above the Hopeful Cape—somewhere there. Not marked on any map, though. A forested shore hiding a narrow path laid with logs, a glade, and a blue-green pool. And in the glade a kind of long wooden shack, with, nailed crookedly above the door, a piece of painted canvas that read: CHYMIST'S.

They came here, those the world had forgotten—or remembered too well. Some old, some young. Some of an age that might be anything between sixteen and one hundred and six. Men, and women, too, sometimes, from every corner and quarter of the earth. They paid for a clay pitcher from the quacking stills that smoked in the back room of the shack, and maybe for a clay pipe of tobacco. They sat on benches in the dark, or went into the hot shade under the heavy trees.

It was out here that the big shaggy man had chosen to sit, nursing a big black glass awash with alcohol. What was he? Pirate—or *priest?* His hat was a pirate's, and the cutlass he toted, the knives and gun. His coat, though, was plain black broadcloth. With the black vest and stained once-white scarf—not to mention the small fat Bible in his pocket—surely, a priest of sorts? (Some *had* reckoned the Bible was hollow, with the usual pistol snuggled inside. But no. The Bible had all its pages, all the way through.)

Mr. Beast, late of the *Enemy*, and slightly less late of the ship of the line FRS *Hit 'Em Where It Hurts*, opened the Bible at random, and read with a resigned look the words:

Then said all the trees unto the bramble, come thou and reign over us.

Beasty murmured, "Judges, chapter nine, verse fourteen. Too right, mates. Ruled by brambles." And downed his black glassful.

Just then another man came up the log path and emerged into

the clearing. *He* was black-stubbled and black of eye patch, and in full pirate gear. He squinted around the area, as if looking for someone he could punch. But not many were there today. Only Mr. Beast, refilling his glass.

The arrival turned into a stone, his mouth opening, then closing up like a lock.

But Mr. Beast at that moment caught sight of the newcomer.

Mr. Beast also changed to a stone.

There they were then, one sitting, one standing. Both gone white and both with eyes (three between them) popping through their heads.

Then slowly the Beast returned to life. He put down his glass and rose, with a pistol in his hand pointing across the glade.

"All right, all right, Beast," said the other. "It's really me. Here I am."

Mr. Beast, however, raised the gun, sighting along it.

But then abruptly his arm dropped. He stood there with the weapon pointing now only at the ground. (While around him the few other drinkers sidled off into the trees or into the Chymist's, prudently shutting the door.)

"Black Knack. I thought," said the Beast. "you was dead, Blacky."

" 'Twas the whole idea, Beasty. Come to that—I thought *you* were. Dead. Hanged by the neck and so on, at Lockscald Tree in Lundon."

"Outwitted them," said Mr. Beast.

"Likewise."

Suddenly Black Knack, the not-dead pirate, himself late of the *Unwelcome Stranger,* and before that of the actors' company Molly Faith had founded, gave a low chuckle.

"Tell you what, Beasty. I'll sit down with you and tell you my story. If you'll share yours, too. And the booze."

Mr. Beast lowered himself to the bench.

And Black Knack, who'd seemed so definitely to die on the Treasured Isle more than a year before, with Little Goldie Girl's bullet in his back, strode over and plonked himself down opposite.

Black Knack drank straight from the pitcher Mr. Beast passed him. He could hold the pitcher perfectly well, and the level of the drink fell, too. The sun didn't shine through him either. Just like the Beast, Black Knack was not a ghost.

They drained the jug before either man began his tale. And it was Black Knack, with a fat purse of coins, who went in to buy the next one.

But it was Mr. Beast who told his story first.

"Yes, I was tooken and all set to swing. They reckoned I was the worst of the whole bunch—worse than Pest—that was a laugh. Oh, and Goldie Girl. But she got herself off. The judge took a shine to her. No doubt later on he wished he hadn't."

"I'd heard she escaped the rope," said Black Knack, but soft, as if he didn't mind now that the woman who had shot him in the back had outwitted the law.

"But y'see," said Mr. Beast, "they put me in a little cell at Oldengate Prison all on my own. I could walk round it in eight paces, and across in four. 'Cramped, are you?' the jailor asked. 'Don't be worried. 'Twon't be for long.' But he'd take a bribe, he would, the old bucket. So, I bribed him."

"You'd concealed some gold?"

"Nay, Blacky. Every nitch and stitch of wealth any of us had off the *Enemy* the arresting captains stripped us of. Even when it was hid, like Pesty's, in his bootsoles. But I, y'see—well, it was always likely I'd come to grief one fine day. So, I provided for myself, you could say."

Mr. Beast had, years before, had three gold muhuras sewn *under the skin* of his left upper arm, and four silver Spanish reals into his left leg, below the knee. "Hurt a mite, but in the end the pain went off. Worth it. Knew it would be."

In the tiny cell Mr. Beast undid his skin, as the surgeon had all those years back, and took out one muhura. This he offered the jailor.

"True creep he was. Took it and brought me what I asked."

"Which was?"

"A bottle of wine, and a priest to talk to—confess my faults. Clear my mind before the rope."

Mr. Beast had been very firm, too, both on the type of wine and type of priest. "Red, full-bodied, preferably from the Californias. And the priest with a stout body to him an' all. Don't want some thin, reedy gosling in here. I need a grown-up like myself, who's seen a bit of life. Stocky, and ready to join me in a drink."

The jailor did his best, apparently. The priest who came bumbling in was a big, shaggy creature, already with a couple of bottles inside him.

"Turned out he'd been around, too, in his youth. He'd been a robber, broken into houses, that sort of thing. But then he saw the error of his ways and became a priest. So we had a glass or two, and then I asked him to pray. When he did, I batted him on the bonce. Down he slipped, graceful as an oyster. Smiling. Full of wine and kindness. And—you'll understand, Blacky—he looked just enough like me."

Beast had swapped clothes with the clergyman, dressing him in Beast's own gaudy pirate tatters and tipping the Beastly hat over his face. Beast himself then put on the reverend's dark outfit. "Took his Bible, too. But I left him the last of the wine."

Mr. Beast called the jailor and went on as if upset. He covered his face with the rev's clean(ish) hankie, and mumbled that the "poor pirate" had loaded him with his sad confessions—and that he'd now have nightmares for a year. The jailor glanced around the cell and saw what *seemed* to be the Beast, lying drunk on the floor with the wine. So he let the actual Beast go, as did the other prison staff. "Gave up my dear hat for that, too. Left it on the priest," said Mr. Beast to Black Knack, "though I was so fond of it. Read in the papers—well, tell a lie—had it read *to* me—that I'd been hanged on the proper day along with the rest of Goldie's crew. I wondered if they'd hung the rev, too, till I saw him in Barterside not ten days after. Either another man swinged in my place, or they made sure no one kept count. A slack jail that, Oldengate, I tell yer."

The second jug was empty.

Beast went into the Chymist's and came out with a pitcher of alcohol and one of papaya juice.

They mixed their drinks now.

And the Beast went on.

"Well, I preached round Lundon, Blacky Knacky. I was quite good. Then I fell in with PIRATE."

"With *what*?"

"P-I-R-A-T-E. Pirate Intolerance Regiment and Teatotalers of England."

Both men cawed with laughter and choked on their drinks.

"*Thou?*"

"*I.*"

The Beast had gone along with the Teatotalers, who were so addicted and crazed with leaf tea they hardly knew what day it was. They couldn't go more than ten minutes without a swig. Beast made sure *he* didn't become addicted to the fatal tea, always dousing his own secretly with large amounts of gin. For this reason he came to carry his own glass—the black one, which was still with him.

"Went down to Dove and Good Deal," he said soberly. "That

was where half the fleet in the bay was set afire during a pirate festival. The government got sour after that, and some minister—Cranberry he was called—started to call for laws to stop the pirate mania. PIRATE were so wound up with that I took myself off to Port's Mouth. And there—"

There, mooching about halfheartedly, looking for some genuine pirate tub to join, Mr. Beast was press-ganged for legal war service with the good ship *Hit 'Em Where It Hurts.*

"I looked less like a reverend by then. And they could see I was a seafaring man. Those press gangs. They don't want ordinary blokes; they want sailors, even pirates. Anyone that can tell a stern from a stem."

He'd been of two minds anyway, he said, no longer really wanting the old life but not sure what else he could do. So he worked on the destroyer, but got fed up with it pretty quick.

"The captain was a proper wretch. Carrot Nose everyone called him, ahind his back. I kept thinking of Goldie and the Goliath. Bad to the bone, but at least they had a touch of class, in the Mad-Agashy style. And you could make some money on a pirate boat. But this—rum laced with dirty water, rats big as dogs, scrub and scramble, old Carrot Nose, and not even a sniff of a Frenchy ship to sack. Then the dark luck started."

They were hauling up and down the Channel when a freak storm bumped into them, entirely dismasting *Hit 'Em.* No sooner had they trailed back to shore and had repairs than the ship wouldn't launch. When she did, she got only as far as the Franco-Spanish coast before she sprang a major leak. There was a coughing fever going around, and old Carrot Nose had received a letter from his wife, by a passing English ship, saying she had run away with the goat's-milk man.

"Off the top of the Ivory Coast we gets word we're to go straight back around to Jibrel-Tar. But another hack of rough weather puts us in a fix. That was when someone found the reverend's Bible in my hammock. 'Here, mates,' squeaks he, 'this beggar is a priest.' Real uncool."

Black Knack knew enough from his combined actoring and pirating to grasp this. Beast had always known. A reverend gentleman aboard a ship was believed as unlucky as a rabbit.

"Carrot comes along. 'This ain't right,' says Carrot. 'You're a Jonah, you are, like old Dewi down in the deeps.'"

They put Mr. Beast pronto into a longboat and cast him off.

"'Twas a nice sunny day by then," he said, "and the Coast of Ivory clearly visible. So I rowed ashore. I've been wandering Africay ever since."

They leaned back then and stretched out their legs.

From the shack marked CHYMIST'S rose an interesting smell of roast meat and corn porridge.

In a short while a tall black woman with tight-coiled hair and shells in her ears brought them each a savory plate of food. It was 'on the house.' They were 'good customers.'

Black Knack and Beasty ate, relaxed as if they'd been friends for years. But the other customers of the Chymist's still stayed out of range. *They* knew this look. Such men might share a pitcher and a plate, then go into the trees, shake hands, and shoot each other dead.

Black Knack had tried to supply first the Golden Goliath, then Goldie, with the original treasure map to the Isle. He'd betrayed Molly Faith, Ebad Vooms, and Art Blastside with equal determination. Beasty had never liked a traitor. But then he had seen Blacky shot by Goldie—whom Art promptly beat in a sword duel. Beast hadn't respected a lash of Goldie's eye after that. Besides, Art had afterward got all *her* men loose from the jail. Goldie left her crew to rot.

They finished the meal. BK went for another round and a couple of pipes.

Insects hummed and clicked in the jungle-woods. A large, rosy scorpion walzened into the pool.

Now it was Black Knack's turn to tell his tale of cheating death.

"I'm an actor, aren't I?" he began. "First and foremost. Lost and last, too, maybe. An actor."

Then he took off the eye patch and laid it between them. It was quite dark under the trees.

"You see, Beast, only a complete twaddle wouldn't know that, given what I've done, somebody might want to murder me. Even virtuous Art might, despite Molly's code, if she learned I'd betrayed her. Or one of the *Unwelcome*'s more predictable crew members, dotty Dirk, perhaps, or Hurdy-Gurdy Cuthbert. As for Goldie Girl, no half-sane man would trust *her*. When we got onto the Treasured Isle and Art and Honest figured out the clues, and we heaved that chest out of the ground with all the maps—for a moment I thought things might be OK. But when Goldie showed up next second, I wasn't astounded. I *was* glad I'd already made my plans."

Black Knack smiled to himself, with a bitter vanity.

"I'd sewn myself a special vest to wear under my shirt. It was packed round the heart and ribs, front, sides, and back, with little pouches of fake blood—the very kind we used to use on stage to make it seem real when we were supposed to be stabbed or shot during the action of the play. *Inside* the vest, too, I had a lining of thin, hard, bookbinding board and quite a few metal coins. By the time I had it ready and put it on, we'd left Mad-Agash Scar. I looked like I'd gained two or three pounds, but I was fairly sure, even if someone fired point-blank, I wouldn't take more than a scratch.

And so I wore it all the time. And when we got to that sweltering island, I *sweated* in the damn thing. But I was glad I did."

Mr. Beast could easily picture the scene. (Somehow, over all the scenes of violence Goldie and he had been involved in, the shooting of Black Knack had stuck.)

He saw the cliff top and Art's pirates looking stunned and angry, and Art with her own style, not showing much, biding her time. And the sky with a greenish weird tinge and the wind stamping—which had been the signal, only none of them guessed, that the mad tides of the Treasured Isle were about to turn and swamp the beach below, rising as high as the head of the cliff itself—

"Even when they're useful, I don't like betrayers, Mr. Knacky," Goldie said.

And Black Knack shrank. He said, ". . . You—promised me my share."

And Goldie answered, *"Here's* your share." And raised her artistic pistol, all chestnut-colored wood and brass fittings—and Black Knack was running, making toward the cliff's edge, perhaps trying to reach the hatch in the headland that led back down the long stair to the shore—and she fired.

Fire flash. Crack of sound. Black Knack seeming to jump forward—right past the hatch and over the lip of the cliff.

"Her shot hit me—I felt the blood sack burst. It was like a kick, the shot, that was all. Gave me a shove forward, too—just right for takeoff."

The ripe splash of blood on his back was explained.

But the *jump*? That cliff had been well high. Fifty minutes it had taken Beast to climb up by the secret stair on the inside.

Blacky said, "I understood about the weather. Do you recall, Beast, the way the sky went green and all that? Art, when we landed, gave us a little talk on how part of the Isle sometimes went underwater. Enough to kill the fruit trees on the shore. And that picture of Hurkon Beare's in Mad-Agash—it showed the blackening went to the top, the sea destroyed everything. So—a high, *high* tide. She and her crew, Goldie and you lot—you were so wrapped up in your plots and dreams. But my main thought was for Old Blacky. The minute the sky went that green color I *knew*. It's coming, the tide—high as the trees. So I saw the sign, and by the time I had to run for it, I figured there was the best chance the beach was already filling up. Thus, mate, I took to my heels and went straight over and down. I'll admit, as I saw the edge of the cliff spring to meet me—I'll admit I had a second thought. But too late, wasn't it. Over I went. And even in the air, I could judge the depth of that water. It was slinking in fast, wonderful deep sea, foaming and crinkling, and I thanked my lucky stars and went headfirst into it."

"And—*then?*"

"I give you this, Beasty, you're a marvelous audience. Well, I hadn't been hurt, only a bit bruised from the clout of that bitch's bullet, that was all. And I can swim like a salmon. What came next was easy as please. I dived deep and swam round underwater, back to the cliff entrance Art so cleverly found. We'd blocked the trick door open with spades on her order—which Goldie must've found very useful. Now *I* did. I swam into the cavern and got off on the stairs. And as the water went on rising, I climbed up again, up and up. My only sticky moment was when I thought the water would go right up to the hatch above—but it didn't. I sat on the top step, just clear of the hatch opening, and the sea rose as high as the top button on my coat. I watched it all the way. And then—it dropped a little. Third button down. So I sat there on the step in the sea and kept still, and I thought, When the water drops entirely, they'll be coming back this way—but I can move ahead and hide below in the back of the dark down there. And overhead, anyway, I knew something rough was going on for quite a long while. Perhaps you'd all kill each other . . . but I couldn't tell. The hatch was still ajar, but the shouts and growls and the slick and clack of swords—could be anything. I sat and cursed you all. You muckers of Goldie's and those donkeys of Art's. And then—it's curious even to me—I dozed off. All the excitement, no doubt. And when I came to, there was a great big silence, and the slit of light from the hatch was gone. I thought—*It's been shut.* But it hadn't. It was only the night. So then I thought, Better get out, Knacky. See what's what."

"It was a stretch up to that hatch. We had to heave each other up, pull the last ones up on a rope," put in the Beast.

"Aye. But the daftest thing—the water had risen again. That's what woke me. It was up to my nose. So I pitched off the stair and I swam—and I was high enough then on the water's back to flip over and kick the lid all the way off and then a sort of upward dive, and I hoisted myself out."

"By Wall-Fallen Jerico!"

"Aye. *Aye.* How's *that* for fortune?"

Across the table, across the months and years of difference and dislike, the two men reached toward each other and clasped each other's hands in a wild fury of irrational delight.

(In the Chymist's the patrons nodded, grabbed a pitcher each, and got under the tables.)

Hands let go of hands.

Almost with sorrow, the two men drew apart again, comrades only for an instant.

"I walked over that cliff," said Black Knack, "from moonrise— till moonrise of the next day. I was careful at first, in case any of you were still there. But you weren't. I reckoned you'd swum for the ships, because they were gone as well. There was a little stream of water to drink on the cliff, but it tasted salt now. Still, kept me going. Nothing I could see to eat but for the odd parrot that came screeching over. Couldn't catch those. Then the tidewater lay right down like an obedient dog on the floor of the island below. I stood on the cliff's edge again and watched, and I saw the sea draw away from the beach and the orchards of trees that had been swamped by it. Every fruit they'd had was blackened. Seaweed draped them. The smell—was like bad wine. And behind me on the cliff, Beasty, left there by all of you, that grim gray wooden chest. It had held the maps—now it was empty. Nothing in it at all. Just that brass page hammered onto the front."

Black Knack sighed. "I heard, later, how the English ships came and arrested every one of you. And the treasure maps were gone, must have been, because nobody spoke of *them*—what did you do?"

"Made them into paper boats and let them swim," said Beast, with a certain swagger.

"I see. Yes. Whose idea—oh, *Art's*. Yes?"

"Art's, yes."

"I booted that empty chest. It was a solid thing. Hurt my foot. I remember, it was heavy to lift. And I kept thinking, What had happened? Where had you all gone?"

Black Knack sighed again.

"I went back through the hatch and down the stair, and wandered about on the salt-blackened shore. I felt I was the last man in the world. In all my born days, never was I so alone as then."

He *was* hungry, though. He tried a few of the blackened fruits, gave up on that.

It was the next day that he thought, as there was nothing left to eat or to do in the ruined orchard or on the beach, that he'd walk across the wet sands to the hill that stood up from the island on the other side.

The parrot swarms had taken refuge on the hill when the big tide came in. And the sea hadn't risen all the way up it.

From the hillsides rocks poked out, and there was salty mud.

Climbing, BK found a stranded fish or two and ate them raw. There was a selection of jewels wedged in crevices as well, just like the scatter on the beach. He picked them up now and put them in his pockets. Either he was the luckiest man alive—or the unluckiest. He wasn't sure which, but either way, any curse on the jewels wasn't going to matter. "Or so I thought."

He even found some scraps of waxed paper. ("The remains of some of the maps, washed back in?") But nothing on them was readable, and he didn't realize what the pirates had done, so screwed the papers up and chucked them away again.

Trees grew thickly on the hillcrest, an area of about a quarter mile. They were lush trees and full of parrots—restless with violent color, and screeching, or still now and then, calling out the map clues that so many people had taught them, in every language under the sun.

Blacky discovered some nut trees and some more of the salty, peachy, orchard fruits in these groves. A kind of wild lettuce and a peppery herb of some sort grew on the ground. He feasted. Asked himself if perhaps he should stay up here, for now. There was shelter from the sun or any weather that happened.

In the end the parrots drove him down.

Not deliberately—he simply couldn't stand the constant row they made among the trees. Not to mention the constant poo. "In parts it looked like it'd snowed."

So then his routine became this: by night he went into the cavern and slept high on the steps. In the morning he went up and inspected the clifftop and swore at the chest, Molly, Goldie, Art, and the vanished world in general. Then he went down and across and up the hill for brunch. Afternoons he sat on the beach if it wasn't too hot, or went in the cavern if it was. In the cooler times of day he hunted for jewels and objects, and caught the odd fish by wading out with a stick. He watched for ships. Saw none.

He thought he had himself well organized, but he was bored and scared. One day he woke up howling. "I said to myself, Black, you'll never see another human face as long as you live. No one comes here—just our ship, that time, and Goldie's. No one else. Ever." According to the reckoning he'd kept on the cavern wall, he had by then been on the Isle for ninety-two days.

Black Knack formed an idea. Which was that he must build himself a raft; that meant somehow fell a tree, somehow make it seaworthy, fix a sail—his shirt? Just like in one of the *Piratica* plays.

"But then, I didn't have to. Oh no. Because then, you see, *she* came along."

"She? Which she was that?"

Blacky looked under his eyebrows at his captive audience.

"Ever hear of a ship called the *Widow*?"

It was the night of the ninety-third day.

Blacky had made his usual rounds, and even selected a possible raft tree on the hill. He would need to fashion a stone-headed ax, so had been looking for stones and chunks of wood, too.

He lit a small cook fire on the beach and roasted salty fruit and nuts.

This was such a *still* place after the parrots finally nodded off. A huge hollow of dark hung over the Isle, with a trail of stars, and the South Down Cross sparkling like a brooch pinned on. The fire spat, and the sea rustled like stiff paper.

Then the moon rose, full and yellow.

Probably he wasn't paying the night much attention—only its silence and loneliness.

Something, however, made him jerk his head up—as if he'd seen it first through some extra eye on the top of his head. *The shape.*

"To start with I couldn't work it out—what it was out there, on the sea. It was more the way the sky seemed behind it. Torn—

undone. And the moon—it looked like someone had run a cutlass through and through the moon—she was all in slices and rags—"

Blacky got to his feet, and the fruit he held dropped in the fire and whistled as its last juice met the flames.

As his viewpoint shifted then, he saw that what stood between him and the moon and stars was a low black ship. It was her masts that had cut up the sky, but it was a peculiar veiling that draped her—like vast nets—that had patterned and sliced the moon. She herself had not a single light.

Black Knack almost bent to seize a stick from the fire and wave it as a signal. But he didn't. The appearance of the unlit black ship stopped him. He even thought, It's too late. She'll have seen the fire anyway.

He had wanted to be found. To be rescued.

Yet this . . .

"I'd never heard of her, you see," he said to Mr. Beast.

"*I've* heard of her. Only the once. Aboard the *Hit 'Em*, before they threw me off. Some men there said the Goliath had been caught by the *Widow*, in a net. She hunts 'em, pirates. Makes them die a horrible death below in the belly of her ship. None know—or can say—what the death is. But no one escapes it and the Goliath didn't. If the tale is true."

"Believe me, Beasty, *'tis true 'tis pity, and pity 'tis 'tis true.*"

The black *Widow* was out on the deep water well beyond the beach. But it seemed she had anchored. And soon BK saw two boats rowing in toward the island. Not a light there either, and they had nets as well, pooling all about them.

"I thought about making a run for it. Like a specter she was, the ship, and her boats no better. I thought about making a run—and I did. I left the fire and legged it into the cavern and up the steps—but I didn't close that trick door—never dared to, in case I couldn't open it again. I was about ten minutes up the stairway when I heard them moving below. It was pitch-black inside the cliff. But I could see all right—and, it seemed, so could they."

"Where'd they catch you?"

"Near the hatch. I'd rigged a grass and creeper rope by then, to pull myself up and let myself down. Planned to get through, drag in the rope, and slam the hatch—find something to weight it shut. But no use. They took hold of me before I put my hands on either rope or hatch. We all went up there later, them and me. But not right then. Black men they were, some of them, and some pale-skinned and pale-haired—like that Felix feller. Only their eyes were pale, too. One spoke to me and said, 'You're pirate kind.' *I* said nothing—hadn't the breath left to speak. And then another said, 'Come, we take you to our captain, Mary Hell.'"

On the floor under the tables in the Chymist's, the patrons were becoming restless. The black woman with shell earrings had given them to understand that a duel between the men outside was very unlikely. One by one they crawled out and ordered more drinks. Three or four even walked out of the shack and went to sit by the pool. It was certainly fairly plain now the two talkers at the table weren't going to fight. Even so, everyone gave them a wide berth.

Black Knack finished his story with an odd, quick lightness.

"The crew's Scandinavian, even the black ones. *She's* a Scanda, too. Pale as an uncooked potato. Dressed black as a crow. She didn't really threaten me with death. She said, 'You're a benighted soul, Mr. Knack'—and yes, she knew my name and plenty about me. 'But I want your former employer, Little Goldie Girl, far more than you. She's done, in her short life, more than enough to gain my attention. Her father killed my husband. Since then I never set foot ashore.' She it was told me what had become of Art and the ship, and Goldie, too. And Mary told me she doubted either woman would hang. Both, in different ways, were too clever for that. 'Will you join me then, Mr. K, in seeking Goldie out?' I said, 'Do I have a choice?' 'None,' she said. 'And you will serve my ship seven years. That's the price you pay me, if not your life. Hard labor. And at the end you can go your own way.' Then she smiled—her smile isn't like a smile—and said, 'You can see in the dark, like all my crew. For us this is because we lived before so far north, that half the year there's no sun and every day is also night. But you, how do you do it?' I explained it was because of wearing the eye patch all those years, now on one eye, now the other. I'd learned to see through it. She *smiled* again and said that had also saved me death. My night vision would help me crew her ship, which never lights a lamp and sails always by night."

Since then, Blacky had traveled on the *Widow*. He was treated mostly like a prisoner, worked like a slave, sometimes even chained, fed scraps. Mary's ship appeared to drift, yet always finding the ones she wanted, in the end. Fair weather seemed to surround her, too. Unless vile weather would be more useful to her.

"Goldie wasn't to be found, though. Then I suggested to Mary Hell that the murderous little yabbit, if she'd lived, might still be in England. I added that I'd kept something of Goldie's—aside from the bullet she'd fired at me, that lodged in the book-board padding. But I had prettier things—a little scarf she once let drop, a wisp of lace off her cuff—why did I keep them? And so safe, in a waterproof, sharkskin bag? It's the acting again. In a play—the fallen hankie, for example, in Shakespur's *Othello*, where I played such a cracking Iago—these things can be very useful. Salt Pete told me once how the cleverest messenger pigeons can be trained to recognize a kind of *scent* on things, and can then locate particular people who once owned the article. Like a bloodhound. And Mary, who knows so much of everything, said there were white doves in England, kept at Good Deal and Dove, which were clever that way. We lay off Deal a while then. And I hired a couple of doves. Trained them to know the scarf and lace—the *scent* of Goldie—even the traces left behind in some place she'd often visited—and I sent the witch two messages.

"It seems seafarers trained those doves, and so the birds knew most of the inns and taverns in Lundon where seafarers might go. Or maybe the dove didn't find Goldie, that first time, for after the first message Goldie never showed. And Mary had told me to say that Art was at Deal, which should have got Goldie there. But later I sent message two. Art was off El Tangerina. And that second time we almost came up with Goldie's ship. But there was another ship Mary wanted to—remove—so we took that one instead. A French ship she was. Pirate. Not anymore. Mary, though, she always prefers to take her prey at sea. She won't step ashore, I've said."

Black Knack winked at Beast. "Am I boring you, matey?"

"Uh—sorry, Knacky . . . just dropped off—" Mr. Beast seemed surprised at himself. "Must be the heat. . . ."

"Or something in the booze, maybe, or the food—or even the jolly old pipe." Foggily, Mr. Beast peered at Black Knack. BK said, "Took you a long time to go under, I'll give you that, too. Keekray usually mixes the drug strong enough to knock out an ox."

"Kee—Keekrayyy . . . ?"

"The nice lady that served us lunch. She's Mary's, too, member of the free crew of *Widow*. How else do you think I'm here for my R and R, forsooth, but with a jailer to keep an eye on me? We'd heard you were here, Beasty. And a wicked old pirate like you, Mary'd *love* to meet you. You're just the type she takes an interest in."

Mr. Beast attempted to rise.

Found this wasn't going to happen.

"Trait—" he tried. "Trai—trrr—"

Then, goggling through his foggy drugged eyes, he listened desperately through his drumming drugged ears.

"Ever hear of Mary's Green Book, Beast? I doubt you have. Oh, she can read the Green Book all right. And there are letters she has, of the alphabet, and some in other languages than English, or the alphabet of the Scandas. They're not quite like the parrot clues on the Isle, though. But she gives her prisoners a few, now and then, as a reward. They all lead to treasure. Wonder how many nabbing *you* will get me?"

Mr. Beast snored. His shaggy head dropped forward on his chest. Keekray prowled, lean and cool, from the Chymist's, the shells gleaming in her ears. She nodded at Black Knack. Together they lifted Mr. Beast from the table and carried him away through the forest, like two leopards with their kill.

~9 TWO ℮~

Lie of the Land ⌒

Questions had been asked in the Government Talkery in Lundon. Why was the expected battle of Jib so *late*? Everyone had assumed it would be over by now.

Concerned dispatches had reached Admiral Hamlet Ellensun aboard his flagship *Triumphant*.

A ship of the line, *Triumphant* was among four other new war models, a try-decker of ninety guns. In the open green sea of the straits between Jibrel-Tar and the Morrocaino shores, she towered up like a piece of architecture, a mansion on the water, balconied, terraced, and looming, fifteen cannon ports per lower deck, forty-five per side, and her masts crowded like a white cloudburst with sail.

"Look at her, Ham," said Thom Healthy, *Triumphant*'s captain and Hamlet's long-term friend. "What a ship she is! I never was so proud."

"Well done, Thom," said Hamlet, rather vaguely.

They were looking, from a hill on the island, out at the whole war fleet, some twenty-odd ships at anchor, and behind these a mass of smaller reinforcement shipping.

The French had been supposed to be here, chased off from Egypt. But not one Monarchist vessel was visible.

"Anyway," said Healthy heartily, "all the French revolutionary leaders are safe now."

"Indeed. Thanks to Michael and Kass Holroyal. If we win this battle," Hamlet added, staring out to sea through the spyglass, "it's a cert the whole of France will rise against the French king. Not to mention Spain. The king has made them pay through the nose for his war, and one more defeat will settle it."

"Wow, I trow."

"Mmm. But where *are* the gaspered French, by the t'gallants?"

They walked back down the hill and paced around the north shore of the island of Trey Falco.

It was a strange place, often visited by those who liked ancient history, now swarming with ships' engineers and other professionals.

A Roman port and town had once sat on Trey Falco. Most of it had collapsed over hundreds of years, from the action of the sea and winds, not to mention robbers from both Jib and Morrocaino. Now only the sea-facing forum, with its plaza or square, remained, laid with uneven grass-grown stones. Four large, heavy-maned, black granite lions, lying down with paws stretched out, dominated the square, and a pair of dry fountains full of granite fish-tailed seapeople from myth. A great column, from which the statue had long since fallen, crumbled up into the air.

Last night, when the square was vacant, Hamlet had noticed a monkey seated on the column's top.

"Admiral, see here. This is where the water washes under at high tide." They peered into the fountain's bowl. "The cistern's cracked below."

"One good shot," said Armstrong Billowes, "those fountains'd play again and no mistake. Hit the top of the sky."

"Something to consider, certainly, Mr. Billowes."

At the east end of the square, Hamlet paused again. "Where are those damned French?"

"According to the spy, last sighted heading back to Calace, Hamlet."

"A falsehood. Our own squadron marks them at Cardice."

"Aye, very likely. Written to Emma, have you?" Mr. Healthy added.

"Yes. Said I longed to moor in the safe refuge of her arms. The sort of stuff everyone expects."

"Lovely girl, Emma."

"Yes, Thom."

They stared out beyond the forest of masts and clouds of sails. The sea as far as Jibrel-Tar looked empty as could be.

"You know the French, Ham. Always late."

"Mr. Billowes."

"Sir."

"Gunnery practice at four o'clock sharp."

"Aye."

Hamlet glanced again at the dispatches and read once more, *It is, as you are aware, Admiral Ellensun, a total destroyment of the Franco-Spanish fleet your country wants—simply to win an elegant victory will not be enough.*

The squadron of six ships, which included the thirty-gunner *Bleurrggh Sorry* and the twenty-five-gun frigate *Is That You Edgar Aah*, were strung out in a loose, wide line, ship behind ship, between the angle of the Franco-Spanish coast and the English fleet at Trey Falco. Their main purpose was to signal news of the French and Spanish fleet, by use of coded flags. Only a single forward ship was actually in sight of Cardice. She was FRS *Is That A Wasp*.

About four in the afternoon, *Is That A Wasp* turned in the water and headed toward the next ship in the squadron, signaling for dear life.

One by one then, the relay of six ships read the flags. One by one they passed the message on, and also headed for the Roman island.

The French commander had kept his own fleet parked at Cardice in the hopes of luring the English toward him. But finally a communication had reached the commander from his king. It insisted that the battle must be joined without delay. The king had added that "Your country wants the English fleet destroyed—to take only a graceful victory will not do."

During the afternoon then, like a huge animal swimming out from shore, the French ships had begun to make their way southeast toward the Straits of Jibrel-Tar.

Is That You Edgar Aah, last of the English squadron, had reversed like a greyhound and sped toward the anchorage of the English fleet. She reached Trey Falco in the sunset.

Armstrong Billowes, up on *Triumphant*'s fighting-top, was in turn the first to read the code message. Billowes bellowed. And the decks were soon ringing and singing.

"The French are on their way!" "The Avey Voos are coming to be made into pastries!" "Into French bread!"

"Hearts of oak are our ships!"

"Shining stars are our men!"

Dear Emma, wrote Hamlet swiftly, *you are always in my heart—*

"We always are ready!"

Dear Mum, wrote Thom, *I'll be wearing the lucky socks thou sent. . . .*

"Best cannon on the globe!"

"England's the best, no lie."

"I never saw men so ready to fight and to conquer."

And on the pillar, in the island square, one more monkey, staring down at all the prewar noise and activity as the evening settled, and the quiet, uncaring stars shone above. Like medals, or bullets, or tears.

Phoenix Sinking

Zero light now entered the hold.

Night was night, and day was night.

Time had stopped.

Forever?

Felix shifted a little on the scrunched-up sacks. He wasn't very comfortable, but things like this had happened before, when he was a child in the workhouse, and his father dead.

He didn't hate Goldie. He felt ashamed, in a way, because he was sorry for her.

Mostly he didn't care.

Once the storm had given him its memory of Art's ship broken on the rocks, and he knew she had drowned . . . No, he didn't really care. About Flag and Fancy grabbing him, and Goldie coming in with her slaps and punches and kicks—

Life hurt worse than any woman's fist.

Outside, too, darkness opened like a slow flower over the Afric waters.

All through the daylight, *Rose Scudder* had tracked a merchant ship, heavy and leisurely with trade goods.

Nicholas Nunn had been very glad Goldie had perked up and taken an interest in this ship. It had allowed him to sneak down to Felix and give him some water. Not that Felix was very concerned with drinking it.

Nick had been—what word worked? Upset? Horrified? *Nightmarized*—yes, that was the one—by Goldie's treatment of Felix.

But Nick stayed very wary of Goldie now.

So he went along with the general pleasure when the merchant vessel was spotted.

There was a feisty wind, and they made a tasty speed.

Did Nick know anything really about pirates? That was, how most pirate crews went on?

No, Nick knew war, which, even at its most awful, was different.

Up on deck in the early darkness, torches blared and Taggers was blasting out an untuneful tune on a trumpet, while a couple of the others thumped drums, and some banged sticks on the rails and howled.

It sounded, Nick thought, a false smirk *glued* to his face, like a pack of especially appalling wolves who had formed a sort of orchestra.

The ship ahead had tried to outrun *Scudder* once they saw what *Scudder* really (now) was—though *Scudder* did not, unsportsman-like, fly the Jolly Roger.

Nick thought the merchantman was from Morrocaino anyway, and most pirates left such ships alone, as the Morrocains were friendly to sea robbers.

Goldie was leaping about, gorgeous, dreadful.

She arranged the guns and they were fired, a ramming broad-side so coordinated it almost knocked *Scudder* back on her starboard flank from the recoil.

Blaambrr—

The merchantman tottered. One mast toppled. Her side was open.

Nick could hear the men aboard shouting and crying out.

He turned to Goldie, trying to join in, keep up, "Hey, Captain! Well shot!"

"Shut up," rasped Goldie, glancing by like a green flame. "Leave me *alone!*"

Nick obeyed. He had seen men in the middle of a battle who reacted less disturbingly.

Then they were close and ropes sizzled across, ship to ship.

Nick, who'd watched and been part of all kinds of military action, leaned on the mainmast of the *Scudder* and thought he—not they, the pirates—must have lost his mind.

It was probably about an hour later that every item worth thieving had been removed from the pirated vessel. Heaps of—*things*—cloth, metal, food, weapons—lay on *Scudder*'s deck.

On the deck of the defeated vessel, only men lay or lurched. A few had jumped in the ocean. But the coast was not to be seen, and even if it were, it was quite some distance off.

Goldie now wore a necklace of bright green jewels—peridots, Nick thought, perhaps.

She was laughing and drinking stolen spice wine.

Then she said to Flag, "By the Wheel, baby, you're at a loose end, sweetling. Go thee down in the hold and fetch me up that rat."

Flag apparently knew at once which "rat" Goldie meant.

So, for that matter, did Nick Nunn.

Felix Phoenix was dragged up from the hold, up on the main deck of the *Rose Scudder*.

The men were amused by the physical distress Felix must be in. Goldie hadn't really marked his face, though, just that one black eye. . . .

"Now, sir," said Goldie to Felix, lying on the deck among the stuff from the robbed ship. "You are a wretch. Rank. And so"—Goldie pointed at the merchantman, which was taking water fast—"how about I put you over there? Would that be comfy?"

Felix just looked at her.

The men (wolves) laughed.

Nick felt sick. (Nothing wrong with a rhyme if it made the point.)

When they got hold of Felix and began to swing him across on the ropes, and Nick could hear how some of them were saying they'd fling burning torches after onto the deck of the broken ship and speed up her sinking, Nicky Nunn came to a decision.

"Hey, best Captain," he roared, "I want in on this fun and frolic."

No one prevented him.

So they all whirled over.

The wreck already smelled of burning. Her remaining crew, men with olive-brown faces and frightened, sad eyes, crept against her sides so that Goldie and her comrades could get on with what they wanted.

Was it just Nick's imagination? Already the night seemed lit up like a whole fleet on fire—

He saw Goldie had tied Felix to the foremast.

"Darling Captain," said Nick. "Can I just check those ropes? Your delicate fingers—I know you're strong, but I want to make quite sure he's held fast."

Goldie giggled. "Were you jealous, Nicky? You *should* have been. But not now. I'll sink this bark and Mr. P with it. Down, down, down to the cellar of the sea."

"No ransom, then?" asked Nick.

"*Ransom*? This is much more fun. My daddy knew. He hated a surrender. Go check those ropes."

Felix was slumped. *Only* the ties, Nick reckoned, held him up. Nick moved around the mast and felt the ropes and cord, which were beautifully knotted.

"*Felix.*"

"What?" He sounded sleepy.

"I'm going to—loosen these a bit. Can you swim?"

"No."

"Well—but can't you—"

"I don't care, sir. Don't endanger yourself. Thanks for trying."

Nick sawed through three-quarters of the bindings with a small knife, all the time grumbling as if he were tightening them. He had reached a point where he didn't think anymore what Goldie would do if she came over and caught him.

It wouldn't make any odds anyway. Felix couldn't swim, and wasn't bothered.

"I've done my best, sir."

"Thanks. I said. Really."

Felix's head drooped forward. He looked as if he wanted to go to sleep and was too polite to tell Nick to belt up.

Nick drew away.

Across the deck Goldie Girl was already swinging back toward the *Scudder*.

"Better run, Mr. Nunn," said Felix softly. (More poetry.)

Nick took the hint. He, too, caught a rope and walloped across the merchantman's tilted deck to land on a pile of stolen mango-lines on the planks of *Scudder*. They squished, and he skidded and fell over.

When he had sorted himself out again, a huge scarlet-saffron flare erupted in the night behind him, and looking back once more, he saw the Morrocain ship already burning.

The last of her crew that could were sprinting into the sea. Things floated there—the odd barrel or bit fallen from the ship. The ones who couldn't swim seized hold of these. Would Felix?

Nick longed to have been much more brave. But then, Goldie's lot would only have shot him.

Oh. The merchantman was going down now.

The sea so black, and the fiery orange ship, ringed with wavelets of vivid pink. Felix Phoenix tied to the foremast still looked—only very tired.

Goldie was jeering across the gap of water. And the Morrocain sailors were silent in their own distress. Fancy took a pot at one or two, missing—he'd been at the wine.

I wish I'd stayed on *Total Devastation*, thought Nick.

His heart was sinking with Felix and the ship.

Art—will I see Art, where I'm going?

Felix heard the gentle voice of his dead father, Adam. "Of course you will, one day. Beyond this world is another, and another, and—"

"Then I'm content."

The heat of the fire hadn't scorched him, and he was very glad the other men had dived off into the sea, where perhaps they stood a chance.

Felix could feel the ropes parting from around him. This had no meaning at all. Besides, something gulped now below, a giant's mouth swallowing the ship and everything on her.

Art, he thought. *Sorry about last time. . . .*

Water, warm and cold at once, smelling of oil and tar and cinnamon and fish, closed over his head.

He had almost drowned once before.

Water flooded him. It was agony, but then it numbed him. A white flash lit his brain. In the flash Felix saw a dark shape, and then a pale hand.

Sinking—

Once . . .

Rising, air still in the lungs . . .

Sinking—

Twice . . .

Sink three times and you stay down.

Something tapped Felix Phoenix quite daintily under his

jaw. He tried, only partly conscious, to avoid it. But there it was again.

A long, cold solidness, hard like wood or iron, patted against his body. A—*face*—white, yet veiled over by some kind of black netting—stared back at his eyes with eyes of cold black paint. The hand pushed at his chin. . . .

The surface parted. Felix coughed and spat out the ocean, and there was the leftover red glimmer of the sunk ship. But here—Art had rescued him that other time, in the sea off Port's Mouth. And it was a woman now, too, who saved him. Only she was made of wood.

He hadn't meant to but he'd gripped her, and she kept him up above the surface. Veils, weeds, and hand—

She was—

She was a figurehead—

Felix opened his eyes wide, even the one Goldie had blacked.

It was the figurehead from Art's ship that had bobbed against him—the coffee lady, the true *Unwelcome Stranger*—she'd sunk before off English shores, but followed Art's ship and been taken and fixed on again. Now the *Unwelcome* was sunk, too. But the figurehead—was *unsinkable*.

Felix laughed a little. The figurehead nodded against him. He held on to her, and she, with her outstretched hand, held on to him.

And so they floated in the black, fire-slit waters off Africay, with all around other men clinging to drifting jetsam, and over there the bright *un*broken ship of pirates, and stars above, and miles of salt sea below, and—

And—

There.

Something else, beyond the last pockets of wreckage.

What was *that*? That . . . *shape*?

(Felix held the figurehead . . . Art's ship . . . Art.)

That shape, it was very black against the indigo sky. And see, where the moon rose, the shape's outline seemed to *carve* the moon—

In slices.

In the Net ——

Did Goldie enjoy seeing Felix "punished," watching him, as she thought, die? Did Goldie know, herself? She sparkled with peridots and spite, that was for sure. His death was necessary. Her father . . . would have done the same. And she'd learned such a lot from the Goliath.

Meanwhile the noisy jollity and flash of torches prevented most of the crew, let alone Goldie in her trance, from hearing or seeing anything else at all special.

By the time any of them began to realize, the other ship had drawn quite close.

Goldie, in fact, was one of the last to lift her head and take notice.

Now she made out only gradually the big, slim shape that blotted the moon but left rags of it showing.

For maybe a minute Goldie stared, her mind wiped blank. And then she heard the voice of Tinky Clinker, breathless and dramatic, *worrying* in her ear. "It's *her*! Like I saw her off Dragon Bay at Hurrys. The *Widow*—like yer worshipful da seen her an' all—if'n he did—Mary Hell—the *Avenging Angel*—"

Goldie swiveled back just long enough to bash Tink on the snout again, as she had the first time he'd told her this story.

Then she moved to the *Scudder*'s rail.

Goldie's eyes were strained open. Her mind cleared to a fearful darkness, full of terror.

The other ship was dark, too; her sails were black as the *Enemy*'s had been, but unpatterned by any decoration of the skull and bones. The weeds or nets trailed from her. They spooled out over the water. Not grasping quite what went on, Goldie saw men who had been floating helpless in the waves, scooped up and drawn in over the dark ship's sides to her lightless deck.

Not a lamp.

Only the torches and lanterns of the *Scudder* described the black ship. And showed those who stood along her rail, looking across at Goldie and all her men.

A mountain of silence had crushed the pirate crew by now.

Up on the quarterdeck, Nicholas Nunn noted with relief that the weird phantom vessel seemed to be rescuing all the Morrocaino sailors—and Felix, too, hopefully.

NN hadn't heard of the *Widow*—or if he had, it was just one more of those shadowy tales (like sea monsters and the *Flying Dutchman*) that you took with a pinch of sea salt. Or, if you'd thought for an instant you'd *seen* it—you reasoned it away. He considered this dark ship might therefore be a patrol vessel, hence sailing lampless—the moon was up after all. Perhaps the tattering veiling was some sort of extra night camouflage. Nick thought he and the others would all be arrested, and no doubt jailed and hanged at the nearest law-abiding port. He squared his shoulders. It served them all right, himself included.

No one attempted a single shot, either from the guns or the firearms on deck. Nor did the dark ship offer fire.

Somehow, this didn't seem odd.

Tinky had slunk away from Goldie. He was sidling along now to the galley. Get down the ladder, hide below—if any of Mary's people caught him, Tink would say he had been captured, that was it, captured while out fishing—

But Fancy barred the hatch and the ladder. He grabbed Tinky hard. "Nah, friend. You stay along o' us. If we're for it, so's you."

Goldie found herself almost immobilized by the line of faces at the rail of the *Widow*. Some were black, and some so white they *gleamed*.

The two ships were now near enough that anyone able-bodied could jump the gap.

And then, Mary Hellström walked between her people and stood herself at her rail. Moon-white face, eyes like caves, mouth a sudden grin—*face of a skull–alive*.

"Good evening, Captain Little Girlie Gold. At last, we meet. I knew your father. Did they tell you? But also, I have a pair of your oldest friends aboard."

Holding frantically to the rail of *Scudder*, Goldie gaped back. Even the muddling of her name didn't register. Terror, Goldie wildly thought, was heavy. It lay on her like the weight of the world. But she'd escaped the gallows. She would escape *this*.

The black and white crew of Mary's ship parted to make way for two more men.

These weren't like any other person on the Widow's ship.

One bleak, craggy face, known so well, under a hat that was like—but was not—the favorite hat he had always worn before. And one face with an eye patch and stubble—*this* one smiled.

Mr. Beast. Mr. Knack.

Dead men on a ship from *hell*—

Goldie dropped bonelessly to the planking. No one caught her, to save her pretty skin bruises. Everyone knew that wasn't going to matter now.

"She's a coward," said Black Knack softly. "Like all bullies." No one replied. Blacky pushed the blade of words home: "You'd never catch Arty Blasty swooning like that at a threat. Nor Molly neither."

"*Huish-la*," said Mary Hell, quiet as a breeze through night grasses, and Black Knack buttoned his lip.

Keekray and Sverre flung the grapplers.

Widow rocked, taking hold of *Rose Scudder*.

Still not a gun barked on the pirate ship.

Mr. Beast took off his hat.

Though it wasn't the first hat, which he'd loved and cherished (brushing it and hanging it on a peg when he slept), he had formed for the new one a certain attachment. He dropped the hat over the side in the few feet of clear water. It would be safer there; it had a chance.

Some days—weeks?—back, he had come to, his head drubbing from the drug Keekray and BK had fed him at the Chymist's, lying on *Widow*'s deck. Mary Hell had presently stood over him in her long black dress. He was close enough to smell the smell of the sea on Mary Hell, and something nearly as intense—like the yellowed pages of an old book. "You're welcome aboard, Mr. Beast," she said. "Your stay with us will be stressed, but I trust educational." "Finish me now," he said. "I knows who you are." But she only drifted away, like a skinny black leaf.

He wasn't treated so badly. Made to work, but that wasn't much different from the press-gang ship *Hit 'Em*, or even Goliath's or Goldie's vessels when the heat was on.

But he knew he, unlike Blacky, was going to be slain. They were saving him for some reason. Blacky told him why. "Mary wants you, and me as well, to greet Goldie, when we find her. Cheer up, Beast. I'd think you'd like to see Goldie suffer the worst death of all. Even if you're for it, too." "*What death is it?*" "None know. That's true, Beasty. None of us ever see. But—it happens. Down they go into the ship's belly. They never return."

Beast had considered during the next few nights—and the days when they lay at anchor, muffled and motionless, everyone else below—whether he could get away. They hadn't chained him, didn't even shut him in. The boats were chained, though. Only the crew seemed able to unlock them. And the shoreline anyway was not visible. He couldn't swim. That, then, was that.

But there might always be a chance in any fix, so he held on.

And now, tonight.

What did he feel when he saw Goldie stuck there, frozen with fear? Pleased she'd suffer? He should be. She had left them all to swing. And besides, after Art had dueled with Goldie and beaten her, Goldie hadn't been worth anything as a captain. She was no longer pistol-proof.

The hat had zigzagged off down the narrow channel between the ships. Beast saw it take to the open sea beyond, along with some bits of wreckage left from the sunk merchantman.

Farewell, bye-bye.

Mary's creepy crew were swarming over to the pirate. No opposition—except in two or three places. Then there was a splurge of fight, swiftly settled in favor of the *Widow*. Back they came with their prisoners, Goldie among them, slung like limp washing over the shoulder of the tall, white-haired Scanda, Sverre.

One of the last to arrive was Nicholas Nunn. Beast could tell Nick was a naval man, not only by his now-mucky uniform, but by his way of standing up straight and dignified.

Mary was once more there then. She could float in and out of a crowd, Beast thought, like a cinder. More than once he had asked himself if she *wasn't* a ghost.

"Yes, I know you, sir," said Mary to Nick.

"Good evening, madam. Nicholas Nunn, late of *Total Devastation*."

"Just so, Captain Nunn. Pray, what are you at among this band of cutthroats?"

Nick said, very low, "I'm a fool, ma'am. I fell head over heels for the wrong woman. But that's no excuse."

"Well," said Mary Hell. "Not everyone is fortunate enough to love the right partner. And if you do, then such as these"—she waved a papery hand—"may take them away from you. As my husband was taken from me."

"I regret it, mistress."

"Regret nothing, Captain Nunn. You're free. You are no pirate, and we'll do you no harm. You've fought only in battle, and another battle waits for you. There you shall go. Perhaps till then, care for the other gentleman whose ropes you loosened so cleverly."

"How did you . . . ?" Nick left off as Mary Hell cindered away over the deck.

"Don't question," said Mr. Beast. "*She* knows *all*."

Nick nodded, and turned to find Felix sitting on a coil of rope, with a strange battered object by him. Seeing it, Nick nearly jumped from his skin. For the object was a figurehead, and so like Mary herself, the skin he nearly jumped from also crawled. But hadn't he seen it before, too?

Felix answered this question without Nick's asking.

"From the *Unwelcome*."

"*Piratica*'s figurehead?"

"All that's left of her, or her ship." Felix closed his eyes. Then Nick sat by him, but left him in peace.

He was aware the grapplers had let go of poor old *Scudder*, leaving her adrift. The *Widow* was stealthily moving off. Light faded, just the moon now, and the moon's mirror on the sea.

By this dreamy illumination, Nick saw the others, conscious, semiconscious, or un, dragged or herded up onto the forecastle.

A wooden chair was there, and Mary seated herself in it. The female First Mate, Keekray, stood to her left, and Second Mate Sverre to her right.

Then the trial began. It wasn't a long one.

"Death."

Goldie woke from her faint. She was bewildered. She thought she had foxed that old judge. But there must still be time. She put on her most winning smile—yet now it didn't fit and fell from her lips. Goldie saw, too, that it wasn't Judge Knowles. It was the woman from hell, Mary.

Even so, Goldie pushed to her feet.

"Oh lady, take no notice of my dress—my story is a tragic one. A cruel father—these wicked men, who forced me aboard and made me watch horrible piratic deeds I dared do nothing to prevent"—(the wicked men snarled in the background)—"for what can a poor weak girl—"

Goldie broke off. Mary had laughed. It was the most unlikely sound—it was a lovely laugh, silvery, better than Goldie's own. Perhaps the laugh was the last of Mary's happiness and youth, a fragment, left behind when all else had gone. But the voice of Mary now matched her frightening, aged appearance.

"True, your father was cruel. True, these men are wicked." (Now—no snarls.) "But you, Little Girlie Gold, are as *bad* as your father. And among these devils you call men, you are one of the foulest."

Goldie blustered.

No one interrupted.

Eyes, pale or black, or *Scudder*-bloodshot, bored into her.

Goldie gave up blustering.

She stood there panting, and then Tinky Clinker thrust by her and threw himself at the feet of Mary Hell.

Amazed, Nick Nunn, who could barely see in the gaining darkness as clouds folded up the moon, heard Tinky bleating of his innocence. "It was out fishing I was, Yer Honor. And they took me, innit." And so on.

Nick looked away. He watched the moon carefully as it vanished. On the forecastle deck another silence.

Mary said, "For most of you, the death can be quick. Not the death of the belowdecks. I save that for the worst, and you, Mr. Clink, are not that."

"No—missus—listen up—by the Will's Gills—I done nothing—I'm—"

"Quick and clean," said Mary again. "And often quicker."

Nick couldn't see, didn't look. He watched the cloud where the moon had been. When the shot came, sudden, piercing the air, Nick flinched, although he'd heard plenty of gunfire in his time. Beside him, Felix didn't stir.

There was a rattly thud as something dropped on the forecastle deck.

Then a sound of sobbing. Goldie. She wasn't crying for Tinky.

The dark sky was now lighter than the ship. All around, the nets rustled and the black sails sighed.

Mr. Beast looked up in surprise as Black Knack appeared, apparently from nowhere, under the mizzenmast. Though Beast's night vision was quite good, Blacky's was better, and his mobility therefore likewise.

"Is it time?" Beast asked. He said it in a casual manner. He had planned to be casual like that, on the other occasion, at Lockscale Tree. There'd have been enough of them making speeches.

"I've spoken to Mrs. Hell, Beasty," said Black Knack. "Convinced her you're not such a bad sort. Or, to be fair, she knew it anyway. Not one of the worst, says she."

"So I get the clean, quick death like all those other men I've been a-hearing go over the side since the moon went."

"Shh, Beasty. We don't speak of it much. Best not to. And it's not for you. She says she likes your attitude. No groveling, no argument, and you're a good worker. Your night vision isn't so poor either and will improve—"

"*Improve?*"

"Mary says you can serve her ship, rather than die. Your sentence'll be ten full years. Come on, thank me."

"You mean . . ."

"Just what I said."

"You ain't kidding? 'Tis for real?"

"Cross my heart with the double bones, Beasty."

Together, both men ambled up the deck, toward the now-vacant forecastle elevation. From stern and bows and the sheets above, the white crew and the black observed them. *Widow*'s people had seen such things before.

Blacky didn't know why he was pleased Beasty should be spared. A familiar face, perhaps, from the old days?

Beasty was relieved, yet somehow didn't feel the threat lift from him. Had Blacky lied? Had Mary Hell? Then he saw who was still there, sprawled on the forecastle deck with Keekray and Sverre standing guard over her. And *then* Beast knew why there wasn't going to be any escape.

He climbed up, saluted Mary Hell, and bent over Goldie.

"Let her be, sir," said Mary. "You may live. She may not. Hers is to be the death her father had. The worst death. It is to be now."

"Belay a moment, missus," said Beast.

He leaned right down and drew Goldie up with an unusually light touch. He stood her by him, and when her legs gave way, he put his arm around her shoulders. She only wept.

"Hush, girlie," said Mr. Beast. Then to Mary he said, "Thankee, ma'am, for offering me such a nice deal. But I can't take it."

"And why not, Mr. Beast?"

"I've known this lass since she was four years of age. I saw what her daddy did to her, and *how* he taught her. She's rotten as he is, but he was the cause."

"And so, Mr. Beast?"

"And so, Mistress Hell, if she goes to this famous death below, then let me go with her. We'll suffer it together. A horror shared is a horror halved, so they say."

Dully then Mr. Beast thought, A bloody speech after all.

To Goldie, who shuddered and wept and seemed not to know where *she* was, let alone who *he* was—her own First Mate that she had taunted and struck so often—he said, "Come on, Cap'n. Soonest in, soonest done. We got off before. Now that ain't to be. But I'm with you. Hold tight."

Mary Hell rose. "You are mad, sir."

Mr. Beast said nothing. He knew it already.

Nick Nunn had also risen on the main deck below—he stood staring at the sea, as if his life depended on counting every wave.

Felix, though, lying on the rope with the figurehead by him, only half saw them go by through half-open eyes. The tall shaggy pirate and the white-faced girl in green with a necklace of green glitters. All this under the gloom of the clouds. Sverre and Keekray escorted them. Somewhere a hatch screaked as it was levered up. Then, a kind of stumbling footstep, a murmur. After that not a sound beyond the lilt and dapple of the black ship. And from the sky, a soft rain falling, smelling of the land. And the wind blowing from the south.

He thought he had dreamed it, when he woke. All or most of it. The deck was empty, and the dawn was a line of rose to starboard, with something between the sea and it—oh, it was the shore.

"Mr. Phoenix." Nick Nunn stood there, seeming embarrassed.

"She goes to sleep by day, you see. So she wants to have a word with you first."

"Who . . . goes to sleep by—"

"Mary Hell."

Felix got up. He was stiff and aching. He wished he hadn't had that dream. . . . He said, "Did they . . ."

"All of them. Yes."

"And Goldie?"

"Yes. Goldie. The worst one that—yes."

"My God. Oh my God."

Two sleepwalkers, they went to the captain's cabin and were shown in by Sverre.

Yes, it had been a dream, and this still was. The cabin was furnished like a smart woman's sitting room. It had two armchairs and a polished table, polished brass candlesticks, and some books in a case. The bed had a coverlet, too, and fat pillows. Over it hung a tiny portrait. Felix the artist found he stared at it, and knew at once this beaming blond sailor must be Mary's dead husband. Who else?

Mary entered by a tiny, inner, curtained door. Bizarre. She wore a dark overrobe, and her hair was long and plaited—it was gray hair. She was abruptly just an old widow lady in her neat little house in Scandinavia.

But the first thing she said was, "Have you heard of the Green Book, Mr. Phoenix? Have you heard *I* know all its secrets and therefore it must belong to me?"

"I—I've been told something like that."

"The book which holds knowledge of all that is carried on the sea or lost there or brought up from there." She nodded. "It's a poetic notion, Mr. Phoenix. But a true one. The Green Book is none other than the oceans themselves. Which, of course, contain knowledge of all that sinks or sails over. And I understand that book so well, as perhaps you've seen, that they say I own it. But it belongs to all and any who will learn its ways and live by its rules."

Felix, weary and unhappy, could summon up no answer. Yet how disappointed they'd be, the greedy ones in Lundon. At another time it might have amused him.

"There are also," said Mary, "the mysterious groups of letters, written on papers, given to this one or that, sometimes even found on those who went back on their bargain of service to this ship, and so sank themselves down into the deeps."

She seemed now to *expect* a reply.

Politely, Felix said, "Yes, the alphabet letters. Clues to some treasure."

"In a way. Go if you will to the table, and look under it."

Totally fuddled, Felix did as she said.

Under the table of Mary Hell he saw something then as unnervingly familiar as the figurehead that had bobbed up and saved him from downing. And as with the figurehead, for some while he stared at it, unable to remember what on earth it was.

Mary Hell assisted him. "The chest of maps, from the Treasured Isle."

". . . Ah. Yes. So it is."

"We took it away with us, when we found Mr. Knack there and took him away also. A heavy chest, needing two men and Keekray to carry it."

"But it was empty by then."

"Do you think so, sir? Well. I will give *you* now a piece of paper with numbers written on it. When Captain Nunn and yourself reach the spot we are bound to take you to, you shall have the chest. I know the secret, but have no use for treasure. It is my pleasure then to gift to you both the chest and the final clue. And my pleasure, also, to make you solve the riddle yourself. Allow me that pleasure then, Mr. Phoenix. I have so few."

Dazzled, bemused, Felix heard his voice flare from him, harsh as the screeching of the hatch the previous night. "I thought your *pleasure*, madam, was the execution of the pirate kind."

"No, sir," she said. "*That* is my work. Farewell. Ride my ship in safety. We will never meet again, I believe, in this life."

～⭒ THREE ⭒～

Bigging in the Rigging ～

"Keep still, Lucinda! Pete, you're good with birds—make her calm down. . . ."

"I'm good with *pigeons*," said Salt Pete to his brother loftily. "And that's a *chicken*. Or," he added disapprovingly, "she would be, if you hadn't painted her with zebra stripes."

" 'Tis only licorice—Jack gave it me. 'Twon't harm her."

"If that egg didn't, then nothing *could*."

Walter had managed to prize an irritated Lucinda off the egg, and both he and Peter gazed at it.

"It's more like a goose egg, by the Stun'sel Stammer. That size, and white like that."

"How did she *lay* it? Who art a clever chick-chick, eh?"

Lucinda pecked Walter. He replaced her on the large egg, and she fluffed herself into a contented broody position, now clucking in a self-absorbed way.

Walter and Peter straightened from her nest, which she had made in the lower forecastle, among many of the hammocks of the crew. The area was otherwise empty.

"Better go up," said Peter.

"Are you scared?" asked Walt.

Peter didn't say. They went up to the deck.

The sun had gone. Dusk was melting to night. Through the dark the ships, the twenty-odd war vessels and their backup craft, spangled with lanterns. The flagship *Triumphant*, and the other three try-deckers, craned skyward, their masts topped with lamps, as if small moons had roosted there.

The great, slow, heavy enemy fleet would take much longer than the English squadron had to reach this place.

And no doubt, the French would, in the normal way, wait out the night. But in case some trick was tried, every English lookout bristled.

Spirits were high.

Ever since the news was flagged and read that the battle was on for tomorrow, rousing cheers and patriotic songs had thundered across the anchorage. There were sounds of parties, too, rations of grog and good food going around.

Lily was one of the few quiet ships.

They were hemmed in now by backup destroyers such as *Tiger Cat*, *Shock*, and *No Surrender*, not to mention one big forty-gunner that was cruising still, a vessel that had been captured only last month from the French. Once called the *Ça Ira*—the *It'll Come To Be*—her now-English crew had renamed her the *It's Happened*.

"Where's Art?" Walter asked Whuskery, who was standing by the deckhouse with Dirk, Grug, Larry, and de Weevil.

"In her cabin."

They looked at each other, then away.

Art, since leaving Ebad and Africay—since before that, maybe, had been acting not quite herself. True, she had come regularly on deck, taken her turns at watches, manned the wheel, spoken reasonably, and as far as this situation allowed, given her orders and made sensible decisions. Nor did she stand for any complaints. "We are stuck with it, sirs," she had said, as *Tiger Cat* "escorted" them to the war zone. "We're not bound for the front line. We cover the battleships and detain any French that try to run away.

Despite England's argument with them, they're a brave people. So perhaps none of them will. They'll attack instead."

And Whuskery had been the one to challenge her then with "And do we keep to the *code*, Captain? Molly's code—your code. *Kill no man*."

"Yes, Mr. Whusk."

"And how do we *do* that?" Shemps had shouted. "Your *code* says we can't even sink the raggers!"

Art hadn't batted an eyelash. "If we must, we sink them. We take prisoners, if we *must*."

They had watched her, anxious and confused, or disbelieving.

"Do your best," said Art Blastside. "None can do more."

And in the silence then, as she went back into the captain's cabin, Dirk had slung his knife point foremost into the stem of the mainmast. "She's brought us to this. Going back on everything. Felix had the right of it. Molly'd spin in her grave." But it was Honest who put his hand gently on Dirk's arm, the snowy parrot Maudy on his shoulder. "Nay, Mr. Dirk. Molly's in paradise. She wouldn't spin."

Now Art stood in her cabin, looking out of the glassed ports at the darkling sea covered with brightling ships.

She had, after that night when she remembered Ebad's words and suddenly guessed what they and her sickness must mean, gone deep inside herself. It was difficult after that fully to emerge again.

How had she missed it?

To be fair to herself, her body had always had a will of its own, and particularly at sea it paid little attention to clocks or calendars. And so she hadn't thought that body was showing her anything more than its usual waywardness. The signs were there. She didn't notice. Or—wouldn't, maybe. But now she must.

For now it wasn't just herself she had to think of. There were two of her—of them—Art Blastside and the baby she carried. The baby, which was part of her and part of Felix—and also, since Art had been a part of Molly, part of Molly in return. The baby was a mixed metal, and all the more precious for that.

I'm not alone anymore. For the first real time in my adult life. . . .

That was her thought after the wave of horror and alarm smashed over her.

And, though he left me, I have Felix back with me now, in a way.

Nothing *outside* all this mattered much now either. But it would have to. They had been nabbed to be involved in what promised to be a huge and awesome battle.

What would you do, Ma?

"Take care of myself," said Molly's voice in Art's mind. "Why do you think I stayed so long with your disgusting father, Weatherhouse, except to take care—of you and me both."

Art found she'd put her hand over her waist. Yes, of course there was a difference. She had thought the tightening of her belt and breeches was due to shrinkage from salt spray—it happened. Funny really. Clever Art. What a dinny!

" 'Twill be all right, kid," said Art to the child inside her. "It'll be fine as sunny days. It's *got* to be."

That evening Honest had charge of the deck.

To Honest, the world was always rather awkward and strange. But he felt a little happier now that he realized Art had woken up to her condition. Honest had known for some while, the way he often did simply *know* things. He had known not to say anything as well.

Above the mizzen, Plunqwette and Maudy were flying around and around each other.

In the galley Feasty Jack was preparing a feast.

Honest had been shown the meat and veg soup, the pancakes

and fried bananas, the fish poached with lime, salt, and nuts, the cake black with rum and decorated with white sugar.

"It's good, son," Jack had said to Honest, "to know where you are."

"Do you?" Honest asked. "Will you?"

"Aye. We'll meet again, somewhere. Just you take care of the bird. He's got speaking talents even *you* don't know about."

From a ship over the water—the *Bruiser*, it seemed to be—roared the strains of "Jewel Free England," with three fiddles and what sounded like the squeals of an unfriendly pig for accompaniment.

And to rival that, farther along, two ships' orchestras and crews were yowling together the verses of "England Strike Home."

On guns across the length and breadth of the fleet were chalked the words TRIUMPHANT—OR DEAD.

Yes. Spirits were high. Left unstopped, the French meant to invade England and "destroy her future," as their king had promised. This would be the big one. But win it, and the course of history would change.

> *England strike home*
> *Across the smoke and foam,*
> *Strike for Freedom*
> *With every sword and gun,*
> *Giving it large*
> *Let loose the charge,*
> *Bigging it up!*
> *Bigging it up!*
> *Yea tho' we stand alone—*
> *England—strike home!*

The French fleet had crossed eastward through the mouth of the straits, and was now at its own night business there.

But some miles out on the broader waters of the Atlantic, four English backup vessels, smaller frigates of around fifteen guns apiece, had met five Franco-Spanish ships of similar type.

As dusk had purpled to dark, red stars lit in two lines along the sea.

Twenty-eight French guns mouthed off, and twenty-six English guns swore back.

The water was clawed up. Trailers of fire and smolder ballooned to smoke clouds on the ocean, through which continuing fire flashes winked. (It was how all inter-country sea battles went on, two lines of warships broadsiding each other.) Some masts were already toppled. One English and one French ship were in serious trouble.

Then, out of the dark and the smoke, from the southwest, a deeper, darker something *slid* into view.

Unhesitating, this new vessel steered straight into the channel between the fighting ships, ignoring the action as if it weren't happening.

Any other unidentified arrival who had dared such a thing would have been blasted apart—by both sides.

Yet it seemed that *almost* at once, *almost* every captain *did* identify this low black ship, trailing her nets like webs.

The French: *"Muselez vos canons! Tenez-les!"*

The Spanish: *"Amordazad vuestros cañones!"*

("Leash your guns! Hold them!")

("Insult your guns by gagging them!")

"Hold your blinking fire!" the English command rang out last.

And farthest in the line, a stray French cannon still let off a fiery burst. The ball soared, fell, vanished. That cannon, too, grew quiet.

Then, nothing.

The black ship sailed between the two lines, noiseless, eerie. Not a light.

In uneasy silence, the warships let her pass, on into the Straits of Jibrel-Tar.

It was a fact that the French fleet, now anchored some way away, would also let the black ship pass. And when she paused to gift one of their ships with three French sailors, saved from bondage with pirates, the French fleet took the men on. Any trained fighter was welcome. Besides, you did not cross the *Widow*.

Once she had grown dim with distance, back in the Atlantic, the gunners' orders were reversed.

Again the red stars exploded to and fro, and the English ship and the French ship, which had been in trouble, were tilting, going down.

"Admiral!"

"Yes, Mr. Billowes?"

"Some—a kind of—a vessel is here. She's unlit and shows no color—except black."

Hamlet raised his eyebrows.

He and his officers had just received a report from the patrolling *Is That You Edgar Aah* and *Bleurrggh Sorry* that the French had formed their line about three and a half miles up from the English position, all ready for the morning.

Hamlet had said, "No night fights here, I think. The one off Egypt was enough for them. But double the watch. Otherwise, it's bright and early tomorrow, gentlemen."

When Armstrong Billowes entered with his message, a dense, startled expectancy filled the flagship's wardroom.

It was Healthy who ventured, "That sounds like the legendary *Widow*. Can she exist?"

Hamlet went up on deck. Under the garlands of lanterns, to a faint background of merry singing all around—which here, by the black ship, had fallen off—he scanned the visitor through the glass.

Certainly she seemed to be the very one he'd heard such a lot of. One knew, having been sternly instructed in Lundon, that such a vessel as this might do as she wished. You didn't detain her, or question her, let alone aggress against her.

Along her decks Hamlet now peered, hoping to spot the Widow herself, Mrs. Mary Hellström. But only a few figures moved there, not easily seen.

A voice called tonelessly under the singing.

"We have two Free Englishmen for your ships. And several for the Morrocain country."

"Oh yes, she does this, too. If she rescues men kidnapped or sunk by pirates, she takes them back to their own."

"That ship," said Thom Healthy, "she's like—"

"A dead thing," finished Billowes.

Hamlet spoke briskly. "She's live enough. Tell them the men may come aboard this ship. Do it politely, Mr. Billowes."

Mr. Billowes did it *very* politely.

On neighboring decks now, crowds of sailors had gathered, to gaze dubiously at the sinister black ship.

But then, spotting a small jolly-boat put out from her with two fellows, one clearly a naval captain, though in a bit of an untidy state, they gave the *Widow*, too, a rousing cheer.

There was a big box in the jolly, perhaps a sea chest. And also a nasty-looking bundle—a body?

Felix Phoenix sat among the white and black rowers, looking at the chest with its brass plate. In his pocket was the list of letters. Neither meant much. Nor this.

Nicholas Nunn patted Felix on the shoulder.

"Nearly there, old chap. By Neptune's Bluest Nose, you're tired and beazled. But this is better. Better than *I* deserve, at least."

They reached the gilded tower block of the *Triumphant*'s side and went up the ladder. The chest and the bundle were roped and also hauled aboard. Nick stood saluting, washed over by sudden vast relief. At home.

Turning without a word, the jolly-boat winged back through the water to the black ship. Was absorbed there.

With no more than this, the uncanny vessel angled her sails, catching some wind not quite available to any other yard or sheet. Away she glided, across the lamp-littered sea, sailing now for darkness and the Morrocain shores.

But Hamlet Ellensun, stalking forward, checked briefly at the bundle—the wrapping had slipped, it was a figurehead of some sort—then drew up with an exclamation.

"Why—Mr. Phoenix, is't *you*, behind the remains of that black eye?"

"It's me."

"Your story must be quite something, sir, to step off *that* ship. Come on, let's have a drink on it. Tomorrow's going to be a busy day."

"So the Green Book is a lie," mused Hamlet about an hour later, sitting with Felix and Thom in the admiral's quarters. "A play on ideas. But the alphabet letters Mrs. Mary gave you—"

"Take them," said Felix. He put the paper flat on the table. The chest stood by, gray and flindery. The brass hadn't been polished. A wretched thing it looked, despite Mary's hints that it still contained treasure.

"I will take the paper for safekeeping, sir," said Hamlet. "When the battle's settled, assuming we're both quite fit, we'll investigate the letters and the chest further."

"Yeah," said Thom. "You know, all this, I'm gobsmacked."

Hamlet laughed. "Thom, thou art often gobsmacked." He turned back to Felix. "But I'm sorry there seems to have been this apparent rift with your wife. . . . Am I correct that you give this impression?"

Felix flicked him a look. "A rift? Yes, permanent. She's dead."

"Oh, by Thunder—but surely—*surely*—"

"Her ship went down. Sunk. All hands."

"You *know* this?"

"Yes."

"Because I thought I caught a rumor that Art was *here*, at Trey Falco. Now who told me as much?"

Thom looked blank. Felix barely paid attention. He hadn't ever doubted he had lost Art forever, not once the storm's memory hit him. He'd lost people before, hadn't he? It seemed to be part of his fate, to lose people. Or be lost by them.

"Thom, will you go up and check the names of all the ships that have come in to the fleet—patrollers, backup, the lot."

"Aye, Admiral." Thom went out, his round pink face showing gladness at getting away from Felix's obvious pain.

Hamlet said, "If the *Unwelcome*'s here, and as a privateer she may well have been invited to join us, Thom will find out for you."

"Thank you," said Felix.

He knew this helpfulness was pointless, and refused to brighten. Nor was he wrong. Ten minutes more and Mr. Healthy returned with long scribbled lists and read off the names of all the gallant English vessels, great and small: *Titan* and *We'll Have You, Whop 'Em Upside the Head, Tiger Cat, Shock* and *IKIS, Swift, Geezer, Fearless* and *Wicked*, and on and on . . . *Ow Blast, Is That A Wasp,*

Valiant . . . It's Happened, Who You Looking At, Paramount . . . Shining Light, Lily Achoo . . .

"Poor chap. Look, he's fallen asleep, Ham. Worn out by it. Poor fellow. And there's no *Unwelcome Stranger* on this list. I checked afore I came back. These rumors go round before a fight. Art Blastside—*Piratica*—they're bound to boast the most famous English pirate captain is fighting with the fleet."

Hamlet Ellensun got up. He stood looking at Felix.

"We'd better get someone to find him a sleeping place. I have a favor to ask of him in the morning."

"What's that, Ham?"

"Felix Phoenix is one of the best artists in England. Better than any other war artist we could get. If he'll risk climbing to the fighting-top, we can strap him in. None better to draw the battle plan from above, or sketch the engagement."

Thom looked doubtful. *Felix?*

But Felix had woken at the changed rhythm of their voices. He spoke softly.

"I'll do it. Why not? I've seen rigging climbed enough times." He thought, And I don't give a damn. Even if I fall. Not now.

Thom said, with forced good humor, "Bigging it up, eh, sir?"

"When all's won, Mr. P," said Hamlet, "you'll be able to paint the most important English victory of the past two hundred years, from firsthand knowledge. Your name will live forever."

It *isn't* my name, Felix thought. My name used to be my father's—*Makepeace.*

But Hamlet Ellensun was gravely and graciously smiling on him, and Thom Healthy seemed proud of everything and everyone. They parted. Long after he lay down in the belowdecks, Felix could hear the drub of feet; the stabilized wheel-shift of cannon—whose firing jaws had now been raised on blocks to give them height; the crank and croak of the three decks. The ways, the life of a ship was all he knew, finally. All he had.

⊰≈⊱

> *Mary, Mary, quite contrary,*
> *How does your garden grow?*
> *With silver bells and cockle shells*
> *And Hell's men all in a row.*

Glad Cuthbert leaned for a long while on the rail of the *Lily Achoo*, gazing far out, toward the island anchorage of all those biggest warships. He had seen, he thought, the oddest thing—again. It was the phantom ship of Mary Hell, slinking between the other shipping. But dazzled by lamps, and the vista obscured by masts and prows, sheets and shadows, he didn't, even now, feel sure.

The others had missed the incident.

After Jack's magnificent supper, most of the *Lily* had got off to bed—even the two parrots, cuddled together up there on the mast.

Was Arty sleeping?

Cuthbert doubted it.

He wasn't going to mention the Widow's ship to anyone, let alone his captain. It still seemed to Cuthbert that first glimpsing the *Widow*, and next telling Art, had somehow undone this whole barrel of weevils. In Cuthbert's pocket was a note.

> *Dear Glayd, Hope this leaves me as it finds you, well. If I*
> *don't get back but som'n gives ya this, take it as all me luv girl.*
> *Me ol' ghost'll still be ducking them pans yer fling at me. Just*
> *look for me in the corner by the door. Like allways, Glladys.*
> *Glalways.*

Trey Falco

Killing clear, the dawn.

The ships were bathed in light. How clean they looked.

But the French ships, stationed there in their seemingly endless line across the sea—they had a special beauty.

It was their flags, their colors.

"Like a flower garden . . ."

Lilies golden and white on blue, blue on silver, silver on mauve, and the scarlet and amber of the Franco-Spanish, their crimson battle pennants, and the French flagship's flapping All-Flame, the standard of the king himself, vermilion and gold.

The English, even with their multicolored Republican flag, were pale beside this.

But then the English signal flags were run up the masts of the huge try-deckers, and on the masts, too, of every signaling squadron ship. These were a rainbow, and quickly read by those who could. The message flew against the sky, and each vessel raised now a cheer like a lion's roar.

England knows (read the flags) *that every Man here is a hero.*

Sunlight sparkled on the mouths of cannon. And if the French ships were a flower garden, it was a garden that stretched, north to south, for nearly two miles.

The French were singing the victory songs of France.

On the English decks, "Jewel Free England."

On the decks of the smaller English ships, too, the twelve-gun *Boo* and the ten-gun *Fuchsia*, the seventeen-gun *Come On Then*. Even on the *Lily*, Peter and Shemps and Grug, Whuskery, Larry and Mosie and Oscar Bagge, Stott Dabbet and Nib Several, lifting their voices so their hearts could rise up with them.

"Jewel Free England,
Free England Jewel the waves!
We shall never never never
E'er be slaves!"

Drums were beating men to their stations.

The island of Trey Falco lay just behind the English fleet as it began to advance toward the French. Unlike the French, they *didn't* move in a horizontal line, nor did they intend to form one.

Ellensun's orders had been as easy to read as the flags.

In two separated columns, the Republican ships took the light breeze of morning and blew almost flirtatiously toward the long French barrier.

We will cut through their line, [Hamlet Ellensun had written] *not stand there on the sea and duel with them, trading broadside shot for shot, like two landsirs on a fine spring morning.* Triumphant *will lead the way, as is her honor and duty. We will pierce the middle of the French line, followed as closely as possible by each of our column of ships in turn. We will blast and overpower each enemy vessel, ranging from the center to the southern rear of their line. This will prevent the second half of that line from coming to their neighbors' rescue in time. Our second column, which is to be led by the* Pegasus, *will meanwhile break through farther up the French line to the north, most probably where the French have placed their seventy-gunner the* Gueux Fou, *and proceed by the same method. Those French ships which evade us and attempt to go west into the Atlantic or east into the Med will be tracked and snared or taken apart by our smaller vessels. Or by any larger vessel that can spare a moment to do it.*

If any captain cannot see the signals and is unsure of what to do next, let him be aware he will not go far wrong in rubbing shoulders with any French vessel, and showing her, at close quarters, how English cannon are operated.

The wind was so playful it took another hour for the leaders of the two English columns to come within range of the French.

Pegasus, a try-decker of slightly lighter build, was the first to cross into their sights. At once the *Gueux Fou* (the *Mad Rover*) opened fire.

Undeterred, *Pegasus* pierced like a dagger between *Rover*'s flanks and those of the neighboring Spanish ship *Monarca* (*Monarch*), sending off two blazing broadsides to both. Almost three-quarters of a mile to the south, *Triumphant* was closing with the command-ing French flagship *Chevalier* (*Knight*). The *Knight* let loose her guns, but *Triumphant*, too, stabbed nimbly between the flagship's bows and those of the *Redoute* (the *Field-Fort*). *Triumphant* let go her own cannonade, employing thirty guns. She managed to rake the *Redoute* stem to stern with this blast, causing great upheaval and damage. *Chevalier*, though, proved a less helpful target, and took the shot sidelong.

Behind *Triumphant* the burly *Titan* was already striding in, and behind her the *We'll Have You*, bunching up with the *Fearless*, the *Wicked*, and the sixty-gun *Whop 'Em Upside The Head*.

While behind the *Pegasus* came the *Valiant*, with *It's Happened*, *Paramount*, *No Surrender*, and *Shining Light* treading on her heels.

The clouds of smoke were already gushing up thickly, the blue sky staining gray. White and orange splashes of fire, the belches of the guns and whip and zoom of flying balls, screams, shouts, the click, crack, and spat of pistols and flintlocks, all lit and split the overcast. And somewhere, already a mast was snapped like a matchstick and cascaded down. But in the quickly curdling soup of the smoke, you could not be sure which ship had suffered.

The daylight grew dirty and stopped being daylight, stopped being *day* at all, and was at last only the prearranged canvas of a vast and burning, swirling war.

Canvas . . .

Felix supposed he *could* see it as a painting.

He had climbed the rigging almost idly—and got, to his surprise, a cheer from *Triumphant*'s men so far below. Mr. Billowes, who had climbed up after him, strapped Felix in. "You'll be safe enough like that, sir." "Unless," said cheery Mr. Leggins, who'd also climbed up with Felix's sketching gear, "unless the old mast cops it and goes down. Don't worry, Mr. P, someone'll catch you." Billowes grimaced, but Felix only said, flippant, smiling his sweet smile, "Don't bother. Just catch the sketches."

Because he didn't care, he thought he wouldn't care about the sea fight either.

But he was wrong.

Going in like this, so high on the mast, getting nearer and nearer to the tall French ships with the gorgeous flags, to start with you could pretend you were—well, above it all. But then you saw the other ships, too, were alive, their decks swarming with men, just like the English decks below.

The first grunts of the guns trembled up the mast and rattled Felix's platform.

Felix stared to every side, behind and in front, over the water, and then began to draw the plan of the advancing English and static French ships.

How odd, he thought randomly as the boom of guns was suddenly all around, the smoke foamed up, and the world shook, that he had gone headfirst into the fight—Felix Makepeace, who always preferred—peace.

In a sort of panic then, not wanting to feel part of this or what it meant, he started to draw more busily and more thoroughly: the toss of timbers through smoke, the curls of fire, the shapes of men, boys—women, too—scurrying, leaping. Swags of sails crumpling. A mast going there. ("Don't worry, we'll catch you.") A dull explosion below, and the fighting-top shuddered now. Had *Triumphant* been hit? He guessed not seriously. The noise directly below was only angry and determined, the cries of the hurt no worse—

Whoosh! A vast red firework bursting in the smoke lather—Felix attempts to catch it on paper quickly, before the image dies down or becomes more extreme. (What was that? Something with gunpowder? About five ships away to port.)

He can feel the big ship sharply turning now, her sheets and stays protesting as they always did at such a maneuver—uselessly, of course. Why ever protest? It seldom did much good—

Except . . . that time at Lockscald. That time on the gallows with Art. Protest, then, had made a miracle—

Two tears, *splat*, on the paper. Messy. Don't cry; you'll spoil their nice drawing that they want so much.

Would Art have liked this battle? No. Men would die, couldn't avoid it. Art was well out of this.

"They're turning! They're standing in behind the French line! Three—six—eight Frenchies surrounded! *Bang! Bang!*"

This was Mosie from *Lily*'s lookout.

Plinke had the wheel.

Art stood on the quarterdeck, and Honest by her. (They had caught the two parrots and put them in the cabin. Walt's chicken they'd tried to catch, but she wouldn't either leave her egg or let them take it.)

De Weevil, whose arm healed slowly, had been trying to perfect left-hand shooting.

Below at the gun stations, Shemps, Stott, Larry, Nib, and Cuthbert, with Tazbo the primer. (Their ears were stuffed with noise-muffling rags bound in place by handkerchiefs.) Five gunners to serve sixteen guns. Grug, still favoring his leg, had to resort to flintlock and pistols on the upper deck.

The actors had even left off whining. They'd put on their best pirate gear, all burnished and aglow with earrings, cutlasses, and boots you could see your face reflected in. Art, too, had put on a brown silk coat with pearl buttons, and brushed her hair with its tiger stripe.

England *knew* every man . . .

Behind was the outline of the island of Trey Falco, with its Roman square. It was dimmed a little by now from smoke. Here was the edge of battle. It was worse ahead. A fog bank had formed from the powder clouds.

This was *Lily*'s station, for she, too, had had her orders. Along with her ranged the smaller vessels *Boo* and *Fuchsia*. *Fuchsia* had a figurehead some of the men thought very pretty, a young girl in a white dress with a garland of fuchsia flowers. Other ships were in this group. Privateers and smaller warships, like the *Is That A Wasp*. About a hundred and fifty feet away, the huge destroyer *IKIS* (which stood for her full name of *I Knew I Shouldn't Have Had That Last Sausage*—one more joke ship that had turned out to be not only real, but formidable) was even now passing by on her route into the fray, part of Hamlet Ellensun's assault column. Behind her rolled the try-decker *Confound Thee*. (*Pegasus* and *Unconquerable* were already well into the action.)

Something seemed to blast the fog apart in a magenta shatter.

Walt gave a quavering yell.

Art shouted, "Mr. Whuskery, alert the guns."

For a ship was coming out toward them now, unseen in the fog but for a glimpse of her topgallant sail, and the sudden flame of her cannon. A French ship, as predicted, not running but cut from her line, wounded and hounded forward, now making for the Mediterranean.

IKIS and *Confound Thee* had already vanished away like huge ghosts into the smog.

The French ship emerged a moment after.

She was, after all, Spanish, and in a poor state. Her only hope was to leave the battle. Two of her three masts were lopped and trailing by her in the sea, caught fast by torn rigging and canvas, red with her flags. Her sides were black from fire, and her upper deck seemed empty. Yet as she came she fired once more, a cannonade that smashed right across *Lily*'s bows, bashing instead against the distant shape of the *Boo*.

Boo retaliated. But the Spanish ship was stocky, her thirty-odd guns still fit—if she had to leave, she would do as much harm as she could on the way out.

On her side was her name. *Adiós* (*Bye-Bye*).

Art bawled. Whuskery, too.

"FIRE!"

Lily juddered in the old familiar prance as five of her port-side cannon punched at the Spaniard.

(Through the fog-dullness, Art could see the *Boo* was holed. Water purged from her. Her shape became *wrong* as her balance left her.)

The dismasted *Adiós* slewed ungracefully, and fifteen guns coughed.

"Hard about, Mr. Plinke."

Lily veered.

But three smoldering black objects, rimmed with white heat, ripped into rails and bulwarks. A cruel spray of wood and metal lashed *Lily*'s deck.

Art saw Dirk spin and go down, and Peter staring in disbelief at the blood that marked his shirt.

Feasty Jack leaned across the gunwales and fired his flintlock at the Spaniard's apparently empty upper deck.

Cries answered.

Feasty turned and grinned solemnly at Art.

"Sorry, Missus Cap'. Broke your code."

Art had nothing to say. She nodded, that was all.

Next second, *Adiós* fired again.

Lily staggered.

"Chain fire!" Art shouted.

And her gun crew began to send their broadsides one on another. Tazbo nearly caught fire himself, the speed with which he dashed from keg to guns, the lint-stock ready in his grip.

Boo was going under. Her men, flailing in the water, were being taken up by the *Fuchsia*. That girl with her flowers, their figure-head, was so out of place in all this—

But from the smoke now, like a magic trick, the English frigate *Come On Then* was rumbling, the voices of her cannon ahead of her.

The third mast of *Adiós* detonated to dust. Two gun ports *melted*—

An awful groan—was it that of men or of the vessel herself?— burned in the air. Her prow dipped abruptly, and a white eruption—like *snow*—rent her side as one of her cannon exploded—

On the deck of *Lily*, men danced, howling with terrible glee. Even Peter in his bloody shirt. They were no longer like anybody anyone ever knew.

"She's sinking!"

"Good *riddance!*"

"Down to the belly of the whale!"

Art saw Whuskery had deserted the *Lily*'s cannon. He was bending over Dirk, who said feebly, "It's all right, darling. 'Tis nought. Just a little bit of a broken leg."

Art turned to Honest.

"You never fire a shot, do you, Honest?"

"Sorry, Captain."

"Thank God for you, Mr. H."

Mr. Witty, sailmaker's mate, stood to the rear of *Triumphant*, under her mizzen spanker sail, which he had been looking over. The sail was torn, but not too badly. He also had his pistol ready. It was by now quite warm with use.

Triumphant had cut through the Avey Voos' line and taken out several ships, though the flagship, *Knight*, had been obscured by now in the fog. They were forging south at a good pace, a wind having picked up from the northwest. Right now *Triumphant* was, as it were, between ships, though this wouldn't last more than minutes.

Witty took the time to notice *Titan* over to port, thumping the heck out of the French ship *Gare! C'est Moi* (*Watch It! It's Me*). This was just visible in the gray-yellow murk. A crippled French ship, the *Pardonnez Ma Force*, lay over to starboard, all masts down. She had surrendered and dropped her flags to the deck, despite her name of *Excuse My Strength*. Altogether, so far, or so the visible signals said, five French or Franco-Spanish ships had stricken their colors and given in. Others were damaged and beating out to the Atlantic, unable to fight for much longer. There the wasp swarm of such as the *Is That You Edgar Aah, Bleurrggh Sorry*, and *Who You Looking At* were by now hammering them, to judge from the extra thunders to the west.

Over *there*, meanwhile, northerly, was the *Ow Blast*, Mr. Witty also noted.

A neat boat, and though not of the largest class, tackling the French ship of the line *Vous En Bas* (*We'll Sink You*). At this point *We'll Sink You* looked the most likely to be sunk.

Having studied the spanker, Mr. Witty, and ten other men, turned to batter at some figures with knives trying to climb aboard. They let go and dropped back into the sea.

Just then red-flagged *Santa Asta* hove into view.

"*Boom throom!*" *Santa Asta* said.

Darn it! There went another sail.

In the now-smoky, explosion-rocked underdeck, Oscar Bagge had removed the three-inch splinter from Peter's shoulder. It was a lightish wound, but Peter had stunned Oscar by acting bravely. Whuskery, however, was *not* brave. He loomed, loudly lamenting, over Dirk.

"You're worse than the patient, Mr. Whusk. Get out."

Whuskery reddened behind his mustache and took a stand as if to defend Dirk from the enemy—rather than Oscar and his carpentry set.

Oscar said, "I mean, Whusk, ye're a-making it worse for *him*." Whuskery left.

The break in Dirk's leg was a grim one. But Oscar had an idea. Of all the men with snapped bones after *Unwelcome* had struck the rocks, Forecastle's had healed with unusual speed. Oscar took the weird fossil bone that had been Muck's from his own private store. It had made a fine splint.

"Brace up, Mr. Dirk. This'll hurt."

"Avast, you twit," whispered gray-faced Dirk. "Doesn't everything? Just don't spoil my toenails."

Adiós was taken, the prize of *Come On Then*.

As, grappled and roped, the Spanish ship was towed away, a freak break in the smoke cloud showed the ruined fifty-gun English ship *Titan* on the western horizon. She was entirely dismasted and partly burning, spent, drifting. She faded off into the southern fog.

Vous En Bas (*We'll Sink You*) had surrendered, too. The crew of *Ow Blast*, having marked her as *their* prize, was turning at the onslaught of the French *Guerrier* (*Warrior*). *Warrior* had herself broken from the line. She was a large ship, an adapted brig, happy to give her attention to the group of smaller backup vessels that had flooded westward through the line in the wake of the giants *Triumphant*, *Pegasus*, and the rest. Their job, to block any retreat to the Atlantic, provoked *Warrior*.

Ow Blast blasted back. She had a pack of skillful gunners, and well-trained pistoleers on her upper decks and rigging.

The smoke was staining black.

It was difficult to be sure of your target and, over the noise, impossible to hear the howling of the yellow dog, who had been locked for safety in the First Mate's quarters.

Muck had never liked combat. But his howling normally was either a plea or an expression of disgust. Naturally, this was only instinct. Besides which, he preferred to hide!

Now, though, he felt an intense concern at having been shut in. He knew—how or why hadn't been revealed to him—that he must on *no account* remain in here. He had to get out—and straight into the middle of the action!

Muck leaped for the hundredth time at the door. It quavered, but that was all.

Then footsteps tramped along the narrow area outside.

Muck heard the key turn in the lock.

As the door opened, four men appeared, holding up three others, wounded in the fight. The surgeon's cockpit was full by now of casualties from both the *Ow* and several other nearby craft that had been sunk. The First Mate had volunteered his cabin.

Everyone had apparently forgotten the dog.

Alarmed shouts happened as a yellow cannonball rioted between their legs and belted at forty knots for the deck above.

"Look, there goes our Lucky!" exclaimed one of *Ow*'s deck gunners. "Would you believe the little devil—he's abandoning ship!"

This wasn't quite true. Muck couldn't have said *what* it was. He had scrabbled up ropes and across barrels and reached the rail. He plummeted over with all the professional clumsiness of much practice. The actors could have told *Ow Blast* that Muck was *always* running off.

But as he hit the cabbage-green of a boiling sea, already awash with wreckage, oil, and worse, Muck dug in his black nose, dived, circled and came up snorting like a pig. Immediately then he began to doggy-paddle fast between the red-hot roaring sides of enormous warships, while fire-flight and the zip of pistol shot and scream of cannonballs arced over him. Like most things there, he soon disappeared into the fog.

Exactly seventeen times, Muck, emerging like a yellow missile from the smoke, would be offered urgent rescue. Boats were searching the sea between the fighting walls of the ships for fallen comrades. They tried to get Muck aboard, too. But seventeen times Muck would, with an apologetic wink or sneeze, avoid being rescued.

He was paddling south by southeast, if he even knew it. In the direction *Triumphant* and her column had eventually taken.

<hr>

Ships burning and ships roped and tied—prizes. Ships locked by grapples, gunport to gunport, hands flinging grenades between to dismount the cannon from their blocks—or explode them, filling the lower decks with flame and scalding metal. Ships above and below boarded, the insane gleam of cutlass slashing cutlass, knife and dagger like silver needles—the felling of sails and masts and men. Handguns of all sorts quacking like ducks or hissing bullets like snakes. Acts of courage, acts of tragedy. The glory and horror, all gift-wrapped in the smoke. With bows of fire.

The wind, too, freshening, and more from the west, had lightly blown the whole mass of the battle back a short distance, toward the island called Trey Falco.

By now the smaller vessels found themselves completely engulfed in fog, and next bumped by the clashing mountains of the bigger craft.

Sail was shortened and yards angled. The eastern slide stabilized. Yet, at this point, even the brilliant tactics that had broken the French line had lost their smart pattern.

At this point, too, it was mostly impossible to make out signals. Or to know the truth: that at this hour of ten in the morning, eighteen French or Franco-Spanish vessels of that vast fleet had been disabled. They had stricken colors and surrendered.

The *Lily*, the *Fuchsia*, and one or two more had found themselves also backed up closer now to the island.

Looking from her quarterdeck, unaided by the spyglass, Art could make out, even through the smitch, that Roman square on the shore, with its lions and dry fountains.

She found Feasty Jack at her elbow.

"Cap'n, I've walked that island once, some year or two ago. I'll tell you an interesting fact. The cistern that fed those fountains is breached by the sea."

Art glanced at Feasty. There was an odd look on his smoke-smeared face. "A tourist guide, Mr. Jack?"

"Aye, if you like. I tell you, if your cannon scores a hit on those fountains—they'll play again."

"How quaint."

"No, Captain. Take heed. It willn't be a sweet little jet you'll see. Open the cistern up and hole the basins, you'll get a water-spout tall as a tall mast. Taller. And notice the slope? The water will fly straight this way."

Art pulled her thoughts together. They always seemed scattered about now, trying to go below in her mind and consider her child and nothing else.

"You're saying—" she began.

Deep within the shifting, barking cloud that was the main battle, an explosion sounded, much bigger than all the rest. Up over the dome of the smoke rose another cloud. This one was of reddest-golden fire, spreading like a great umbrella, clearly to be seen.

Cries of distress and amazement all around. The vast bloom of flame uncurled and uncurled, and in it black objects were whirling—and then falling back toward the sea like a sooty hailstorm.

It was as if Jack's talk of a waterspout had been made actual—only in fire, not water. But Feasty only remarked, expressionless, "That's a big ship gone there. Her powder store's caught fire and blown up. No doubt of it. All that raining down? That's everything aboard, I reckon. Wood, metal. Or men."

The fire furled inward with a sudden lick. The tremendous glare folded away with it, into the rusty smoke.

And from the chaos of the whole churning fog bank, a huge and terrible bellowing mixture came shouldering.

Pegasus, first through the northerly line, had fought like the mythical creature of her name, a fierce stallion with wings. But she, like *Titan* and the French *We'll Sink You* and many more, had been wounded mortally.

Now she drove toward the open sea, unable to do more. And on her back clung, like tigers to prey, the French *Aigle Noir* (*Black Eagle*) and the Spanish *Espada* (*Sword*). It seemed *Pegasus* was thought too cunning to be allowed to escape—as if she might come back inside an hour and cause more harm.

But *Pegasus* was done. All her masts were gone, her bowsprit also, and half her forecastle had been blasted open like a wooden cave.

Still her guns, or some of them, choked at her pursuers. But by now the *Eagle* was close enough that she had grappled *Pegasus* through her starboard gun ports, spiking her last cannon with small bombs. Exploding painful gouts of fire, harried on both sides, the English ship was kneeling forward, ready either to go down or break apart.

Into this punch-up reemerged the gutsy *Come On Then* and two of the English fifteen-gunners, *Geezer* and *Certainty*—but against the burly *Eagle* and *Sword*, they had only the joint power to annoy.

Slender *Fuchsia* bravely pushed toward this mess—but a casual sidelong slap from *Eagle*'s guns disintegrated the top of her foremast. As her fore-royal and topgallant flailed across her deck, her ten light guns fell silent.

"Remember, Missus Art," said Feasty Jack from behind her shoulder, "*waterspout*."

But a wave of shot from *Sword* stung across the *Lily*'s quarterdeck.

Art dropped, found herself unmarked, and sprang up again.

She had, in that instant, forgotten she was with child.

Smoke clouded, the hounding of *Pegasus* was no longer properly in view. *Lily*, too, presented less of a target—Art couldn't even see her own deck properly. . . .

"Mr. Plinke, hard to starboard. Mr. Whusk, Misters Salt, to the rigging, swing the yards—we want that isle over there. Mr. de Weevil, how's your arm? Good. Mr. de and Mr. Smith and Mr. Jack, man the rail and shoot like stars."

Art, too (jumping over some unseen fallen thing), bounded to the rail, grabbing up the nearest flintlock.

They cracked pistolsful into the heaving smoke.

Lily, catching the brisker breeze, light and slightly right-handed as she was, nosed over quite readily toward the island of Trey Falco. Where the fountains were.

Sketching, Felix was aware of a zinging snap and growl above and to one side. Something like a huge flapping bird of red, green, white, yellow, and blue sailed past him, descending.

The Republican Jack had been shot from *Triumphant*'s masthead.

Felix went on with his work, tearing off each page as he finished—or as he gave up on it.

Next minute Leggins came scurrying, cheerful as ever, up the mast, another flag wrapped around him.

Reaching the top, he leaned out into the smoke, from which French bullets still thunked and whistled.

"Ahoy, my amies! Laisseh-les, can't ye? Let a poor old boy fly his flag, si vous plaîtes!"*

Bizarrely, in keeping with this whole madhouse, the French ship that had been aiming at *Triumphant* and her flag left off. A faint cry rose, also in Fringlish: "We saluteh voos, mister. Carry on, alors."

Leggins, with a quick, chirpy grin at Felix, reattached the flag, pinning it for extra safety against part of a sail.

---

*"Ahoy, my friends! Hold it, can't ye? Let a poor old boy fly his flag, please!"

He then saluted the French ship—the *Belle Beau* (*Pretty Handsome*)—and cried over: "*Merci! Je t'aime*, innit!"* before shimmying down.

The French ship didn't start her barrage again until he had vanished.

Nor had they fired directly at Felix, the artist drawing the battle.

It was about this same time that Mr. Witty, inspecting other sails (between shooting at the *Belle Beau* and also the *Redoute* [*Field-Fort*], who seemed, despite her casualties, to have been shadowing *Triumphant* since their first spat), beheld a funny yellow fish guggling around in the water below the stern.

A leather bucket bound with iron stood under the rail. It shouldn't have been there, the decks having been cleared for war. Mr. Witty attached a rope.

Inside the welter of pistols and snarl of cannon all about, calm as the word *calm*, Mr. Witty lowered the bucket and scooped up the exhausted yellow dog. He raised him from the porridge of sea, smashed portions of masts, spars and figureheads, planks and gilded ship ornaments, pieces of heat-fused cannon, knife hilts and heartbreaking handkerchiefs and patches of blown-off clothes.

Muck landed. He was taken from the bucket and held up for inspection by Mr. Witty: "*Hhhmnr!*" said Mr. Witty, like a kindly, elderly door opening. " 'Ello, doggy."

Muck saw a long, pale face full of old sorrow and eternal strict *niceness*, and two tufts of gray hair above the ears that made the ears seem—upstanding, like those . . . of a dog.

So Muck gave Witty a warm, sloppy face wash with his tongue that tasted of sea and fire, wriggled free, met the deck and shook

---

*"Thanks! I loves ya, innit!"

himself all over Mr. Witty's boots. Mr. W watched, without comment. Then he saw Muck change to quite a small four-legged table of a dog, bristling and nose pointing.

As if out in a worrying jungle, Muck-the-table crept around *Triumphant*'s stern planking. Until he was directly under the ladder that led to the quarterdeck.

Up there, Hamlet Ellensun, Thom Healthy, and Armstrong Billowes didn't see any dog.

Another thing was happening.

The French flagship, the *Chevalier* (*Knight*), had reappeared, separated from *Triumphant* only by thirty feet of water.

Triumphant had battered so many enemy ships, and been battered *by* them, that by now not all were recognizable.

But the *Knight*, flying her flags plus the French king's All-Flame, was unforgettable.

On her quarterdeck stood her commander.

He was a good-looking man, and he fixed Hamlet with smoke-reddened black eyes.

He spoke in perfect English.

"Admiral. You have destroyed our fleet. I have called for a general surrender. And I, too, sir, surrender. Here is my sword of command—" He lifted up the shining blade. "I ask that in return for this, you will take my men as noble prisoners."

Hamlet nodded. "You've fought like lions. The men of all your fleet who give themselves up to us need fear no dishonor."

The French commander bowed. His name meant something like Ninth-Town.

Felix Phoenix, high above, stared down through the smoke at him and thought, I could have painted you, monsieur. You have an excellent face.

All the ships now held their fire.

Even *Belle Beau* had let down her colors. (Had the *Redoute?*)

Only in the distance, where signals couldn't be seen, the wrestle of battle went on.

Boats brought the crew of the *Knight* across to *Triumphant* or to neighboring English ships. The Frenchmen came quietly, some of them in tears, but with heads high. Yes, they had fought like lions—lions of gold.

In the end, only the commander called Ninth-Town stood on his deck, with three or four others around him.

In one hand, Ninth-Town held his sword. Hamlet saw that in the commander's other hand was a small wooden model of his ship, the gallant *Knight*.

"Won't you come aboard, monsieur?" said Hamlet. "You'll get no less honor than your crew. Dine with me tonight. It will be my pleasure."

"Thank you, but no. My honor is lost," said the commander. "Therefore, I and my sword, and these few friends who have decided to stand beside me, will go down with our ship."

A bustle and kerfuffle on the English ships. *Knight* was the French flagship—they *must* take her.

"But sir," began Hamlet reasonably.

The French commander scraped his sword suddenly along his ship's rail. Sparks flew up, and he put the little model of his vessel against them. It caught at once.

There in his hand it flamed, the model of the *Chevalier*. It must have been *burning* his hand, but he didn't flinch.

"We have also lighted a fire," said the commander, "in the belowdecks, up against our powder magazine. Twelve minutes, I would guess, before my ship is blown apart. Draw back, then, my friends. Draw back, or you, too, will go with us."

Sanity and discipline were strong enough still in both the English and French fleet (and the wind, too, strong enough) that inside ten minutes, not one Republican or French vessel was within range of the explosion, when it came.

Up they all soared, everything—sea, ship, the banner of the king, all that small wooden world—held in a column of fire, that broadened out above to an umbrella, in which black objects jostled before spraying down.

Hamlet Elllensun and his officers watched this awful sight; every man on every near deck watched, too. And Felix stared from the remote height of the fighting-top, papers clenched in his hands.

Throughout the whole area of the battle, the event was seen. ("That's a big ship gone there," Feasty had said to Art. "Her powder store's caught fire.")

When the thunder died, one voice alone wailed from the high rigging of that following French ship, *Redoute*. The voice spoke in French, and was understood.

"That tree of *flame*—*that* is my country of France—*burning*!"

Felix Phoenix, high on the platform with his sketches, saw the lean, dark figure who shrieked from *Redoute*'s rigging. He saw him aim and fire, with a terrible simplicity. The thin squirt of light after all the vast rushes of light that had gone before.

And Felix stood up, breaking the straps that secured him, not knowing quite what had happened. Knowing *something* had.

But Muck—

Muck had known *minutes* before. Well, maybe even hours or days—or weeks—before—

About a count of twenty passed after the ghastly *thrummb* of the *Knight*'s explosion, and in that count of twenty, Muck swarmed for the ladder.

Up on to the quarterdeck of *Triumphant* galloped Muck, the Cleanest Dog in England.

As the voice rang from the *Redoute*'s rigging, Muck was already airborne.

Like a flying sack of potatoes he slammed, nose first, into the chest of Hamlet Ellensun, knocking him not only senseless but straight over, flat on his back. And that was in the moment that the bullet also flew across from ship to ship, aiming for Admiral Ellensun's heart.

One pure inch above Hamlet's knocked-out, unseeing head, the killing bullet passed. It plumped into the gilt rail and shredded it. But Hamlet it had missed.

He lay on the deck, under the sprawled body of Muck, who, next second, righted himself, aware always of the importance of being alert. "*Woof!*" Muck roared at everyone around. And they *listened*.

Behind them on the foggy, chopped water, the muddle of still-fighting ships: *Pegasus* pulled down by *Black Eagle*, *Sword* at bay to the guns of the *Come On Then*, *Geezer* and *Certainty* in trouble now, and *Geezer* listing badly to port. The small vessels were circling, some hit, some firing gamely— And then, out of the tumult one more terror bearing down on them all, her topmasts splintered but yet holding up both sails and colors. The eighty-gun French destroyer *Tonnerre* (*Thunder*) had also failed to read the signal for surrender.

None of these ships took note of the *Lily*, a quarter mile off in the lea of the island.

Even when five of the *Lily*'s cannon discharged, and then again.

In the clearer air they had now reached, those on *Lily*'s deck strained their eyes shoreward. And below, too, through the gun ports, Cuthbert, Shemps, Larry, Nib, and Stott squinted at the island. Saw only soft puffs of smoke, shines of light—

It was a yelling Tazbo who saw the charge go home.

Then every voice on *Lily* shouted.

(Behind them, not one of the fighting ships took heed.)

Onshore, up on the hill above the Roman forum, monkeys shrieked in outrage. If anything live had been near the square, now it fled.

Only the four granite lions posed there, apparently unmoved.

But they were *not*—

The cistern under the square at first gave only a gurgle. This seemed no more dramatic than water running in a drain.

Then, a grinding *crunch*. It rang through the space and echoed out to sea, so *Lily* heard it plainly, even through the uproar of *Tonnerre*'s guns.

After that there was a silence, like a sort of period—or was it more a *comma*?

A comma.

With no further warning, the bases and pipes of the pair of huge fountains split—one!—two!—like dropped pumpkins.

From one, then the other, a sparkling *thing* rushed into the sky. It didn't look like water at all. It looked quite solid.

Off their pedestals spun the nymphs and mermen of the water feature. Their big figures hurtled in all directions. But even before most of them fell to break on the grassy paving, the entire square broke apart, and flung itself in chunks and shards upward—

"Art," Honest in a quiet, grave voice, "the lion—"

"I see it."

While three of the great sculpted beasts tilted over in strange positions, the fourth lion was rising into the air, borne by a third enormous pillar of water. As it ascended, it passed the square's *real* pillar, the stone one, which was collapsing.

Up and up, the lion was carried.

It was obvious now that all three of these jets—from the fountains, from the square with the lion riding it—were finally reaching a ceiling and curving over.

"Here it comes! Get down!"

Art pushed Honest to the deck. Other men sprawled, their arms over their heads.

Art, though she crouched once more, couldn't look away. . . .

The flight of the mighty fountains spangled overhead. They sprinkled *Lily* with a light, sharp, salt rain. And from them, with the water drops, fell only gentle materials—grass, stone dust, a wild flower, the bronzy feather of a bird—

Then the *lion* went over.

The sun, which had just got up above the war smoke and the Battle of Trey Falco, was put out. A black cloud of granite; the lion blotted it from sight—and then released it once again.

All the smaller ships were in retreat—they'd seen the pent-up deluge leave the island, and used oars, sail, and boats. *Pegasus* was sinking anyway; her men were already swimming or rowing for the north and east. *Come On Then*, who knew about Armstrong Billowes's ideas on the island waterworks, was dragging lopsided *Geezer* and the slow *Certainty* away with her.

The *Sword* and the *Eagle* were now doing their very best to leave the scene.

But the *Thunder*, that colossal gun machine, found herself too unwieldy and her scorched sails too thinned.

Off her decks whole battalions of men were pouring, flailing away to every side as fast as arms and legs could take them.

The arches of water reached their limit. They crashed toward the sea.

Even the smoke clouds were smashed apart. The Straits of Jibrel-Tar fragmented like a thousand windows.

And through the tumult of springing waters and falling waters, the black lion from the square dropped down.

Only one paw caught the *Thunder*'s armored forecastle. Which gave like brittle toffee. *Thunder* yawned and, with a sigh, dipped half her massive bulk beneath the waves.

Soaked to the skin, Art and her crew, looking on, with grass and feathers in their sopping hair.

Art found her hand had placed itself once more at her waist. She *remembered*.

"*Sorry*, baby. But—well, Ma, well, baby—what a show . . ."

Her knee rested against something like a large, firm bolster. At long last Art glanced down. And saw the body of Feasty Jack, killed by the Spanish bullets of *Espada*, lying there, half smiling, on the quarterdeck.

Curtain Call: Return to Parrot Island

"Emma! Emma! To be or not to be . . ." muttered Hamlet Ellensun. "Are we to be an item or not? I am certain that dog will *bite*—"

"Nay, Ham, he don't *bite*. He's a regular hero!"

Hamlet opened his eyes to find all his officers and several of the general crew bending over him, looking astonished. Thomas Healthy was holding Hamlet in his arms. But the other face that had filled Hamlet's come-back consciousness belonged to Muck.

"He came from nowhere," detailed Thom. "Knocked you over one split second before that sniper's bullet reached you."

Muck and Hamlet glared at each other.

Someone had to give.

Admiral Ellensun extended his hand. Muck sniffed it, then walked back onto Hamlet's chest.

"Good dog," said Hamlet. Muck allowed his tail the briefest wag. "Kiss me, Muck," decided Hamlet. "You saved my life."

With great dignity Muck lowered his muzzle and licked Ham-

let's face, and sitting up, Hamlet hugged him. One more resound-
ing cheer tore from *Triumphant*'s decks.

The beauty of the French fleet was over. Twenty-four ships had surrendered, some of these crippled beyond use. And others had gone
to the bottom. The casualties among the men were worse.

The English fleet had lost vessels, too. *Titan*, for example, had
burned to charcoal, and *Pegasus* lay on the sea's floor beside the
wreck of the *Tonnerre*, a stone lion guarding them both. The English casualties were lighter. But men had died, and other men had
received hurts they must now carry all their lives.

Cheering and sobbing, joy and despair, triumph and agony.

The Green Book of the sea had closed its covers once more on
secrets.

Art and her men gave Feasty Jack the sea burial necessary so far
from home.

As the wind brought rain to clear the smoke, they lowered his
body into the straits. And on the rail, Jack's white parrot, Maudy,
spoke suddenly, in a deep and musical voice learned long ago from
some actor, the curious words of an ancient prayer. "Yea though I
go down beneath the earth or the waters, yet tomorrow shall I rise
from them again, and we shall meet each other elsewhere. For though
even the world must pass, the spirit of Man shall always remain."

"Not a dry eye in the blinking house," sniveled Peter accusingly.

But Plunqwette, seated on Art's head, watched Maudy with an
air of proud ownership.

"Feasty was a fine man," said Art.

"He was a fine cook," added Shemps, blowing his nose. "I can't
believe like I'll never taste his fish stew again."

Walter went belowdecks and cried on Lucinda the chicken, who eventually went for him and beat him off, far more concerned about her large white egg.

Aboard the *Lily*, an air of tired depression filled the gap where fighting madness, sadness, and relief had been.

Beyond the rails, rescue boats were combing the waters for survivors or trophies, and the rain littered down.

In the admiral's stateroom, as afternoon altered to evening, documents had been signed and sealed. Courteous exchanges had gone on between upper-ranking victors and prisoners. Wine had been drunk. Muck had been fed meat and gravy.

Hamlet, with Muck now seated on his knee, lingered admiringly over the sketches Felix Phoenix had brought safely down from the fighting-top.

"These are splendid, Mr. P. You've done a wonderful job, by the Bounding Main. Your eye must be straight as a string and your hand like a rock. Look at this excellent plan, too, of the battle scheme. And this—and *this*—what fantastic paintings will result from them!"

"Thank you," said Felix, turning his wineglass around and around on the table.

Hamlet could see Felix didn't now give a haddock's hammock for either his artistic talent or its praise. Hamlet supposed if you lost the love of your life, you might feel a bit down. (It had been far simpler finding a solution to the other problem, which was Nicholas Nunn. There'd been something off-color in his recent past. But luckily he'd shown such flair and courage during the battle, Hamlet would recommend that past be forgotten.)

"And *this* one is a masterpiece in itself," Hamlet tried again, waving a drawing and genuinely impressed by the work. "Did you know what it was you saw, over toward the island?"

"Mr. Healthy kindly explained afterward that it was a water-spout from the old cistern under the square. I could barely see it through the smoke—only those arches of water, and then the black dot in the middle, falling."

"The black dot was a granite lion, I'm pleased to say. It took out the great warship *Tonnerre* and saved us a deal of extra trouble. But you've caught the impression exactly. 'Tis supersweet."

"Again, my thanks."

"I gather," Hamlet rambled on, "one of the smaller vessels fired at the cistern and breached it. We'd thought it was *Come On Then*, but no. Seems it was"—he consulted a paper over Muck's head—"the *Lily Achoo*. Sixteen guns, but the story goes only five gunners able-bodied. I've sent for her captain and officers, to thank them personally. I thought, maybe, you might do a quick sketch of them—for the newspapers back in England."

Felix raised his face. It was washed of dirt, the black eye nearly better. But never, Hamlet thought, had he seen any face so resignedly and totally stripped of purpose and hope. Except, perhaps, on the steps of a scaffold.

"Well . . . oh, well then, sir," said Hamlet, "let that go. You needn't if you don't want to."

"Again, Admiral—"

"Oh, Ham will do in private, Felix."

"My thanks," said Felix. "I'd rather not see any extra heroes from this war. Not just now."

"Of course, old man. Forsooth, go and have a lie-down. Probably you won't miss anything. I'm sure *Lily*'s captain won't even be worth drawing."

Once Felix had left, Muck, Hamlet, Thom, and some others moved into the next room, where the empty treasure chest had been placed in the middle of the floor. Armstrong Billowes and his team had been examining it, polishing the brass plate, tapping at the sides, and even trying to lever up the chest's bottom, which was perhaps solid, and certainly immovable.

"According to our Mr. P, Mary Hell took this with her from the fabled Treasured Isle. Whatever strange character she is, she's no fool. This chest has something to it." Armstrong, looking annoyed and hot.

Muck trotted over to the chest and sniffed it.

Everyone held their breath—this uncanny dog, did *he* know something?

Muck turned his back on the chest, sat down, and had a good, thorough scratch. After which he left the cabin.

"What about the paper with the letters from the alphabet?" asked Thom. "That's the clue. It has to be—doesn't it?"

"It may all be a practical joke," said Armstrong.

Hamlet took the paper from him and stared down at the line of letters, not for the first time.

It was a simple list, really. It showed each letter of the English alphabet, although not in order. Three of these letters, however, were written twice. It ran:

N E̲ T Y A V G I S D̲ C P U J W M H O R X L B

Q Z D̲ K̲ K E̲

"Something occurs to me," said Hamlet. "Could it be possible that this alphabetical list refers to *several* treasure hoards—hence the disorder of the letters? But we have here only *one* such treasure—the chest—and the doubled letters apply only to this chest. We can ignore the rest—unless, of course, we happen to discover any more such puzzling objects."

The men glanced at one another.

Armstrong said, "So the only letters that concern us here are the D̲, the K̲, and the E̲. . . ."

"Plus the order they're in?"

"Well, I'm still stumped," said Billowes.

"Me an' all, Ham," added Thom.

Above, sounds of music ran over the evening ship.

"Celebrating," said Hamlet. "I tell you what, sirs. We'll heave this chest back up on main deck. See if anyone among the men can solve the riddle. Offer a prize to the one who does it. They've cracked the French fleet. What's a treasure clue to that?"

Triumphant blazed with lights through a dusk still misty and tinged with smoke as Art, the Honest Liar, Glad Cuthbert, Forecastle Smith, and Larry Lully were rowed toward the try-decker's bulk. The flagship didn't look as trim or glamorous as she had. She'd been knocked about a bit, and some of her bling shot off. But as the night came on, her wounded cared for and her dead given to the burial of the sea, her dinner was being served and she seemed a jolly ship.

Art and her men looked at *Triumphant*. Like kids locked outside a cake shop.

That kind of party—none of them felt they could ever enter.

Belowdecks, in the officer cubicle Felix used to sleep in, Muck, having battered at the entrance and got in, was leaping what looked like twelve feet in the air, barking and yodeling.

Seeing Muck on Hamlet Ellensun's ship at all had shaken Felix quite a lot. For Muck had been aboard the *Unwelcome Stranger* the last Felix knew, and *Unwelcome* was sunk. But then Felix recalled he had glimpsed Muck ashore in El Tangerina that fateful afternoon. Probably the dog had jumped ship as he had before. And so survived.

He was certainly one hundred percent alive *now*.

"Muck—what is it? Oh, Muck, for God's sake—good dog. Just let me alone."

For Muck had now jumped on the bunk. He sank his teeth in Felix's coat sleeve—pulled and pulled, till the sleeve was ripped.

"Muck, pack it in."

Muck wouldn't. Muck scampered and rolled and bounced all over Felix, panting and snuffling and yelping.

"What?"

Muck drew back. He rushed to the cubicle's exit and wagged his tail so hard it seemed likely to fly off. Then, when Felix did nothing but lie there watching, Muck launched again into his stampede.

"Dog, you are mad. All right. Yes. See, I'm getting up. See, I'm following you to the door. Now what?"

Muck gave an operatic soprano aria of approval and broke for the 'tween-deck ladder.

Felix considered blocking the cubicle's door with pillows off the bunk. But Muck had other ideas. Back he came, fastening his teeth now in the skirt of Felix's coat. A long note of tearing. Muck let go and attempted to get his fangs instead through Felix's boot.

Felix surrendered. He left the cubicle and went after the now-shrieking Muck, up the ladder to the topdeck.

Ah. Just what he had wanted to avoid.

Men playing flutes and fiddles, dancing jigs, eating food and swigging grog, and all around other festivals on other ships. But there—out there, beyond them all—that smoky, darkening ship-swallowing loneliness called the sea.

Felix walked to the ship's rail.

That was the truth, then. Battles were lost and won, men and women arrived and went away. Even history moved on. But out there . . . *that* was reality.

And *from* reality then, a single ship's boat, bearing the grand name of *Triumphant* on its side, was rowed out of the mist.

More terrible sometimes than heartbreak, the healing of a heart.

Felix stared. He stared as if he would eat off the dark and murk with his eyes and so see better. His eyes were the biggest things on earth. No, bigger than the earth.

"Why is that man screaming?" inquired Hamlet on the quarterdeck, in disapproval. "What are the surgeons doing? Surely we have painkillers—"

"No, Ham, look, it's—"

Felix, clinging to the rail while at the same time trying to throw himself *off* the rail. Felix yelling, over and over at the top of his lungs: *"My wife! My wife! My wife!"*

Art, below on the sea that is so real, that steals things away and sometimes brings them back—in bottles, in wooden chests, in boats—Art stares upward in return.

Somehow she knows, even before she hears him clearly, or sees him against the lights of the big ship.

And if Art doesn't fathom yet quite why Felix is so glad to see her, she can't really miss that very glad he is.

In those moments, too, Mr. Witty moves forward on the deck to where the chest from the Treasured Isle now is. It's Mr. W's turn to have a go at solving the clue.

Mr. W can't read—that is, he can't read words or letters. Only weather, and the oceans, and people's faces. Well, there you go.

But even so, as the owler Tinky Clinker could, Mr. Witty can understand the *shapes* of letters.

So he looks at the alphabet paper, and the three shapes that are written twice and are exactly the same. And then he looks at the brass plate hammered onto the lid of the chest. The plate carries a message from the pirates who put some of their most precious stuff into this chest for any who could find it. Their note to this fortunate person was read before by Art and her crew on the Treasured Isle.

But Mr. W can't read, so he merely gazes at the brass and the words cut in it. And so he sees at once that some of the words in the message are in capital letters, just like all the letters on the alphabet list.

Then Mr. Witty notices that, of all the capital letters scattered through the message he can't read, only three there are repeated twice. These capitals are on words as follows: **K**ind, **K**ingdom, **E**xample, **D**eed, **E**nd, and **D**rink.

"Hnr," says Mr. W. He turns to Armstrong Billowes. Mr. W points out carefully to Billowes, with patience, the similar letters. Armstrong gives a gulp. Mr. W steps modestly away. But Billowes bellows again. *"He's GOT it!"*

Men bound forward, slapping Mr. W on the back. He smiles, happy because they are, encouragingly saying, "Tha's right, yerrh."

Hamlet, who had been going to welcome the captain of the *Lily* aboard, sees his welcome is unneeded. It's Art Blastside—the rumors she was here were evidently true. Felix Phoenix has taken hold of her the instant she stepped on deck. He has wrapped her up like a parcel in his arms and hair. Three of the other men from Art's ship Hamlet also recognizes. They seem delighted. "Walk good, Phoenix! Walk good!" Larry is shouting. Glad Cuthbert is dancing with Honest, and round about, men from *Triumphant* are laughing and joining in.

So Hamlet goes instead to the forecastle deck, where Armstrong's signaling like a potty scarecrow in a high wind.

"This man's solved it, Admiral! Sailmaker's mate, Witty."

Hamlet is shown the matching letters.

"Only thing is, we've pressed them, *hit* them—nothing."

"Wait," says Hamlet. This is his day. He knows that. His life was saved by Emma's dog, and he has won the war for England. "Let's see. The alphabet—there are twenty-six letters. And every letter of the alphabet is on the paper, too, but these three repeated. And besides, the letters are not in alphabetical order . . . nor are the repeated letters all in one spot. <u>E</u> near the start, then again at the end, <u>D</u> ten in, and then again four from the end . . . the <u>K</u>'s both together."

The answer floods Hamlet. It's so silly. Easy. Exactly like breaking the line instead of fighting in the old-fashioned way. "Listen," says Hamlet (who on his return to England will be awarded the CBN—Commander Beloved of his Nation). "It isn't the number these letters are in the alphabet. It's the number of letters *in* on this list. And so, <u>E</u> comes second—that's two. Then <u>D</u> is ten. Then near the end here another <u>D</u>, which is twenty-fifth along; the first <u>K</u>, which is twenty-six; the second <u>K</u>, which is twenty-seven; and the last <u>E</u>, which is number twenty-eight.

"Give me your knife, would you, Mr. Witty? Thank you, sir, you'll get the prize." Hamlet leans forward. He goes to the first <u>E</u> in the text and strikes it twice. To the first <u>D</u> and strikes it ten times. To the second <u>D</u> and strikes it with great care twenty-five times; the two <u>K</u>'s twenty-six and twenty-seven times respectively. The final <u>E</u>, with *extreme* care, twenty-eight times.

At the last neat blow, the chest—

Shatters.

It splinters apart. And the brass plate clangs on deck. And with that plate, all the things packed inside the layers of the chest's wooden walls and lid and floor.

Rubies dark as blood, pale as dawn, topaz like Budgerigar wine and emeralds like the greenest sea, pearls white, tawny, black, and coral, coal-blue sapphires. Coins of gold and silver; chains and figurines of gold and silver. Jade necklaces. Turquoise necklaces. Amber necklaces. Sharkskin wallets with banknotes from a hundred lands. Diamonds of nineteen different shades from blue to sheerest white. Rings set with every stone known to man—and one or two *not* known.

The forecastle is in hysteria. Men come running from all quarters to see. Even Honest goes over, with the others from Art's crew.

Honest knows he needs to come back in a while, though. Something he has to give to Art.

Art and Felix, however, don't even look.

Like the moment on the gallows when the first miracle happened. This second miracle. The world, for Art and Felix, is only—Art and Felix.

A brief glance then, months ahead, to the future of some.

To Hamlet, about to get his CBN, returning to the Holroyal mansion with Muck at his side.

"Emma!" Hamlet will exclaim, quite startled. "You're not wearing yellow! You're wearing—pink . . ."

"In honor of your victory," Emma will say, looking at Hamlet now rather as Plunqwette had recently looked at Maudy.

"If I'd known," Hamlet will say, "I'd have put a pink bow on the dog."

But Muck and Emma are already in each other's arms. Hamlet will have to wait. He puts up with this with a good grace.

In fact, about the time a grateful government votes to reconstruct Trey Falco Square, fountains, lions, pillar, and all—this time with a statue of Hamlet on top of it—Hamlet presents Emma with a ring. It shows in red gold two hands that clasp each other. And over these the paw of a dog, done in white gold. Muck's paw, holding Emma and Hamlet together.

But Glad Cuthbert's return won't be quite so adorable. Reaching his lodging, he will find the place deserted. Gladys has left a note. *So, if the sea's so cool, Cuth, I thought I'd try it for meself. Don't wait up.*

Yet Dirk and Whuskery are due to make a great success. Once Dirk's elegant slight limp is seen, and everyone learns he and Whusk fought at Trey Falco, nobody can do enough for them. Their Republican Theater will open to vast acclaim, the performance only slightly spoiled by the difficult Mrs. Worthytown and her untalented daughter Marigold.

While Oscar Bagge, who had saved Dirk's leg, not only by splinting it with Muck's special bone, but by giving Dirk (and Grug and de Weevil) small doses shaved *off* the bone, in wine), has realized the fossil has incredible healing powers. Oscar will therefore set off to find his bone-studying, stuck-up half brother, Erasmus.

It's winter, anyway, by the time they all get home to England. In the trees of the parks, commons, and fields, parrots will be adapting to the cold weather by now, despite the Republic's strict antipirate laws, regularly fed and cared for by PIRATE—the Parrot Interest Regiment and Teatotalers of England.

In France, where still no revolution has happened, aristocrats have scornfully renamed England *Parrot Island*.

So things *will* go.

But for now, back on the deck of *Triumphant* on the night after the battle, Felix says softly to Art, "I'll never leave you again. And you—you must never leave me. We two, from now till forever. Just we two."

And Art says, "Actually, sweetheart, we *three* . . ."

But that's when Honest reappears and hands Art Feasty Jack's letter, written on the morning of the battle, before sunrise.

> *Respected Captain,*
> *Take no care for my death. I was warned of it—to*
> *the very year, day, and hour, when I was only a boy.*
> *This was in the Inde, and the fortune-teller told me*
> *not to fear. For death passes, like everything else.*
> *Only life is constant.*
> *Your Obedient Late Cook,*
> *Fils de Jacques (Feasty Jack).*

Post Scriptum

Meanwhile, Cap'n, you'd better know that the big
white egg Walt's chicken is nursing comes from
Khem, the Black Land our Ebad Vooms now rules. I
found it in the river mud. It's the egg of a sacred
crocodile. They grow to sixteen or eighteen feet in the
same amount of years. But to hatch—you'll only
have to wait thirteen weeks.